THANQUOL'S DOOM

'Burn-burn!' the grey seer snarled. 'Slay-kill!'

Boneripper shuddered into motion, lumbering away from the walls and into the middle of the tunnel. The dwarfs must have missed the hulking rat-ogre or mistaken it for some piece of dilapidated mining equipment. Thanquol chittered with amusement as he saw the shock in the dwarfs' eyes as they beheld his fearsome bodyguard.

The rat-ogre didn't give the dwarfs a chance to overcome their shock. Lowering its warpfire projector, Boneripper sent a blast of green fire jetting down the tunnel. The screams of dwarfs and the shrieks of skaven echoed through the mine, the sickly stink of roasted flesh, scorched hair and burning fur filling the air. In the first blast, Boneripper caught a half-dozen of the dwarfs and five skaven who were too slack-witted to move fast. The burning ratmen lay strewn across the ground; the dwarfs writhed in agony as the green flames melted their armour into their flesh.

A WARHAMMER NOVEL

Thanquol & Boneripper

THANQUOL'S DOOM

C. L. Werner

BLACK LIBRARY

To Chris and Shaunna, for putting up with poor work habits.

A BLACK LIBRARY PUBLICATION

First published in Great Britain in 2011 by
The Black Library,
Games Workshop Ltd.,
Willow Road, Nottingham,
NG7 2WS, UK.

10 9 8 7 6 5 4 3 2 1

Cover illustration by Winona Nelson.

Map by Nuala Kinrade.

See the Black Library on the internet at
www.blacklibrary.com

Find out more about Games Workshop
and the world of Warhammer at
www.games-workshop.com

Printed and bound in the UK.

A dark age, a bloody age, an age of daemons
and of sorcery. It is an age of battle and death, and of the
world's ending. Amidst all of the fire, flame and fury
it is a time, too, of mighty heroes, of bold deeds
and great courage.

A E EA of the Old World sprawls the Empire, the
largest and most powerful of the human realms. Known for
its engineers, sorcerers, traders and soldiers, it is
a land of great mountains, mighty rivers, dark forests
and vast cities. And from his throne in Altdorf reigns
the Emperor Karl Franz, sacred descendant of the
founder of these lands, Sigmar, and wielder
of his magical warhammer.

B E E A E far from civilised times. Across the
length and breadth of the Old World, from the knightly
palaces of Bretonnia to ice-bound Kislev in the far north,
come rumblings of war. In the towering Worlds Edge
Mountains, the orc tribes are gathering for another assault.
Bandits and renegades harry the wild southern lands of
the Border Princes. There are rumours of rat-things, the
skaven, emerging from the sewers and swamps across the
land. And from the northern wildernesses there is the
ever-present threat of Chaos, of daemons and beastmen
corrupted by the foul powers of the Dark Gods.
As the time of battle draws ever nearer,
the Empire needs heroes
like never before.

PROLOGUE

GREY WITCH-LIGHT SLOWLY manifested itself, coalescing from the darkness. The eerie luminance revealed a small chamber with walls cloaked in shadow, ceiling and floor concealed in an almost tangible miasma of blackness. There was a weird, unreal quality about the chamber, as though it were a place detached from the crude boundaries of physical matter. The air held the chill of magic, the frosty atmosphere of the aethyric planes.

Far from this sinister refuge seemed the world of men. Yet if the chamber were not a part of that world, then at least it bordered upon it. Only a few feet from the shadow-wrapt walls the teeming streets of Altdorf stretched across the greatest city in the Old World. Only a few of the denizens of that metropolis suspected the existence of such a room, a shadowy sanctum torn from the mystic veil. Yet the name of the room's inhabitant was known to many, a name whispered in tones of awe and fear by the city's thieves and murderers, sorcerers and heretics.

As the grey light flickered into being, a shadowy apparition detached itself from the darkness. Like a great black bat, the cloaked figure descended upon the solitary chair standing in the hidden chamber. Darkness crept away from thin, claw-like hands, drawn back as though black gloves had suddenly melted from the pale fingers.

A hiss of laughter rasped through the chamber as the owner of those hands leaned across the table standing beside his chair.

A motley assortment of curious objects rested upon the table. There was a golden bowl, shallow and broad-brimmed, filled with a translucent treacle. Beside the bowl yawned a hideous golden idol, incense pouring from its fanged and leering mouth. Next to the idol was a disc of glass set into a circle of silver. The glass was neither smooth nor clear, but rough and frosted, possessing a texture that somehow suggested a mass of cobwebs.

It was to the glass that Jeremias Scrivner, shadowmancer and secret protector of Altdorf, directed his attention. The wizard's intense gaze bore down upon the curious glass, focussing his very soul upon the frosted mirror. He could feel the magical energies rising up from the mirror in response to his focus. They were not unlike the emanations which had disturbed his other activities, drawing him from the dark streets into this hidden sanctum.

The shadowmancer understood the mystic summons. There were some conjurations a wizard could not fail to recognise. That of the scrying mirror was one such magic. Through careful ritual and long meditation,

Jeremias Scrivner had mastered an art few other wizards had ever dared attempt. Many had been driven mad by the very effort.

As Scrivner stared down into the glass, his astral self began to pass through the frosted mirror, seeping down into that nether realm where thought becomes substance and dream becomes reality. It was that plane of existence which only the most colossal of wills could penetrate and only a powerful intelligence could retain its sanity. Entering the realm, the shadowmancer's body became ever more wraith-like, passing into a more perfect semblance of shadow than even his own magic could evoke on the physical plane.

The wizard felt his head swim as stars strode past his spectral form, as suns and moons wheeled through the amber nothingness all about him. Planets spun in their orbits, dancing to the phantom whistle of a cosmic flautist. Worlds shattered as discordant melodies warped their cores, comets flared into icy brilliance as they capered through crimson nebulae.

Scrivener forced his straying thoughts back into focus. To lose sight of purpose was to court madness. The astral self would be fractured, blown across the cosmic reaches, scattered about the eternal void, torn asunder among the symphony of the spheres. The wizard who lost purpose would lose his soul and leave behind him a gibbering husk of madness.

Through the effort of his steely will, the shadowmancer silenced the discord. The cosmic vastness collapsed in upon itself, taking the semblance of a monstrous form. A bloated, toad-like figure with golden eyes, the spots on its mottled skin shifting in ceaseless fluctuations of hue and pattern.

Scrivner knew he looked upon the mighty mage-priest

Lord Tlaco'amoxtli'ueman, among the most potent of the reptilian wizard-kings of Lustria, the eldritch slann. Alone among thinking races, the slann could cast themselves effortlessly into the nether realm, their cold brains immune to the numbing lure of the cosmic vastness. Here they would withdraw from the crudity of physicality, devoting themselves to a fuller appreciation of the Great Math.

The slann's unblinking golden eyes focused upon Scrivner's astral form. The wizard bowed in humility before Lord Tlaco's superhuman mentality. Thoughts rushed from the mage-priest, thoughts of such magnitude that they would have seared the brain of a lesser being. Scrivner reeled against the swirling confusion of algorithms and equations, sifting through the multitude of the reptile's contemplations for that one stream of thought which it wanted to impart upon him.

The effort was not made easily, but at last Scrivner was able to fix his mind upon the knowledge Lord Tlaco wished to impart to him, the wisdom which had caused the slann to summon him into the astral world.

Like a robber with his prize, Scrivner fled from the slann's presence. It was unwise to linger in proximity to such vast intellect lest the very magnitude of its thoughts crush the supplicant's mind.

Back through the dancing planets and flickering comets, Scrivner's astral shape retreated. The wraith-like essence of the wizard seeped up from the frosty surface of the mirror, snapping back into his shadow-wrapt body.

Scrivner leaned back in his chair, his flesh numbed after the brief excursion of his soul. The wizard focused his thoughts, drawing warmth back into his chilled bones, willing his body into a speedy recovery.

Lord Tlaco had been perturbed by a potential miscalculation, a disharmony in the equation it had been considering. That miscalculation had a name, one with which Scrivner was not unfamiliar.

Grey Seer Thanquol.

CHAPTER I

IF THERE WAS a comfortable spot in the Under-Empire, the warren of Skabreach was as far from it as it was possible to get. A filthy network of half-empty tunnels burrowing beneath the blazing heat of the Estalian sun, Skabreach was the sort of two-mouse flea-hole that any right-minded skaven did his utmost to escape from. It was a no-place in the middle of nowhere, a pathetic slum of fungus-farmers and chow-rat breeders. The air stank of poverty and weakness, the miserable inhabitants scurrying about with their heads cringing low against their chests and their tails dragging in the dirt. One could almost watch the piebald fur of the ratkin falling out as anxiety and malnourishment wreaked havoc on their wasted bodies.

Grey Seer Thanquol stalked among the tunnels of Skabreach with such contemptuous arrogance that he might have been the Horned One himself. The debased skaven of the colony prostrated themselves before him, cowering against the squalor of the tunnels until his imperious presence had passed. Sometimes Thanquol amused himself by trampling one of the abased rat-men, other times he vented his anger by lashing out with his staff against a skaven skull or knocking a few fangs down a farmer's throat with a sharp kick.

Lately even these violent distractions had failed to improve the grey seer's mood. After three weeks his supply of warp-snuff was perilously low and even the lowest cut-throats of Skabreach's pathetic black market had been unable to scrounge up any more. The abominable smell of the warren was growing noxious to him: a vile mixture of fear musk and starvation. He was growing sick of eating mushrooms and chow-rat, finding the taste equally tedious despite the thousands of ways his hosts found to prepare it. He found himself almost longing for the salty taste of rat-ogre. There had been a lot of meat on old Boneripper. Had he known what to expect when he returned to skavendom, he might have rationed the flesh of his late bodyguard a bit more judiciously.

Thanquol's eyes glistened with spite as he reflected upon his latest misfortunes and the events that had led him to such a pass. Coerced into an insane scheme by Nightlord Sneek to help Clan Eshin murder the reptilian Xiuhcoatl, Prophet of Sotek the Snake-devil. Of course, the small matter of having to go to Xiuhcoatl's temple in Lustria hadn't bothered Sneek – the skulking old backstabber wasn't going!

If Thanquol lived to be forty winters, he would never set one paw on a ship again! First the crossing of the Great Ocean on a stolen man-thing pirate ship. Then to be cast alone in a little dinghy with his injured rat-ogre, abandoned to the doubtful mercies of tide and tempest.

And between those two terrifying ordeals at sea! Thanquol ground his teeth together as he remembered the green hell of Lustria, a stagnant morass of swamps so overgrown they were like jungles and jungles so damp they might as well have been swamps. How he hated those jungles! Alive with insects and reptiles and huge hunting cats! Everything in the thrice-cursed jungles had been devoted to one purpose: killing and eating ratmen! Even the plants were lethal, a riotous array of poisonous foliage even a skaven couldn't choke down and a menagerie of ghoulish growths that supplemented their diets by dragging shrieking ratkin into their slobbering maws.

Lizardmen, snakes, zombies, even the treacherous blades of his underlings from Clan Eshin had all been poised to thwart his mission! But Thanquol had prevailed! Like one of the triumphant Grey Lords of old, he had manipulated all of his enemies into destroying each other. The zombies had settled the murderous Chang Fang. His own masterful exploitation of the human Adalwolf had spelled Xiuhcoatl's doom. Given the choice of killing the grey seer or saving his breeder-woman from the skink's knife, Adalwolf had acted precisely as Thanquol knew he would. The human had been his instrument of death. It was a stratagem that would make even Nightlord Sneek bow to his cunning and subtlety.

Thanquol tugged nervously at his whiskers, remembering his horrifying encounter with the bloated toad-priest of the lizardmen. He had once stood over the Black Ark, that most sacred of skaven artefacts, and he could safely say that the magical energies he had sensed emanating from the slann had been greater. For a sorcerer, it was a chilling prospect to consider that such power could exist within a living being. His glands clenched at the mere idea of facing a creature like that again. It would be a cold day in Kweethul's larder before Thanquol set a paw in Lustria again!

Shaking his horned head, the robed ratman smacked a prostrate farmer across the backside with his staff, evoking a squeak of frightened pain. The pathetic maggots of Skabreach lacked even the spleen to bare their fangs when they were struck. Not that Thanquol could entirely blame them. After all, it wasn't every day one was abused by the mightiest hero in the Under-Empire.

The narrow earthen tunnels pressed close against the grey seer as he made his way through the wretched warren. Sometimes he was forced to turn sideways to make any progress, the passage so tight that his whiskers brushed against both sides at once. The Estalian sun baked the ground into something approximating the toughness of concrete, making the excavation of even the smallest burrow a gruelling ordeal.

A more prosperous community might have bought one of the warpstone-powered digging machines crafted by Clan Skryre or hired the use of one of the gigantic moles bred by the beast-masters of Clan Moulder. But Skabreach was far from such developments. Its only recourse towards expansion was to send gangs of skaven into the tunnels with shovels and picks. As a result, everything in the settlement was close and confined, even by the standards of the underfolk.

Thanquol could not leave the warren behind him soon enough. When his boat had washed ashore on the Estalian coast, the grey seer had spent several frantic days searching for a hole that would lead him back into the tunnels of the Under-Empire. A hint of skaven-scent in the air had at last drawn him to one of the pit-vents leading down into Skabreach. There had been a moment of anxiety on his part when he discovered where he was. As an outpost of Clan Skab, Thanquol had every reason to suspect a violent reception. A warlord clan whose power he had played a part in diminishing through his hand in both the assassination of Warlord Vermek Skab and the near-eradication of Skab's holdings beneath the human city of Nuln during the Battle of Nuln, the ratmen of Clan Skab weren't likely to forget him anytime soon. Only a subtle mix of bribery and blackmail had enabled Griznekt Mancarver, Clanlord of Skab, to retain his seat on the Council of Thirteen. It made Thanquol's tail twitch to think there was somebody among the Lords of Decay with more reason to want him dead than Arch-Plaguelord Nurglitch.

His momentary fear, in hindsight, had been absurd. Probably a result of eating the much too-salty flesh of his late and unlamented bodyguard for so many nights at sea. There wasn't a rat in all Skabreach with the spleen to look at him, much less think of lifting a claw against him. Even the ruling warlord, a blight-eyed fawning rodent named Ibkikk Snatchclaw, had proven himself to be a grovelling lick-spittle. From almost the first moment, Thanquol had the warlord kissing his feet and falling over himself to keep the fearsome grey seer appeased.

It would have been a pleasant experience, but for the annoyance that the best Skabreach had to offer was almost as bad as being back in the jungle. What the warren could produce on its own was barely enough for subsistence and the cringing ratmen were so terrified of the human knights who patrolled the surface that they wouldn't so much as poke their noses above ground, much less scavenge for supplies. All in all, Thanquol was so disgusted he would recommend the place be demolished when he got back to Skavenblight. He was pretty certain he'd heard Ibkikk muttering seditious talk that was both heretical and blasphemous. Or at least certain he could make Seerlord Kritislik believe he had.

Thanquol kicked another cowering ratman from his path and hastened his pace. There was a dank, musty stink on the air now, meaning he was getting close to his objective. Soon, the tunnel began to widen, the walls becoming jagged and smooth, unmarred by the tools of miners and the claws of slaves. His whiskers twitched in amusement. It was the smell of the river! The subterranean waterway that linked this forsaken outpost to the rest of the Under-Empire.

As the tunnel widened, so did the press of skaven filling it. The grovelling wretches abased themselves as they caught the grey seer's scent, but in doing so they only placed themselves more directly in his path. Ordinarily, he would have bludgeoned and kicked the cringing vermin until they got out of his way, but the smell of the river made Thanquol anxious to escape the narrow tunnel. Callously, he scurried over the bent backs of the other skaven, indifferent to the squeaks of pain rising from the living carpet beneath his paws.

Soon the tunnel broadened into a cavern. Ramshackle huts built from bone and tanned rathide littered almost every corner of the cramped cave, some of them suspended like the nests of bats from the ceiling. The steady rumble of the river pulsed below the clamour of hundreds of skaven chittering and squealing as they scurried about the settlement. Thanquol's lip curled back in contempt as he noted the crude lanterns that illuminated the squalor. Skabreach was so poor it couldn't even afford proper warp-lanterns. Instead of the comforting green glow of smouldering warpstone, the hovels were lit by the flickering orange light of ratskin lanterns, the pungent stink of burning dung clinging to the black smoke billowing away from each light.

To be quit of this place, Thanquol was ready to brave anything. Even the thought that a slum like Skabreach might be too lowly to draw the attention of Nightlord Sneek and the assassins of Clan Eshin wasn't comforting enough to make him embrace the flea-infested warren as a refuge.

Thanquol hurried through the crowded runs between the rathide shacks, kicking and clawing his way through the press of scabby skaven bodies. His eyes were fixed upon his goal: the massive pier and warehouse maintained by Skabreach's small clutch of water-rats from Clan Skurvy. Among the few skaven with an affinity for water and the lunatic capacity for braving the subterranean rivers of the Under-Empire, Clan Skurvy was a powerful force within the skaven economy; its clanlord, the self-appointed Fleetmaster Viskit Ironscratch, enjoyed a position upon the Council of Thirteen. Ironscratch held tremendous power through the indispensable services of his armada of barges and scows. Without clans like Skurvy and Sleekit, valuable cargoes of food and slaves would rot before they reached the markets of Skavenblight. The iron hook which served the Fleetmaster for a left paw was poised against the belly of every ratman in Skavenblight and the Council knew it. Grudgingly, they had allowed Clan Skurvy to increase its reach until even a forgotten slum like Skabreach was not beyond its influence.

The warehouse had been cobbled together from old planks and timbers scavenged by Clan Skurvy from wrecked man-thing ships and barges. The rickety structure had been assembled in a crude, haphazard fashion, with extra storage rooms and slave pens slapped on seemingly at random, many of them sagging out over the black water of the river.

A great press of skaven surrounded the warehouse, clustering about the pier in a shoving, shouting mob of verminous flesh. Thanquol could see a long, flat-bottomed barge moored at the end of the pier. It did not take any deductive genius to figure out the reason for all the ratmen clamouring for attention. Like himself, they were trying to get out of Skabreach by means of the river, desperately waiting for even the worst scow to put in a rare appearance at the pier.

Perched atop an upended barrel, the outlandish colours of his vest and breeches making a stark contrast to the drabness of the mob, Weezil Gutgnaw, potentate of the local water-rats, was auctioning spots on the barge to the highest bidders. A pair of glowering black skaven who looked as though they'd been sired by rat-ogres flanked the flamboyant Weezil, while another gang of black-furred killers, each armed with a curved cutlass, guarded the narrow entrance to the pier.

'No-no!' Weezil was snarling at a grotesque-looking brown ratman. 'Sick-smell,' he added with a tap to his nose. 'No sick-smell on board!' Weezil kicked the miserable skaven away, at the same time slipping the paltry bribe of warp-tokens he had been offered beneath the bright red sash that girdled his waist.

The grotesque skaven lunged at Weezil, intending to recover his money. In mid-leap, the wretch was cut down by a guard's cutlass. Black blood sprayed across the mob. An excited squeal rose from the throng, dozens of skaven rushing at the corpse and scrabbling among its clothing for any wealth the dead ratman might have hidden. By the time a pair of piebald scavengers armed with flesh-hooks pushed their way through to drag the body away, the mob's frenzy had reduced the corpse to an unrecognisable mess of naked meat.

Thanquol watched the gory mass being dragged away, then pushed his way towards Weezil's barrel. He felt a great wave of satisfaction when he saw the wharf-rat wince at his approach.

'You were supposed to say-tell when a ship came in,' Thanquol hissed through clenched fangs, his red eyes glaring into Weezil's frightened yellow ones. The grey seer cocked his horned head to one side, a fierce grin splitting his face. 'Perhaps you-you mistake-forget?'

The menace in the grey seer's voice silenced the throng gathered about the pier. Nervously, the skaven fell back, clearing the space around Thanquol and Weezil. Even the black-furred bodyguards drew away, distancing themselves from their patron and the infamous sorcerer.

Weezil licked his fangs and tugged anxiously at the warpstone earring he wore. 'G-great and g-glorious Thanquol, mightiest of g-grey seers,' Weezil stammered. 'I... I... I was just-soon to send-fetch...' Weezil tugged even more fiercely at his earring, casting an angry look at his bodyguards. The black skaven ignored his signal, finding more interesting things to look at on the cavern ceiling.

'I told-ordered you to find-fetch me a ship!' Thanquol

growled. He gestured furiously at the barge tied to the pier. 'What-what do you think-see that is!'

Weezil turned and squinted at the barge where skaven sailors were making fast the meagre cargo Skabreach had provided them. 'Oh! But that is too poor-poor a vessel to carry-take Mighty Thanquol!' the wharf-rat tried to explain.

The lame excuse only provoked Thanquol's anger. With callous brutality, he brought the heavy metal head of his staff smacking into Weezil's leg. The wharf-rat spilled from his perch atop the barrel, smashing into the bloody ground in a tangle of curses and flailing limbs.

'I'd sail-scurry from this dung-hole in the hollowed carcass of a cave beetle!' Thanquol raged. He jabbed the end of his staff into Weezil's chin, splintering some of the ratman's fangs. 'Now listen-hear, tick-sucking tail-sniffer! Tell-say the captain-chief of that wormy scow I am leaving this filthy midden-mound!'

Weezil pressed his nose into the mud, cowering before the grey seer's wrath. 'Calamitous lord! Please... listen-hear... it-it not my fault! Warlord Ibkikk say-order make-keep you here-here!'

The wharf-rat's words came in a frightened squeal, whistling through his broken fangs, but they were enough to arouse a twinge of fear along Thanquol's spine. Was it possible that cringing, pathetic warlord would actually have the gall to detain someone of his power and importance? Certainly the lick-spittle had made a few fawning requests for his help in ridding the area of the knights who so plagued Skabreach. But certainly the maggot wasn't so deranged as to think such an enterprise was worth Thanquol's time?

'You-you stay-stay!' a savage voice growled from

behind Thanquol. There was such a note of ferocity and such a lack of deference in the voice, that the grey seer didn't at once connect it with Ibkikk. Only the warlord's scent convinced him that his ears weren't playing tricks on him.

Thanquol turned slowly. At the mouth of one of the runs he could see Ibkikk, his bulk now encased in a rough suit of armour crafted from human shields laced into a vest of mail. The warlord's lips were curled back from a mouth of gleaming fangs. Around him, a score of armoured clanrats stood with bared weapons.

'I ask-speak before,' Ibkikk snarled. 'Now I say-tell! Thanquol will-will use his magic-power against steel-men! Thanquol will-will fight-kill for Skabreach!'

The grey seer listened to the warlord's tirade, but found his attention constantly shifting back to the barge. The crew had erupted into a positive frenzy of activity. It wasn't difficult to guess their intentions. They were making ready to debark as fast as they could.

'Mighty Grey Seer Thanquol!' Ibkikk scoffed, spitting a blob of phlegm into the mud. 'We-we feed-treat you for many day-night! Now you-you return-pay! You kill-slay steel-men! Or I gut-stab you and let-leave rats to eat-feast!'

As he hissed the threat, Ibkikk drew his notched sword from his ratskin belt. The warlord ran one of his fingers along the blade, drawing a thin bead of blood from his finger.

Sight of the gesture sent a spasm of terror coursing through Thanquol's body. The image of a homicidal ginger-furred dwarf-thing running his thumb along the edge of his enormous axe flared through the grey seer's mind.

Before he was fully aware of what he was doing,

Thanquol tongued the last bit of warpstone he had hidden in his cheek-pouch and crushed the tiny pebble between his teeth. A pulse of raw magical energy rippled through his body, burning away his fear and enflaming his mind with visions of destruction and havoc.

Ibkikk squirted the musk of fear as he saw Thanquol's eyes suddenly erupt with a green glow. The same magical light gathered about the head of the grey seer's staff. The warlord had just enough time to drop his sword and turn to flee before his enemy raised one of his paws and pointed a claw at him.

'Burn-rot!' Thanquol snapped. As he spat the words, a stream of crackling green lightning leapt from his finger to strike Ibkikk squarely in the back. The warlord shrieked as the magical energy scorched a hole clean through his body, shrivelling his flesh and blackening his bones. The charred husk smashed to the floor, burned bones scattering across the narrow street.

The sight of their leader's instant destruction killed any enthusiasm his warriors had for confronting the sorcerer-seer. They glanced anxiously at one another, each waiting for one of the other clanrats to make the first move.

Thanquol glared contemptuously at the cringing vermin. It would be so easy to burn them all down where they stood. He started to raise his paw to do just that when simple practicality quenched the warpstone-fuelled impulse. This scum was nothing to him. All that mattered now was getting to the barge.

Thanquol brought his staff smashing down, obliterating the charred skull of Ibkikk which had bounced across the ground to land nearly at his feet. 'I think-say Skabreach need-wants a new warlord,' he growled, letting his menacing gaze linger on the cowering clanrats before turning and marching down the pier towards the barge.

The black-furred guards of Clan Skurvy didn't even dare to look at him as he stormed past them.

'A good-safe journey, dread Thanquol!' Weezil's whistling voice called out from behind the barrel.

Briefly, the grey seer considered turning back and attending to the double-dealing wharf-rat.

A FEW HOURS out from port, Thanquol was beginning to question allowing Ibkikk Snatchclaw to goad him into embarking upon such an unseemly vessel as the leaky old barge he now found himself on. Staring at the black waters of the underground river, he recalled the nightmarish horrors of his ocean voyage. The only difference being that at least the longboat had been seaworthy! His current conveyance seemed designed for no other purpose than to drown him and leave his body to be picked at by whatever noxious things slithered in these lightless waterways.

Paranoid thoughts swirled about in Thanquol's mind. It was all a plot, of course! Ibkikk pushing him to leave Skabreach so that Clan Skab could have its revenge on him! What better way than to drown him on the river, with no one any the wiser about his fate. They could tell the Council they had never seen him and everyone would assume he had perished in Lustria!

Or was it Clan Skab at all? It wasn't the brightest or most subtle of the warlord clans. Such a cunning plot would have to have a more cunning mind behind it. Clan Eshin! Nothing was secret from Nightlord Sneek's spies! He would have learned of Thanquol's return and the success of his mission. The famed assassins wouldn't want it getting around that he had succeeded where they had failed.

Thanquol studied the deck of the barge with a new suspicion, inspecting every pile of mushrooms or crate of chow-rats for any lurking shape. His nose twitched as he drew the smells of his fellow voyagers into his senses, trying to detect any skaven that didn't smell right. After his terrifying encounter with the Death-master in Skavenblight, he almost expected Snikch to be hiding among the huddle of grubby passengers or the mass of naked slaves chained to the foredeck. Most of these were skaven, wretches sold by the ratmen of Skabreach, but a few were dwarfs captured by the more prosperous skaven of Stabfall, deep beneath the Iranna Mountains.

The barge itself was a leaky mass of planks soaked in pitch and lashed together with a mishmash of chains, ropes and crossbeams. Water slopped across the deck every time the vessel hit even the most minor spot of rough water. A ratgut lantern suspended from a pole at the stern and another at the bow provided the only illumination. A gang of villainous ratmen dressed in the same sort of colourful rags as Weezil Gutgnaw served the dingy ship as its crew, languishing under the tyrannical voice of their captain. This worthy was a whip-wielding despot with cold green eyes and a tuft of white fur sprouting from his chin, resembling nothing so much as the dainty face-hair sometimes worn by prosperous humans.

Lynsh Blacktail snarled a stream of orders to his crew and stalked across the rolling deck to stand beside Thanquol. The vicious captain doffed the battered black hat crushed down about his ears and bobbed his head in deference to the grey seer's eminence.

'No fear about follow-track now, Terrible Thanquol,' Lynsh told him, the iron fangs in his mouth rasping against his lips as he spoke. 'Nobody swim-sneak this far-long down the river.' A chitter of amusement coursed through the barge-rat's voice. 'Skabreach better-nice with no-none Ibkikk!'

Thanquol glared at the captain. Did the slime really think he was worth speaking to simply because he was the captain of this wreck? Or was the wretch trying to distract him? The grey seer's eyes narrowed with new suspicion. He didn't have any more warpstone, but in a pinch he could certainly call up a spell on his own. Certainly one strong enough to send this tub to the bottom and ensure his enemies followed him to a watery grave.

Lynsh noted the shift in Thanquol's attitude. Seeming to guess the turn in the grey seer's thoughts, he pulled his tail upwards, displaying it for Thanquol to see. Only about six inches of the captain's real tail was left; the rest of the extremity had been replaced with a length of black leather studded with a sadistic array of spikes and blades.

'Pretty-pretty,' Lynsh cooed, stroking the artificial tail. 'Big-hungry lurker take-snatch real one,' he explained, jabbing a claw towards the black water. 'Snick-snap! No more tail! Eat it all up!'

Thanquol winced in disgust at the image of some loathsome water beast waiting just under this leaky barge to snap off his tail. For an instant, his attention turned from Lynsh to the dark surface of the river. The jab of a blade against his ribs reminded him that he didn't need to look to the river for danger.

'One word I don't like-like and I tickle-stab your lung,' Lynsh hissed into Thanquol's ear. He put emphasis on the threat by pressing the blade a little closer, evoking a whine of pain from his captive. The captain raised his voice, shouting new orders to his crew.

'Alright you bilge-worms! Sort the passenger-meat!'

At their captain's command, the barge-rats abandoned their other duties and swarmed over the passengers who had embarked on the barge at Skab-reach. Most of the skaven were taken completely by surprise by the sudden treachery and the few who did put up a fight were quickly put down. The triumphant pirates herded their prisoners to the middle of the deck, searching them with expert skill for any valuables they had hidden about them.

'Steal-fetch all of it!' Lynsh bellowed. 'Put any rat-meat we can sell-trade with the slaves! The rest can swim-sink!'

Thanquol watched as the skaven pirates brutally carried out their orders. The healthiest of the prisoners were herded towards the chained slaves. The others, shrieking and squealing in terror, whining for mercy, were callously thrown into the river. Some made a desperate effort to swim back to the barge, but these were savagely driven away by jabs from the crew's spears.

'Enterprising,' Thanquol told Lynsh, hoping to use flattery to ingratiate himself into the pirate's good graces. 'The Horned One smiles on clever-smart skaven.'

'Good-good,' chittered Lynsh. 'Now we see-take what Great Thanquol has to give-leave.'

'No-no!' shrieked one of the crew, a dusky creature with notched ears and a tangle of talismans about his neck. 'We-we not rob-take from grey seer!'

'Who say-squeak we don't?' demanded Lynsh.

'I say-squeak!' the indignant pirate snarled. 'Bring-find curse of Horned One...'

Before he could finish, the pirate's head exploded in a

gory mess. In one smooth motion, without ever removing the knife from Thanquol's ribs, Lynsh had drawn
a heavy warplock pistol from his belt and sent a ball
of hardened warpstone smashing through the ratman's
skull.

The shot had unexpected consequences, however.
Hurled back by the impact of the deadly bullet, the
pirate was flung into the mass of chained slaves. While
the skavenslaves cowered, the dwarf prisoners surged
towards the body, seizing the dead pirate's weapons. In
a matter of seconds, the dwarfs used the ratman's cutlass to smash open the rusty lock restraining the single
chain which ran through the manacles each of them
wore and which linked all of them together.

Several of the pirates leapt forwards to subdue the
dwarfs, but it was already too late. Two of the bearded
prisoners had weapons now and were in no mind to
fall captive to the scheming ratmen a second time. The
brawny, red-haired dwarf who had taken the cutlass
now plied it about in a murderous arc. Grim determination was etched upon his face as he opened the throat
of one pirate, then hacked the paw from a second. A
younger dwarf, armed with a knife and protecting his
kinsman's flank, finished the wounded pirate with a
quick stab through the eye.

'Belay that row!' Lynsh thundered. 'Get-take that
slave-meat!'

The captain's distraction was only momentary, but it
was enough for Thanquol. The instant he felt the pressure of Lynsh's knife against his ribs lessen, the grey seer
spun into action. Viciously, he smashed the head of his
staff full into the pirate's face. Something broke inside
Lynsh's snout, black blood streaming from his nose.
Stunned, the captain reeled back, his knife clattering

to the deck as he clapped both hands to his mangled muzzle.

Thanquol did not give Lynsh time to recover. Drawing his own sword, he pursued the staggered captain. A swipe of his staff cracked against the side of Lynsh's head, a slash of his blade opened the ratman's thigh. Before he could deal the pirate further damage, Thanquol was forced back by Lynsh's flailing tail. The bladed appendage gouged splinters from the deck as the grey seer retreated from its deadly thrashings.

'Your bones will make good-nice chum, prayer-spitter!' Lynsh howled, slashing at Thanquol with another sweep of his gruesome tail. For good measure, the pirate pulled his whip from his belt, adding the lash to his vengeful assault against the grey seer.

A flick of the whip set the lash coiling about Thanquol's staff, a swipe of the tail smacked against his chest, knocking him flat. Lynsh gloated as he used his brawn to rip the staff from his enemy's paws. His tail came slamming down against the grey seer's head, only Thanquol's horns saving him from the murderous blow.

Before Lynsh could attack again, the captain was suddenly confronted by a very different foe. Roaring a fierce dwarf battle-cry, the escaped slaves came lunging across the deck, breaking through the ragged line of pirates trying to subdue them. The red-bearded dwarf with the cutlass charged straight into Lynsh.

For the second time, the captain was caught by surprise. He turned to deal with the enraged dwarf, but the cutlass easily chopped through Lynsh's whip, taking three of his fingers in the same stroke. The embattled captain recoiled in agony, howling for help from his crew.

At the same time, the young dwarf who had armed

himself with a knife came around the side of Lynsh. Intent upon helping his comrade and believing the pirate had finished Thanquol with the brutal sweep of his bladed tail, the dwarf made the mistake of placing his back to the prone grey seer.

Seething with indignation and the fury of a cornered rat, Thanquol pounced upon the unwary dwarf, stabbing his sword into the prisoner's back. The blade erupted in a welter of gore from the dwarf's chest. Thanquol's victim was dead before he slumped to the ramshackle deck.

The red-bearded dwarf turned away from the cowering Lynsh. His eyes went wide with shock as he saw his comrade fall to the deck. An instant later, they became narrow slits of hate.

'That is my brother you've killed, vermin!' the dwarf roared, brandishing his bloodied cutlass.

'Your birthkin was in my way, dwarf-thing,' Thanquol snapped. The grey seer's eyes burned with unholy energies as he drew the power of the Horned Rat into himself. Without the aid of warpstone, magic was a fatiguing effort, one that didn't really appeal to any grey seer. At the moment, however, Thanquol was too angry to care about exerting his affinity with the aethyr.

'You're in my way too,' the grey seer announced, raising his paw and pointing a claw at the enraged dwarf. Before the prisoner could rush him, Thanquol sent a globe of searing green light smashing into him. The magic crashed into the dwarf with the kick of a mastodon, flinging him across the deck of the barge as though he had been shot from a cannon, pitching him out into the river where his hurtling form was lost in the darkness. Thanquol flicked his ears in cruel amusement as he heard a faint splash.

Now it was time to deal with his real enemy. Turning towards Lynsh, however, Thanquol found that the fight had gone out of the pirate. The captain came crawling towards him, whining and pleading for mercy. The grey seer lifted a paw to his forehead where one of the spikes on the pirate's tail had cut him.

The other pirate-rats came scurrying towards the two foes. With the vanquishing of their armed leaders, the rest of the dwarf captives had been quickly subdued. Now, however, the crew found themselves uncertain which of the two leaders it was safer to support. They knew the viciousness of Lynsh Blacktail, but they did not know what other fell magic Grey Seer Thanquol might unleash upon them.

Thanquol could smell the fear and doubt in the scent of the other pirates. Gloatingly he turned towards them. 'I think-say this scow needs a new-better captain.' No voices rose in objection and Thanquol knew then that none would. Imperiously he pointed a claw at Lynsh. 'My first command is that you get rid of the old captain.'

Thanquol stepped back as the crew surged forwards. Eagerly they seized Lynsh and in a matter of moments pitched him into the river. Thanquol wondered if that lurker was somewhere about. If so, it might finish the meal it had started long ago.

Looking out over the crew, Thanquol tugged at his whiskers and considered his next move. 'I don't know how much-little Lynsh claimed-took as captain, but I'll settle for half.' He could see from the way the pirates glared at him that whatever Lynsh's cut had been, it was a good deal less than half.

Thanquol bared his teeth and flexed the fingers of his hand, the hand that had so lately dealt sorcerous death to the crazed dwarf. The threat was not lost on the crew.

'If there are no objections, I want a course laid for Skavenblight,' Thanquol told the barge-rats.

There were no objections.

CHAPTER II

BLACK WITH THE heavy darkness of the underworld, cold with the chill of the forsaken deep, the tunnels coursed their way beneath the mountains, writhing like worms in the corpse of a shattered kingdom. Long ago, these passages had echoed with the clamour of hammers and the scrape of picks, the roar of explosives and the hiss of steam-drills. Miners and engineers, architects and prospectors; once these halls had been filled with the clatter of their heavy boots and the sound of their gruff voices as they laboured to wrest from the darkness the treasures of the earth and carve for themselves a kingdom of steel and stone.

Now, the old tunnels were abandoned by those who had gouged them from the rock. They were a relic of a bygone time, a time when the dwarf kingdoms dared to dream of glories that would never be. A relic of the days before the dwarfs were beset from above and below by their merciless enemies. A relic of an age that now lingered only in the ancient Book of Grudges.

Like worms burrowing through a corpse, the black tunnels writhed beneath the remaining strongholds of the dwarfs. Abandoned to the darkness. Left to the creatures that had risen to inherit much of the dwarfs' ancient realm.

Miner and architect no longer dared to brave the old dark of the underworld, but the dwarfs could not completely ignore the leavings of their past glories. The things that had crept into their abandoned holdings were not content to steal what had been left to them. They would use the old tunnels to besiege what little the dwarfs still had the strength to maintain. Goblin and orc, troll and ogre, the dwarfs had to remain vigilant against their rapacious enemies.

In the darkness, a group of dour figures kept that vigil. Armoured from head to toe in extensively engraved plates of gromril, their flowing beards locked behind iron beard-sheaths, the dwarfs maintained their unending watch upon the tunnels. Silent as the rock walls, knowing that the least sound might betray them to the ears of a lurking goblin, the sentinels communicated by touch and gesture rather than by spoken word. Among a race accustomed to labouring in the darkness, the eyes of these lonely warriors were especially keen, able to see in almost pitch blackness. For in these forsaken tunnels, light, even more than sound, would betray a dwarf to his enemies.

These were the ironbreakers, an elite cadre of warriors with brothers throughout the scattered strongholds of the dwarf kingdom. Theirs was the role of watchman and sentinel, the first line of defence for their people against the horrors of the deeps. Against the monsters of the underworld, the ironbreakers pitted their self-less valour and martial prowess. Armed with the best weapons to emerge from the forges of their warsmiths, encased in armour crafted from indestructible gromril, many a foe had met its end before these unbreakable warriors.

Among the dozen armoured dwarfs spread across the opening of the tunnel, one of their number stood close against the wall. The lone dwarf had removed one of his gauntlets. His bare hand was closed about a length of wire fastened to the wall, his sensitive fingers pinching the copper thread between them. His role was one of especial vigilance, so much so that he did not engage in such silent banter as the gesture-speak allowed the other ironbreakers. He knew that the thin little wire held the only advanced warning they could expect in the case of an approaching enemy.

Strung across the floor of the tunnels, the wire would brush against the feet of any invader, sending a vibration along its length which the monitoring ironbreaker could feel with his fingers. Many times, by such a ruse, the dwarfs had been warned of things creeping through the tunnels. Their foreknowledge had been the difference between victory and disaster on more than one occasion. Goblins, cave squigs, even a basilisk, had all been repulsed before they could enter the inhabited halls of Karak Angkul.

Now, the wire again pulsed with the step of an enemy. The monitor reached out with his armoured right hand, closing his fingers about the shoulder of the dwarf standing beside him. The touch of the monitor's hand was all that was needed. The meaning was clear. Without a word being spoken, the alarm was passed among the ironbreakers. One of their number, the youngest and most junior of their company, was dispatched back into the passages of Karak Angkul proper to warn their people of potential danger. The other warriors drew axes and hammers from their belts. Closing ranks, standing shoulder to shoulder, they formed an unbroken wall of armour across the mouth of the tunnel.

Long minutes, the dwarfs waited for their foes. The monitor continued to clap the shoulder of his comrade, indicating that their enemy was no lone straggler from the deep. The continued vibration of the wire meant a large group of adversaries, many feet trampling the concealed wires.

Before the sharp-eyed dwarfs could see or even hear the coming foe the loathsome stink of the enemy struck them. Not one of the ironbreakers could forget that smell. Memories of battle and fallen comrades rose within each dwarf's mind, litanies of ancient grudges made speechless lips move in silent whispers. Ancestral hate, the heritage of centuries of unending war, caused hands to tighten about the grips of weapons. Yes, the ironbreakers knew this smell, the reek of their most despised enemy: the verminous skaven!

'Fast-quick, dung-scum! Smash-kill all dwarf-things!'

Rikkit Snapfang added a bit of emphasis to his snarled command by lopping off the ear of a skaven who had the misfortune of standing too close to him. The stricken ratman squealed in agony, clapping a paw to his bleeding head and cringing his way into the teeming horde of furry bodies scurrying down the tunnel. Rikkit raised his sword to his mouth and licked the blood from his blade. The faint trace of warpstone in the black ooze sent a thrill coursing through him. There was nothing like the taste of blood to stir a warrior's heart before battle.

'Scurry-hurry, maggot-suckers!' Rikkit growled, making a menacing sweep of his blade. It would be just like the treacherous lice to malinger in the tunnels and allow the dwarfs to escape. Worse, they might be so slothful that there would still be dwarfs alive when he reached the battlefield. Rikkit had all the ferocity and valour of a true skaven warrior, but very little appetite for engaging an enemy able to fight back. That was the duty of slaves and clanrats, to take all the danger out of the enemy before important skaven such as himself entered the fray. As a warlord of Clan Mors, Rikkit Snapfang would see that his underlings didn't shirk that duty. Even if it meant killing a few dozen of them to keep the others moving.

Not for the first time, Rikkit cursed the craven hearts of his minions. But for their cowardice, he would have risen to prominence within the hierarchy of Clan Mors, gaining the notice of Clanlord Gnawdwell, perhaps even joining the Supreme and Merciless War-king Tyrant-General in Skavenblight. Instead, Rikkit was rotting away as warlord of a single warren, the fortress-burrow of Bonestash, a three-mouse hole some three miles beneath the stronghold of Karak Angkul.

Long had the skaven of Bonestash coveted the halls of the dwarfs above them, dreaming their vicious dreams of the hoarded wealth so near they could smell it. Many a warlord had tried to batter his way into Karak Angkul, each expedition ending in disaster. Rikkit Snapfang, however, was smarter than his predecessors. He knew that it took wealth to gain greater wealth. He had shunned the tactics of his stupid precursors, the massed charge of half-naked slaves straight into the waiting axes of the foe. His was a far more crafty and subtle mind. It had cost him almost half the treasury of Bonestash and much of the riches he had skimmed for himself, but he was certain he had spent his warp-tokens well.

Baring his fangs, Rikkit Snapfang shrieked his final command, urging the horde of nearly naked skaven-slaves to charge into the ranks of their enemy. The dwarfs might be able to kill their lights and hold their tongues, but they could not mask the scent of their skin. In the pitch darkness, the skaven would still be able to find their enemies and destroy them.

The terrified slaves, urged forwards by the brutal lashes of Rikkit's clanrat soldiers, swept up the tunnel in a tidal wave of stinking fur and flashing fangs. Rusty swords, stone clubs, splintered spears and corroded maces lashed out as the scrawny ratmen crashed against the armoured wall of their enemies.

The ironbreakers met the first wave of the attack with stony discipline. Unmovable, the dwarfs absorbed the crush of frenzied skaven. Rusted blades shattered against gromril plate, stone clubs chipped and cracked as they rebounded from the rune-etched armour. Squealing in terror, the foremost skaven tried to flee from their invulnerable enemies, only to be pressed back into the fight by the multitudes swarming up the tunnel behind them.

With the need to keep silent gone, the ironbreakers gave voice to a great shout. Their roar thundered through the tunnel, like the grumble of an angry mountain. They swept their axes into the press of claw-ing, stabbing bodies before them. In such quarters, every blow the dwarfs dealt split open a skull or slashed through a ribcage. Arms and legs and tails were lopped from the frantic ratmen as they alternately tried to escape or vainly strove to break through the formation of their enemies.

Rikkit listened to the carnage and a twinkle came into his beady eyes. The ironbreakers had taken the bait. They were committed to the fight now. There would be no escape for the hated dwarfs this time. No doubt they thought he was just another idiot warlord squandering his troops on the same suicidal attacks that had been tried so many times before.

Lashing his tail in amusement, Rikkit gestured to the mass of brown-furred skaven gathered at the foot of the tunnel. These ratmen were of a finer breed than the scabby slaves he had sent so callously to be slaughtered. Better fed, with sleek pelts and wearing long leather aprons, they formed a marked contrast to Rikkit's abused minions. The warlord felt better just smelling the cold assurance they exuded in their scent, the encouraging odour of warpstone and gunpowder and the exotic oils these skaven used to maintain their weaponry.

Such weaponry! Great muskets with barrels longer than the ratmen who used them, each fitted with a glass eye to magnify their victims and ensure a killing shot! Pouches of refined gunpowder, little ratskin bags filled with bullets crafted from shards of warpstone! Grimy little skavenslaves bearing metal crooks upon which to rest the muzzle of each jezzail and ensure the steadiness of the shot! Rikkit had spent a small fortune hiring these mercenaries from Clan Skryre, but when they smashed the vaunted defenders of Karak Angkul, he would count the warp-tokens as well spent.

Climbing onto a ramshackle wooden platform Rikkit's clanrats had erected, the jezzail teams loaded their weapons and took their positions. With the added height of the platform, the skaven sharpshooters would be able to fire over the heads of the slave horde and into the dwarfs beyond. Not that Rikkit was overly concerned by the accidental shooting of his worthless slave-troops, but when each bullet was costing him three warp-tokens, there was no sense in wasting ammunition.

The jezzails took aim, crouching over the barrels of their muskets, squinting through the telescopic lenses until they could draw a bead on their targets. A chittered peal of laughter rose from the first shooter as he pulled the trigger and sent a shard of warpstone rocketing towards one of the ironbreakers.

The bullet struck one of the skavenslaves, punching through his spine and tearing out of his chest in a welter of gore. Passage through the ratman's body hardly diminished the terrible velocity of the bullet. The round ploughed onwards, smashing into the armoured breast of the ironbreaker.

The sharpshooter cursed under his breath, fear creeping into his scent. Through the sights of his jezzail he was able to see his bullet shatter as it crashed into the dwarf's gromril breastplate. The dwarf was knocked back a few steps, but when he recovered, there wasn't even a scratch to show where he had been hit.

The stunned sharpshooter snarled at the other jezzails. Instantly there was unleashed a full fusillade against the dwarfs. The shrieks of skaven caught in the path of the deadly bullets rang through the tunnel, but the enchanted armour of the ironbreakers again proved too much for the skaven weapons to penetrate.

Although he could not see the inefficacy of the jezzails, Rikkit could still hear the sounds of battle coming from the mouth of the tunnel. If the weapons had performed as they should have, then the dwarfs would be in no condition to put up a fight. Tugging at his whiskers in his agitation, Rikkit glared up at the sharpshooters as they reloaded their weapons. Quickly, the warlord began to calculate how much this fiasco was costing him.

'Stop-stop!' Rikkit howled. He didn't wait to see if his mercenaries were going to obey. Gesturing to his dependable clanrat warriors, Rikkit ordered them to knock down the firing platform. Before they could shoot again, the jezzail teams found their perch tipped over and themselves sprawled across the floor.

Rikkit glared at the worthless sharpshooters. If he didn't have to pay Clan Skryre extra for every one of their warriors who perished while fighting for him, he would have each of the mangy parasites skinned alive and fed to the squigs! They had proven useless. Worse, they were expensive and useless! Fortunately, he had been too clever to stake all of his ambitions upon a bunch of cowardly snipers who couldn't shoot straight.

'Bad-air! Bad-air!' the clanrats were squealing now. A half-dozen ratmen came slinking up the tunnel. They formed a strange and sinister sight, their bodies covered from crown to tail in heavy ratskin cloaks soaked in preservative unguents and chemical solutions. Bulky, grotesque devices were slung to their backs, deranged contraptions of pipes and tubes that groaned and shuddered as they circulated air through their frames. Ugly masks enclosed the faces of each of the ratmen, giving them an almost insect-like look. At their sides, each of the skaven carried a heavy bag filled with glass globes, a sinister green mist swirling within each of the spheres. As the globadiers made their way towards the massed slaves, the wretched verminkin struggled to flee from their approach. The clanrats at the rear of the slave horde were more pressed than ever to keep the mob from turning tail and stampeding back down the tunnel.

Rikkit grinned savagely as he watched the globadiers force their way along the flanks of the packed slaves. The Poison Wind was one of the most hideous weapons known to skavendom, a vapour so toxic it could eat through iron and would melt the lungs of those who inhaled it. Even the most reckless warlord did not employ such a weapon without severe consideration, but the jezzails had failed to eliminate the ironbreakers for him. Now it was time to set aside his scruples and give the dwarfs the death their stubborn refusal to die had earned them.

Unseen by the ironbreakers, the globadiers drew closer to the fray. The hideous skaven in their gas masks and protective cloaks hesitated when they came within twenty feet of the embattled dwarfs. Heedless of their fellow ratmen who were still braving the enemy axes, the globadiers thrust their gloved hands into the bags slung at their sides. Chittering maliciously within their masks, the murderous skaven hurled the fragile glass globes into the raging melee.

Green fog burst across the tunnel as the globes crashed violently against the combatants. The shrill shrieks of ratmen ripped across the tunnel as the deadly gas engulfed them, burning through flesh and fur with savage rapacity. Dozens of skavenslaves wilted to the ground, blood streaming from their mouths as they coughed out their lives.

Though it had cost the lives of many ratkin, the brutal assault by the globadiers broke the dwarf line. For the first time, the discipline of the ironbreakers was fractured. Their stout gromril armour, proof against the fiercest blows, could not guard them against a weapon which could seep beneath the armour to attack the dwarf within.

First one, then another, then the entire company slumped to the ground, axes and hammers tumbling from numbed fingers. The dwarfs coughed as violently as the dying ratmen around them, a gory pulp of burned tissue dribbling into their beards. Their eyes, once so keen in the darkness, were blinded as bursting capillaries turned them into crimson pits of misery.

'Fast-quick! Kill-slay!' Rikkit shrieked at his warriors, driving his clanrats to turn the fleeing slaves about and herd them back up the tunnel. With the defenders on the floor, he wanted to take no chances that the dwarfs would somehow rally to thwart his schemes. Not waiting even for the Poison Wind to dissipate, he forced his army upwards. Dozens of slaves perished as they were thrust full into the still potent cloud of gas, but they were losses Rikkit was prepared to accept.

After the gas had dispersed and the vanguard of his warriors were stripping the dead ironbreakers of their vaunted armour, he breathed a little easier. His gamble had paid off. They were free to invade the upper halls now and claim the stronghold for Clan Mors!

'Leave dwarf-things!' Rikkit snapped at the looters. He pointed his claw towards the upper corridor. 'More-more dwarf-meat to kill-take!'

The skaven host, their bloodlust stirred by the smell of dead enemies, needed only a few threats to get them moving again. Like a river of fur and fangs, the ratmen surged into the lower workings of Karak Angkul. Here the walls were not the raw, unworked stone of the tunnels, but were crafted from great blocks of granite, richly adorned with massive columns. Mighty pillars supported the arched ceiling high overhead, huge steel lanterns hanging from the hook-like crockets adorning their finials.

Rikkit revelled in his triumph as the skaven horde pressed onwards, sweeping into deserted mine-workings and empty galleries. No long-abandoned halls, these, but living chambers still thick with the smell of dwarf. Clearly the ironbreakers had spread the alarm to their fellows above! The realisation brought conflicting thoughts racing through the warlord's mind. On the one paw, he appreciated the tactical advantage to catching his enemies unaware. By the other paw, however, his ego was glutted by the knowledge that the dwarfs had fled from him, Rikkit Snapfang, rather than face him in hopeless battle!

Packs of skaven now detached themselves from the main host, swarming into the empty galleries, hunting among the chambers for any dwarf stragglers and whatever loot they had left behind. The main horde, however, driven by the threats of their warlord and the lashes of their clawleaders, made straight for the ramps leading to the upper halls of Karak Angkul. Why pick over the leavings of miners when they could pillage the chambers of kings?

As the surging mass of ratmen raced up the ramps, the skaven saw the first dwarfs since they had broken through the guards in the tunnel. A skirmish line of dwarf warriors had arrayed themselves in one of the upper galleries. When the skaven saw how few their foes were, their creeping laughter echoed from the walls. If this was the best the dwarfs could muster, then the entire stronghold would soon belong to the ratkin.

In their murderous rush to come to grips with the dwarfs, the ratmen paid scant attention to the upturned mining carts scattered between themselves and the battle line. It was only when the attackers were a few dozen yards from the carts that they realised their mistake.

The wooden sides of the carts collapsed, revealing themselves to be nothing more than a lightweight façade. Concealed behind the simple panels were squat, bulky machines bristling with pipes and gears, their steel faces pockmarked with the ugly openings of gun barrels. As they were revealed, the machines shuddered into life. Steam jetted from their pipes, gears rumbled into motion. From the score of gun barrels set into the face of each machine, an iron bullet went tearing into the skaven horde.

Mercilessly, the automated guns ripped apart Rikkit's army. Hundreds of skaven warriors were butchered in a matter of moments, their mangled bodies cartwheeling through the air as the vicious barrage scoured their ranks. One of the Poison Wind globadiers was struck, the round punching through his bag of gas bombs. Instantly a deadly cloud spread away from the dead globadier, its fumes searing the flesh of every skaven who came into contact with it. Rikkit shrieked in dismay as he saw his expensive jezzail teams trampled under the paws of his fleeing warriors, their heavy muskets smashed beneath the terrified clanrats.

The automated guns continued to fire at the routed skaven, reaping a bloody harvest from the shattered army. Copper belts fed fresh bullets into the steam-driven machines, allowing them to maintain their withering fire without respite. One of the guns let out a loud screech, its fire falling silent as a belt caught in its mechanism. The other dozen machines, however, continued to punish the skaven until they had fled back down the ramp and into the lower workings of Karak Angkul.

Leading the retreat, Rikkit Snapfang cursed the cowardice and stupidity of his soldiers. They should have expected some kind of dwarf trick and been ready for it! The treacherous rats had instead broken faith with their warlord and allowed themselves to be massacred! Worse, they had allowed his hired mercenaries to die, putting him further in debt to Clan Skryre!

The thought gave Rikkit pause. A cunning gleam wormed its way into his formerly panicked eyes. He still had most of Bonestash's treasury to spend. He could buy more weapons from the warlock-engineers, weapons that would smash, burn and blast whatever the dwarf-things could bring against him! If he could force the treacherous remains of his army to stand fast and keep the enemy from retaking the mines, then there just might be a chance he could still bring the whole of the stronghold under the dominion of the underfolk!

THE DWARFS LET out a mighty cheer as they watched the craven ratmen turn tail and flee back down the rampway. Squads of vengeful warriors broke away from the battle line to finish the stragglers the routed army had left behind. Teams of engineers dashed across the gallery to attend the automated sentinel guns.

Among the dwarfs, a small group stood alone. They displayed only a scant interest in the decimated skaven and the functional sentinel guns. The gun which had jammed, however, warranted their full attention. Even as the last of the ratmen was vanishing back into the lower workings, these dwarfs were in action, hastening to the machine that had failed.

The dwarfs made a curious grouping, a cross-section of Karak Angkul. The first of them to reach the machine was a broad-shouldered hairy brute of a dwarf, his homely face marked by a bulbous nose and close-set eyes, his black beard wound into a trio of long braids. A weird framework of pipes and pistons supported his brawny arms and girded his thick legs. At each step, little bursts of steam rose from the framework, forming beads of condensation on his elaborate armour.

The second of the dwarfs was a spry, youthful example of his kind, his blond beard growing close about his cheeks and chin. There was a keen look in his blue eyes, reflecting the keenly inquisitive mind inside his head. Like his comrade, he was dressed for battle, his body draped in a heavy suit of mail. Thick chains were looped about his waist and neck, each of the chains sporting a wide array of small stone charms etched with ancient Khazalid runes. The oversized hammer the young dwarf bore was likewise marked by a sharp dwarfish rune, the fiery symbol of algaz, a sign endowed with potent magic.

A white-bearded dwarf bearing a horned helm and wearing a rough bearskin hide over his armour came next. He prowled about the sentinel gun with the wary air of a panther stalking prey, his roving eyes never at rest but always watching the shadows for any sign of movement. In his gloved hands, he bore a brace of heavy pistols of ornate and exotic fashion.

Each of the dwarfs had attained his own renown within the halls of Karak Angkul. The brutish dwarf was Horgar Horgarsson, once captain of King Logan's bodyguard and one of the fiercest warriors in the entire stronghold. Goblin poisons had polluted his body and brought him to the brink of death. Only the amazing medicinal skills of the master he now served had preserved his life, and only the same mind's genius for invention had allowed him to be anything more than a cripple afterwards. Horgar had been retired from King Logan's hammerers after his wounding and the grim dwarf had come to serve his saviour as assistant, guard and comrade at arms.

The young dwarf was Kurgaz Brightfinger, the youngest runesmith to ever walk the halls of Karak Angkul. Often dismissed by his elders as little more than a beardling, it had taken an intellect outside the order of runesmiths to appreciate Kurgaz's talents. With the support of his new master, the young dwarf had been able to expand his knowledge of the ancient craft and theorise new ways to use the magic symbols.

There was a reason the white-bearded dwarf studied his surroundings with such caution. Alone among his companions, Thorlek could be said to have spent more of his life above the mountains rather than inside them. A veteran ranger who prowled the surface wilderness hunting and trapping, always keeping a watchful eye out for gathering enemies, Thorlek was an accomplished fighter and tracker renowned for his puckish humour and formidable sword arm.

While the other dwarfs maintained the perimeter, the fourth member of their group inspected the malfunctioning sentinel gun. He was a tall dwarf, towering over his comrades. Powerfully built, with dark leathery skin and a beard of deep gold colour, he cut an impressive figure as he dashed to the machine and began his inspection. His eyes, peculiar orbs of flake-gold hue, pored over the mechanism. At length, he reached into the belt feed and removed a misshapen lump of lead.

'I still say you didn't need to sabotage your own invention,' Horgar grumbled.

The gold-bearded dwarf flashed a sombre smile. 'Guildmaster Thori will need something to complain about, otherwise he won't be happy. And if he isn't happy, then the Engineers' Guild could make problems. I shouldn't like to take the slayer-oath like old Malakai Makaisson.'

'They wouldn't dare!' objected Kurgaz. 'Even King Logan wouldn't try to silence the genius of Klarak Bronzehammer!'

Klarak smiled at his friend, warmed by the young dwarf's enthusiasm and confidence, if not his appreciation for politics. The guilds which controlled dwarf society were founded upon centuries of tradition and experience. They did not accept new ideas easily, and none of them resisted innovation so sternly as the Engineers' Guild. Still, there were ways around the obstructions of dwarfs like Guildmaster Thori. It only took some appreciation for the traditions of the guild and a respect for its power.

Of course, the tacit collusion of a stronghold's ruler was a big help too. Klarak had been able to create many inventions to help the inhabitants of Karak Angkul, but his devices would have withered on the vine without King Logan's help to get around the obstructions of Guildmaster Thori. King Logan was a ruler of unique vision, who appreciated that the way to restore the dwarf kingdom did not lie in some slavish devotion to the past, but in new ideas and bold innovations.

Still, even King Logan felt the power of the Engineers' Guild and there were limits to what he could allow Klarak to do without completely offending the conservative sensibilities of the other engineers.

This field test of Klarak's sentinel guns had been the most audacious exhibition yet. Any dwarf with eyes could see the value of these machines, but the engineers would be slow to approve such a startling invention. It might take hundreds of years before they were satisfied that such a device was safe enough to be approved for production. In the meantime, Karak Angkul would be exposed to her verminous enemies.

Hence, Klarak had deliberately arranged for one of his guns to malfunction. It would give Guildmaster Thori something to complain about and it would give himself an excuse to conduct more 'tests' of his invention.

A deep, rumbling bellow echoed through the gallery, rebounding from the walls. Klarak smiled as he heard the sound. Turning he basked in the boisterous cheers of the dwarf warriors, bowing his head as he accepted their adulation.

'They don't need Guildmaster Thori to tell them your guns worked,' Horgar said.

Klarak frowned and shook his head. 'That makes things worse,' he stated. 'It will make Guildmaster Thori even more critical of their performance. If the common folk start questioning the caution of the guild, then the guild is just going to dig its heels in even more.'

'Idiots,' Thorlek spat.

'Defenders of tradition,' Klarak corrected him in a severe tone. 'Theirs is the thankless duty of advancing progress without sacrificing all that has come before.'

Klarak Bronzehammer fixed each of his aides with a warning look. 'Never forget tradition,' he said. 'For it is the great strength that binds our fractured kingdoms together.'

CHAPTER III

THANQUOL RUBBED HIS claws against his chest to polish them into a menacing sheen. His unyielding stare bore into the beady eyes of the bloated scavenge-merchant. 'Four thousand warp-tokens,' the grey seer reiterated, putting a little more malice into his posture.

Nabkrik Fatgut tugged at his whiskers, avoiding the intensity of the grey seer's gaze. The merchant had been on the wrong paw from the start, ever since Thanquol had smelt fear in the scent of Nabkrik's bodyguards. The hulking, black-furred skaven might have been ready enough to rip out the throat of a common rat-man, but against a grey seer, they seemed more inclined to scratch their fleas than think about using the motley array of weapons hanging from their belts.

'Three-three,' Nabkrik said, holding up three of his fat little claws. Sprawled out in a sedan chair, the piebald skaven looked like some sort of misshapen pillow. The stink of the swamp was everywhere in the crumbling stone cellar Nabkrik employed as his headquarters, which was hardly surprising considering the amount of mud and black sludge oozing down the walls. Half of Skavenblight's old waterfront had already been dragged down into the morass of the Blighted Marshes. The area around Nabkrik's burrow was well on its way to joining its sunken neighbours.

Glancing at the frightened bodyguards, Thanquol's lip curled back in a grisly leer. 'Five thousand warptokens,' he announced. The grey seer enjoyed watching the loathsome trade-rat wince at the figure.

Huddled between the haggling ratmen was a motley collection of dwarfs and skaven, the slaves and ex-passengers Lynsh Blacktail had been transporting before his 'accident' on the river. The captain's crew had been helpful enough in locating the buyer Lynsh had waiting for their cargo. The crew had been quite angry at Thanquol's cut of the spoils, but now that they heard how much the grey seer was going to extort from Nabkrik, they were quickly regaining some of their old confidence and avarice.

They were vile things, these disgusting pirate-rats. Thanquol wondered what sort of diseased breeder could have suckled such vermin at her teats. Preying upon hapless travellers who had placed all of their trust and hope into the treacherous paws of these marauding villains! Scum, without a shred of nobility or decency about them! Knowing no loyalty except their own slinking greed!

'Five thousand warp-tokens,' Thanquol repeated. 'And I'll toss in the scow and its crew.' The grey seer glared malignantly at the pirates who seemed to have a moment of trouble understanding that their new captain had just downgraded their status from sailors to slaves. When they did, the ratmen howled in fury, brandishing their weapons. One of their number lunged at Thanquol, a crooked blade in each paw, spittle flying from his clenched fangs.

Thanquol watched the vengeful rat spring at him. Calmly, the grey seer raised one of his fingers and rasped a string of arcane squeaks. A blazing ribbon of electricity crackled from his finger straight into the leaping pirate. The stricken ratman was flung back through the air, his body smashing against the ceiling before plummeting to the floor. Smoke rose from the charred crater in the centre of the dead pirate's chest, filling the cellar with a noxious reek of ozone and burnt meat.

Nabkrik's guards were quick to pounce on the other pirates, overwhelming them with clubs and sword hilts while they were still in shock at their comrade's violent demise.

'Don't think-think you'll get much-much for that one,' Thanquol stated, nodding at the dead pirate. As he spoke, the grey seer opened his little rat-skull box and took a pinch of warpstone snuff. Old Lynsh had had quite a stash of the stuff secreted away on his scow. Thanquol had been surprised at its high quality, feeling the stuff flow through his brain like fire each time he took a sniff. It made him feel as though he were a walking dynamo of arcane malignance, as though all he had to do was snap his fingers and the Horned Rat would reduce all his enemies into mush. He had to but stretch forth his paw and he could topple the foundation of the world and grind the land into dust. It was really quite a thrilling sensation. He rather regretted dumping Lynsh into the river before finding out where he'd gotten the stuff.

Nabkrik turned a horrified grimace towards the dead pirate, then nervously faced Thanquol once more. 'Five thousand warp-tokens,' the fat old ratkin fairly cried. 'Yes-yes, Dread One!' He fumbled about beneath his chair, removing a few heavy bags that had been soaked in some foul-smelling excretion. It was a sensible precaution when hiding money from thieves who would find it better by scent than sight. The merchant tugged open the neck of one of the bags, displaying the black and green discs inside.

Thanquol's eyes lit up as he saw the mass of wealth. His tail twitched in excitement as he scurried forwards to accept the money.

'Three thousand?' Nabkrik pleaded, hugging one of the bags to his chest. 'I-I can't use-take barge-scow.'

'Sell-trade it to Clan Sleekit,' Thanquol said, jerking the bag away from Nabkrik's fat fingers. 'Or sell it back to Clan Skurvy, if you have the spleen.' A sharp smell crept into Thanquol's nose. Glancing down he noted another bag of warp-tokens still hidden in the drawer beneath the chair. 'And another thousand warp-tokens for saving you from that vicious murder-rat!'

Nabkrik sputtered in protest, but had sense enough to refrain from mentioning that the dead pirate had been intent on killing Thanquol, not himself.

Even so, the grey seer didn't take kindly to the argument. Sniffing another pinch of snuff, he leaned forwards and glared into Nabkrik's eyes, his lips pulled back to expose every fang in the grey seer's mouth. 'Or perhaps you don't feel-think your skin-fur is worth a thousand warp-tokens?'

GREY SEER THANQUOL prowled through Skavenblight's skrawl market, his newly-hired guard-rats battering a path for him through the teeming masses of skaven crowding the streets. Unlike the rest of skavendom, part of Skavenblight existed above ground, situated in the ruins of an ancient human city. Tradition held that the skaven had inherited the city as a gift from the Horned Rat himself, and since that tradition was taught as religious truth by the grey seers, nobody was of a mind to question its basis in fact. While the teeming masses of the Under-Empire eked out an existence in the muddy burrows beneath the city, the rich and powerful carved out nests for themselves among the grandest of the old human buildings. Each of the great Lords of Decay had his own fortified palace within the sprawl of Skavenblight and the most imposing structure in all the city, the colossal bell tower that jutted up into the sky like the bared fang of a god, held the Council of Thirteen's meeting chambers.

With all the most powerful ratmen in the world gathered in Skavenblight, the city's markets were second to none. Merchants and traders from every corner of the Under-Empire brought their wares to the capital, knowing that here alone could they command top price for their exotic goods. Prowling through the skrawl, Thanquol smelled the odours of a hundred lands, heard the chittering squeals of a thousand clans mixed in a cacophony of haggling. He watched a greasy Clan Verms bug-breeder selling trained fleas with shells that glistened like tiny stars. He saw a white-nosed skaven with one ear displaying narcotic salt-licks from the jungles of Ind. He listened to a balding ratman extolling the uses of mole-skin whisker brushes.

Standing amid the jumbled confusion of the market, Thanquol couldn't remember now why he had been so dead-set on seeing Nightlord Sneek as soon as he arrived in the city. He laughed at his foolish paranoia, the puppyish fear that had dogged him all the way down the river. Clan Eshin had no authority over him! He was the mighty Grey Seer Thanquol, hero of skavendom! It was he who had slain Xiuhcoatl, the terrible Prophet of Sotek, not any of Eshin's vaunted murder-rats! If Nightlord Sneek wanted to see him, then the cowardly old shadow-stalker could come to him!

Thanquol snapped shut the rat-skull box and sneezed as the fiery warpstone snuff seared his nasal passages. He cast a shrewd eye on the goods his train of steve-dores was carting behind him. New robes fashioned from the finest weasel-fur. A sword of Cathayan steel. A marvellous dwarf-bone puzzle box, inlaid with tiny tiles of powdered warpstone.

His favourite purchase, however, had to be the horn-rings etched with the thirteen secret names of the Horned One. Thanquol lifted a claw and played idly with them as he walked along, enjoying the way the tiny bells dangling from the gold loops tinkled when he swatted them.

Yes, he would cut quite an imposing figure when Nightlord Sneek came to thank him for saving Clan Eshin from humiliation and disgrace. But, of course, there was one thing that was still missing. Guard-rats were nice, but they had a worrying tendency to take the short-sighted view that their lives were more valuable than that of their employer. Thanquol always felt a more brainless kind of loyalty was advisable to feel truly safe.

Patting his belly, the grey seer lifted his nose and sniffed around for the distinct scent of Clan Moulder's flesh-shapers. He still had a small fortune to spend, more than enough to buy a first-class rat-ogre from one of the beast-masters.

Calling out to his entourage, Thanquol sent his guard-rats ahead to bully a way through the swarming crowd. Other guard-rats kept a close watch on his stevedores, ensuring that none of them got 'lost' in the shuffle.

For many minutes, Thanquol's henchmen tried to force a way through the press of ratmen, but the tide of traffic coming down the street was too great for them to overcome. Growing impatient, and having a momentary flash of fear as he recalled how Chang Fang had tried to use just such a crowd to kill him not long ago, Thanquol directed his minions down a back alleyway. The few denizens of the blighted backpath scampered away when they saw the fearsome grey seer approach.

The smell of rat-ogre leading him on, Thanquol gave directions to his guard-rats, urging them to make speed along the narrow, winding run of alleys. A twinge of disquiet kept nagging at the grey seer, stubbornly resisting his repeated efforts to silence it with a pinch of reassurance from his snuff-box.

The alleyway was about as black as the inside of a snake's belly when Thanquol discovered the reason for his nagging concern. A piece of shadow suddenly detached itself from one of the walls, falling silently upon his leading guard-rats. Before any of them could so much as squeak in surprise, the shadow was cutting them to ribbons, wielding blades not only in each paw, but one gripped by its tail as well!

The tangy stink of skaven blood and voided bowels flooded the alleyway. Thanquol watched the shadow leaping from one guard to the next, striking them down as though they were mewling pups instead of ten warp-tokens a day Clan Rictus sword-rats! The lack of any distinct scent emanating from the murdering shadow abolished any idea that it was anything but one of Clan Eshin's merciless assassins!

Worse, Thanquol was pretty certain he'd seen this particular assassin in action once before. Deathmaster Snikch, Nightlord Sneek's prize killer, a skaven who had never failed to carry out any murder asked of him.

All the reassurance the warpstone snuff had been filling his head with seemed to evaporate. The grey seer's body began to shiver from horn to tail. He tried to focus his mind on a spell that might reduce the Deathmaster to a bloody paste, or at least something that would allow Thanquol to escape from this deathtrap of an alley. But no matter how hard he tried to concentrate, the magical words just swirled around, refusing to coalesce into anything resembling a complete incantation.

Deathmaster Snikch rose from the mangled heap of his last victim, wiping his three swords clean on the dead guard-rat's cloak before stalking straight towards Thanquol. The assassin's body was clad in black silk, his paws and tail dyed to blend with the darkness, but Thanquol could see the malignant gleam in the killer's red eyes. Snikch seemed to be daring the grey seer to try casting a spell against him.

Thanquol did something more practical. He reached into his robes, removed the heavy bags of money Nabkrik had given him and dropped them onto the ground. Snikch cocked his head to one side as he heard the warp-tokens clatter against the hard earth.

'Take-use,' Thanquol urged the Deathmaster. 'I want-want you to have-keep.'

Snikch didn't even look at the bags of money, instead fixing Thanquol with his malignant stare. 'Thanquol returns from lizard-land,' the assassin hissed.

'Yes-yes!' Thanquol hurriedly agreed. 'I kill-slay

Xiuhcoatl! Other skaven ran-flee, but I stay-fight! Keep-keep promise-word to Nightlord Sneek!' Snikch cocked his head to one side as the grey seer spoke the last part so Thanquol hastily added: 'I want-need look good-nice before see-speak to Nightlord.' He hoped it sounded like a reasonable excuse for his delay in seeking out the sinister master of Clan Eshin.

Deathmaster Snikch took another step towards Thanquol, his tail lashing from side to side, a dripping blade still clenched in its prehensile coils.

'Stay away from the dojo, Grey Seer,' Snikch snarled through the folds of his mask. 'Stay far-far away. You were never there.'

Thanquol blinked in confusion. 'But... Xiuhcoatl... kill-slay?'

The sword clenched in the Deathmaster's tail arced upwards. 'Nightlord Sneek never say-send you to lizard-land. Say-squeak anything, and never say-squeak anything again.'

Thanquol continued to mutter confusedly. What madness was Snikch talking about? Of course Sneek had sent Thanquol to Lustria! The mission had been a success! Xiuhcoatl was dead! Clan Eshin had exactly what they wanted. What did it matter if Thanquol was the only one to return to tell the tale? The Prophet of Sotek was dead!

His threat made, Deathmaster Snikch faded back into the darkness, vanishing in the wink of an eye. If not for the dead guard-rats strewn about the alley and the fear musk dripping down his leg, Thanquol might have questioned whether the assassin had ever been there.

With the source of his fear gone, Thanquol turned to berate his stevedores for not lending a hand when their employer was in peril. He ground his fangs together when he saw that not one of the luggage-rats was anywhere to be seen. Every last one of them had fled, probably the very moment Snikch started carving up the worthless vermin he had hired from Clan Rictus. The stevedores hadn't been so terrified, however, as to abandon the valuables they had been carrying. By now all of his carefully selected gear was being sold in a dozen back-burrow dives.

Irritably, Thanquol stooped to recover the money he had dropped. Again he felt his jaws tighten. The bag of warp-tokens was gone. Spirited away by the sinister Deathmaster.

Thanquol drew the rat-skull snuff-box from his sleeve and glared at it. If not for the idiotic bravado the snuff had subjected him to, he would never have behaved so irrationally. Certainly he would have made provision to keep a spell ready to blast that annoying little flea Snikch back to his slinking master! He wished he hadn't drowned Lynsh, because at the moment, there were a lot of things he wanted to do to that miserable pirate.

Upending the snuff-box, Thanquol spilled the contents onto the ground. He was through with the phoney strength of such vices. He did not need them! He was Grey Seer Thanquol, mightiest sorcerer in all skavendom, favoured servant of the Horned Rat! He was above such petty weaknesses!

Looking around him, Thanquol took stock of his situation. His guard-rats were piles of meat (which Clan Rictus would expect him to pay for), his luggage-rats were gone (with his luggage), and his hard-earned warp-tokens had vanished into the night (along with a master-assassin who might just decide to come back). All in all, things were looking decidedly bad.

Thanquol stooped down on all fours and began collecting the snuff he had dumped out. The stuff might be dangerous, but there was no sense allowing it to go to waste.

IT WAS A less confident but far more irritable Grey Seer Thanquol who began retracing his way through Skavenblight's swarming streets. He was heading towards the stone tenements where some of the lesser warlords maintained their warrens. As a grey seer, there was always a bit of money to be made offering to bless a clanleader or packmaster. Alternately, there was always a bit of money to be had by threatening to put a curse on a clanleader or packmaster. Making up what he would need to placate Clan Rictus for their dead warriors would take a bit of time.

Ordinarily, Thanquol wouldn't have bothered, but with things as they were, there was always a chance Clan Rictus might approach Clan Eshin about the misunderstanding and engage their services to make an example of him. Thanquol considered that the only reason Deathmaster Snikch had let him live was because Nightlord Sneek needed an excuse to eliminate him that wouldn't draw attention to the plot to assassinate Xiuhcoatl. Until he could put himself under the protection of one of the other Great Clans or the Council itself, the last thing Thanquol wanted was Clan Eshin taking any more interest in him.

Ahead, the grey seer noticed a dilapidated building lying half across the street, its bulk kept standing only by its more stout neighbour across the way. The effect was to make that part of the street almost a tunnel, with the collapsed building pressing down upon the pedestrians below. Far from shunning the spot, the

pace of each skaven slackened as he bent low and scurried under the crumbling brickwork, finding the press
of tons of stone overhead far more comforting than the
open emptiness of the night sky.

Thanquol crouched down and joined the throng
scurrying beneath the ruin. Initial thoughts of immi-
nent squashing should the building suddenly decide
to finish its descent were banished by the comfortable
sensation of something solid above him. Ever since
seeing the hideous snake-birds of Lustria, Thanquol's
agoraphobia had been especially pronounced. He'd
even made a little hutch for himself from Boneripper's
fur during his long sea voyage to evoke some sense of
security.

Skaven snapped and snarled at one another as they
passed beneath the structure, angrily urging others forwards while stubbornly trying to prolong their own
time under the ruin. The bickering voices and sharp
squeaks echoed from the walls, the air was filled with
the hot stink of so many skaven pressed close together.
It was no wonder then that Thanquol failed to notice
the lurking ratmen above him.

The broken windows of the toppled ruin formed
holes in the roof of the tunnel, in one of which a pair
of burly skaven crouched, their glistening eyes fixed
upon the approaching figure of Grey Seer Thanquol.
When the horned ratman passed beneath the window,
the two lurkers sprang into motion. The two skaven
leaned down from their perch, grabbing Thanquol by
the shoulders. Before he was aware of what was happening, the sorcerer found himself being lifted through
the window and deposited onto a cold stone floor.

Thanquol pawed at the wall as he began to slide down
the weirdly angled floor. He was inside the collapsed

building, and the floor down which he had begun to slide was in fact the outer wall of the original structure. Behind him, forming a partition across the chamber, was the rotten remains of the old wooden floor. Everywhere, filthy hammocks and strings of dried weeds hung from the ceiling, the reek of mangy fur making it clear that the collapsed building was far from uninhabited.

The only skaven he saw at present, however, were the two bruisers who had snatched him from the road. Thanquol gripped the heft of his staff, wishing he hadn't lost the Cathayan sword he'd bought. Each of the brutes looked like he'd been sired by a rat-ogre, nasty bundles of corded muscle showing beneath their leather vests and brown fur.

'Back-back!' Thanquol growled as the bruisers turned away from the window-hole. 'I'm a grey seer and I'll hex-curse you!'

The two bruisers looked at each other and backed away, which Thanquol took as a good sign. Then they laughed, which he decided wasn't so good.

'Thank you for joining us, Grey Seer Thanquol,' a raspy voice spoke from somewhere behind him. Thanquol turned slowly around to find a gang of armed skaven emerging from behind the wooden partition-floor. The speaker was dressed in a long leather coat, his arms covered in thick gloves up past the elbows and a bizarre contrivance of rods and wires winding around his head. It didn't take a genius to figure out he was one of Clan Skryre's warlock-engineers. The ratmen who flanked him were encased in insect-eyed iron helmets and bore an extra brace of pistols on their hips. A few cringing creatures with burnt fur and blistered skin formed the rest of the engineer's retinue.

Mustering his offended dignity with a scowl and a quick brushing of his rumpled robes, Thanquol glared into the warlock-engineer's glass-covered eyes. 'Give me a good reason for not turning you into a stain on the wall,' he hissed, instantly wondering why he'd let the words leave his tongue. Lynsh's damnable snuff again!

The skirmishers reached for their pistols, but their master merely chuckled. 'Peace-peace, Thanquol,' the engineer rasped. 'We need-use each other.'

Thanquol lashed his tail in annoyance at the engineer's audacity. 'You assume much-much,' he snarled.

The warplock-engineer grinned back at him, exposing his steel-capped fangs and rubbery gums. 'Yes-yes,' he agreed. 'I know-learn that Thanquol has many enemies. He should find-seek friends. Powerful friends. Friends like Warlock Kaskitt Steelgrin.'

Thanquol rolled his eyes at Kaskitt's overly dramatic way of introducing himself, but kept a tight rein on his quarrelsome tongue. What the warlock-engineer said was true. At the moment, Thanquol needed some strong friends.

Kaskitt rubbed his paws together, taking Thanquol's silence as a good sign. 'I do not know how much you have heard-listened, but Clan Pestilens and Clan Eshin have had trouble. Assassins tried to kill-stab Lord Skrolk, now the two clans are at each other's throats.'

For the second time today, Thanquol could only blink in confusion. He wasn't sure which news was more strange, the idea that Lord Skrolk was still alive or that the carefully hatched scheme Nightlord Sneek had concocted to ally with Clan Pestilens had fallen apart. Given that the last time he had seen Lord Skrolk the plague lord had been trying to kill him and that there was no reason to think Skrolk had changed his mind about that, Thanquol decided to be more upset to hear the plague lord was back in Skavenblight.

The grey seer pulled at his whiskers as a thought came to him. It was just possible everything was all a part of Lord Skrolk's plotting. The diseased plague lord could have placed the idea of an alliance in Nightlord Sneek's head to begin with, sending Thanquol on the suicidal quest to kill Xiuhcoatl. Then, to ensure that even if Thanquol succeeded things would be ill for the grey seer, Skrolk goes and gets a few assassins to try and kill him! As the favourite of Arch-Plaguelord Nurglitch, all he would have to do is go whining to his master and then any chance of an alliance would be off! In that situation, Nightlord Sneek would hardly receive anybody who'd killed Xiuhcoatl favourably!

Thanquol ground his fangs together as he imagined the depth of Skrolk's intrigues. The diseased monk was a victim of his own wicked scheming, Thanquol was blameless for whatever had befallen him beneath Altdorf! It was senseless persecution for the plague lord to turn his dear, close friend Sneek against him!

'You can use the protection of Clan Skryre,' Kaskitt repeated. 'Great things are stirring, the fortunes of Clan Skryre are on the rise. We will be generous to our friends.'

Thanquol scratched at his ear as he considered the engineer's words. There was no love lost between the grey seers and Clan Skryre. Except for the heretics of Clan Pestilens, the science-obsessed tinker-rats of Clan Skryre were the biggest thorn in Seerlord Kritislik's side. The warlock-engineers were woefully lacking in piety towards the Horned One and his servants. Indeed, sometimes Thanquol wondered if any of the treacherous tinker-rats even believed in the Horned One. If they were not so powerful a force on the Council, if their inventions had not done so much to advance skaven society, the vermin would have been wiped out long ago in a holy war. Perhaps they still would. It was something to aspire towards, anyway.

With such a state of affairs, Thanquol had to wonder why Kaskitt wanted a grey seer involved in whatever crazy scheme he was about to propose. Particularly, why would he want the mightiest and most renowned grey seer in all the Under-Empire?

'What-what is it you want-need?' Thanquol asked, straightening into his most imperious posture.

Kaskitt rubbed at his eye-pieces, his steely smile growing impossibly wider. 'A warlord of Clan Mors, one Rikkit Snapfang, needs help to drive the dwarf-things from their burrow of Karak Angkul. The skaven who help him will be paid well.' Kaskitt gnashed his steel teeth together, as though biting into a chunk of warpstone.

Thanquol wasn't fooled by Kaskitt's performance. He wasn't interested in any reward from Rikkit Snapfang, at least not directly. He was scheming to bring a better relationship between Mors and Skryre by helping Mors take the old dwarf stronghold. Clan Skryre's great weakness was its lack of warriors. An alliance with Clan Mors would solve that problem for them. Indeed, such an alliance would be strong enough to challenge the rest of the Council, even more threatening than an alliance between Eshin and Pestilens!

Once again, Thanquol felt himself being dragged down into the treacherous world of inter-clan politics with himself caught squarely in the middle.

Still, there was the little question of why Kaskitt wanted him along. Glancing over his shoulder,

Thanquol saw the reason. The two bruisers who had snatched him off the street weren't from Clan Skryre, they were warriors of Clan Mors and they had their eyes fixed firmly on the grey seer. He could guess why. Over the years of his selfless service to skavendom, he had gained a completely ill-deserved notoriety for being an opportunist who would betray his fellow ratmen to further his own career. It was a wholly fallacious rumour, but one that had spread. Kaskitt was playing on that deception. With Thanquol along, Clan Mors would be keeping such a close watch on him that they wouldn't be paying attention to what the warlock-engineer was up to.

That left only one question: what was Warlock Kaskitt Steelgrin up to?

IT WAS EARLY morning before Thanquol was able to extricate himself from his meeting with Kaskitt. The more he heard about the scheme, the less inclined he was to risk his neck. There was the rather obvious problem that his primary role in Kaskitt's plans was to act as a decoy for whatever his real plans were. Clan Mors numbered some of the strongest and fiercest warriors in all the Under-Empire among its ranks. The last thing Thanquol needed was to get himself involved in anything likely to provoke them. Especially when it was something he wasn't certain he'd be able to use for himself, even when he discovered whatever it was.

Then there were the dwarfs to take into account. The beardy maggots were hardly just going to lie down and hand over their stronghold to the skaven. Thanquol knew from past experience exactly how tenacious and terrifying the dwarfs could be. That ginger-furred maniac who had single-handedly destroyed some of

Thanquol's most intricate schemes immediately came
to mind.

The dwarfs of Karak Angkul had been described as a
particularly tough and sneaky sort. Clan Mors had lost
a good many warriors to their tricks and traps, and Rikkit Snapfang had spent a small fortune buying slaves to
make up their numbers. Even if the skaven managed to
take the dwarfhold, they might not have enough warriors left to keep it.

Even if they did, a strengthening of the bonds
between Clan Skryre and Clan Mors was hardly in the
best interests of skavendom. The warlock-engineers
were a godless batch of secular progressives who were
woefully lax in their veneration of the Horned Rat and
the respect due his holy priests, the grey seers. A powerful warlord clan like Mors certainly didn't need the
pernicious influence of such vermin upon them. The
order of grey seers was quite capable of bestowing all
the helpful guidance Mors could ever want. They didn't
need a bunch of self-serving tinker-rats confusing the
easily-manipulated warlord clans.

Besides, a closer union between Skryre and Mors
and the resultant weakening of the position of the grey
seers wouldn't exactly help Thanquol's own prospects.
No, he had every reason to run as fast and as far from
Kaskitt's proposal as he could. Not that he'd told the
warlock-engineer anything of the sort. Thanquol was
shrewd enough to understand that if Kaskitt thought
he wasn't interested, then he would have left their little
meeting with a few dozen bullets in his body. Instead,
he'd managed a very enthusiastic show of support and
agreed to meet Kaskitt's expedition when they set out
in the morning.

Hurrying through the maze of Skavenblight's crowded

streets, Thanquol scurried to his own burrow. There was just a chance that another grey seer hadn't taken over his lodgings while he'd been away – Seerlord Kritislik wouldn't have wanted any obvious signs of Thanquol's absence unless he was sure Thanquol wasn't coming back.

Allowing that his home was intact, he'd have to be fast gathering his belongings and he'd have to be quite severe in deciding what to take and what to abandon. Some of his prize books and scrolls would have to go, of course, and his priceless collection of bottled breeder scent. A few of his most potent talismans, one or two of his snuff-boxes, a couple of extra robes. It wasn't much to show for his years of faithful service to the Council, but it was better than losing his pelt to a bunch of upset warlock-engineers and their Clan Mors bully-rats.

The tunnel leading into the complex of caves and pits where many of the grey seers kept their nests was lined with flagstones plundered from throughout the city and supported by marble columns looted from the palazzos of Miragliano. A gang of white-furred stormvermin guarded the entrance, their pink eyes glaring balefully at every skaven who came too close to the tunnel, their clawed fingers wrapped about the hafts of axe-headed halberds.

The guards stiffened as Thanquol came near them, two of them even crossing their weapons to bar his way. The sergeant in command of them crept forwards, his nose twitching as he sniffed Thanquol's scent.

Lashing his tail impatiently, Thanquol waited for the dull-witted albino to recognise the grey seer's spoor.

Unfortunately, the sergeant did. Snapping his jaws in a silent howl, the burly stormvermin seized Thanquol by the arm. Instinctively, Thanquol smashed the head of his staff into the ratman's face, sending blood spraying across his white fur.

'Do you know-think who I am?' the furious grey seer demanded, heedless of the fact that the mute skaven couldn't answer him.

Instead other guards rushed forwards to help their injured fangleader. Seizing Thanquol, the stormvermin ripped his staff from his fingers. A rush of panic flooded through the grey seer's brain as he felt himself being overwhelmed. Desperately he flailed about in the grip of his captors, raking his horns across their snouts, biting their fingers with his fangs.

A trap! And one he had allowed himself to scurry straight into! It was all that scheming weasel Kaskitt's doing! The warlock-engineer had goaded him into such recklessness through his wild talk of schemes and alliances! He wasn't sure how Clan Skryre had gone about bribing the elite stormvermin, but he was sure nobody would believe such a thing possible. Whatever happened to him, Clan Skryre would never be suspected!

The mute stormvermin lifted Thanquol from the ground, a different warrior holding each of his thrashing arms and legs. Thanquol began to shriek for help, but the louder his cries, the more resolutely the skaven in the street turned away. Everyone knew the white stormvermin were the private troops of the Council of Thirteen. If Thanquol had run afoul of them, then clearly he had evoked the wrath of the Lords of Decay.

Still struggling and squealing, Thanquol was carried off through the crumbling streets of Skavenblight.

Carried to the Shattered Tower.

CHAPTER IV

Heavy, cloying incense filled the air, creating an almost smothering fug that seeped clear down into the lungs of those forced to breathe it. For a skaven, the sensation was as frightening and disorientating as being blindfolded. The noxious fumes provoked fits of coughing that left a ratman almost doubled over in pain. Even if he could smell an enemy coming, he wouldn't be able to do anything about it.

The stone-walled chamber had an alarmingly high ceiling, the faded ruin of a fresco peeking out through layers of soot and dirt. Great bronze sconces stood scattered all about the floor, green light glowing from their bowls where chunks of refined warpstone smouldered. The great symbol of the Horned One was painted upon the floor with a skill and precision that denoted the most diligent of care. Probably slave work, with a most violent penalty for any mistakes. Upon one wall, a great stone rat-head with double horns leered malignantly, its ruby eyes twinkling in the light.

Beneath the stone head, standing atop a small dais, his back to a long marble altar, stood one of the most powerful skaven in the Under-Empire. Seerlord Kritislik, the Grand Grey Seer of all Skavendom, Ipsissimus of the Entire Order of Grey Seers, Keeper of the Temple and the Faith of the Temple, Lord Exalted of the Shattered Tower, Ringmaster of the Black Bell, First Member of the Council of Thirteen and Voice of the Horned Rat.

The villainous old ratman held a brass pomander under his nose, sniffing liberally from the black vapour rising from its vents. Whatever the vapour was, it seemed to nullify the effects of the incense filling the room. Kritislik grinned down at his rumpled guest as the guards tossed Thanquol onto the hard floor.

'You smell-look well, Grey Seer Thanquol,' Kritislik announced, his eyes watching as the grey seer curled into a little wheezing ball as the incense overwhelmed him. 'I am pleased you have not died,' he added. The show of compassion chilled Thanquol to the marrow. A skaven was never more menacing than when he professed kindness and sympathy.

Thanquol blinked back tears as the incense began to burn his eyes. He struggled to right himself, but was careful not to make eye contact with his superior. The last thing he needed was for the megalomaniacal and thoroughly unbalanced Kritislik to mistake an innocent whisker twitch as some gesture of challenge.

'Most-most magnificent Seerlord, Favourite Spawnling of the Horned One,' Thanquol wheezed between coughs.

Kritislik made an impatient flick of his paws. 'Hold-keep that fawning tongue, Thanquol,' he snapped. 'I don't know how you survived Lustria…'

Thanquol's glands clenched, spurting the musk of fear. Kritislik knew about his journey? How much more did he know? Did he think Thanquol had tried to betray the grey seers by helping Clan Eshin try to secure an alliance with the plague monks?

'Great Devourer of Unbelievers,' Thanquol whined. 'I have served you and the Horned One faithfully without think-thought of myself. Bravely I have penetrated the crooked plot-scheme of Nightlord Sneek…'

'Nightlord Sneek was the one who told me you were back,' Kritislik said, taking a deep sniff of his pomander. 'Since their recent unpleasantness with Pestilens, Eshin has been quite zealous in serving the Temple of the Horned One.' There was a malicious smile on Kritislik's face that made Thanquol wonder just how much of Eshin's problems with the plague monks had been orchestrated by the Seerlord. Kritislik could not abide another grey seer upstaging him and was envious of Thanquol's brilliant mind. It was just like the slippery old priest to go and poison the relationship between the two clans before Thanquol could claim the reward and recognition which was his due.

Kritislik turned away, toying with an array of knives laid out across the top of the altar. The Seerlord's nonchalance didn't fool Thanquol. He knew the scheming rat would have guards hidden somewhere about or some sort of spell ready and waiting to be unleashed. Perhaps there was a trapdoor in the floor between Thanquol and the altar. The grey seer's glands clenched as he recalled the ghastly mutant crocodiles the Lords of Decay were said to keep in pits below the tower to dispose of unwanted minions.

The Seerlord gave Thanquol another toothy smile,

then set down the warpstone knife he had been fondling. 'Killing the Prophet of Sotek was inconvenient,' Kritislik stated. 'Ever since Xiuhcoatl's death was discovered, Nurglitch has been trying to sell-tell the rest of the Council on a re-conquest of Lustria.'

'Most-most Vicious Pontiff,' Thanquol sputtered. 'I did not-not slay-kill Xiuhcoatl. A man-thing shot him and ruined all of my plans to make sure-certain the Prophet was live-safe.' The grey seer coughed as the incense continued to assail him, the little bells on his horns tinkling in time to his convulsions. 'The lizard-meat was a good enemy of Nurglitch and useful to us.'

'Yes-yes,' Kritislik agreed. 'The scaly little pest was a useful threat to keep Pestilens in line. But now that Nurglitch is determined to try to restore Pestilens' burrows in lizard-land, things are changed. The expedition is sure to fail and Pestilens will lose many plague monks fighting the lizardmen. Their power will be diminished for some time.'

Thanquol perked up, straining to keep himself erect even as another fit of coughing wracked his body. 'It is well-good that I told the man-thing to shoot-slay Xiuhcoatl,' he stated.

Kritislik wasn't really listening any more. Instead, he had removed a strip of tanned ratskin from under the belt of his robe. He read the hash-mark letters stained into the hide, then fixed his gaze back on Thanquol. 'You have a talent-gift for setting our enemies against each other,' Kritislik said. He tapped a claw against the scroll he had just read. 'Some of Sneek's spies tell me you have been squeaking with Kaskitt Steelgrin. He has some plan-plot to make an alliance between Skryre and Mors.'

Thanquol's empty glands tried to squirt, sending a

wave of pain flashing through his innards. 'Lies! Not-trues!' Thanquol whined. 'I am a loyal servant of the Horned One! I would never betray the temple and the Council of Thirteen!'

Kritislik bruxed his fangs, the sound of his teeth grinding together echoing through the stone chamber. 'Stop grovelling, Thanquol,' the Seerlord commanded. 'I want you to join Kaskitt and hurry-scurry to Karak Angkul. Let-make Kaskitt think you are helping his plan. But what you will really be doing is working for me.'

The Seerlord snapped his fingers together. From behind one of the heavy curtains, a pot-bellied old grey seer scuttled into view. The sorcerer-priest had limbs that were as thin as a rail and part of his nose had been eaten away. Combined with his paunch, Thanquol recognised all of the marks of a degenerate snuff-user. The ratman's scent reeked of unrefined warpstone and his eyes had the unfocused look of the inveterate addict. A surge of disgust welled up in Thanquol's belly as the other grey seer stared down at him. How such a morally repugnant and weak-willed creature could be numbered among the Horned One's priesthood was a mystery to him.

'Skraekual will go with you,' Kritislik pronounced. 'Tell-say he is your helper.'

'I don't need-want a helper,' Thanquol said, remembering the last apprentice Kritislik had foisted upon him. Adept Kratch had come very close to killing his mentor several times with his selfish treacheries. Thanquol wasn't about to repeat that experience, certainly not with the memory of what he'd done to his own mentor still fresh in his mind.

Kritislik began to chitter with amusement, the bleary-eyed Skraekual soon joining in the Seerlord's

laughter. 'Skraekual is not your helper,' Kritislik informed
Thanquol. 'You are his, but only the two of you will-will
know that.'

It was Thanquol's turn to brux his teeth together in
annoyance. Kritislik intended to use him the same way
Kaskitt intended to: as some sort of damned decoy! He
was going to exploit the fame and renown of skavendom's greatest hero so some drug-addled half-wit could
blunder about on one of Kritislik's insipid ploys!

The Seerlord glowered back at Thanquol, irritated
that his minion would dare show distemper in his
presence. The malignant stare had its effect. Thanquol
cowered back down to the floor, oozing support for Kritislik's genius and silently cursing the exotic snuff that
continued to have a pernicious effect on his normally
cautious judgement.

'Mighty and Wise Squeaker of the Law,' Thanquol
whined. 'It is a stroke of genius to use your humble servant as a cover-cloak for my noble colleague Skraekual.'
The grey seer coughed, almost choking on the words, a
reaction that had nothing to do with the incense filling
the room. Suddenly a cunning gleam came into his eye.
'What sort of mission is it you wish me to conceal?'

There might still be a way to twist the intrigues of
his scheming superior around towards his own benefit. If Thanquol could learn what it was Kritislik and
Skraekual were up to, then he might be able to beat
them to the scratch. Or at least make sure Skraekual
wasn't in any condition to finish the job, thereby making it essential that Thanquol take over for him.

Sadly, Kritislik had a deceitful mind that trusted no
one, however loyal they had proven themselves in the
past. 'Skraekual knows what he must do,' the Seerlord
growled. 'It is enough for you to keep Kaskitt and Rikkit

from interfering with him. Do you think you can manage that, Grey Seer Thanquol?'

Thanquol felt a mad urge to lunge at the Seerlord and make him eat his words, but he knew that was just Lynsh's snuff trying to make him commit suicide. Instead, he bowed his head and tried to keep from coughing as he waited for Kritislik to dismiss him.

KLARAK BRONZEHAMMER STOOD alone before the Silver Throne of Karak Angkul. Carved from living rock and silver ore, the immense seat stood as tall as any four dwarfs and was as broad as a mine cart. The great hall in which the Silver Throne sat had been constructed around the seat, for the stone of which it was made had never been moved since its discovery by miners four thousand years ago when the great hold was still being cut from the roots of the mountains. Tradition held that if the Silver Throne were ever moved, then the ancestor gods would turn their faces from Karak Angkul and the stronghold would fade into ruin.

The hall around the throne was gigantic in its proportions, with enormous fluted pillars supporting its tiled ceiling and the crystal mirrors which brought the light and warmth of the sun down deep into the mountain. The tiles depicted the sagas of the ancestor gods, of Grimnir's doomed exodus into the Realm of Chaos, of Valaya founding the great dwarfholds of legend, of Grungni leading his people deep beneath the earth to mine gromril from the black depths. Each of the ancestor gods was depicted in marble with a halo of gold surrounding them and the weapons they bore had heads of pure gromril.

The frescoes covering the walls were of equally superb craftsmanship, though of more humble subjects. They

depicted the founding of Karak Angkul, the heroic
history of the dwarfs who called the stronghold home.
Sections of wall were dedicated to the Goblin Wars,
showing the dwarfs waging their unending battle
against the wretched greenskins for control of the
mountains. A section dozens of yards long showed
the dwarfs of Karak Angkul making war against the
arrogant elves during the War of the Beard, artillerists
from the stronghold maiming the dreaded wyrm
Malok at the Battle of Burned Blades. A smaller tableau
showed the dwarfs marching to the aid of the fledgling
Empire, cutting off the advance of the undead warlord
Zahaak the Usurper before he could join the horde of
his unholy master Nagash against the outnumbered
army of the manling emperor Sigmar.

Trophies adorned the sides of the pillars, mementoes
of the victories of Karak Angkul. The mummified husk
of the devil-spider Togrildam hung from chains against
one column, the gigantic beast's carapace still showing the marks of King Glorin Thornefinger's hammer.
The immense war-axe of the orc warlord Ghazagruff,
its cleaver-like blade split where it had broken against
the runeshield of King Uldrik Blackhand. The armour
of Lord Corirthar Swiftsword, slain by Nimbrindil Iron-
foot at the Battle of Fellwind Dale. Two crimson scales
as big as shields that had been ripped from the hide of
the dragon Malok by Skalfri Brandbeard with his bolt-
thrower during the War of the Beard.

The glory of Karak Angkul was on display all around
him and Klarak felt a swelling of pride to belong to such
a proud heritage. Reflecting upon his ancestors always
gave him a redoubled sense of purpose, a fierce determination to bend his sharp mind towards the service
of his people. It did not matter if he received acclaim

and recognition for his works. What mattered was that he helped ensure the continuance of Karak Angkul and its rich history.

'Your sentinel guns took a formidable toll on the enemy.' The statement came from the grey-bearded dwarf seated upon the Silver Throne. Well into his fourth century of life, King Logan Longblade still cut an imposing figure. The stamp of time had been merciful to the old king, though the swords of enemies had not. The king had lost three sons in battle against the many enemies who threatened Karak Angkul. His last son, the youngest, he had dispatched as ambassador to Karaz-a-Karak some two decades past, ostensibly to represent the stronghold at the court of the High King, though many whispered he had sent him away in an effort to protect his bloodline from complete extinction.

Perhaps it was the personal tragedies he had suffered which made King Logan such a forward-thinking ruler, uncommonly open to new ideas and innovations. Without his complicity, Klarak knew that most of his inventions would have languished unused and unseen within the isolated halls of the Engineers' Guild.

'The contraptions performed adequately,' the crackly voice of Guildmaster Thori admitted. If time had been kindly to King Logan, the same could not be said of Thori. The engineer was wizened, his long grey beard the only thing about him that still looked healthy. His body was withered, his skin shrivelled, his eyes bleary behind the thick crystal lenses of his spectacles. Thori's legs would barely support him, forcing the engineer to employ a gold-tipped staff as an elegant kind of crutch.

'Guildmaster Thori is too kind,' Klarak said in his most diplomatic tone, bowing to the old dwarf. 'I am troubled by the malfunction of one of the weapons. It should not have happened.'

King Logan smiled behind his beard. He was too old a hand at the game Klarak was forced to play with the Engineers' Guild to be fooled by the verbal duelling. 'The sentinel guns broke the back of that damned horde of ratkin filth,' Logan declared. 'There was barely anything left for the axes of our warriors.'

'The skaven still control the lower mines,' Thori pointed out. 'Never before have they penetrated so far into our domains.'

'Perhaps we should have posted a few of Klarak's guns in the lower mines,' Logan replied, his tone sharp.

Klarak intervened before an argument could erupt. 'The sentinel guns are still unproven. One marginally successful test in combat does not mean they are proven to be dependable.' His words brought a frown to Logan's face and a confident gleam to Thori's eye. His next words reversed the expressions the two dwarfs wore. 'I should like to experiment further, Highness. I should like to post my sentinel guns at the approaches to the lower mines. With the ironbreakers overrun by the ratkin, we will need a new line of defence against them when they make another assault on the upper halls.'

Thori pounced on the idea, his voice dripping with scorn. 'And who will watch these contraptions of yours? Do you mean to risk the lives of valiant dwarfs defending unproven…'

'There will be no need for anyone to watch the guns,' Klarak stated. He reached to his belt and removed a length of leather hose. 'This is the key to making the guns completely independent. Under pressure, this hose will remain taut. Break the pressure and it will go limp.'

'Any apprentice could make such a claim,' Thori grumbled.

'It is a simple concept,' Klarak agreed. 'But what I propose is a new way of using this simple concept. A pressurised hose will be connected to each sentinel gun, the other length trailing into a central watch-post. Each hose will be numbered and the location of each corresponding gun recorded on a map. If any gun is damaged – as it is sure to be should an enemy overwhelm it – then the hose attached to it will lose pressure. In that way, we will know where the enemy has struck and can react accordingly.'

Thori threw up his hands. 'Of all the…'

'A bold idea, Klarak,' King Logan interrupted. 'Whatever you need to implement your plan, you shall have it.' The dwarf king glowered at the fuming Thori. 'I am sure Guildmaster Thori will show you every courtesy.'

'I look forward to working with my fellow engineers,' Klarak said, bowing in turn to each of the dwarf leaders before turning on his heel and marching swiftly from the great hall.

As he left his audience with King Logan, Klarak's mind was troubled. It was not the performance of his sentinel guns which worried him, nor even the obvious displeasure of Guildmaster Thori. His eyes had fallen upon the flayed pelt of a ratman stretched across the side of a pillar, a grey pelt which still sported ivory horns.

After the battle in the lower mines, Klarak had found a messenger awaiting him in his chambers, a messenger from the human city of Altdorf. The letter the Imperial dwarf delivered had been brief, but alarming. It had been written with a special ink and in a special script that would not make itself intelligible unless a certain incantation was spoken over it. There were few outside the cadre of operatives who served the wizard Jeremias Scrivner who had ever been made privy to that secret. Klarak Bronzehammer was one of those few.

The shadowmancer's message had been brief. It was a warning, a prophecy of great disaster looming over Karak Angkul and Klarak Bronzehammer. Central to the warning was a horned ratman, one of the abominable grey seers.

Thanquol, the skaven was called, and he would unleash a hideous doom upon Karak Angkul unless Klarak could stop him in time.

MEGALITHIC IN ITS proportions, the immense tunnel known as Swampscratch wormed its way deep beneath the Blighted Marshes, connecting the festering city of Skavenblight with its far-flung subterranean empire. Armies of slaves tended the tunnel day and night, labouring under the lashes of snarling ratmen to shore up the sagging ceiling with a motley array of wooden beams, stone columns, and brick pillars. Patches of masonry dripped from the walls, steel plates bulged from the roof, timbers groaned under the strain of archways. Everywhere, the stink of the swamp oozed into the tunnel, stagnant black water sweating out from every inch of exposed earth. Pools of filth formed in every footprint that marred the floor.

In many places, heaps of mud and earth formed obstructions, great yawning pits in the ceiling letting swamp water and sunlight stream into the tunnel. Sometimes the crushed bodies of skaven poked out from beneath the slimy rubble. Occasionally, a muffled whine rose from some wretch trapped within the muck.

The teeming hordes of skaven scurrying through

the tunnel ignored the cries of their less fortunate kin. Carefully they navigated around the obstructions, snarling and cursing the slaves who were tasked to clear the rubble away. The seemingly endless tide of vermin swarmed along the monstrous passage, wheeling about the confused array of pillars and columns keeping the swamp from crashing down about their heads. Many of the skaven pushed carts or carried great baskets lashed to their backs, struggling beneath burdens of goods plundered from across the world. Tribute for the Lords of Decay from their scattered vassals.

Grey Seer Thanquol glared malevolently at the dripping ceiling as a stream of stinking swamp water splashed across him. Irritably, he wiped his paw across the front of his fouled robe.

'Where-where is that tick-licking wire-chewer?' Thanquol growled. He tapped his claws on the little rat-skull snuff-box, restraining the urge to take a little sniff of the crushed warpstone to ease his nerves.

'The Horned One will provide-give when it is time,' the scabby voice of Skraekual hissed. The decayed grey seer skirted around another stream of swamp water, his rheumy eyes fixed on Thanquol's. 'Only fool-meat hurries to find trouble.'

A low rumble shook the tunnel. Skraekual quickly skipped forwards, his eyes narrowing into sly little slits. Thanquol's hackles rose in suspicion. It was more instinct than thought which moved him to leap ahead and join his fellow sorcerer-priest. Behind them, a part of the ceiling came crashing down, smashing a knot of hurrying skaven beneath a morass of mud and stagnant water.

'Fool-meat!' Thanquol snarled, his tail curled about his ankles. 'Why did you not warn-cry?'

Skraekual grinned back at Thanquol, exposing his yellow fangs, pitted from over-use of warpstone and clinging to gums that were riddled with cankers. 'The Horned One saves who he will save.'

Thanquol's fingers closed about the heft of his staff. He wondered if he could get away with bashing the dust-addict's brains out. A quick glance about reminded him there were far too many witnesses.

'Next time, give the Horned One some help,' Thanquol grumbled.

Skraekual just kept grinning at him. The noseless grey seer raised a claw, pointing at the amulet around Thanquol's throat. 'I like-like talisman,' Skraekual gibbered. 'I might find-take if Thanquol has accident. Kritislik won't mind.'

Thanquol's paw closed about the talisman. It was an ancient artefact, dating from back before there was a Council of Thirteen, back to the time when the Under-Empire was ruled by bickering Grey Lords. It was hoary with eldritch magic, endowed with powers even Thanquol had never fully explored. The Amulet of the Horned One had been the prize possession of his old mentor, Grey Seer Sleekit, a badge of honour bestowed upon him by Seerlord Kritislik.

Thanquol felt his glands clench as he thought of the tyrannical Master Sleekit. Only a few of the villainous old rat's pupils had survived to become grey seers. He chuckled to himself as he considered the fates of the few who had been initiated into the Order alongside him. Tisquik, Seerlord Kritislik's favourite, had been murdered by an assassin's blade shortly after he'd been caught meeting with Seerlord Tisqueek, Kritislik's greatest rival within the Order of Grey Seers. Thanquol sometimes wondered if the meeting had really happened or if Kritislik had just suddenly developed some unreasoning paranoia over the similarity between the names of his protégé and his most hated enemy. Whatever the reason, the elimination of Tisquik had been a happy accident as far as Thanquol was concerned. He was only sorry he hadn't thought of helping such a fate along sooner.

He had been less happy with the fate of Bokha. Really too weak-willed to make a good grey seer, Bokha would have proven an easily manipulated ally for Thanquol to exploit. Sadly, the idiot devoured too much warpstone while leading a skaven army against orcs in the Black Mountains. The concentration of warpstone had unbalanced the humours in Bokha's body, causing the ratman to degenerate into an almost formless mess of lashing tentacles and snapping fangs. To his credit, the Bokha-spawn had killed a lot of orcs before he was finally crushed under a boulder. Unfortunately, the monster also killed half of his own army before he was finished.

The last of his comrades had been the ambitious Squiktat. Of them all, Squiktat had been the only serious rival to Thanquol's genius. Squiktat had had a genuine aptitude for sorcery that made him the star pupil of old Sleekit. The scheming little maggot had been able to unleash the most devastating spells without even taking a tiny sniff of warpstone to help him master the raw power of the Horned Rat. It had troubled Thanquol greatly to know Squiktat might possess more power than himself. He'd intended to give himself a head start on his rival by sneaking a look at Master Sleekit's collection of magic tomes. Word of his plan must have been betrayed to Squiktat, however, for the other grey seer tried to cheat Thanquol and steal Sleekit's books first.

The result was another happy accident. Thanquol never knew what it was Squiktat had read in those books, but whatever it was had driven the sneaking little thief out of his mind. The mad, gibbering wretch was last seen wandering into the depths of the Blighted Marshes.

It was only natural that, with all his fellow apprentices gone, Thanquol should inherit Master Sleekit's prize possessions when his revered mentor should suffer a significantly fatal accident. The Amulet of the Horned One was chief among the treasures Thanquol filched before anyone could question Sleekit's demise too closely.

It had powers. Thanquol had never failed to feel the invigorating influence of the Amulet. His already considerable endurance was expanded to fittingly heroic levels by the power of his talisman. Inconveniences like bug bites and the odd knife wound healed with supernatural quickness. He could even brave a meeting with the diseased disciples of Clan Pestilens without getting sick.

Thanquol looked away from his amulet and back at Skraekual with his rotten face and drug-ravaged body. Did that mass of loathsomeness have any idea of the Amulet's powers? What would that hedonistic hophead give to possess the restorative powers of such a relic? Under such magic, the maggot might undo the havoc his addictions had wrought. He would be reborn as a virile, healthy skaven at the prime of his powers even as Thanquol himself!

Thanquol bruxed his fangs together as another idea came to him. Was it Kritislik who had concocted the unscrupulous idea of using him as a decoy, or had that wormy thought originated with Skraekual? He could see in the addict's bleary eyes the avarice scurrying about in his brain! There was no real mission at all! This was nothing more than some crazy plot by Skraekual to get Thanquol out into some forsaken corner of skavendom and then steal his Amulet!

Fur bristling, Thanquol tongued a little sliver of warp-stone from his cheek-pouch. So that was the game then! Well, he would soon finish it! He'd blast Skraekual into a pool of pudding and then report the slime's deception to Seerlord Kritislik!

Even as Thanquol's mind began to focus upon the spell that would send Skraekual to his traitor's reward, a sharp shout brought him about. The spell died unformed in his mind as he found himself being encircled by a pack of leather-coated Clan Skryre skirmishers.

'Grey Seer Thanquol,' Kaskitt Steelgrin's shrill voice called out. The warlock-engineer emerged from behind the ring of skirmishers, scratching at the wires curling around his face. 'I see-scent you are timely.' The eyes behind the lenses of Kaskitt's face-wrappings narrowed with suspicion as he noted Skraekual. 'What-who is that?' he growled.

Thanquol lashed his tail in annoyance. Was Kaskitt actually trying to accuse him of bringing along Skraekual as some sort of plot against the warlock-engineer? Had the rattle-brained mouse-squeezer spent so much time in his laboratory that he couldn't recognise pure hate between two skaven when it was right under his nose?

A cunning gleam crept into Thanquol's eye. Why dispose of Skraekual himself and risk the ire of Seerlord Kritislik when he could have Kaskitt do the job for him? All it would take would be a little cautious encouragement of the warlock-engineer's already existing suspicions.

'Grey Seer Skraekual help-work great and tyrannical Thanquol,' Skraekual's unctuous voice chimed in. The wretched priest was pawing at the rotten stump of his nose, his bleary eyes making a feeble attempt to focus upon Kaskitt. The stink of warpstone snuff, black-root and ratnip was pronounced as he shuffled closer towards the Clan Skryre skaven.

Kaskitt chittered with amusement, directing a shrewd glance at Thanquol, then making a subtle gesture with his paw to his own bodyguards. The posture of the skir-mishers became more relaxed, their hands drifting away from the warplock pistols slung beneath their belts.

'Fine-good assistant,' Kaskitt laughed. Clearly he had caught the smell of Skraekual's excessive vices and instantly dismissed the decrepit grey seer as anything to be wary of. Perhaps Kaskitt thought Thanquol had brought the other grey seer in an attempt to turn the warlock-engineer's own trickery back upon him – to give him someone to watch and worry about so that he would relax his vigilance over Thanquol. If so, Kaskitt felt his sneaky ally had chosen a poor instrument for such deception.

'Grey Seer Skraekual is a powerful sorcerer,' Thanquol insisted. 'The Horned Rat favours him like no other! Great and terrible are the magics of Skraekual! Renowned throughout the Under-Empire!'

A fit of coughing came over Skraekual, the priest doubling over in a trembling fit as spasms wracked his body. A shivering hand pawed across his belt until finally closing about a dried twist of blackroot. The quaking fingers dropped the hallucinogenic to the floor. Instantly, Skraekual fell to all fours, retrieving the root with his teeth. Mud caked the front of his face as he noisily wolfed down the desiccated herb.

Caustic laughter rose from Kaskitt and his skirmishers. Even some of the foot-traffic filling Swampscratch paused to jeer at the spectacle of a decrepit grey seer wallowing in the muck like some kind of rabid mole. Thanquol felt his contempt for Skraekual swell. It wasn't enough that the villain had abused his body and mind to the point where he was nothing but a walking mass of addictions. It wasn't enough that he had sunk so low that he didn't even have the wit to preserve the dignity of the grey seers. It wasn't enough that every breath the scabby wretch took was a blight upon the glory of the Horned One. No, the scum had sunk so low that he couldn't even evoke a bit of concern in the hearts of Thanquol's duplicitous allies.

Filthy, drug-addled vermin, Thanquol thought as he scowled at Skraekual's disgusting spectacle. He took a pinch of Lynsh's snuff from his rat-skull box to take the edge off the jeers of his fellow skaven.

'Your help-meat has seen-smelled better days,' Kaskitt cackled. A sly quality entered his voice. 'Seerlord Kritislik must dislike you much-much to send this with you.'

Thanquol felt his glands clench. The inference was plain. Kaskitt had had Thanquol watched since they had parted company. He knew the grey seer had visited the Shattered Tower. Somehow he'd discovered Thanquol's meeting with Kritislik. But how much did Kaskitt know about what had transpired during that meeting?

'Kritislik does not value you much,' Kaskitt persisted. 'A great-mighty hero-lord like Thanquol could do better. He could help-serve Clan Skryre.'

Thanquol's eyes narrowed with concern. It wasn't the fact that Kaskitt was about to make some sort of treasonous, perhaps even blasphemous proposal to him. Indeed, he'd been waiting to hear what sort of bribe

Kaskitt was going to toss his way. No, what alarmed Thanquol was the very public manner in which Kaskitt was broaching the subject. There were literally thousands of ears all around them, any one of which could bring word back to Kritislik.

And clearly, that was the point. Whatever his own position, Kaskitt feared no reprisal by making Thanquol an offer. Conversely, by making his offer publicly, he wanted word to filter back to the Seerlord. Whatever Thanquol did, whatever his answer to Kaskitt, he would not be able to escape the fear that Kritislik would already believe him guilty of switching his loyalties. The only safe course for Thanquol would be to loyally maintain his bargain with Kaskitt and hope for the protection of Clan Skryre against any reprisal from Kritislik.

Even so, Thanquol thought it best to make a bold display of unwavering loyalty to the Seerlord. 'I am content to serve-work for the Horned One and grim Seerlord Kritislik, who is the Voice and the Might of...'

Thanquol's words caught in his throat, choked by a sudden clenching of his glands. Across the tunnel, the crowds had suddenly wheeled away, spurts of fear-musk rising into the air. He could see a clutch of Clan Skryre forge-rats scurrying his way, their bodies stinking of oil and steel. He gave them only a passing notice, his eyes drawn instead to the towering shape that lumbered behind them.

The thing was gigantic, easily twice the height of a skaven and nearly as broad. It smelled of warpstone and blood and death, all mixed with the scent of old bones and new steel. Looming over the cowering crowds of skaven, it marched across the tunnel like some primordial titan, each step gouging a fresh crater in the muddy floor.

Once, it had been a rat-ogre. Only so fierce and enormous a creature could have provided the thick bones which served as its framework. Fleshless, polished clean by time, the heavy bones glistened in the flickering warplight of the tunnel. Short thick legs supported a massive, bulky trunk. Long skeletal arms depended from broad shoulders. The chest cavity had been reinforced with plates of steel, wires and tubes running in crazed disorder from machinery hidden behind the bare ribs to sink into metal rods bolted into each arm and leg. A third arm jutted from the creature's left side, but where the others ended in massive paws of bone and claws of steel, this arm ended in a monstrous nozzle from which a long slimy hose emerged to connect with an iron-banded barrel fastened to the creature's back.

'A gift-bribe,' Kaskitt chittered, sweeping his paws in a grand gesture. 'A token-present of Clan Skryre's appreciation.'

The strange, ghastly abomination continued to stomp its way towards Thanquol, finally halting a few steps away. It stared down at the shivering grey seer, tiny warp-lights glowing in the sockets of its huge, rat-like skull.

'For... for me?' Thanquol stammered, half ready to scurry back to the Shattered Tower if the hideous machine-monster took another step.

'Spent much-much to steal bones of Thanquol's rat-ogre from man-things,' Kaskitt explained. 'Cost much-much to automate dead-thing.'

Thanquol peered more closely at the hideous construction. He could see the iron bands holding the skull together where it had been cleft in half by a mighty blow. Instantly a thrill of terror coursed through his glands. The ginger-furred dwarf-thing! That thrice-damned Gotrek Gurnisson! As vividly as though it were yesterday he could picture the dwarf slayer confronting him in the tunnel beneath the nest-home of Fritz von Halstadt. Some treacherous mouse-spleened flea had betrayed Thanquol's brilliant scheme to use the hapless human as his ratspaw to bring the man-thing warren of Nuln under skaven control. The dwarf and his man-thing pet, Felix Jaeger, had been waiting for Thanquol, manically attacking him in a frenzy of unprovoked and unwarranted violence before the grey seer could call up a spell that would blast them into cinders. Only the self-less devotion of his rat-ogre, the first to bear the name of Boneripper, had saved his life. While Boneripper was stopping the dwarf's axe with his head, Thanquol was able to effect his speedy, if undignified, escape.

The grey seer ground his fangs together. There would be a reckoning between him and that pair! By the Horned One, he would yet have both their hides to cover his floor! He would have his revenge upon the cowardly slayer and his companion, such a revenge that all skavendom would quiver in admiration when they heard of it! He'd make their names a byword for torture and suffering! He'd give their bones to his pups to chew! He'd bottle their blood and drink it every time…

Shaking his head to clear the delicious images of vengeance from his mind, Thanquol stared at the hulking bone-ogre with a new appreciation. Twitching his nose, he realised he could now smell the scent of his first and favourite bodyguard lingering beneath the stink of Clan Skryre's techno-sorcery.

'I thank you for your gift,' Thanquol told Kaskitt, enjoying the nervous look Skraekual directed at him as he did so. If everything he did was going to be reported to Kritislik anyway, then it would pay to exploit the situation to its fullest. Besides, even the Seerlord would think twice about toying with him now that he had such a formidable, magnificent bodyguard.

Kaskitt bobbed his head in obvious pleasure. 'This is the finest automaton to emerge from our laboratories,' the warlock-engineer explained. 'Powered by a warp-stone heart that will keep it moving for thirty moons before replacement. The bones have been hard-made with layers of warpstone dust. The arm,' and here the engineer's eyes glistened with malicious apprecia-tion, 'conceals a small warpfire thrower, fill-fed from cistern mounted on its back.' Kaskitt bared his fangs with murderous glee. 'Burn-slay many dwarf-things,' he promised.

The warlock-engineer removed a curved sliver of warpstone deeply scratched with Queekish markings and bound about with a bizarre array of wires. 'This warptooth will let you command the rat-ogre,' Kaskitt explained, demonstrating how one of the wires could be coiled about the ear. 'Anything you squeak-say while wearing the warptooth will be listen-heard by the rat-ogre.'

Thanquol listened as the excited warlock-engineer elaborated every nuance of the morbid machine-beast, Kaskitt quickly losing himself in zealous aggrandise-ment of Clan Skryre's technological wonders.

The grey seer paid little attention to Kaskitt's expla-nations. He gazed up at the fleshless skull of his new bodyguard, revelling in its horrifying appearance.

'Boneripper,' Thanquol hissed. 'I shall name-call you Boneripper.'

CHAPTER V

'ALWAYS SPARE A sniff for Skraekual.' Thanquol kept his voice restrained to a conspiratorial whisper. Not low enough that the other grey seer couldn't hear him, of course. If Kaskitt Steelgrin didn't start getting worried about Skraekual, then it would serve Thanquol's purposes almost as neatly to have Skraekual worried about the warlock-engineer.

Kaskitt's eyes narrowed behind their lenses and he scratched at the wires sewn into his skin. He peered intently at the stooped figure of Skraekual as he crept down the narrow tunnel. He tried to affect an attitude of aloof unconcern, but Thanquol noticed that Kaskitt's nose was twitching just the same.

Since the warlock-engineer's extravagant gift, Thanquol had done his best to ingratiate himself with Kaskitt. Not that he felt any real gratitude to his benefactor, of course. Indeed, providing him with such a lethal instrument of destruction as a mechanical Bon-eripper simply proved that Kaskitt was as much of a delusional slack-wit as Skraekual. Thanquol was rather looking forward to the time when he could turn the tables on Kaskitt and have his gift peel the hide off the fool's bones!

Until then, however, it behoved Thanquol to play up to the moron. He was the very model of an apprecia-tive, fawning lick-spittle, a toady for every crackpot idea Kaskitt mentioned. Why yes, of course Kaskitt Steelgrin was the greatest warlock-engineer in the Under-Empire. He was so much more brilliant than opportunists like Ikit Claw and Gnawlitch Shun. It was a crime that War-plord Morskittar hadn't recognised the immense genius of Kaskitt Steelgrin and elevated him to the heights of Clan Skryre's hierarchy.

It grated on Thanquol's pride to flatter the delusional little tick. Kaskitt was a worm, a nothing that would be smashed flat the second he popped his head out of his hole. The only thing to do was to exploit the idiot's delusions and make certain to be far away when dis-aster struck. Or, if possible, make a deal with Kaskitt's enemies before disaster struck.

Before then, however, Thanquol intended to get rid of Skraekual. He wasn't sure what the other grey seer's secret mission was, but clearly it couldn't be anything of great importance. Seerlord Kritislik would never have entrusted anything valuable to such an undependable wretch. Skraekual was so debilitated by the pandemo-nium of drugs coursing through his veins that half the time the hophead wasn't even capable of form-ing a complete sentence, much less carrying out some nefarious scheme. Obviously Kritislik was becom-ing slack-witted to dispatch something like Skraekual on anything of consequence. Perhaps it was time for Thanquol to look seriously into furthering Seerlord Tisqueek's ambitions to become the Supreme Seerlord. Certainly Kritislik's lapses in judgement and inability to differentiate between a useless, worn-out drug addict and a valuable, loyal and courageous servant like himself boded ill for Kritislik's continued reign over the other seerlords and the Order of Grey Seers.

Thanquol took a pinch of snuff from his rat-skull, chittering happily as the fiery hint of warpstone scorched his nostrils. Skraekual! That loathsome little flea was an itch he would scratch very soon. It was taking all of his craft to work on Kaskitt's paranoia, but by degrees he was starting to convince the warlock-engineer that the other grey seer was a threat. Taking the tack that Skraekual was actually a spy for Warplord Morskittar seemed to yield the best results. Every time Kaskitt was about to dismiss the decrepit grey seer as a worthless addict, Thanquol would pose the question: where did Skraekual manage to find the warp-tokens to indulge his vices?

Thanquol stared at the walls of the tunnel. They were of close-packed earth braced with timber and rathide. The marks of shovels and claws could still be seen scarring the passage, obvious sign that there had been a collapse some time in the recent past. They could kill Skraekual and bury his body in the wall and nobody would find him for months. By then, Thanquol was certain, not even Seerlord Kritislik would care what fate had overtaken the mouse-livered scum.

Kaskitt's skirmishers trooped down the tunnel, their backs bowed beneath the weight of their sinister weapons. Hordes of leather-coated technicians and engineers scurried between the columns of fighting ratmen, their

arms laden with a bewildering variety of esoteric apparatus. Ranks of emaciated skavenslaves brought up the
rear, labouring under heavy sacks of provisions. No
threat of the slaves sampling their burdens. Each of
them knew that when the rations fell short, the difference would be made up in fresh rat meat.

Boneripper's metal muscles whirred as the hulking
monster lumbered after its master. Thanquol felt a rush
of satisfaction as he watched the warlock-engineers
part to allow the immense bodyguard to pass. Even
these ratkin, the very ones who had built it, were afraid
of Boneripper. They were wise to fear, because their
foolish master had placed control of such a terrifying
weapon into the paws of the most dangerous skaven in
skavendom!

It was tempting to order Boneripper to start tearing
apart Kaskitt's minions. The rat-ogre would wreak havoc
upon the closely-packed vermin, leaving Thanquol free
to unleash his mighty sorcery against Skraekual and
Kaskitt. He would turn the two maggots into burn-
marks on the wall of the tunnel! He would send their
souls shrieking into the black abyss of Kweethul the
Abominable! He would visit upon them the wrath
of the Horned Rat and rip their innards with his own
claws!

Thanquol smacked a paw against his horn, the sharp
pain helping to fight down the murderous visions blazing through his mind. It was easy to forget how potent
old Captain Lynsh's warp-snuff was. There must be a
high content of warpstone in it to affect a connois-
seur of Thanquol's experience and constitution in such
a manner. He scowled at the little rat-skull box, once
again considering dumping out its contents. He cast a
withering glance at the skaven around him. If he did

that, one of these maggots would just pick it up and use it himself. Why should Thanquol let some undeserving ratkin gain such a windfall? Besides, he wasn't Skraekual. He had an iron will. He could dispose of the wretched stuff any time he wanted and would do so just as soon as he was alone.

The tunnel ahead soon branched out into a much wider corridor. Unlike the crumbling rat-run they had been traversing, the new corridor boasted walls of solid stone supported by great balustrades of granite. Each of the skaven uttered a little squeak of relief as he passed from the tunnel into the stone passage. The new passage did not bear the crude marks of claw and pick, but was a carefully engineered and skilfully constructed corridor, part of the ancient dwarf Ungdrin Ankor, the subterranean road that once connected all the far-flung dwarfholds. Since the decline of dwarf civilisation, many stretches of the Underway had fallen to greenskins and other creatures of the dark. Whenever possible, the skaven had incorporated stretches of the Ungdrin Ankor into their own Under-Empire. No amount of prideful propaganda could prevent the ratmen from appreciating dwarf craftsmanship and the longevity of their constructions. It was rather refreshing to scurry down a tunnel one knew wasn't going to come crashing down about one's ears.

Thanquol shoved his way through the scrabbling mass of verminkin pouring out from the tunnel, just as eager as any of them to be quit from the earthen passageway. Boneripper lumbered after him, easily forcing a path through the press of furry bodies. Thanquol considered just letting the rat-ogre clear the way for him, but then decided it would be beneath his dignity to allow a mere lackey to go before him.

Besides, he was having too much fun smacking his staff into the noses of those skaven too slow to get out of the way of the mighty Grey Seer Thanquol.

A tug on the sleeve of his robe brought Thanquol spinning around. His staff whipped down, missing the face of the skaven who had accosted him by mere inches. If Skraekual's nose hadn't rotted away years ago, there would have been a most satisfying whack. It was just another example of the thousand ways the other grey seer was getting under Thanquol's fur.

'Mind-watch what you squeak-speak,' Skraekual hissed. 'Kritislik order-say you are decoy-meat, not Skraekual!'

Thanquol bared his fangs at the other grey seer. Who was this hophead to dare reprimand the greatest mind in skavendom! He'd feed the little weasel his own spleen!

Lips curled back over yellowed fangs. There was an uncomfortable focus about Skraekual's usually bleary eyes and a hint of menace in his usually stooped posture. Thanquol cast an anxious look around to see if any of Kaskitt's rats had noticed the threatening change that had come over Skraekual. Unfortunately, it seemed they were too focused on getting out into the dwarf passageway to pay any notice to Thanquol's distress.

Desperate, Thanquol cast a hopeful look at Boneripper. The skeletal rat-ogre's mechanics whirred as it pivoted at the waist and turned in his direction. Thanquol glared malignantly at Skraekual.

'Call it off-back,' Skraekual snapped. 'I can-will burn your brain before it takes seven steps!'

Thanquol felt his glands clench as the other grey seer hissed his threat. He found himself staring at Skraekual's fingers with their long filthy claws. Wrapped about one of the fingers was a band of black metal fashioned into the shape of a dragon's head. Thanquol knew that particular bit of jewellery. It had been among the possessions of his late and unlamented master, Sleekit. How Skraekual had come by it, he didn't know. He might have stolen it from Sleekit before Thanquol could find it, or perhaps it had been given to him by that treacherous rat Kritislik. At the moment, all that mattered was he had it and Thanquol knew precisely what he could do with it.

Bobbing his head submissively, Thanquol waved away Boneripper, nervously watching the lumbering brute to make sure it obeyed him. There was no sense in alarming his dear colleague Skraekual.

'Wise and noble Skraekual,' Thanquol said, brushing some of the filth from the other grey seer's robes. 'Surely you did not think-think I wanted Kaskitt to do anything to you.' Thanquol forced a peal of chittering laughter through his fangs. 'What I say-squeak was to make the fool suspect me, not you. The more I tell him you are untrustworthy, the more he suspects me of being dis-loyal. After all, if I would betray a fellow grey seer, how can he think-think I won't betray him?'

Skraekual lashed his tail in amusement. 'I did not get-make that impression,' he hissed. 'Stop telling him bad things about me. Or else...' He raised his finger, displaying the ring so that his enemy could not mistake the threat.

Thanquol squirmed uneasily, his fur feeling as if an army of fleas was scurrying through it. He watched as Skraekual dropped back into his usual stooped posture and limped away to join the flood of skaven rushing into the dwarf tunnel.

The filthy mouse-livered worm! He wouldn't dare

treat so flippantly with a sorcerer of Thanquol's stature were it not for that damn ring! It was just like the cowardly rat to cringe behind some magical artefact instead of relying upon his own powers! Any grey seer of real ability, anyone truly favoured by the Horned Rat didn't rely on sneaky tricks and fancy weapons to deal with his foes.

Thanquol waved his paw at Boneripper, the giant monster lumbering ahead of him to make a path through Kaskitt's minions. Thanquol needed time to think and the pleasant distraction of brutalising his fellow skaven would only muddle his wits. He needed a clever plan to deal with that upstart Skraekual.

Something sneaky.

Something that he could have Boneripper attend to while he was somewhere safely out of reach of Skraekual's magic.

'RIKKIT SNAPFANG HAS promised much-much warpstone to help him,' Kaskitt was telling Thanquol for what seemed the hundredth time. The grey seer rolled his eyes, but allowed the warlock-engineer to pursue his favourite subject: betraying Warlord Rikkit Snapfang. The plan involved getting Rikkit's warriors engaged in an all-out assault against the dwarfs. Once Rikkit's troops were committed, then Kaskitt and his skirmishers would turn tail and scurry back into the largely undefended burrows of Bonestash. They would find Rikkit's treasury and plunder it to their hearts' content.

'We take-fetch more than he think-say,' Kaskitt chittered.

Thanquol was less than enthusiastic about the plan. Not that he objected to the idea of stealing warpstone from a warlord who was trusting them to help him destroy some of skavendom's most tenacious enemies. Any warlord stupid enough to leave his own burrow undefended deserved to be stabbed in the back and robbed. That was simple common sense.

No, what bothered Thanquol was the fact that Kaskitt had confided in him. That meant the warlock-engineer wanted him involved in the plot in a big way. Rikkit Snapfang didn't belong to some three-flea clan, he was part of Clan Mors, the most powerful warlord clan in the Under-Empire. High Warlord Gnawdwell sat upon the Council of Thirteen and could bring considerable influence to bear against those who wronged his clan. Kaskitt knew this. For all of his mad talk about rising to a position of dominance within Clan Skryre, Thanquol knew he wasn't a complete fool.

The answer was obvious, so obvious Kaskitt himself had mentioned it at their first meeting in hopes that Thanquol would dismiss it as being too obvious. He was going to use Thanquol as the decoy, place all the blame for treachery on the grey seer's shoulders while he made good his own escape. Thanquol appreciated that in some quarters he had acquired an entirely underserved reputation for scheming against his own allies and always trying to improve his own wealth and position. Kaskitt's lies would be readily believed and Thanquol might not have the chance to explain the reality of the situation when Gnawdwell's outraged warriors caught up to him.

Day and night through the long march Kaskitt had been elaborating on his plan. Day and night Thanquol had been wracking his brain for a way to extricate himself from his predicament. Revealing the plot to Rikkit Snapfang when they reached Bonestash was one option, but hardly one that would put any warpstone in Thanquol's paws. No, there had to be a way to go through with Kaskitt's plan and shift the blame back onto somebody else.

The high ceilings of the Ungdrin Ankor didn't help ease Thanquol's mind. He kept expecting a Lustrian lizard-hawk to come swooping down out of the darkness to snatch him up in its claws. Or maybe a tregara, creeping along the black ceiling watching for prey. Thanquol's glands clenched as he remembered his own near escape from one of the carnivorous insects in Kritislik's Maze of Merciless Penance.

Unsettling smells lingered in the mammoth tunnel, saturating the dust-covered stones. Thanquol's nose caught the stink of cave squig and goblin scat, the reek of troll and the odour of spider webs. Somewhere in the darkness, a reptilian geckamund had cast off its scaly skin. Behind the pillars, the husk of a giant beetle was quietly rotting away.

Even the softest sounds echoed through Thanquol's keen ears. The squeaking of blind bats as they flew through the darkness, the rustle of rats as they crept along the walls. He could hear the faint drip of water from one of the stone cisterns the dwarfs had carved into niches in the tunnel walls.

Thanquol cursed the dwarf-built corridor. The miserable rock-sucking beard-brains were always trying to overcompensate for their diminutive size. That was why they built everything on such ridiculous, gargantuan scale. Why, a family of dragons could come cavorting down the Underway and still have room to spare! Anything might be lurking out there in the darkness, just waiting to pounce upon an unsuspecting skaven! A mob of blood-crazed orcs, a gang of ravenous ogres, even a distempered lion!

Glaring at Kaskitt, Thanquol could only wonder why the fool-meat hadn't struck a deal with Clan Sleekit to take them as close to Bonestash as possible on some of their barges. It was much safer to travel by river and much quicker. The rivers were forever connecting to the Ungdrin Ankor, because the dwarfs always needed water to power their steam engines and mining machines. The moron hadn't thought of that! If only Thanquol's brilliance hadn't been distracted with the petty schemes and jealousies of these small-minded lice he should have suggested such a plan back in Skavenblight.

'We will reach Bonestash soon-soon,' Kaskitt promised, scratching at the wires winding about his head.

'About time,' Thanquol sniffed. 'I grow weary of marching through these cursed dwarf-runs!' He dug a pawful of black corn from a pocket and chewed spitefully at the stuff. It had annoyed him to no end that Kaskitt had decided to start in on the black corn before carving up a few of the slaves. He rather suspected the idiot was trying to show off to his minions by feeding them on Skavenblight's famed crop. Unfortunately, black corn was about as appetising as a mouse turd and had about the same taste.

Kaskitt turned about to give some manner of rejoinder when the sharp squeal of a skaven in distress echoed off the walls of the Underway. Thanquol spun about, putting Boneripper's thick leg between himself and the source of the cry. It had been several hours since they'd lost a ratman to one of the Underway's predators. That time it had been a giant spider hiding above a cistern. Thanquol only hoped the current danger was likewise content to stuff itself with a single skaven and then scuttle back into the dark.

More cries sounded. Mixed among them now were

the distinct booms of guns. The dwarfs! It had to be! Thanquol ground his fangs together in rage. That idiot Kaskitt had marched them straight into a formation of dwarfs! His head snapped about, claws spread, but Kaskitt was already scrambling for cover. The cowardly mouse! He would strangle that tick-licking scat-sniffer when he got his claws on him!

Boneripper trembled as something smacked into its chest. Thanquol peered out from his refuge behind the rat-ogre's leg just far enough to see a smoking crater above where the monster's heart should have been had it been a thing of flesh and blood. The grey seer's glands clenched at this display of marksmanship. His eyes darted across the tunnel, not to find where Kaskitt had hidden himself but to find a suitable refuge for his own precious skin.

A fallen pillar looked as though it might afford a suitable barrier between himself and the fire of dwarf guns. Hastily, Thanquol snapped orders to his bodyguard. Boneripper's head creaked on its hinge as the rat-ogre stared down at him, then the monster's body swung about. In an instant, the brute was dashing across the tunnel, effortlessly pushing through the confused bedlam of Kaskitt's entourage.

'Wait-wait for me!' Thanquol cursed Boneripper. He wanted to use the brute as a shield until he was safely behind the smashed pillar. Now he found himself scurrying after his own bodyguard, frantic to keep pace with it. The boom of guns sounded again and Thanquol winced as a ratman beside him crumpled to the ground. The tangy smell of warpstone struck his senses. For an instant, he hesitated, staring down at the writhing skirmisher, greed arguing against his instinct for self-preservation. From the smell, the dead skirmisher must have a fair amount of warpstone on him.

'The Horned One need-want your flesh,' Thanquol snarled, seizing a ratman fleeing past him. Swinging the struggling skaven about, Thanquol bashed the head of his staff into his captive's skull until the prisoner went limp. Holding the slack body up like a shield, he bent to inspect the dead body at his feet.

A thrill of alarm squirted from his glands when Thanquol saw the extent of the damage the bullet had done to the skirmisher. The ratman's chest was a gory crater; his armoured breastplate looked as though a giant had punched it. Gazing at it, the grey seer realised that his living shield wouldn't prove much barrier against any weapon that could dole out such damage.

Callously dropping his senseless captive, Thanquol scurried with all haste across the tunnel, freely battering and clawing at any ratkin who got in his way. The sound of bullets whipping through the air, the agonised shrieks of dying skaven, the smell of fear-musk and black blood spurred him on. He could see the comforting safety of the rubble ahead of him, Boneripper stupidly standing out in the open waiting for its master to give it new orders.

He'd give it new orders all right! Thanquol cursed the dim-witted machine and its infernally fast legs. It was all a subtle plot by Kaskitt Steelgrin to get him killed! He'd known he couldn't trust any gift handed to him by the delusional lab-rats of Clan Skryre!

The stench of burning fur struck Thanquol's nose and a whoosh of flames rushed past his ears. He could feel intense heat blaze across his back. A pack of confused skaven who had decided to follow him to safety gave voice to a miserable howl. Thanquol glanced over his shoulder to see a dozen ratmen writhing on the ground, their bodies engulfed in green flames.

A hideous suspicion flared up as Thanquol sniffed the dying skaven. They reeked of warpstone, even though many of them were scrawny slaves who couldn't possibly have any of the precious mineral on them. Moreover, he'd never seen a dwarf flame cannon that tossed green fire at its victims.

The grey seer made a wild leap and scrambled behind the pile of rubble. He took a half-dozen breaths, then reached for his snuff-box. A pinch of warpstone snuff would help just now. His paw froze as his fingers closed on the rat-skull box. If he was right, then he would need his full wits about him. The emboldened mindset of a warp-addled brain wasn't going to do him any good, however much it calmed his nerves.

Thanquol peered out from behind his refuge. The floor of the tunnel was littered with dead and dying ratmen. He could see the pile of rocks from which the ambushers were picking off Kaskitt's minions. He could even see Kaskitt Steelgrin cringing behind the base of some dwarf king's statue, Skraekual and a clutch of leather-coated tinker-rats trying to exploit the same sanctuary.

Resolutely, Thanquol stuffed the rat-skull box back into his robe. 'Over here, idiot,' Thanquol growled at the still unmoving Boneripper. The rat-ogre shifted position, dropping down behind the rubble to join its master. Thanquol noted that the lummox had been shot several times while it had been standing out in the open. Each of the ghastly impacts had pitted the brute's skeletal frame and battered its armoured machinery. Little flecks of glowing green stone clung to the edges of the wounds. Gingerly, Thanquol extracted one of the slivers and pressed it to his tongue.

The grey seer felt a hot shock sizzle through his body, a burning sensation that was at once excruciating and invigorating. His suspicion was justified. The bullets that had struck Boneripper and Kaskitt's hench-rats were made of refined warpstone. The fire that had consumed the skavenslaves had been of a chemical nature, liquid flame that used warpstone as its base.

The ambushers weren't dwarfs. They were skaven! No wonder there had been no betraying glimmer of lamps and lanterns! The ambushers didn't need to see their victims; with their sharp noses and the updraft of the tunnel, the ratmen could smell their enemies!

As if to confirm his suspicion, several ratmen emerged from behind the rubble. They wore elaborate armour, their arms and legs locked inside complicated frameworks of pipes and gears. When they moved, they clanked and clattered in the same fashion as Boneripper and with a similarly uncanny speed. While Thanquol watched, the enhanced skaven fell upon a pocket of Kaskitt's minions, butchering them with long, hook-bladed halberds.

More attackers followed the war-rats. These were leather-coated skaven who resembled in almost every way the skirmishers Kaskitt had brought. The only difference was the red tabards they wore, each marked with a black, slash-like symbol.

And the fact that the jezzails they carried were loaded and ready to kill.

Teams of muscular ratmen scurried about the flanks of the jezzails. These wore long cloaks that glistened wetly in the faint light of the tunnel and their faces were carefully masked with leather visors. Each team consisted of two skaven, one lugging a huge cask on his back, the other holding a curious metal implement

before him. Thick hoses of ratgut connected the cask
the rear skaven carried to the implement the leader
bore. A faint drip of flaming green liquid dribbled from
the gaping mouth of the device in the leader's paws.

Thanquol recognised the weapon for a warpfire
thrower, one of the most fiendish of Clan Skryre's inventions. He'd suspected the presence of such a weapon
the moment he'd seen the burning skavenslaves. These
seemed to belong to a more complex pattern than
those his own minions had employed on his behalf
during the Battle of Nuln, but their function was certainly the same. As he watched, the grey seer saw the
attackers immolate a knot of Kaskitt's followers with a
sheet of green fire.

Thanquol tugged at his whiskers. He didn't know
what sort of game was being played, but he knew he
had to take a paw in the action now while there was still
time. A judicious use of magic could rescue Kaskitt's
expedition from disaster. A grateful Kaskitt Steelgrin
would then be obliged to help Thanquol with his own
problems. They could always tell Kritislik that Skraekual
had been killed in the fighting.

Climbing atop a chunk of rubble, Thanquol gazed
out across the battleground. Maliciously he selected his
first victim, one of the warpfire teams. It wouldn't take
much of a spell to do what he wanted. He wouldn't
even need any warpstone to reinforce his concentration. The fire-thrower would provide that.

Opening his mind to the aethyr and his soul to the
tyrannical glory of the Horned Rat, Thanquol pointed
his staff at the doomed fire-team. A crackling ribbon of
lightning leapt from the head of his staff. The magical
energy seared across the tunnel, striking the fuel cask.
Instantly the entire tunnel was lit up by a burst of green

light. The weapon team vanished in the explosion, streams of unleashed warpfire spattering about the passageway, striking down ambushers and victims alike. A second warpfire thrower was caught by the blast, causing its fuel cask to explode in a similarly dramatic manner.

Unfortunately, the chain-reaction ended with the second warpfire thrower. Revelling in the destruction he had unleashed, Thanquol was almost caught in the vengeful sheet of flames that swept across the tunnel. A third warpfire thrower had marked him as the cause of their comrades' demise. Determined not to share such a fiery fate, they viciously persecuted the grey seer.

Diving down from his perch, Thanquol glared helplessly at the green flames sizzling all around him. Another weapon team had joined the first. The combined fire couldn't penetrate his cover, but then, it wouldn't have to. The slinking villains could just sit back and roast him alive without ever clapping eyes on him!

'Two can kill-slay this way,' Thanquol muttered. He turned his eyes on Boneripper. The murderous machine was a magnificent example of Clan Skryre's techno-sorcery. A far more advanced weapon than the cheap toys his enemies were using. It would make short work of his foes once it was turned against them, burning them alive with its own fire-thrower.

'Boneripper!' Thanquol howled at the rat-ogre, trying to keep his voice from sounding too panicked. 'Go-go! Kill-slay! Burn-burn!'

The automaton's skull creaked around, staring at its master with glowing eyes. Obediently, Boneripper emerged from behind the rocks. Thanquol hopped about in glee as the monster turned about to face the

terrified warpfire throwers. He could almost smell the
fear spurting from their glands as the rat-ogre lifted
its third arm and pointed the nozzle of its own fire-
thrower at them.

Instead of burning and dying, instead of fleeing
and screaming, the warpfire throwers just stood and
laughed. Thanquol blinked in disbelief. Boneripper
just stood there, its arm raised to deal fiery death to
his enemies. The grey seer scurried to the edge of his
refuge, trying to goad his metal-brained bodyguard into
action.

'Boneripper! Burn-burn!' he shrieked. 'Burn them!
Burn them with fire!' he elaborated.

The hulking machine-monster just stood its ground.
Contemptuously the weapon teams ignored it and
began to fire on Thanquol's refuge once more.

Reluctantly, Thanquol realised his bodyguard wasn't
going to help him. Gripped by a mixture of terror and
fury, he began pawing at his robes for a sliver of warpstone. He didn't like employing the magic that would
allow him to slip into the immaterial Realm of Chaos,
but at the moment the threat of being ripped asunder
by daemons seemed preferable to being roasted alive.
His only consolation was that Kaskitt and Skraekual
were certain to be doomed once he abandoned them to
their own feeble resources.

A metal scratch of a voice rumbled across the tunnel.
The sheets of flame billowing about Thanquol's refuge
suddenly abated. The grey seer popped a finger-sized
nugget of warpstone into his mouth, but hesitated to
grind it between his fangs. Carefully, he peered around
the rubble.

The ambushers were falling back, adopting a wary
posture, their weapons at the ready. Emerging from

the mound of rubble that had concealed them was a
ghastly-looking skaven clad in slick robes of ratgut and
leather. Half of the ratman's head was locked inside a
grisly metal mask; what part of his face was exposed
was burned and scarred in an especially hideous
fashion. Wisps of white fur emerged from the grey mess
of scar tissue to form a long mane running down the
side of his face. A gigantic steel claw was fitted about
his left arm, a confusion of wires and tubes running
from the metal hand to a cylindrical device fitted to
the forearm behind it, uncomfortably reminiscent of
the warpfire projector fastened to Boneripper's arm. A
brace of warplock pistols were holstered at the ratman's
belt and in his right hand he bore a black sword that
stank of warpstone. The blade was bolted to a long
metal pole and about it was fastened all manner of
curious mechanisms. From the skaven's back, a tall rod
supported a tattered banner upon which was displayed
the image of the Horned Rat blasphemously merged
with the hatchet symbol of Clan Skryre.

Again, the metal snarl of the skaven's voice echoed
through the tunnel, confirming for Thanquol what his
ears had thought they'd heard the first time.

'Submit-live,' the snarl spoke. 'Only Kaskitt Scrapface
needs to die-die!'

Thanquol cast a hopeful look towards the statue
where Kaskitt was hiding. If he could contrive to
eliminate the warlock-engineer, then he'd be able to
ingratiate himself with this new, terrifying personage.

Skraekual, unfortunately, had the same idea.
Before Thanquol could act, the underhanded sorcerer
unleashed a blast of magic against Kaskitt that sent
the warlock-engineer tumbling from his sanctuary. He
ended his tumble in a helpless sprawl, his fur smoking

and his body quivering from the fury of Skraekual's magic.

The metal-faced skaven chuckled, a sound not unlike a knife grinding against stone. The sound of his enemy's amusement seemed to revive Kaskitt. The stricken ratman scrambled back onto his feet, slapping at some contraption hidden under his coat. Instantly the wires wrapped about his head began to blaze with energy, crackling fingers of electricity running through the strange framework. The lenses of Kaskitt's goggles began to darken. Raising his paw, Kaskitt now displayed a strange armature of steel tipped with a globe of polished warpstone. The speed of its deployment made Thanquol wonder if Kaskitt had conjured the weapon into being or if it had been concealed under his robes and deployed by some spring-loaded mechanism.

Whatever the source of Kaskitt's weapon, Thanquol was genuinely shocked when he saw the warlock-engineer dispatch a bolt of warp-lightning from the glowing green globe. It was impossible! There had been no smell of magic about Kaskitt, yet here he was unleashing what was unquestionably a manifestation of aethyric energy! Thanquol gnashed his fangs at the heretical thought of a skaven exploiting magic without the wisdom of the Horned Rat behind him.

Much like Thanquol's own spell, Kaskitt's warp lightning crackled across the tunnel, streaking straight towards its target. Unlike the grey seer's magic, however, Kaskitt's lightning failed to find its victim. With an almost casual flick of his metal claw, the steel-faced ratman caused the warp lightning to dissipate, to shatter as though it had struck an unseen wall. Little sparks of energy cascaded down to the floor, scorching the flagstones of the old dwarf road.

More sorcery! A counter-spell conjured with an ease that made Thanquol's heart tremble with jealousy and his glands clench with fear.

Kaskitt shrieked in horror as he saw his intended victim unharmed. The warlock-engineer turned to flee, but as he did so, the steel-faced skaven raised the black sword in his hand, thrusting it out before him on its long pole. The machinery connected to the warpstone blade whirred into life, energy quickly crackling across the black sword, the symbols scratched along its edge glowing with power. Before Kaskitt could run more than a few paces, a beam of dark energy snaked outwards from the sword, striking the warlock-engineer in the back.

Thanquol could feel the awful power of the coruscating black energy. It was like the harnessed soul of raw warpstone, a thing terrible in its potency and awful in its potential. He expected to see Kaskitt's body ripped in half by the blast. Instead the energy writhed across the warlock-engineer, racing about the weapon fastened to his arm.

The warpstone globe shattered in a burst of malignant green fire that sent Kaskitt's charred arm dancing across the floor. Streams of energy crackled away from the broken weapon, converging upon the network of wires wound about Kaskitt's head. For a moment, it seemed as though Kaskitt had gained a dark halo. Then the moment passed and the warlock-engineer's head burst like an overripe melon.

'This fight-fray is done-over,' the steely scrape of the metal-faced skaven declared. 'Squeak-swear to serve me or join that fool-meat in death.'

The gruesome ratman swept his fiery gaze across the tunnel.

'Ikit Claw now commands this expedition.'

CHAPTER VI

THE SKAVEN WERE quick to bare their throats in submission to Ikit Claw, scrambling out from their refuges and stumbling over themselves in their eagerness to surrender. For their part, Ikit Claw's ratmen took petty revenge on each former enemy as he presented himself. The filching of warp-tokens and food was the rule, even among these clan-kin, but a few went so far as to pull whiskers and cut ears.

From his own hiding place, Thanquol watched as the ambushers took charge of Skraekual. They treated the decrepit grey seer with a great amount of reverence, sparing him the indignity of robbery and abuse. A few even chittered their gratitude to the rot-nosed traitor. Clearly Skraekual's opportunistic and utterly craven betrayal of Kaskitt hadn't gone unnoticed.

Thanquol ground his teeth in frustration. His hated rival was insinuating himself with the victors while he was left cringing alone in the dark with no one to help him except a bony rat-ogre with a touch of the stupids! Betraying Kaskitt was something Thanquol had planned from the start! It was criminal that Skraekual should reap the benefits of Thanquol's subtle plot!

A cunning gleam crept into Thanquol's eyes. Skraekual wouldn't profit from trying to undermine his own position. Indeed, the mouse-livered weasel was acting to the benefit of Thanquol, even if he was too warp-witted to know it! Let him flatter and whine his way into the good graces of Ikit Claw! The fool would save Thanquol the trouble of doing it himself.

The grey seer turned his attention away from Skraekual and focused on the real threat. Ikit Claw, Chief Warlock of Clan Skryre, the right fang of Warplord Morskittar himself. Ikit Claw was a name held in envy and fear throughout skavendom. Rumours claimed he was old enough to have helped Morskittar try to seize control of the Under-Empire in the dark days before the Great Summoning when the Horned Rat had manifested himself before the Shattered Tower and imposed the foundation of the Council of Thirteen upon his squabbling children. Thanquol didn't believe such nonsense, of course, for that would make Ikit Claw thousands of birth-cycles old and only dwarf-things and elf-meat lived that long. He was prepared to accept, however, that the Claw shared his master's ability to extend his lifespan through the techno-sorcery of Clan Skryre. There were dark rumours that the upper echelons of Clan Skryre maintained kennels of specially reared and extravagantly pampered skavenslaves which they harvested once every few birth-cycles to replace their own corrupt organs with fresh healthy ones.

Thanquol cringed in disgust at the thought. A skaven

should accept the years bestowed upon him by the Horned Rat. Or else try and find some magic trinkets that would improve his longevity.

Still, that wasn't entirely an impossibility where Ikit Claw was concerned. It was said he'd penetrated the secrets of countless wizards and sorcerers. The warren of Spitespittle was still haunted by the liche priest the Claw brought back from the Dead Lands and tortured into revealing the black art of necromancy. Ratkin in Grabkeep still spoke of his terrific battle with the sorcerer Nostramus after his theft of the human's scrying stone. There were even stories that he'd infiltrated the polluted lands of the black-fur dwarf-things and discovered how they made their hideous daemon-machines.

Reluctantly, Thanquol decided that it would be in his best interest to keep on the right side of so formidable a personage. The Claw could even protect him from Kritislik should eluding the Seerlord's displeasure become a problem.

First, of course, he'd wait and see if Ikit Claw blasted Skraekual. If the sly, double-dealing warp-brain could manage to talk Claw out of incinerating him with the flame projector built into his metal arm, then Thanquol would take that as a good sign. Though he'd be sorry not to watch the other grey seer burned alive, there'd be time to work towards that end later.

Thanquol held his breath as he watched Skraekual approach Ikit Claw. He felt a twinge of disgust at the way the other grey seer abased himself before the warlock-engineer, a disgust made all the more profound because it seemed to work. Cheated out of the prospect of seeing his rival summarily exterminated, he decided it was time to act.

Resisting the impulse to take a pinch of snuff to

fortify his convictions, Thanquol emerged from behind
the pile of rubble. He could feel his fur crawl as he saw
patches of liquid warpfire still burning on the floor.
As he rounded the immobile bulk of Boneripper, he
delivered a vindictive crack of his staff against the
skeletal brute's leg.

The resounding impact was louder than Thanquol
had expected, the smacking report of his staff echoing through the tunnel. At once, hundreds of skaven
eyes fastened onto him, fingers flying to the triggers
of pistols and jezzails, paws wrapping about the hafts
of swords and spears. The two warpfire throwers came
scuttling back into view, frantically trying to ready their
cumbersome weapons.

The temptation to dart back behind the rocks was
sore upon Thanquol, but his pride fought down millions of birth-cycles of skaven instinct. As he looked
down upon Ikit Claw's warriors, as he drew in their
scent, Thanquol felt his heart pounding with ferocity.
They knew who he was. And they were afraid. Even the
warlock-engineers recognised the awful power of Grey
Seer Thanquol and even they were afraid.

It did not dawn upon Thanquol that the reason for
their fear might lie in their belief and the warpfire teams'
repeated insistence that he was dead. With such a dramatic entrance, with everyone concentrated upon the
task of looting their vanquished clan-kin, Thanquol's
sudden reappearance seemed nothing less than a visita-
tion by the Horned Rat himself.

'Good-good,' Thanquol said, straightening his back
and marching in his most magnificent manner towards
the horrified ratmen. 'Kaskitt Steelgrin was traitor-meat.
You all act-serve the Horned One when you kill-slay
traitor-meat.' His eyes narrowed as he looked over at

Skraekual. 'I told my servantling to make certain Clan Skryre had the chance-time to take-finish Kaskitt themselves.'

A subdued murmur spread among the ratmen. Thanquol tried to retain his dictatorial bearing, but felt his imperious tendencies shrivel as Ikit Claw fixed his terrible gaze on the grey seer.

'I... I had to... make-look like I... with Kaskitt watch-sniffing...' Thanquol winced as he saw Ikit draw back some of the burned skin from his muzzle and expose his scarred teeth. 'Look-sniff!' Thanquol whined, gesturing behind him. 'I tell-say for Boneripper to stop-stand, not to kill-smash loyal-true skaven!'

Ikit Claw continued to glare at Thanquol for a moment, then a strange and hideous noise rattled through the warlock-engineer's throat. It took a little time before the grey seer understood it was the Claw's laughter.

'You told rat-ogre to stop?' Ikit Claw cackled. The laughter was taken up by his minions and even the subjugated skaven who had so recently served Kaskitt Steelgrin.

'You told-say for bone-thing not to stomp-slay?' There was a very nasty note in Ikit Claw's mirth that had Thanquol glancing back to his abandoned refuge. A pox on that duplicitous rat Skraekual for not standing his ground and getting himself burned to a crisp! That maggot had tricked Thanquol into thinking everything was safe!

'Yes-yes!' Thanquol squeaked, fingering his staff and wondering if he would be able to cast an escape spell faster than Ikit Claw could have him shot. 'I tell-say for Boneripper not to hurt-hurt Great and Powerful Ikit Claw... or any noble-mighty skaven who help-aid him.

By the Horned One, I squeak-speak true-straight!'

The last comment brought a peal of blasphemous laughter chittering from every skaven throat. Thanquol felt a surge of outrage course through him. How dare they mock a grey seer invoking the name of their god? How dare they find amusement in a grey seer making a sacred oath before his divine master that he was not trying to trick them? If it wasn't complete suicide, Thanquol would have liked to wring every one of their scrawny necks! Of course, it was suicide to do anything like that, so Thanquol just stood still and tried to join in on the laughter, but his voice sounded hollow even to himself.

Ikit Claw raised his huge metal hand, motioning the other skaven to silence. He marched towards Thanquol, his teeth bared in a fierce smile. 'Thanquol,' he hissed. 'That machine-thing stopped because it has a safety valve. It didn't smash-crush my ratkin because it can't smash-crush anything that carries Clan Skryre's scent.'

The explanation provoked another burst of laughter. Thanquol felt his insides wither. It wasn't the humiliation of being caught in an impious lie, but rather the likelihood that he was about to be burned to a crisp that bothered him.

'I still make-tell Skraekual to help kill-slay Kaskitt,' Thanquol insisted. 'Ask him,' he said, then considered better of pressing that particular point when he got a good look at Skraekual's rotten face. 'Ask any of Kaskitt's tinker-rats! They will speak-squeak that Skraekual is my helper, that he does what I tell-say!'

Ikit Claw continued to glower at Thanquol, lashing his tail as he weighed the grey seer's words. 'I know all about Kaskitt's plan-plot,' he said at length. 'I know what he planned for you.' The way he said it made Thanquol's glands clench, but the grey seer didn't say anything. 'It was-is good scheme. We will go to Bonestash and help Rikkit Snapfang fight-kill dwarf-things. Clan Mors will keep their noses turned your way, Thanquol. That will make it easy for me to do what I need-want in Karak Angkul.'

Thanquol breathed a little easier when it became obvious that Ikit Claw wasn't going to order his immediate destruction. Instead, the Chief Warlock ordered some of his tinker-rats to attend Boneripper and get the rat-ogre moving again before the locked safety valve caused it to explode. The grey seer could only mutter his thanks and watch as his new ally stalked off to inspect the survivors of Kaskitt's troop.

Let Ikit Claw savour his small triumph, Thanquol thought. There would be a long way to Bonestash and an even longer tunnel back to Skavenblight. More than enough time for the Horned One to visit a terrible judgement upon the prideful tinker-rat and his abominable entourage.

THE SKAVEN EXPEDITION, now under new leadership, soon resumed its journey through the desolation of the Ungdrin Ankor. In their wake, the ratmen left little behind, stripping the dead of anything of value and butchering all but the scrawniest of their bodies to supplement their rations.

The skaven were brutally thorough in their scavenging, moving with a speed and skill honed by lives spent trying to survive in the merciless Under-Empire. Even in victory, the ratmen were cautious, watching every shadow, flinching at every unexplained sound, jumping at every unexpected smell. They did not like to linger in a place that smelled of battle, knowing only too well that the odour would draw scavengers bigger and nastier than themselves.

In their vigilance, however, the skaven missed one pair of hostile eyes that watched them from the darkness of a milestone. The pure hate shining in those eyes would have sent many a ratman spurting the musk of fear, but harsh experience had taught the mind behind those eyes to keep to the downwind darkness where his enemies could neither see nor smell him.

The red-bearded dwarf pounded his fist against his side. It grated upon every fibre of his being to act like this, creeping about in the dark following a bunch of filthy skaven. Every time their loathsome stink filled his nose, every time their shrill voices cut his ears, he wanted to leap out and kill them with his bare hands.

But he wouldn't do that. To do so would shame his ancestors and offend the gods of the Karak Ankor. It had been an act of Grimnir himself that had brought him to this place and at this time. Among all the millions of ratmen who infested the world, he'd again crossed paths with the one skaven he wanted to kill more than anything.

Mordin Grimstone had come far since casting off the chains of a slave. By rights, the ratkin's spell should have killed him, and whatever life the skaven magic left in him should have been smothered by the river. The dwarf ran his hand along the ugly burn-mark where Thanquol's spell had struck him, then touched the scarred flesh where his back had been ripped raw by the rocky banks of the river. He had survived both foes. The river had even colluded with him once it tired of trying to drown him, its swift current bearing him through the darkness until finally washing his battered body onto a dilapidated stone pier.

Mordin had spent several days nursing his wounds before straying very far from the pier. That the river had brought him to some abandoned stretch of the great dwarf Underway was apparent, but it took locating an intact guidestone for him to fully gain his bearings.

The dwarf clenched his fist as he remembered the long journey alone in the dark, surviving on a few blind fish from the river and what mushrooms he could gather from the ruined tunnel. Only the thought of his dead brother and the awful shame of watching him die kept him going. It was in his mind to journey to Karak Kadrin and present himself before the Slayer Shrine. He would shave his head and take the Slayer Oath in memory of his brother and the death Mordin felt he could have prevented.

Grimnir, however, didn't seem patient enough to await Mordin's arrival at his shrine. Mordin discovered a horde of skaven prowling through the Ungdrin Ankor. At first he had hidden himself, determined not to fall into the cruel paws of the skaven again, determined not to die until he had atoned for his shame before the Slayer Shrine. Then, against all odds, Mordin had made an amazing discovery. The skaven who had killed his brother, the one who had cast him into the river, was among the ratmen. There was no mistaking that scratchy voice and the distinct curl of his horns. Any chance he was wrong was eliminated when the other skaven referred to the creature as Grey Seer Thanquol. Mordin fell to his knees and thanked Grimnir for granting him such an opportunity for revenge.

Since then, Mordin had followed the skaven, shadowing them through the tunnels. Having been caught by the ratmen before, having spent months as their prisoner, he knew what mistakes would alert the vermin to his presence. Though it plagued him to do so, he kept his distance, forcing himself to watch and wait. He did not care about dying, he had resigned himself to that fate the moment he saw his brother murdered. But to die without accomplishing his revenge was something the dwarf would not countenance.

So he followed, waiting for any opportunity to catch Thanquol alone and gut the grey seer with the rusty goblin knife Mordin had found in the tunnels. It wouldn't matter if the entire horde came screaming down upon him after that. His brother would be avenged and his honour satisfied.

Unfortunately, Thanquol had proven as wary as he was cowardly. The grey seer was never alone, always keeping well within the middle of the skaven horde. Mordin was just about resigned to mounting some crazed berserk charge in the hope of getting through the skaven and coming to grips with his enemy when a second horde of ratmen attacked the first.

It took every ounce of willpower to remain a spectator to the ensuing carnage. Mordin watched the fight with a sense of nausea at the back of his throat, terrified that some slinking ratman would kill Thanquol and cheat him of his chance at revenge. The dwarf was actually relieved when the battle ended and the second pack of skaven absorbed Thanquol into their ranks.

His relief was soon squelched, however. From his hiding place, Mordin was able to overhear Thanquol and the other skaven leader plotting their campaign against Karak Angkul. The dwarf had spent long enough as the slave of the ratmen to understand something of their chitter-spit language. He couldn't mistake the scheme he heard. Suddenly the dream of vengeance that was so close began to slip through his fingers. Even if the chance presented itself, he couldn't attack Thanquol now. A greater duty had been placed upon his shoulders, one the vengeful dwarf found as heavy as a millstone.

Mordin Grimstone had uncovered a new and terrible threat against an entire dwarfhold. The life of every dwarf in Karak Angkul might depend on learning what he had overheard. If he could reach the stronghold ahead of the skaven, there was just a chance his warning could make the difference between victory and disaster. The skaven would follow the Underway as far as they could, but they would be slowed by their numbers and their ravenous metabolisms. More, it was doubtful if any of the ratmen could read the ancient Khazalid runes on the guide-stones. They wouldn't know the secret ways by which a traveller could trim days from his journey by making his way to the surface and travelling overland.

Vengeance would have to wait. It was a decision that made Mordin sick to his stomach, but it was the only decision he could make. Thanquol would have to wait.

Though there was one consoling thought the dwarf took with him as he slipped unseen into the darkness.

At least he knew where his enemy was going.

'I DO NOT understand why an engineer is so interested in these ancient tomes. I seem to recall that a certain engineer is always extolling the necessity for looking forwards and not clinging slavishly to the past.'

The statement was made by a stern-faced old dwarf with a snow-white beard that fell nearly to his ankles. He wore a voluminous robe of rich purple trimmed in silver thread. About his neck he wore a small stone anvil upon which was etched a single rune like a lightning bolt.

The white-bearded dwarf was Morag Frostbeard, Runelord of Karak Angkul. The chambers were his own, located several halls from the librarium within which the Guild of Runesmiths kept their tomes of lore and craftsmanship. Morag was old enough to remember Karak Angkul at its glory, though he had been a very young beardling in those days. It had been that nostalgia which King Logan had exploited to elicit the runemaster's complicity in what was certainly a breach of custom and tradition.

Morag's chambers were not extravagant, but there was a sense of opulence about them. Several copper etchings of extraordinary skill were bolted to the smooth stone walls, a collection of polished geodes rested upon a richly carved set of limestone shelves, an elaborate fresco depicted the family of the ancestor god Grungni, and the floor was covered in the pelts of bears and wolves. In one corner stood a small shrine to Thungni, the son of Grungni and patron god of the runesmiths.

In the centre of the room stood a large table with legs of deeply etched bronze and a surface of ancient wutroth wood richly carved with a map of the Worlds Edge Mountains and the once vast domains of the dwarf kingdoms. Much of the table's surface was covered with voluminous tomes bound in steel, their copper pages polished to a bright sheen by the tireless efforts of the Guild's librarians. Even so, each page bore a patina of decay about it, for the tireless march of time could not be wholly thwarted even by the most attentive of care.

A lone dwarf sat behind the table, scrutinising the open page set before him with such intense concentration that he might have been carved from stone. He wore the deep red robe of a journeyman runesmith, its edges picked out in a trim of golden thread, forming into intricate whorls as they converged upon the hem of the garment. A heavy stone pectoral was looped about the dwarf's neck, depicting the anvil and lightning bolt symbol of the Guild of Runesmiths. His long blond beard fell only to his waist and only the first streaks of grey had started to appear within it. The runesmith's face was broad and full, his brows knitted in their customary attitude of deliberation. Kurgaz Brightfinger never did anything without the most careful consideration. It was why the Brightfinger family had despaired of ever making him a first-rate jewelsmith, for he would spend weeks before making the first cut upon a stone. They had been quite relieved when the Guild of Runesmiths had accepted Kurgaz into their company.

Kurgaz's mind had been a natural fit to the work of a runesmith and he had excelled within the Guild. His time as an apprentice had been the shortest ever recorded in the lore of Karak Angkul, and only decorum and tradition had kept him from achieving the rank of journeyman decades sooner than he had. It was the thought of these lost years and what he might have done with them had he been allowed the opportunity that had planted a seed of discontent in the breast of Kurgaz Brightfinger, a seed that had eventually lead him to the friendship and patronage of Klarak Bronzehammer, the daring genius and nonconformist pariah of the Engineers' Guild.

Klarak himself stood behind Kurgaz's chair, watching his friend labour over the ancient pages of the Rhun Kron. It was forbidden for any but a runesmith to consult the great tomes within which the ancient runes of power were recorded, and the engineer was careful to keep his eyes averted from the subject of Kurgaz's studies. That Runelord Morag had allowed him to even set foot within the chamber while the books were unlocked and open was a mark of how unusual the king's request had been and how deeply – albeit grudgingly – Morag respected the bold Klarak.

'We should not cling slavishly to the past,' Klarak said. 'To do so is the doom of our people. But neither can we ignore the wisdom and pride of our ancestors. If we do that, then we are no longer dwarfs and no better than grobi.'

Morag huffed and grumbled at the remark. 'Yet you flout tradition and custom at every bend in the tunnel.' He gestured with his calloused hands at the diligent Kurgaz bent over the copper pages of his book. 'This, for instance, is a terrible breach of precedence and propriety. The books young Kurgaz is being allowed to examine are the exclusive province of only the most learned within the Guild. Why, perhaps if he was a runemaster with a hundred more years under his chin he might be capable of understanding a fraction of what he is reading, but to think he can possibly accomplish what you intend...' Morag threw up his hands in a hopeless gesture.

Klarak shook his head. 'Yet you agreed to let him try,' he pointed out, a touch of reprimand in his voice.

'It was King Logan's request,' Morag said. 'I was faced with the choice of permitting this foolishness or having my name entered in the king's Book of Grudges. I've lived a long life and know I'm close to meeting the ancestors. I don't intend to do so with a king's grudge-stone tied about my neck.'

'There was a very important reason I asked King Logan to make this request,' apologised Klarak.

The runelord allowed a flicker of smile to pull at his

white beard. 'I know that,' he said. 'If it were not so, then I would have refused the king, grudgestone or no. But I still cannot see the purpose of this. A Master Rune is something even a runelord's wisdom finds difficult to understand. And without the proper understanding, they become dangerous. How many glory-hungry fools have taken the sacred Anvils of Doom out into battle, boldly thinking they can command the vast powers of such scared relics? And how many of these precious artefacts have been lost forever because they broke beneath the hammers of these same fools?'

'I know the danger,' Klarak said solemnly. 'But I have faith in Kurgaz Brightfinger. Even you will acknowledge he is the most brilliant dwarf to ever study under one of your runemasters.'

'Yes,' conceded Morag, 'but intelligence is only half the alloy that makes up wisdom. The other half is experience, and no amount of brilliance can make up for young Kurgaz's lack of years.'

'We will have to agree to disagree,' Klarak said.

Morag fixed him with a stern look. 'It would help if I knew what you intended to do. Allowing of course that trying to forge a Master Rune doesn't shatter the brain of Runesmith Kurgaz.'

Klarak frowned and shook his head. 'That, I fear, is something I must keep to myself. But know that if it works, then you will have helped save Karak Angkul from destruction.' The flake-gold eyes closed for a moment and Klarak pictured again the strange mystical writing on the message he had received.

'More than that,' he said as he made his way to the door, leaving Kurgaz to his study. 'You may help save the whole of the Karak Ankor.'

* * *

THERE WAS URGENCY in Klarak Bronzehammer's step as he made his way through the vast halls of Karak Angkul's Third Deep. Excavated by miners long ago, the old workings had been expanded into broad galleries and gigantic corridors. Monolithic pillars supported the vaulted ceilings far overhead, many of them etched with scenes from the dwarfhold's long history. A steady throng of dwarfs travelled along the passageways, hurrying about the business of the hold. Goatherds bringing milk and cheese to the larders of their patrons from the pastures far above the hold. Apprentice ironsmiths and weaponsmiths pushing trolleys of ingots to the forges and workshops of their masters. Wranglers leading lode ponies down to the stables of the various miner clans. Wiry young runebearers hurrying through the crowds to deliver the messages they had been entrusted with.

Among the normal traffic of the dwarfhold, there was an added air of tension. Armoured warriors moved among the crowds in greater numbers than was commonly seen. King Logan had dispatched a great number of troops into the lower deeps, trying to drive out the skaven from their stubborn foothold in the mines. The entire household of Thane Tarbrak was armed and assembled in the Sixth Deep, charged with the duty of maintaining the sanctity of the dwarfhold against any further encroachment by the ratkin. Thane Tarbrak's cousin had been among the ironbreakers overwhelmed by the first attack, so success in this new duty would allow him a chance to atone for the failure of his kinsman and wipe out the grudge charged against his clan.

Klarak knew the need for such precautions. A show of force was the only thing that would keep the scavenging ratmen from rushing up into the dwarfhold itself.

But he also knew it would not be enough to keep them there. From bitter experience, he knew the devious ways of the skaven. Even now the ratmen were sniffing for another way into the stronghold, a way past the waiting axes and guns of the dwarfs. He had every reason to suspect the vermin would find that way, even if they had to claw it from the roots of the mountain.

The engineer's expression became grim. The warning he had received made no bones about what he could expect once the skaven gained access to Karak Angkul. It was up to him to keep that from happening.

Klarak passed through the great gallery overlooking the icy mountain stream that provided the dwarfhold with its water. The workshops and forges of Karak Angkul were arranged about the stream like the spokes of a wheel, a tiny culvert with a little dam providing each smith and armourer with the water he required. The sound of banging hammers filled the air; the flickering glow of forgefires crept out from every tunnel, painting the walls a smouldering crimson.

Klarak's own workshop was situated here, poised at the very edge of the stronghold. He smiled as he saw teams of lode ponies being lead away by muleskinners. Each team pulled an iron cart laden with beams of reddish-gold metal. As the muleskinners passed him, their eyes were filled with wonder and admiration. It was an expression of esteem the dwarfs were too cautious to give voice to. Here in the forgeworks of Karak Angkul, the ears of the Engineers' Guild were everywhere.

There was a reason for their admiration. Though concerned with ponies and their care, the muleskinners were still dwarfs and knew a thing or three about metal and its properties. The beams they carted away, destined for the lower deeps and the tunnels recently recovered from the skaven, were of a remarkable nature. They had a flexibility about them that was almost organic, yet a hardness and toughness that was the equal of adamant. Never had these dwarfs seen such an amazing metal.

Of course, there was no way they could have. Until a few months ago, such metal hadn't existed. It was a new alloy developed by Klarak Bronzehammer. It was stronger than anything short of gromril, yet with the give and flexibility of wood, he had named his metal barazhunk. There was need of his alloy now. The skaven had a villainous reputation for sabotaging the tunnels they abandoned, leaving behind sinister traps that would bury their pursuers. With barazhunk, the dwarfs would be able to quickly and safely shore up the passages as they went along, allowing a far speedier pursuit of their foes and preserving the many warriors who would otherwise fall victim to ratkin trickery.

Guildmaster Thori would, of course, pull his beard over such reckless innovation. The Engineer's Guild would have demanded years, even decades of testing barazhunk before condoning its use by the populace. And in the meantime, dwarfs would perish trying to fight their way through skaven traps using the old tactics their fathers and grandfathers had used against the ratkin and which their scheming enemies knew only too well.

Klarak shook his head. No, there was a time for caution, but there was also a time for boldness. Dwarfs like Thori, while well-meaning, were also restraining the potential of their people. The greater the risk, the greater the reward.

He sighed as he watched the ponies carting their cargo towards the ramp leading to the Fourth Deep. Barazhunk could save many lives by shoring up the mines, but Klarak saw an even more important contribution it could make, one that would depend on Kurgaz Bright-finger and his ability to recreate one of the secret Master Runes.

One that would depend on the loathsome ratkin and what they would do once Grey Seer Thanquol arrived in Karak Angkul.

CHAPTER VII

'IF I CATCH you sniffing around that tarp again, I'll have to bite off your nose.'

Thanquol leapt back immediately when he heard Ikit Claw's metallic growl. The source of the grey seer's interest was a sledge the Claw's slaves were dragging through the Underway. At first he had thought it simply contained ammunition or provisions, but the way the warlock-engineers hovered about it left him with serious doubts. The sledge was almost always escorted by a half-dozen skirmishers with another pair of jezzails perched atop the ratskin tarp in an attitude of paranoid vigilance. It didn't take an intellect of Thanquol's stature to realise that there was something important hidden away under there. If he could find out what it was, he had a feeling it would explain why the Chief Warlock of Clan Skryre was interested in the pathetic schemes of a two-flea moron like the late and certainly unlamented Kaskitt Steelgrin.

Wondering what Ikit Claw was hiding had plagued Thanquol ever since he'd been persuaded to join the reformed Clan Skryre expedition. He was mindful of the old wisdom that curiosity killed the rat, but it was like an itch he couldn't scratch, only growing worse the more he tried to ignore it.

Finally he had hit upon a clever scheme to draw attention away from the sledge. He ordered Boneripper to behave as though it were going berserk, being careful to stipulate that the rat-ogre wasn't to actually harm any of Ikit Claw's tinker-rats. It wasn't that he cared a pellet about the heretical Skryrelings, but he didn't want to run the risk of the monster's safety valve locking up and spoiling his plan.

There was one constant, dependable quality among the maddening array of crackpot machines Clan Skryre foisted upon the teeming masses of skavendom. That was their unpredictability. The ratmen might have installed a safety valve to keep Boneripper from turning on them, but Thanquol was certain they wouldn't be so smug as to think the device was fail-proof.

True enough, Boneripper's amok antics drew the guards away from Ikit's mysterious sledge, leaving Thanquol with a free paw to inspect the Claw's secret cargo.

Unfortunately, it seemed Ikit Claw had guessed the reason for the commotion.

Thanquol lowered his head submissively as he found the Chief Warlock glaring at him, a warplock pistol clenched in his paw. 'I was worry-feared that Boneripper might…'

'You told-say the machine-ogre to start trouble-fear so you could look-sniff,' Ikit Claw accused. He drew back the hammer of his pistol. 'Call back-off your bodyguard.'

'I'll see-smell what I can do-say,' Thanquol said, wearing his most innocent look. Ikit Claw lowered his pistol and snapped orders to his wayward guards, berating them for leaving their posts and threatening a particularly gory end should they ever do such a thing again.

Thanquol picked his way through the rubble Boneripper had torn from the stone walls and the litter of gear abandoned by the skaven the rat-ogre had seemingly threatened. 'Stop-stop!' he cried out to the hulking brute. The skeletal monster froze in mid-motion, a thousand-pound dwarf statue held above it. The grey seer could hear the machinery inside Boneripper whining and shuddering beneath the tremendous weight. The monster couldn't hold such a burden for long, yet it just mindlessly stood there, waiting for its next order. If not for that cursed fail-safe, the brute would have made the perfect bodyguard.

'Drop it!' Thanquol snapped irritably, then leapt out of the way of the statue as it came smashing down where he had been standing. Coughing on the cloud of stone dust that rose from the impact, Thanquol glared at his moronic protector. It was just like Clan Skryre not to include harming its master among the things that would lock-up Boneripper's safety valve!

The rat-ogre's skeletal head stared back at its master, oblivious to the destruction it had nearly wrought. The beady red eyes glowed evilly in the darkness, sending a tinge of fear crawling through Thanquol's glands. For a moment he wondered if there wasn't some glimmer of awareness back there in that ruined skull. Maybe Boneripper somehow remembered its previous life and meeting its violent end beneath the axe of the thrice-damned Gotrek Gurnisson. Maybe it resented obeying once more the master who had gotten it killed deep beneath the streets of Nuln.

Thanquol gnashed his fangs, dismissing the idiotic idea. 'Come along, fool-meat,' he growled, whacking Boneripper's side with his staff. There wasn't anything inside the rat-ogre's head but a bunch of cogs and gears. It didn't think anything except what it was told to think, and even then it had a hard time.

Plodding through the dark, Thanquol and Boneripper put some distance between themselves and Ikit Claw's sledge. It would be wise to keep clear of the Chief Warlock until his temper cooled a bit. Just now, he was exhibiting a good deal of utterly foundless suspicion regarding his stalwart companion and ally. Thanquol would wait until the Claw was a bit less emotional before making another try at seeing what the warlock-engineer was being so secretive about.

'Don't think-try that again.'

It was the second time Thanquol had received the same warning in the last few minutes. This time his accoster wasn't the fearsome Ikit but the pathetic, drug-wracked mess of fur and bones called Grey Seer Skraekual.

Thanquol's lips pulled back in a fang-ridden grin, his claws tightening about the haft of his staff. 'I'm in a bad mood, warp-wit,' he hissed. 'I'll be in a much better one if I have Boneripper twist that ugly-nasty head off your shoulders.'

The bleariness faded from Skraekual's eyes as he glanced in alarm at the looming rat-ogre. 'You brave-dare not-not kill-slay Skraekual,' he whined, cringing back against the cavern wall. A flash of anger suddenly flashed across the grey seer's rotten face as he remembered the magic ring he wore. The cringing posture was abandoned and he leered back at

Thanquol. 'Do what I say-tell!' he snapped, pointing the ring at his rival. 'Kritislik put me on top. You do what I say-tell.'

Thanquol glowered at the degenerate sorcerer-priest. How he would like to crush the maggot and leave his carcass for the beetles. But he'd seen old Master Sleekit's ring in action and wasn't of a mind to risk ending up a charred smear on the floor. Besides, he reflected, Skraekual would be a useful scapegoat should anything go wrong. Perhaps it would be wise to confer with his fellow grey seer and gain his collusion against Ikit Claw.

'That tinker-rat is hiding something,' Thanquol said, his voice a low and conspiratorial whisper.

'Not interested,' Skraekual said, his tone making it clear that he spoke for both of them.

Thanquol's fur bristled. The arrogant flea! Daring to talk down to the greatest mind in the Under-Empire! He'd pull out the rat's liver and feed it to him!

'It must be something powerful the way he guards it,' Thanquol explained in what he considered his most convincing tone.

Skraekual coughed, spitting a broken tooth against the wall. 'Tinker-rat heresy!' he growled. 'The only real-true power comes from the Horned One!'

'That's because you don't know how tinker-rat machines work,' Thanquol pressed.

'And you do?' Skraekual scoffed, directing a sly look at Boneripper.

Thanquol ground his fangs at the subtle reminder of his bodyguard's spectacular failure during Ikit's ambush. He forced himself to ignore the irritation of Skraekual's words. Now that he'd started to form his plan, he had decided Skraekual should be a part of it.

After all, if things went bad, Seerlord Kritislik did place him in charge.

'No, I don't,' Thanquol admitted. He tilted his head ever so slightly, twitching his whiskers at the distant figure of Ikit Claw. 'But he does. All we have to do is make the Claw work for us.'

Skraekual peered suspiciously at the Chief Warlock as he made his inspection of the sledge and whatever was hidden under the tarp. 'For the Horned One,' he hissed, correcting Thanquol's statement.

'Of course,' Thanquol agreed, a gleam in his eye. 'That is what I meant-said. We'll make him work for the Horned One.'

The skaven settlement of Bonestash opened directly upon the Ungdrin Ankor, connected to the ancient dwarf tunnels by a series of narrow passageways. All of the openings had been clawed from the earth by skaven labour, the walls still bearing the scars of their digging. A litter of bones and pellets made it obvious which of the tunnels were in use and which were nothing more than booby-trapped blinds to snare the unwary goblin and the odd subterranean predator.

Ikit Claw ordered his entourage towards the largest of the active tunnels, the only one broad enough to accommodate the sledge his slaves had been dragging. The tunnel was situated between the legs of an enormous statue, the decapitated figure of some ancient dwarf lord. The stone head glared fiercely from the floor, its nose broken and its teeth pitted by the marks of blades. As they approached within scenting distance, a pack of sentries scrambled down from the statue's head and scurried off into the tunnel. The sound of rattling chains and the groan of a heavy gate echoed down the passageway.

Jezzails and warpfire teams scuttled into positions facing towards the tunnel, arming their weapons on the run. Other skirmishers began struggling into cumbersome harnesses and covering their faces with garish masks. Thanquol felt his fur crawl when he saw these ratmen, recognising their gear as that of a globadier, wielders of the hideous Poison Wind, one of Clan Skryre's most fiendish inventions.

He did not, however, recognise some of the other strange devices Ikit Claw's minions were readying. One was a bulky mass of metal that looked as though a half-dozen muskets had been soldered together and then bound in copper wire. The brawny ratman who carried it was followed by a brown-furred helper who laboured beneath the weight of a portable furnace lashed to his back. A long hose of ratgut connected the mechanism of the strange gun to the side of the furnace. Thanquol could smell warpstone in the tiny puffs of steam venting from the furnace as it shuddered into life.

The second new weapon was even more bizarre and unsettling. Ikit Claw was renowned through the Under-Empire as inventor of the warp-lightning cannon, a mighty war machine capable of burning a hole through a mountain. Thanquol had seen that weapon displayed for the benefit of the Lords of Decay in Skavenblight, though his attention had been more focused on the huge chunk of raw warpstone the cannon derived its power from than the intricacies of the contraption itself.

What he gazed upon now seemed a smaller, more compact sort of warp-lightning cannon, carried upon the back of a single massive warrior. The skaven wore a weird sort of quilted armour over his black fur and his eyes were covered by a set of almost-black lenses. The gun itself was a long, slender tube of metal down the length of which a series of coloured lenses were fitted at intervals. The mechanism of the lightning-rifle was still a chunk of raw warpstone, much smaller than that employed on the cannon Thanquol had seen. It was housed in a mirrored box built into the back of the rifle, directly behind the end of the barrel and the focusing lenses.

While his attention was distracted by the preparations of Clan Skryre, Thanquol failed to notice that Ikit Claw had turned towards him. He cursed under his breath when he realised the Chief Warlock was staring straight at him. No doubt the vermin was expecting him to lead the attack while the brave Ikit kept himself well away from the fighting.

'Grey Seer!' the Claw's steel voice rasped.

Thanquol glanced about in a vain hope that perhaps he was addressing Skraekual, but the worthless warp-wit had scurried off to some hiding spot. Grinding his fangs in annoyance, he saw no choice but to answer Ikit and excuse himself from the dubious honour he was about to bestow upon him.

'I fear-think I cannot lead-guide the attack,' Thanquol said. 'I am only a poor priest who speaks-squeaks with the Horned Rat. I don't learn-know Clan Skryre's most magnificent weapons. I wouldn't know how-when to use them in the attack. So you see-scent that I'm the wrong-bad choice to lead-guide the attack.'

'I don't want you to lead my troops,' Ikit Claw told Thanquol. The grey seer blinked at him in momentary confusion. A scratchy chitter of laughter hissed up Ikit's ruined throat. 'I wouldn't trust-leave you with my troops.'

The Claw flexed his massive metal hand meaningfully, displaying the warpfire thrower built into its palm and the sword-like blades fitted to each steel finger.

'What-what do you want-need?' Thanquol asked, not bothering to hide the fear in his posture. The warlock-engineers were an impious, secular breed and Ikit Claw was the worst of the litter. He'd think no more of killing a grey seer than he would popping a tick.

'Clan Mors was expecting Kaskitt,' the Claw explained, gesturing towards the dwarf head so recently vacated by the sentries. 'Rikkit Snapfang may not receive us as warmly as he would my unfortunate clan-flesh.' The burned skin pulled back from Ikit's lip, exposing his scarred teeth. 'Your job is to go in there and let him know the deal has changed.'

Thanquol felt his glands clench. Going alone into a dark tunnel that was probably crawling with hostile warriors from the fiercest clan in all skavendom was hardly his idea of the duties of a grey seer. Then again, getting incinerated by a crazed tinker-rat wasn't much of an alternative.

'What should I squeak-speak?' Thanquol asked.

Ikit Claw's ghastly laughter sounded once more. 'Tell-say that Ikit Claw, Chief Warlock of Clan Skryre, Master of the Warpstorm, Flayer of Forgemaster Gharhakk Bloodtongue, Butcher of Chicomecoatl, Gutter of Jarl Alfhild Daemonkin, Burner of Magister Klaus von Doenhoff, Razer of Helwigstadt...'

The warlock-engineer was still giving himself titles when Thanquol started his reluctant dash into the black mouth of the tunnel.

THE TUNNEL WAS as black as the inside of a snake – not the most pleasant of images for the grey seer to think of, but appropriate. If there had been any torches or warp-lamps in the tunnel, the sentries had doused them. Thanquol found himself hugging the right-paw wall, keeping his whiskers in constant contact with the reassuring presence of earth and rock.

Darkness alone didn't overly bother a skaven. Indeed, they usually found it comforting. If they couldn't see, then at least they couldn't be seen either. No, what had Thanquol's glands clenching was the smell. A skaven was more disturbed by an inability to smell than an inability to see, and some twisted sadist had decided to eliminate that key sense for any ratmen entering the tunnel.

When he entered the tunnel, at first there had been the expected smells of fur and dung and musk... and a tantalising hint of warpstone. The sorts of smells anyone would expect to find in a skaven warren. But only a few yards into the passageway, all of these smells had been blotted out by the overwhelming stink of ratbane, a noxious weed that dulled the usually keen senses of a skaven to a point where he could barely function. Some craven fiend was burning a bushel of the filth somewhere down the tunnel and fanning it directly towards Thanquol.

The grey seer couldn't help pawing at his nose, the horrible smell seeming to clog his nasal passages. Only a few steps of such vexing treatment was all he was going to put up with. Extracting his rat-skull snuff-box, he took a pinch of Lynsh's weed to clear the reek from his nose.

Immediately, the stench vanished as the fiery blast of warpsnuff sizzled through his body. Thanquol shook in the grip of the intoxicating rush, forcing him to stumble back and lean on Boneripper's skeletal frame for support. Little pixie-lights twinkled across his vision, flittering about in the gloom. Irritably, Thanquol swatted his paw through the air, trying to disperse the annoying phantoms.

He felt himself propelled forwards by the lumbering Boneripper. The brute would keep going until doomsday unless it was given the order to stop. Such brainless obedience was admirable – up to a point. Thanquol had no great desire to be trampled by his own bodyguard.

Truthfully, he couldn't remember just now why he needed a bodyguard anyway. He was, after all, Grey Seer Thanquol, the most feared sorcerer in skavendom. No – the world! What did he need some hulking idiot about for? It was insulting actually. The very suggestion that a mage of his powers should need protection! He should blast Boneripper into bits for having the impertinence of thinking he needed it to guard him!

Thanquol shook his head. That was the warpsnuff talking. He wasn't going to blast anything. Not without being able to see what he was blasting. It wouldn't do to hit a support beam and bring the whole mountain falling on top of him. Even his magic powers would be incommoded by such a happenstance.

Muttering a quick spell, Thanquol lifted his staff. The metal head blazed with luminance, as though a piece of the sun had been dragged down into the tunnel. The grey seer shut his eyes at the blinding brilliance, finding it quite a bit more than he had been planning on. A bit more restraint, perhaps, was in order.

Pained squeals sounded from further down the tunnel. Sneaks lying in wait, their scent obscured by the ratbane!

Thanquol didn't wait for his vision to clear. Stretching

C. L. Werner

forth his paw, he unleashed a stream of warp-lightning
in the direction of the cries. He could hear earth sizzle as
the magical force slammed against the wall. Rocks burst
like boiled ticks as he continued to play the lightning
about in a wild arc. His vicious assault was rewarded
with an anguished howl and the scent of smouldering
fur and scorched flesh.

Baring his fangs, Thanquol drew more power into
his spell, feeling the aethyric energies blazing across
his mind. He could see now, could see the slinking
black-furred ratmen who had thought they could
ambush him. Each of them carried a crooked sword
and their noses were damp with some sort of salve – a
provision against the ratbane, undoubtedly. Well, the
vermin would have worse things to worry about than
ratbane!

The warp-lightning crackled into another of the
skaven, scorching him into a charred huddle of burnt
fur and shrivelled flesh. Several of the ratmen tried to
flee, drawing Thanquol's ire. Redirecting his energies,
he blasted a hole through the spine of the foremost of
the runners, splitting him nearly in two. The lashing
energy continued on, ripping across the stone lintel
that braced the roof of the passage. A deep groove was
gouged into the lintel and the earth overhead groaned
angrily.

Let the mountain try to kill him! He was Thanquol
the Mighty! He would show it the folly of daring to
trifle with him! When he was through with it, there'd
be nothing but pebbles left!

Thanquol dropped his staff and clapped a paw to
his horned head. A thrill of terror coursed through
him, beating down the crazed fury of the warpsnuff.
The stream of warp-lightning faded as he willed the

surge of magical energies coursing into his body to abate. The madness past, he wilted to the floor, gasping for breath. Every bone in his body felt as though it had been gnawed on by ratlings and then used to swat mosquitoes. Exhausted, he couldn't even maintain the light that still glowed upon the end of his staff.

A new fear filled Thanquol's heart. Not the fear of his rampant and crazed display of magic. That was over and done and he would recover from that. No, it was the realisation that he was once again blind and stifled by the ratbane. And there were still several angry skaven scattered about the tunnel.

His enemies would be blind and unable to use their noses, but the vermin still had their ears to work with! Exhausted, his body taxed to the limit by his sorcery, Thanquol could not keep from gasping at the air, could not stifle the frantic pounding of his heart. No, the cowardly mouse-lickers wouldn't need to see or smell him to find him and take advantage of his helplessness!

A flash of cruel inspiration came to Thanquol. Between gasps, he snarled words to Boneripper. 'Tear-crush all rat-flesh comes near-close!' he growled, ensuring his voice was loud enough for the other skaven to hear... and appreciate.

A few moments later, there was a flurry of activity in the dark. Thanquol heard the pathetic mewing of a rat-man an instant before the dull crack of a spine being snapped in two echoed through the tunnel. The smell of blood and fear-musk accompanied the crash of the body against the floor. After that, the other skaven kept their distance.

Fool-meat! Did they think Thanquol did not have

contingencies to deal with their petty scheming? He would never have stepped so brazenly into their trap without taking the proper precautions. Let them try to blind him and stuff his nose with ratbane! He had the colossal Boneripper to protect him! A rat-ogre rebuilt by Clan Skryre's remarkable techno-sorcery! An unliving juggernaut who could see in absolute blackness and who had no nose to be smothered by ratbane fumes!

'I tell-say for Boneripper to kill-slay all-all!' Thanquol threatened, then hastily called out to his bodyguard to stop when he heard the automaton lurching into motion. Unthinking obedience was becoming a bit of a nuisance.

'Bring-fetch Rikkit Snapfang!' the grey seer commanded. 'Tell him that Grey Seer Thanquol will take-have words with him!'

There was a satisfying rush of feet when Thanquol made his demands as the lurking warriors fled up the tunnel to carry his words to their warlord. The effect of hearing who they had so stupidly thought to ambush had filled their black hearts with fear. No ratman would dare defy the will of Grey Seer Thanquol!

'Boneripper! Stop-stand! No more kill-slay!' the grey seer grumbled as he heard the rat-ogre lumbering after the retreating skaven.

THE WORKSHOP OF Klarak Bronzehammer was a flurry of activity. Every smelter and kiln was glowing with heat, pushed almost beyond endurance by the production demands he had placed upon them. His aides raced about the workshop like frightened grobi, rushing from smelter to anvil and from anvil to slack tub.

Klarak paused on the threshold, letting himself

adjust to the sweltering heat. He watched with admiration as his aides hurried about their labours. No need to impress upon them the urgency of the task he had set for them. They knew that Klarak never asked anything of them without good reason.

Horgar Horgarsson was working the bellows of one of the forges, keeping it at the white-hot glow that was necessary for the smelting of barazhunk, his steamwork frame lending him the strength to maintain the fires. Thorlek had shed his customary furs and pelts, standing bare-chested and covered in sweat as he pounded away at one of the anvils, folding and refolding the near-molten alloy until it achieved the tenacity Klarak required.

Two other dwarfs laboured in Klarak's workshop. One was a wizened old longbeard, his floor-length grey beard plaited into three tails and stuffed into the broad belt he wore. Azram Steelfoot was among the most venerable dwarfs in Karak Angkul, older even than Runelord Morag. One of the hold's lorekeepers, the historian had benefited from the innovative engineering of Klarak Bronzehammer when one of his eyes had started to fail him. The left side of Azram's face now bore the fruit of Klarak's invention, an augmetic device of multi-faceted lenses and clockwork gears that now served the dwarf in place of his wasted eye. The lorekeeper's gratitude had been boundless and firmly indebted Azram to his benefactor. Hence the old historian was here, inspecting each beam of barazhunk for imperfections before allowing it to be placed on the pile awaiting transport into the lower deeps.

The last of Klarak's company was a short-bearded, dark-haired dwarf busying himself with feeding coke into the forge Horgar was using. Despite the length of his beard, however, Kimril was no beardling, having almost two centuries under his belt. He'd shorn his beard long ago as a token of respect and fealty to the father of his wife, Thane Borin of the Nogardsson clan. In those days, Kimril had been a tradesman, making his living transporting cargo to and from Karak Angkul. Then, while he was away on one of his trips, his wife took ill. She never recovered from her lingering sickness, though Kimril had spent every coin and favour owed to him on physicians and healers. After her death, he had taken up the physician's staff, becoming the most accomplished doctor in the dwarfhold.

Still, the tragedy of his wife's death hung heavy on Kimril's heart. He blamed the conservatism of dwarf medicine for her slow decline and had devoted himself to finding new cures, however untraditional they might be. The physician's mindset had made him something of a pariah in the hold and a natural dwarf to accumulate the friendship of Klarak Bronzehammer.

Together with Kurgaz Brightfinger, these four dwarfs made up Klarak's Iron Throng. They had adventured far and wide with their master, but always the road led them back to Karak Angkul.

Thorlek was the first to notice Klarak's return. The ranger set down his hammer, a wide smile splitting his face. 'I was beginning to think you were leaving all the fun to us.'

The other dwarfs paused in their work to greet the gold-bearded engineer. 'I had the idea that perhaps Guildmaster Thori had finally managed to give him the cogging he's been asking for all these years,' quipped Kimril, wiping his hands on his soot-stained apron.

'That old grobi-fondler doesn't have the beard to even try,' Horgar said. He closed his armoured hand into a menacing fist. 'And if he did, he'd trip and fall all the way down to the Sixth Deep.'

'That would be something to see,' Azram said, adjusting the lenses on his iron eye so he could focus on the figure of the engineer as he entered the workshop.

'Guildmaster Thori means well,' Klarak reprimanded his aides. While he applauded their enthusiasm and loyalty, sometimes he worried that they forgot to show the proper respect to their elders and superiors. 'He is right to be cautious about moving forwards too fast and too recklessly. Remember the horrible abuses the dawizharr have put their technology to.'

Mention of the abhorred Tainted cast a pall upon Klarak's aides. Each of them remembered the corrupt dwarfs of the Dark Lands and the monstrous things crafted by their abominable daemonsmiths. It was an image no dwarf could forget and which no dwarf could consider without a twinge of guilt and a flash of hate.

'The beams are almost done,' Kimril said, breaking the tension. 'Do you think King Logan will let them be used?'

'More to the point, will Minewarden Grundin?' Thorlek observed.

'King Logan has already agreed,' Klarak stated. 'Minewarden Grundin is under a grudge for being improperly prepared to repulse the ratkin from the lower deeps. He won't make any obstruction to our plans.'

Horgar clapped his metal-sheathed hands together. 'Then barazhunk is going into the mines. The filthy thaggoraki will break a few teeth trying to chew through this!'

Klarak's expression was dour. He was thinking of all that could still go wrong with his plan and the dreadful warning he had received from Altdorf.

'We'll get barazhunk into the mines,' he said, 'but we don't want it to stay there.' His friends stared at him, each wearing a look of confusion. 'Things have changed,' Klarak told them. 'The ratkin menace is greater than any of us thought it could be. We need a trap to catch the rats leading these vermin.

'And barazhunk is going to be our cheese.'

BONESTASH WAS A sprawling warren consisting of hundreds of miles of winding tunnels, chambers and burrows. There was no rhyme or reason to the layout of the settlement, it had expanded as need had dictated, chasing deposits of warpstone, water sources and food supplies. The staple diet for the warren was largely based upon the cave squigs and giant beetles cultivated by the large numbers of goblin slaves they kept, but the skaven weren't above adding the occasional dwarf and the frequent goblin to their meals. The only crop they used as a supplement was a sort of bread-like fungus that seemed quite partial to skaven pellets as fertiliser.

The warren was thriving, if not exactly prospering. No less than thirty brood-mothers were actively producing litters five times a year, a statistic Rikkit seemed especially proud of. Thanquol could guess the reason. The slithery little villain was expanding the treasury of his warren by selling some of his extra population on the side. Most likely Clan Skaul, Thanquol decided. The drug-peddlers were always looking for ways to expand their numbers and they'd certainly be interested in pups sired by strong Clan Mors warriors. Moreover,

Skaul had certain opiates that would increase the fertility of female skaven. Seerlord Kritislik had patronised them quite heavily in his efforts to develop a strain of brood-mother that would only birth horned pups.

Thanquol was beginning to appreciate the idea of looting Rikkit's treasury. There was every reason to suspect the blood-brained war-rat had skimmed quite a bit for his own purposes before sending along his duty to Clan Mors. The best part was, if he wasn't supposed to have it to begin with, then he couldn't squeak about it when it was taken from him.

Still, there was the problem of Ikit Claw to worry about. The Chief Warlock was up to something and, against all reason, Thanquol didn't think it had anything to do with stealing Rikkit's warp-tokens. It also made Thanquol wonder if there might not be more advantage to be gained trying to ferret out exactly what the Claw was up to.

Unfortunately, Thanquol knew it would be an up-burrow battle to get Rikkit or any of his clawleaders involved in any plot against Ikit. They already thought the grey seer had been bought and paid for. From the first moment Rikkit had gotten a sniff of Thanquol's scent, he'd considered him nothing but a lackey of the Chief Warlock.

It was all the moronic automaton's fault! A big hulking abomination that shouted 'gift from Clan Skryre' with every gear and gizmo bolted to its ugly bones! Thanquol had been right to be suspicious when Ikit had so graciously allowed him to take Boneripper with him on his way to treat with Clan Mors. One sniff of that mechanical brute and every skaven in Bonestash thought Thanquol was up to his neck in Clan Skryre bribes!

If it had been true, Thanquol might have been more at ease, but he was barely tolerated by the tinker-rats and Ikit Claw wasn't inclined to lift a whisker to help the grey seer. Worse, the Chief Warlock kept making extravagant demands on their hosts. He'd appropriated one of the largest chambers in the warren for his own uses, necessitating the relocation of a dozen brood-mothers and their pups. Then he'd started plundering the stores of timber and material Rikkit had squirrelled away, taking everything into his new lair. Finally, there had been calls for hundreds of slaves to be handed over to the Clan Skryre expedition. Instead of acting like the mercenary hirelings Rikkit had been expecting, Ikit Claw was conducting himself like a conquering warchief!

With Clan Skryre keeping almost entirely to the chamber Ikit Claw had appropriated, Thanquol and Skraekual were left to fend for themselves among an increasingly hostile population. Or at least Thanquol was. Skraekual appeared to have smoothed over a good deal of the resentment directed at him, no doubt by spinning elaborate lies about his fellow grey seer's association with the Claw and intentions to spy on Clan Mors.

Thanquol was no stranger to being in the unenviable position of being caught between two hostile factions. However, this was the first time he couldn't see a way of playing the one against the other and gaining some benefit from the infighting. The presence of Skraekual only made it that much worse. The scurvy flea-monger always seemed one jump ahead of him, poisoning the water before he could reach the stream.

'Horned Rat guard-keep me from the intrigues of fool-flesh!' Thanquol grumbled. The scheming maggots were so involved in their own plots that they had completely forgotten the real enemy. They had all come here to drive the dwarf-things out of the halls above Bonestash. Why couldn't any of these idiots remember that? And why couldn't they do it soon so they'd have something beside Grey Seer Thanquol to be plotting against?

Thanquol stared out across the pack of clanrats marching through the main run of Bonestash. The cave he had appropriated for his own use was ideally located to keep a careful watch on the activity of the warren, situated above a pit that opened into the very heart of the settlement. There had been a bit of disagreement with the previous owner, a decidedly impious belly-sniffer who didn't seem to appreciate that it was his sacred duty to defer to the will of a grey seer. Boneripper had sorted him out though, which was what the trash-sifters would be doing next time they came around to scavenge through the tunnels.

The warriors of Bonestash were a fine breed. Many burly black-furred stormvermin among their numbers, which was always a promising sign. The dwarfs of Karak Angkul must be unusually tough or Rikkit Snapfang unusually stupid for them to be having such trouble taking the stronghold. Thanquol was willing to bet on either.

Boneripper suddenly rose from where it was crouched at the entrance of Thanquol's cave. The grey seer turned around with irritation. There were two ways into the cave, one being the pit, the other being a hole that connected to one of the warren's tunnels. Since taking up residence he'd positioned Boneripper to watch the main hole, the logical route for any intruder to come. However, the rat-ogre was again showing that annoying trait of interpreting its orders a bit too broadly. There was a pile of thirty rat carcasses lying in the corner, and a fair number that were too squished to dig out of the doorway. Thanquol wondered how much it would cost him to have Clan Skryre upgrade whatever it was rattling about inside Boneripper's skull.

This time, however, the intruder was a bigger kind of rat than the common vermin Boneripper had been dispatching. Displaying a tattered cloth bearing the symbol of the Horned One upon it, a lone skaven poked his nose inside the cave.

'Stop-stand,' Thanquol ordered Boneripper. The hulking brute subsided, sinking back to its crouching position with a hiss of steam and a groan of gears.

'Grey Seer Thanquol,' the suitably intimidated ratman spoke. 'I have been sent-ordered to bring-lead you to meeting-talk.'

Thanquol's fur bristled at the words. He was no slithery lackey to be taking orders! If someone wanted to seek his counsel, then they could damn well come to him! He wasn't about to go scampering off to see them. It was beneath his dignity.

'Who sent you?' Thanquol demanded, displaying his fangs.

The messenger spurted the musk of fear. 'Warlord Rikkit Snapfang and Chief Warlock Ikit Claw,' he said. 'They both seek-want your advice-wisdom for attack-battle.'

Thanquol smoothed his whiskers with his paw, lashing his tail in amusement. So the two flea-scratchers had finally come around, had they? They had come to realise the limits of their intelligence and wanted the mighty Grey Seer Thanquol to bail them out of their troubles. Well, he might consider it if they made their appeal with due humility and deference to his rank. And, of course they'd have to placate him for the indignities they had subjected him to. That shouldn't take more than Boneripper's weight in warpstone though.

Thanquol glared at the messenger. 'What are you gawping at, filth-fur!' He gathered up his staff and sword from beside his nest and motioned for Boneripper to get up. The grey seer strode towards the shivering messenger. 'Hurry-scurry, dung-breath! Take-lead me to this meeting!'

CHAPTER VIII

GREY SEER THANQUOL bruxed his fangs and glowered menacingly at the skaven he had been coerced into following into the dwarf mines. Scabby, flea-bitten clanrats bearing splintered spears and rusty goblin swords. They were the mangiest pack of mouse-chewing rejects he'd ever had the misfortune of commanding, and he included the time Seerlord Kritislik had put him in charge of a litter of horned ratling pups! These sorry specimens of malnutrition and inbreeding wouldn't last five seconds against the dwarf-things!

Of course, that was the point. It was all a conspiracy to get rid of him! Ikit Claw and that conniving little tick Rikkit Snapfang were jealous and afraid of Thanquol's vast intellect and natural leadership. They didn't care a pellet about taking the dwarfhold, they just wanted to get him out of the way! It was selfish traitors like them who had prevented the skaven from conquering their enemies and overwhelming the surface world! If just a few of the leaders of skavendom would set aside their personal ambitions and work towards the betterment of the Under-Empire, nothing could stand in their way!

But, then, few skaven had the brains to learn from Thanquol's own selfless example. The trouble now was to figure out a way to extricate himself from this predicament. Preferably before they walked into dwarf axes or the ghastly shooting machines Rikkit had described so monstrously during the war council. There probably weren't enough clanrats to hide behind if Thanquol stumbled into that kind of firepower.

The war council! Bah! More like the 'let's have Grey Seer Thanquol take care of all the dirty work we're too mouse-spleened to do ourselves' roundtable! He had never met a more conniving, cowardly bunch of maggots! And these vermin called themselves warriors!

Rikkit Snapfang was still out of sorts because he had petitioned Clan Skryre for a few warlock-engineers to help him clear away these shooting machines that were causing him such trouble. The Chief Warlock himself was a bit more Clan Skryre than he had bargained for and he was openly afraid of Ikit Claw's presence in his warren. The sub-chiefs and clawleaders under Rikkit were no better, alternately fawning over and cowering before the fearsome Claw.

Ikit Claw, of course, conducted himself with the iron tyranny of a petty despot, pillaging Bonestash of its resources. Not for the coming battle with the dwarfs, though. Oh no, the Claw needed everything for whatever experiment he was conducting in the old brood-chamber. So much for the bravery of Clan Skryre!

That left Thanquol to pursue the campaign against the dwarfs. At the meeting, it was decided that the grey seer would lead a scouting party into the mines and investigate the new defences the dwarfs had been constructing over the past weeks. Rikkit pledged a few hundred of his 'best warriors' for Thanquol to lead, while the Claw had given him a dozen of his 'finest sharpshooters'.

The Claw's sharpshooters had deserted as soon as they were out of smell of Bonestash, slipping into the dark with the skill of an Eshin deathmaster. Rikkit's 'best warriors' were too pathetic and dull-witted to manage even that much cunning. Thanquol wondered who those armoured stormvermin belonged to if this rabble was Rikkit's 'best warriors'. No doubt, the black-furred brutes were just fungus-farmers in disguise!

Lashing his tail in annoyance, Thanquol cursed once more the names of his duplicitous allies. One of them should be leading this suicide run, not him! They were just petty warlords and tinker-rats, but he was a grey seer and above such grubby dealings. He should be back in the warren helping plot the next phase in the campaign. And he would be too if that warp-wit Skraekual hadn't been so debilitated by an excess of warp-weed that he couldn't even twitch a whisker much less stand on his feet. It had taken a supreme effort of will (and sight of that cursed black ring) to keep from bashing in the wretch's head then and there.

The scent of skaven musk gradually lessened, replaced by the smell of dwarfs and metal. Thanquol could tell from the way the passageway was sloping upwards that they would soon be quit of the ratruns dug by Clan Mors and must then enter the mines of the dwarfs. If he was going to escape this fool's exercise, then he would have to do it soon.

Thanquol looked back over his shoulder at the skeletal bulk of Boneripper. With the desertion of the skirmishers, every skaven in the scouting party was from Clan Mors. He could tell the rat-ogre to turn on them, roast them alive with its warpfire projector. Afterwards he could claim the brute had malfunctioned, or better yet try to insinuate that Boneripper had somehow been acting upon some treacherous instruction from Ikit Claw. Would he be able to make Rikkit buy that? More importantly, could he be sure there wouldn't be any survivors to tell the warlord otherwise?

Tugging at his whiskers, the grey seer made the depressing conclusion that he'd need to wait until the clanrats were actually locked in battle to be sure his plan would work. Caught between the dwarfs and Boneripper, there'd be only the smallest chance anybody would get back alive. Except himself, of course, but that would clearly be a sign of the esteem in which the Horned Rat held him.

A sound from one of the side passages connecting onto the main shaft brought Thanquol up short. He gnashed his fangs in outrage as the clanrats scattered, leaving their horned commander dangerously exposed to whatever was sneaking about in the gloom. The grey seer quickly spun around, putting the solid mass of Boneripper's leg between himself and whatever was creeping towards his patrol.

'Boneripper!' Thanquol hissed. 'Burn-slay! Burn-slay!' Kill first and find out what it was later had been a good rule of claw as far as the grey seer was concerned.

With a whir of gears and a rumble of pistons, Boneripper raised its warpfire projector, directing the nozzle at the connecting passage. Then the automaton froze, becoming as still as a statue.

'Burn-slay!' Thanquol shouted, smacking his staff against the rat-ogre's ribcage, wincing as the unyielding metal and bone sent a shudder through his arm. He knew it! Safety valve indeed! The damnable abomination didn't work! It was all a trick to get him killed depending on a faulty rat-ogre!

An instant later, the grey seer smelled the distinct scent of Clan Skryre ratmen. He glared through narrowed eyes as a pair of cloaked skaven emerged from the shadows. If their clan-scent hadn't betrayed them, the crazed array of pneumatic arms fastened to the harnesses they wore would have. The visage of each ratman was hidden behind a weird metal helmet, pipes and hoses running from the iron masks into a series of cylinders fastened to the harnesses they wore. Warlock-engineers! Thanquol was really coming to despise that cursed safety valve!

'Stop-safe,' Thanquol growled, calling off his body-guard before Boneripper could overheat or blow up or whatever it was the lummox would do unless he told it to back down.

The warlock-engineers looked about, inspecting the cluster of trembling clanrats. Thanquol could hear the breath of the tinker-rats gurgling through their respirators.

'Where-where are shooters?' one of the warlock-engineers demanded.

'Gone,' Thanquol hissed. 'Scurried off at the first sniff of dwarf-smell!'

The answer obviously didn't please the warlock-engineers. Whatever they were up to, they looked of a mind to forget it and head back to Bonestash. They might have, too, had it not been for the ratman who had come with them, carefully hiding behind the Clan Skryre tinker-rats until Boneripper had been called off.

'Ikit Claw will be displeased with them,' the third

skaven said. Thanquol ground his fangs as he recognised the voice. Grey Seer Skraekual loped out from the
gloom, bowing his horned head in sneering deference
to Thanquol.

'We felt-thought you could use some help,' Skraekual
explained. There was no hint of debility about the other
grey seer now. Indeed, Thanquol hadn't even recognised
Skraekual's scent, lacking the usual stink of warp-weed
and brain-dust.

A horrible thought came creeping into Thanquol's
mind as he stared at Skraekual. He was standing so
straight and tall, without a sniff of addiction and weakness about him that if Thanquol didn't know better
he'd swear Skraekual was one of those zealots who
never touched anything stronger than mole-milk for
fear of tainting their connection to the Horned One.

It was impossible that he could have been deceived
by the scurvy warp-wit! Nobody could fool a skaven of
his perception and guile! Besides, if it had been a trick,
why had Skraekual chosen this moment to scurry out
from behind his mask?

'I have all the help I need-want,' Thanquol said. He
gestured with his staff at the motley pack of clanrats.
'These are best-fiercest fighters in Bonestash,' he said.
'Worth-equal twenty dwarf-things!' The clanrats seemed
to take the compliment with a mix of stupid pride and
craven anxiety – no doubt wondering if Thanquol really
expected them to take on twenty dwarfs.

Skraekual grinned at the obvious lie, displaying his
rotten teeth. 'Then we should be safe accompanying
you,' the grey seer said. 'Surely nothing to worry-fear
with great Grey Seer Thanquol and his brave-strong
war-rats to protect us!'

It wasn't so much the fact that Skraekual and the

warlock-engineers started laughing that got under Thanquol's fur, it was the way the ungracious vermin did it.

Angrily, Thanquol turned to his clanrats. 'Onward!' he snarled. 'Hurry-scurry! I'll feed the slowest fool-meat to my rat-ogre!'

The clanrats set off at an admirably frantic pace, not hesitating to wonder why a warp-powered skeleton would want to eat them. Thanquol preened his whiskers as he watched them race off down the tunnel. If he couldn't demand the respect of his peers, at least he could still command the fear of his subordinates.

THE SCOUTING PARTY was soon deep within the no-rat's-land between the mines Rikkit's warriors had been able to secure and the upper deeps still held by the dwarfs. The stink of fear rising from Thanquol's warriors was obscene. It took a fresh tirade of curses and threats to get them moving again every dozen yards. The clanrats just about jumped out of their fur every time they heard a beam creak or a common rat kick up some dust. It vexed the grey seer to think these maggot-munchers thought they had something more terrible than his own anger to worry about. He was sorely tempted to wither a few of them with a violent display of magic just to get the point across.

Instead, Thanquol just grabbed the handiest of the skaven by his throat.

'What-why are you coward-flesh afraid?' Thanquol growled, making a full display of his fangs. 'I am here. The might of my magic is great-better than any dwarf-thing!'

The frightened ratman went limp in Thanquol's grip. 'Mercy-pity, Horrific One!' he whined. 'We survive-escape first attack-raid on dwarf-things! Seen-saw nasty-mean gun-things! Many skaven die-die from shooty-kill!'

Thanquol felt a little tingle of fear run through him as he heard the description of what might be waiting for him just around the next bend. He quickly got control of himself, angered that this craven little parasite was trying to infect him with his cowardice. 'The Horned One will protect-guard you!' he snarled angrily. 'No-none dwarf-thing can-will match the magic of Grey Seer Thanquol! You will be safe-safe with my power watching over you!'

Well, at least maybe the other skaven would be safe. In his fury Thanquol had put a bit too much pressure on the clanrat's neck and strangled the wretch. He dropped the body to the ground and prodded it against the wall with his staff, trying to make its presence as inconspicuous as possible. Raising his head, he glared at the other skaven, daring any of them to comment.

'Fast-quick,' he growled at the clanrats. 'I want to get this over-done quick-quick!' Thanquol slammed the butt of his staff against the floor, causing the many talismans tied to it to rattle and jangle. The clanrats didn't need any further display of his impatience. With indecent haste, they began scrambling through the mine shaft. Thanquol lashed his tail in amusement. Who would have thought strangling one of the fleas would be as effective as immolating them with a spell?

'Thanquol,' Skraekual hissed. The other grey seer was developing an annoying habit of getting around behind him. It made Thanquol's fur crawl to know the conniving Skraekual could exploit even the most momentary distraction to put himself into such position.

'What do you want?' Thanquol growled, in no mood for the warp-wit's pompous demands. Ever since joining the scouting party, the tick-tongued pizzle-drinker had been trying to assume command. He kept referring to some mangy old ratskin map and giving Thanquol directions. It was a situation Thanquol was getting very tired of.

'At the next gallery we need turn-go left,' Skraekual directed after inspecting his map. Thanquol tried to sneak a look at whatever was written on the old ratskin, but as soon as he did, Skraekual pressed it close against his chest and bared his fangs.

'Not another step until you say-squeak what this is about,' Thanquol growled.

Skraekual gestured with one of his paws, displaying the black ring circling one of his fingers. 'Think-think,' the grey seer snarled. 'I am leader-chief, not you. Seerlord Kritislik chose-charge me with...' Skraekual scratched at his rotted nose and lashed his tail, irritated that he'd almost told Thanquol what he wanted to know despite himself. 'Just do what I say-tell!'

Glaring at the ring, Thanquol backed down. Sometime the treacherous toad-spittle would make a wrong move and then it would just be too bad for Kritislik's little toe-licker! Looking past Skraekual, Thanquol found another source of annoyance. The warlock-engineers were dawdling far behind the rest of the scouts... again! He bruxed his fangs angrily. If it came to a fight, those two tinker-rats would bolt without lifting a paw to oppose the enemy!

'You two!' Thanquol yelled. 'Keep-stay with the rest!'

He almost expected the two tinker-rats to yell back at him. Instead they jumped in surprise, then came scurrying up the shaft, the contraptions fitted to their harnesses rattling and clanking as they ran. Thanquol thought he detected something sneaky and furtive about the way they avoided looking at him as they passed. As if he'd caught them doing something he shouldn't have seen. It seemed even tinker-rats didn't like to have others spot their cowardly streak.

'Next left,' Skraekual hissed in Thanquol's ear.

Thanquol gritted his teeth. 'Next left,' he agreed, forcing the words through his fangs.

THE ROAR OF guns boomed through the stone-walled gallery, making it seem as if a thunderstorm had been unleashed within the mine. Unlike the raw earth of the narrow shafts, the gallery was a broad chamber with thick stone walls and a high ceiling. Pulleys hung from archways high overhead, connecting to platforms which in turn connected to other mine shafts. Across the floor ran a rail-system, upon which several abandoned mine carts still stood. Piles of raw ore were scattered about the ground, the odd pick and hammer attesting to how quickly the dwarfs had fled this gallery during the initial skaven assault.

They had come back, however, recovering their dead and leaving something behind that would ensure the destruction of any second attack.

'Stop dying!' Thanquol bellowed from behind the corner of the mine shaft. It was just like the worthless stew-meat Rikkit had foisted upon him to ignore his order. While he watched, two more of the useless maggots were cut to shreds by the unrelenting fire.

It made the grey seer's fur crawl to look at their attacker. It was no living thing, but rather a boxy contraption of pipes and belts and gears and pistons. From its front projected an array of gun barrels, each belching forth a thunderous burst of flame and smoke. The huge bullets the guns sent flying across the gallery might not be made of warpstone, but they struck the clanrats like the fist of a giant, splitting their bodies in a gory holocaust. Ten skaven were already strewn about the floor, the rest had either fallen back into the tunnel with Thanquol or were scurrying madly about the gallery trying to find cover.

While he watched, the sentry gun swivelled on some pivot and sent another volley of lead chasing Thanquol's terrified warriors. It made for an eerie sight, these mindless machines following his troops with such uncanny precision.

'If you don't take a paw, we'll never get through,' Skraekual whined.

Thanquol studied the hellish gun array. He could see no sign of an operator. That was how the damnable thing had taken them by such surprise. There had been no dwarf scent. The thrice-damned dwarfs had made certain to cover the tell-tale stink of their hands and gunpowder when they'd set the diabolic thing up.

Given the way the sentry gun was ripping up his clanrats, Thanquol didn't think he wanted to try his hand at knocking it out, magic or no.

'We'll find-take another way,' the grey seer decided. The surviving clanrats chittered their eager agreement to this idea.

Skraekual stared at the ratskin map, then bared his fangs. 'Seerlord Kritislik won't like-like if we go around.'

Thanquol ground his fangs together. Of all the impertinence! 'You're a grey seer!' he snapped. 'You take a paw and get us through!'

The other grey seer pointed his claw at Thanquol, the black ring gleaming evilly in the light of the dwarf glowstones set into the walls of the gallery. 'I will if you can't,' Skraekual threatened.

Glaring at the other grey seer, Thanquol wondered if he'd be able to get behind Boneripper before Skraekual could unleash the magic of the ring. A quick glance at the bony rat-ogre made him question the efficacy it would make as a shelter from enchanted dragon-fire.

Thanquol smoothed his whiskers as a similar thought came to him. He risked a quick glance at the gallery where the sentry gun was picking off the last clanrats scampering about among the mine carts. He watched the bullets pinging off the sides of the steel carts. A cunning gleam crept into the grey seer's eyes as he looked at his bodyguard once more, taking especial notice of the reinforced ribcage.

A plan was forming in the horned sorcerer's mind. It wasn't the sort of plan he would normally think he should play any part in beside that of spectator, but Skraekual had made it a bit necessary. Damn the thieving flea's spleen anyway!

Snapping commands to Boneripper, Thanquol got the automaton to crouch down beside him. Forgetting the indignity of his position (at least until he could get a good shot at Skraekual's back) the grey seer scrambled up onto Boneripper's back, fitting his feet between the rat-ogre's ribs to ensure a secure hold.

Dutifully, Boneripper lumbered out into the gallery. The sentry gun pivoted and directed its murderous fire at the brute, bullets glancing from the rat-ogre's armoured chest. Thanquol shivered against his bodyguard's back, scarcely daring to breath. Clenching his staff between his teeth, he frantically dug into his robes and seized his snuff-box.

Just a little pinch of warp-snuff, he promised himself. Just a little something to take the edge off his precarious situation.

The intoxicating rush of burning madness flowed through the grey seer's body. All the terror drained out of him, replaced by a bold fury that made him peep his head over Boneripper's shoulder. Thanquol glowered down at the sentry gun. What was this puny contraption to dare pit itself against the greatest wizard in all skavendom! It was a gnat, a flea, something to be crushed with a snap of his claws!

Using Boneripper's fleshless ribs like the rungs of a ladder, Thanquol climbed up onto his bodyguard's shoulder, heedless of his exposed position. The grey seer's eyes glowed, burning green as he drew aethyric energies into his body.

He was Grey Seer Thanquol! The Paw of the Horned Rat! Greatest Magician in all the Under-Empire! He'd blast this filthy dwarf-thing contraption into a thousand bits and feed them to whatever scruffy beard-meat built the ridiculous thing!

Bullets clattered against Boneripper's chest, gradually climbing up the brute's armoured body as the sentry gun sought out the new target perched on the rat-ogre's shoulder. Crazed fires blazing through his brain, Thanquol ignored the certain death creeping towards him. Pointing his staff at the sentry gun, the grey seer poured all of the magic he had drawn into his body into a spell that would annihilate the infernal machine.

Green flames crackled about the head of Thanquol's staff, forming into a great sphere of destruction, a mass of flaming ruin that swept across the gallery, hurtling directly at the sentry gun. It was a spell of such awesome power that it could knock down a castle, sink a warship, collapse an entire warren. In a more lucid state, Thanquol would never have drawn so much power into himself without the aid of warpstone. But the grey seer's snuff-fed fury had risen to a frenzy. He would see the sentry gun obliterated in a way that would make Skraekual's nethers shrivel.

The orb of fire crashed down upon the sentry gun. There was a flash of blinding light and a crash like that of a spitting volcano.

Thanquol sagged against Boneripper's shoulder, exhausted by his amok display of sorcery. At least he had shown Skraekual. He would never have dared call upon the Sphere of Annihilation! The scab-sniffing little nether-nibbler would turn himself inside out if he even tried! It took a true master of magic, a skaven who was truly at one with the Horned Rat to evoke such awesome power!

Thanquol scrambled behind Boneripper's chest as bullets continued to hammer at the lumbering rat-ogre. The terrified grey seer peeked under Boneripper's arm to see the sentry gun, intact and unharmed, still blazing away. All around the weapon, the flagstones were scorched, but the gun itself was unmarked. Thanquol felt his glands clench as he spotted the protective runes inscribed upon the sides of the weapon glowing with the last wisps of his spell.

The cursed dwarf-things and their filthy rune-magic! What kind of coward put talismanic runes on a stinking machine!

Thanquol was too exhausted to even attempt another spell – he'd given his all to that damnable Sphere of Annihilation! What a useless spell! Whatever flea-brained moron-meat had come up with that one should be dragged out of his burrow and stomped like a rabid weasel! It was all that conniving Skraekual's fault! Goading him into expending his powers on such a reckless spell!

Thanquol was just starting to wonder how he would get back to the safety of the mine shaft when he sensed a powerful expenditure of magic close to him. He turned his head to see Skraekual standing at the mouth of the tunnel, his arms spread wide, his eyes glowing with arcane energies.

The filthy coward was using Boneripper as a shield to protect him from the sentry gun! Thanquol gnashed his fangs in outrage at the idea of his rival using his own bodyguard to keep him safe. He'd strangle the rat for that!

Quickly, it became obvious Thanquol had other problems to worry about. In response to Skraekual's evocation, the entire gallery began to tremble, the chains of the pulleys swinging about as though caught in a tempest, mine carts tumbling onto their sides.

Boneripper swayed and staggered. Thanquol leapt off the brute's back an instant before the rat-ogre toppled over. Bullets skittered across the ground as the grey seer scrambled for the cover of an overturned mine cart, flinging himself behind it just as the sentry gun adjusted for his range.

The gallery continued to rumble. From his refuge, Thanquol could see a jagged crack appear in the ground, gradually snaking its way across the gallery towards the sentry gun. As the crack spread, it widened, becoming a veritable fissure by the time it closed upon the sentry gun. The protective runes glowed brightly as Skraekual's magic struck it, but the runes could only guard the gun, not the floor upon which it stood. With a shriek of escaping steam, the sentry gun toppled into the widening fissure.

Grinding his teeth and lashing his tail, Thanquol climbed out from behind the mine cart. The look he directed at the exultant Grey Seer Skraekual was murderous.

'Thank you for the distraction,' Skraekual chortled, scratching at his rotted nose. The grey seer chittered with amusement. 'But that's why you are here-here!'

Still cackling, Skraekual ordered the surviving clan-rats to pick themselves up and head for the far side of the gallery and one of the mine shafts located there. The two warlock-engineers hurried after the gloating grey seer, pausing only to stare down the black pit of the fissure. The tinker-rats didn't linger overlong trying to find the sentry gun, making sure to keep close to Skraekual.

Thanquol watched them all go, his belly boiling with disgust. Angrily, he kicked the fallen Boneripper.

'Up-up, bone-butt,' he snapped. Boneripper obligingly lifted itself off the ground, gaining its feet with an awkward pivot of its socketed waist. Thanquol glared at the backs of the withdrawing scouts.

'Hurry-scurry before that whelp-gnawer goes and conquers the rest of the dwarf-things!' Thanquol cursed, urging his skeletal bodyguard onwards with a whack of his staff. The pair were soon scrambling after the other skaven.

Like his minions, Thanquol didn't pay any notice to the flattened hose that had been connected to the sentry gun or the faint wisps of steam still venting from its severed end.

CHAPTER IX

'I DON'T LIKE it.'

The protest was voiced in the gruff tones that passed for a whisper with Thane Erkii Ranulfsson. The dour, white-bearded dwarf was Minemaster of Karak Angkul, charged not only with the expansion of the mines beneath the hold, but also with arbitrating disputes between the Miners' Guild and the independent mining clans and wildcat prospectors who had claims scattered throughout King Logan's domain. Of late, a new duty had fallen upon Thane Erkii's shoulders: defending those mines that had not yet fallen to the skaven.

Thane Erkii seldom had cause to don the heavy suit of steel chain and plate that had been in his family for over a thousand years, but he still managed to move quickly in the weighty mail. No dwarf was so unfamiliar with armour as to be burdened by it. What he did find burdensome was Klarak Bronzehammer's insistence on accompanying his warriors into the lower deeps.

No, Thane Erkii corrected himself, more than just accompanying them. Klarak insisted on leading the way.

When the hose connecting to one of the engineer's sentry guns had fallen slack, the alarm had been given. It had been quickly sounded, despite the possibility (or probability as Guildmaster Thori insisted) that it was only a malfunction of Klarak's new and unproven invention. According to the inventor's own assertion, and the evidence of those dwarfs who had witnessed the sentry guns in action, only a major skaven incursion would be able to get past the automated weapons.

That made it even more unseemly that Klarak had insisted on coming down into the mines. It simply wasn't done! A dwarf of his prominence shouldn't be risking himself on some rat-hunt. His place was back in the upper deeps, to wait for word of exactly what Thane Erkii and his warriors found. If Klarak got himself killed, it would be a great blow to Karak Angkul's defences. Moreover, Thane Erkii knew that if that happened, King Logan would blame him rather than the daring engineer.

'I know you don't like it,' Klarak said, his voice low yet still carrying that suggestion of brooding power which never failed to impress those who heard it. 'But we have to be sure.'

Thane Erkii had been hopeful when he'd seen the jagged crack in the gallery floor and the broken sentry gun lying at the bottom of a crevice. Certainly there was evidence the gun had dispatched a handful of ratkin, but there was no sign the vermin had been responsible for its destruction. No sign, that is, until Azram Steelfoot, Klarak's personal lorekeeper, observed that several old histories made mention of skaven sorcerers casting spells that could create such havoc.

It made Thane Erkii even more anxious about his prestigious companion to think that a ratkin wizard was creeping about the mines. More so because such a villain would hardly be doing so alone. Any moment he expected every passageway and tunnel to vomit forth a swarm of chittering ratkin.

He was also irked that Klarak had shunned any sort of traditional armour, instead trusting to a curious steel vest of his own creation. Looking at the odd garment with its array of dials and gauges, pipes and rods, Thane Erkii could only scratch his beard. It didn't look like it could stop a snotling's language, much less a skaven knife. He could only wonder if the engineer was trying to get himself killed and earn Thane Erkii a place in the king's Book of Grudges.

'You must have a poor opinion of me and my warriors,' Thane Erkii grumbled. 'Whatever you need to know, we can find out for you.'

Klarak smiled at the Minemaster. 'If you and your warriors were not the toughest fighters in Karak Angkul, I wouldn't be down here. I know you find it eccentric for me to go hunting rats with you, but I have my reasons.'

Thane Erkii would have asked for further details about what the engineer's reasons were, but at that moment one of Klarak's aides interrupted them. The fur-draped Thorlek came rushing up to his master, the weathered ranger holding a fresh rat pellet in his hand.

'Skaven,' Thorlek explained. 'They've headed into the old iron pits.'

Klarak nodded. 'How long ago?'

Thorlek snapped the pellet in half, displaying a

revolting mush of crushed seeds and mouse bones peppered with small black rocks. 'Less time than it took us to get down here,' the ranger said. 'A bit before midday.'

'I should have known you'd be familiar with ratkin dung,' Horgar Horgarsson, the third of Klarak's aides to accompany him into the mines, scoffed. 'You probably eat the stuff.'

'I'm not the one with the bad breath,' the ranger retorted. 'In fact, this would be an improvement.' Malignantly, he threw the pellet at Horgar. Locked in his steel framework, the former hammerer couldn't duck the loathsome projectile, the pellet glancing from his helm.

Horgar fumed at the indignity, stomping forwards and reaching out to grab Thorlek. The ranger dodged the clumsy assault. Horgar tottered for a moment as he almost unbalanced himself, such was his agitation.

'If I get my hands on you,' Horgar threatened, 'they'll need tweezers to pick up all the pieces.'

Thorlek shook his head, an expression of mock gravity on his face. 'Is that before or after you fall down?'

Horgar's face turned crimson and the dwarf sputtered wrathfully into his beard. The warriors around him watched anxiously, certain that the hammerer would soon fall upon his antagonist in a murderous frenzy. They didn't know the long friendship between the two comrades, a friendship that most often expressed itself by one of them trying to drive the other into an apoplectic rage.

Klarak, however, had seen it all before and many times at that. The engineer moved between the two combatants as though nothing had happened. 'Thorlek,' he said, 'I need you to pick up the ratkin trail.'

Thorlek immediately forgot his feud with Horgar. 'That will be easy enough. They don't seem to be making any extra effort to hide their tracks.'

That news met with a mixed reaction when the dwarfs heard it. If the skaven weren't hiding their tracks then it was either because they were in too much of a hurry, too lazy, or too stupid. It was a fourth possibility that caused the dwarfs worry. The skaven might be behaving in such a bold manner because they didn't feel the need to hide their presence. Each of them thought about the sentry gun and what Azram had said about ratkin wizardry.

'We'll follow the tracks,' Klarak said. 'But be on the watch for any trickery. If there is a sorcerer with the ratkin, then we might have a bad fight on our hands. Don't take any chances.'

With Thorlek showing them the way, Klarak and the dwarf warriors marched into the old iron workings. In the gloom of the abandoned mine, the other dwarfs couldn't see the troubled look that settled over the engineer's rugged features. He was thinking of the warning he had been given. A warning about a skaven sorcerer named Thanquol.

THE SKAVEN PRESSED on through the mine shafts, following the tunnels at the western approach of the main gallery. Although the shafts had been dug without any plan, simply pursuing veins of ore, there was nevertheless a regularity and order about them that put them far beyond the meandering confusion of a skaven warren. Even without Skraekual's little map, Thanquol felt confident he could find his way out of the dwarf complex. If his rival was trying to get them lost, he was failing miserably.

It was obvious from even a cursory sniff that the tunnels the skaven now wandered represented diggings that had been played out and abandoned long before the ratkin attack. The wooden beams that supported the tunnels were old and caked in dust, the walls unmarked by any fresh assault by either pick or hammer. The nests of brown rats poked out from niches that had once held lanterns, thick cobwebs stretched beneath the archways that supported each intersection. Beetles and other cave vermin skittered about the floor.

Just like Skraekual to lead them as far away from another confrontation with the dwarfs as possible. He had a yellow streak as wide as a rat-ogre running down his spine. Thanquol could guess the warp-wit's plan now. He would lead them on some wild chase through the abandoned mines for a few days, then head back to Bonestash and report that they'd made a full reconnaissance of Karak Angkul's lower deeps. Skraekual would be heralded as a brave hero when he got back and he'd be thick as fleas with Rikkit Snapfang.

Not a bad plan, Thanquol reflected. He should have thought of it first. Of course, there was no reason why he couldn't still make it his own. All it would require would be for Skraekual to have a little accident.

Unfortunately, the other grey seer was being exceptionally wary, keeping well back of the rest of the skaven where he could keep an eye on both the clanrats and Thanquol. The warlock-engineers were nowhere to be found, having lost interest in the scouting mission once it became obvious the dwarfs hadn't been active in these tunnels for many years. If Thanquol didn't know better, he would have thought the lousy tinker-rats actually wanted to run into some enemies. Whatever the reason, they'd started playing their old game of lingering well behind the rest of the party until after turning one bend of the tunnel, they simply disappeared. Thanquol hoped the cowardly lice fell in a hole and broke their scheming necks.

'Right-right!' Skraekual suddenly called out, gesturing imperiously with his claw. The clanrats at the head of the pack dutifully turned about at the intersection, heading back southwards.

Thanquol lashed his tail in annoyance. It was the warp-wit who was lost! The idiot had a map and he was still unable to tell where he was going! Any skaven with half a brain could tell that these shafts were ones they'd already been through. In fact, if Thanquol was right, another half-mile and they'd be back in the main gallery where the sentry gun had been posted.

Thanquol stroked his whiskers. So he was right, Skraekual was just playing for time so he could scurry back to Rikkit and claim the job was done. The only problem was the idiot didn't have the spleen to make a proper job of such deception. Even a mouse-brained moron like Rikkit wouldn't believe they'd made a full reconnaissance of the dwarf positions in such a short time.

It was looking like he'd have to arrange that accident for Skraekual sooner than he'd been planning.

Suddenly, a new smell struck Thanquol's nose, bringing him up short. The grey seer flattened against the wall of the tunnel, his heart pounding in his breast. He glanced at the clanrats and saw that they'd smelled it too. The cowards were cringing in the dark, muttering fearfully among themselves and casting eager looks at the dark tunnel behind them.

Dwarf-stink, that unmistakable mix of sweat, beer and goat-cheese that exuded from the skin of every dwarf Thanquol had ever encountered. There was more, the tang of steel, the musky fug of oiled leather, the sharp sting of blackpowder. As he keened his ears to the effort, he could hear the tromp of boots marching through the tunnels.

Thanquol glowered at the clanrats, cursing them for fifty kinds of flea-bitten fools. The dwarfs hadn't been in these old mines in decades. There was only one reason why they'd be here now. They'd found spoor left by these third-rate sword-rats and picked up their trail! If he didn't think they'd be more useful against the dwarfs, Thanquol would have blasted the whole lot of them with a bolt of warp-lightning for daring to endanger him by their stupidity.

'Quiet-quick!' Thanquol snarled at the cowering rat-men. From the sound of things, there were far more dwarfs moving through the mines than there were skaven in his patrol. However, Skraekual's moronic map-reading abilities gave them a very good chance to avoid their enemies. The skaven had crossed and recrossed their own trail so many times it was bound to confuse the dwarfs. Dwarf-things were worthless when it came to picking up a scent. They'd use their eyes to follow the trail and the odds were good they'd pick the wrong one.

All Thanquol and the clanrats had to do was keep quiet and stay in the shadows until the dwarfs passed them by. Then they could scarper while the fools were still looking for them in the mines.

Thanquol fingered the little rat-skull snuff-box, longing for a pinch of warp-snuff to calm his nerves. Just a little bit, not enough to really make him go overboard. Just enough to keep himself steady. He had the box open before prudence and self-preservation made him stuff it back into his robe. The last thing he needed now was to start losing control – nerves or no nerves. He would need a clear head if anything went wrong.

The marching dwarfs came nearer. Thanquol could see them now, tromping down the tunnel, every one of them armed and armoured for battle. Except maybe the one up front with the gold face-fur. He just had on some weird chain-vest thing festooned with a bunch of straps and gadgets. The dwarf reminded him somehow of the thrice-cursed tinker-rats, but there was something about his scent that the grey seer really didn't like. He couldn't place his paw on it, but he'd be just as happy to let some other skaven tangle with that dwarf if it came to a fight.

Fortunately, it didn't look like it would come to that. Thanquol's eyes boggled happily when he saw the dwarfs studying the tracks on the ground. True to his prediction, they turned and started to march off down in the wrong direction.

So much for the quick wits of dwarf-things! Now all they had to do was keep quiet and wait a few minutes for the dwarfs to be well on their way. Then the scouting party could break cover and make a run for their burrows back in Bonestash.

Thanquol decided to use the delay to consider what he would tell Ikit Claw and Rikkit Snapfang. Obviously it was necessary to put all the blame on Skraekual, but it helped to plan these things out in advance.

A bright flash of light and a loud clamour suddenly exploded all around the grey seer and his warriors. Thanquol nearly leapt out of his fur, so sudden and without warning was the disturbance. He looked about him in a frantic fury, trying to spot the source of the light. The clanrats were whining and squealing, terrified by what seemed a violent explosion. Yet Thanquol could find no scent of blasting powder in the air and

there was no sign either the skaven or the tunnel had
been damaged.

Magic! It was the only explanation! Thanquol's eyes
scoured the confused ranks of the ratmen, but there
was no sign of Skraekual. The other grey seer was gone!

A moment later, Thanquol had bigger problems than
his missing rival to bother him. Scores of armoured
warriors were charging down the mine straight towards
the skaven. The dwarfs had heard the explosion and
seen the ratmen exposed by the brilliant flash of light.
Now they were running back, eager for the blood of the
verminous invaders!

Skraekual! The filthy little pustule had betrayed them
to the dwarfs! He was using the whole lot of them as
a distraction so that he could safely slip back to Bonestash!

Thanquol admitted it wasn't a bad plan, except for
the part where he was included among the hapless
dupes left to get butchered by the enraged dwarfs.

The clanrats were caught completely by surprise.
Three of them were cut down the instant the first dwarfs
reached them, two more crumpling to the ground with
crushed skulls an instant later. Unlike the skaven, the
dwarfs wore heavy armour and carried broad shields.
Their weapons were massive hammers and wickedly
sharp axes, the blades gleaming in the glow of their
lanterns.

Escape was foremost in Thanquol's mind, but there
seemed little chance of flight with the dwarfs hot on
his tail and only a few measly skaven warriors between
himself and their axes. He needed to buy some time
for him to put some ground between himself and the
dwarfs. Glaring up at Boneripper, he pointed a claw at
the oncoming dwarfs.

'Burn-burn!' the grey seer snarled. 'Slay-kill!'

Boneripper shuddered into motion, lumbering away from the walls and into the middle of the tunnel. The dwarfs must have missed the hulking rat-ogre or mistaken it for some piece of dilapidated mining equipment. Thanquol chittered with amusement as he saw the shock in the dwarfs' eyes as they beheld his fearsome bodyguard.

The rat-ogre didn't give the dwarfs a chance to overcome their shock. Lowering its warpfire projector, Boneripper sent a blast of green fire jetting down the tunnel. The screams of dwarfs and the shrieks of skaven echoed through the mine, the sickly stink of roasted flesh, scorched hair and burning fur filling the air. In the first blast, Boneripper caught a half-dozen of the dwarfs and five skaven who were too slack-witted to move fast. The burning ratmen lay strewn across the ground; the dwarfs writhed in agony as the green flames melted their armour into their flesh.

Before Boneripper could fire again, the gold-bearded dwarf Thanquol had noted earlier sprinted into view. He rushed towards the burning dwarfs, reaching to his vest. Thanquol saw something that looked like a ceramic egg in his hand. The grey seer watched in horror as Klarak threw the object ahead of him, thoughts of Clan Skryre and the Poison Wind filling his brain.

As the grenade burst and a thick white cloud billowed over the tunnel, Thanquol hastily ordered Boneripper to stand in front of him. The rat-ogre could soak up the bulk of whatever fiendish gas was inside the dwarf's weapon. Thanquol could hear the remaining clanrats coughing and hacking as the gas came upon them. Frantically he focused his mind upon a spell to protect himself from the noxious fumes, evoking the minor enchantment just as the white cloud rolled over him.

Thanquol blinked as a gritty powder settled over him, something that seemed equal parts dust and snow. Petrified by what it might be he began swatting at his body to dislodge the weird powder. Around him, the other skaven were doing the same. Boneripper simply stood in place, looking like a white statue with all the dust caked on it.

The sound of a gargled war-cry drove Thanquol from his cleansing ritual. Remembering the dwarfs, he quickly grabbed a nearby clanrat and held the wretch in front of him. A broad-shouldered dwarf warrior, his armour a half-melted mess of slag, shambled out of the white cloud as it began to settle. Swinging an enormous axe, the dwarf cut down Thanquol's living shield.

Baring his fangs in the fearsome snarl of a cornered rat, Thanquol smashed the head of his staff into the side of the dwarf's melted helm. His burnt enemy stumbled back, but quickly recovered, lunging towards the grey seer once more.

Again, Thanquol drew upon his magic. Pointing a claw at the dwarf, he sent a bolt of green lightning smashing into the warrior, lifting him off his feet and flinging him down the tunnel like an arrow. The burnt dwarf landed in a clatter of armour, a great crater smouldering in his chest.

Thanquol looked away from his victim, finding that the cloud had now dispersed, leaving a powdery residue across the tunnel. Every trace of warpfire had been extinguished, and the stricken dwarfs who only a moment before had been burning inside their own armour were now being helped away from the battlefield by their comrades. Those dwarfs who weren't busy with the wounded were staring straight at him and fingering their axes, none more so than the gold-bearded Klarak Bronzehammer.

'Burn-burn!' Thanquol snarled up at Boneripper. The rat-ogre moved to obey, but not even a puff of smoke managed to emerge from the nozzle of its warpfire projector. The powder coating the automaton had clogged the weapon.

'Grey Seer Thanquol!' Klarak called out. Thanquol was taken aback by the cry, shocked that this dwarf-thing should know who he was.

'Try your tricks on me, coward,' the engineer shouted, marching towards the grey seer.

Thanquol glared at the brazen dwarf. There was more than one way to cook a dwarf. 'Die-die, fur-face!' the grey seer howled, pointing his claw at Klarak and sending another bolt of warp-lightning crackling through the tunnel.

There was an unhappy feeling of déjà vu when his spell struck the dwarf, unpleasantly reminding Thanquol of the way the sentry gun had resisted his magic. The warp-lightning danced and crackled all across Klarak, but the dwarf's strange vest seemed to absorb the fury of the spell. The armoured garment glowed as though it were fresh from the forge as the aethyric energies were reflected away from Klarak. Dials and gauges fluctuated wildly, some of the copper rods fitted to the vest corroded into nothingness or melted into unrecognisable blobs of metal, but when Thanquol's spell was spent, Klarak himself stood unharmed.

The dwarf quickly drew a bulky pistol from a holster on his belt, aiming it directly at the grey seer. Thanquol could see steam venting from the weapon as Klarak fired it. He was knocked back as the bullet slammed into him, flopping down onto his back. The grey seer wailed in horror, a bright light flashing before his gaze.

It took an instant for Thanquol to realise he wasn't dead. Patting his body, he felt the shattered pieces of his snuff-box rattling about in his smoking robe. Before he took another breath, Thanquol dived behind Boneripper. Baring his fangs, he glared at the surviving clanrats, pointing the head of his staff at them.

'Fast-quick! Kill-slay gold-fur!' he snarled. Instead of obeying him, the treacherous ratmen took to their heels, tails between their legs.

A second bullet smashed into Boneripper, heralding a veritable fusillade as Klarak unleashed the firepower of his automatic steam pistol. Thanquol squealed in fright as the bullets rattled through the rat-ogre's hull, blasting away bits of bone and metal. Gas jetted from a shattered piston, oil exploded from a punctured pipe. The entire automaton shuddered as some gear went spinning off down the tunnel.

Cursing everything he could think of, Thanquol dug a sliver of warpstone from beneath his robe and bit down on the sorcerous rock, grinding it into bits between his teeth. He exulted as the magical energy trapped within the warpstone rushed through his veins. His body felt as though it were burning with power. He might turn around and pick up Boneripper and hurl it at the impudent dwarf who dared to attack him! He could swat aside the fool's bullets as though they were gnats and shove that damnable pistol...

Thanquol forced himself to think clearly. The memory of the vest and the way his earlier spell had failed to harm Klarak was too fresh to forget. He couldn't risk having the dwarf just walk through another of his spells. He needed to take a page out of Skraekual's tome of tricks. He needed to do something that would rid him of the cursed dwarf without targeting him directly. Get rid of him the same way Skraekual had gotten rid of the sentry gun.

Bullets continued to chew away at Boneripper as Thanquol gave form to the magic boiling inside him. He could be thankful for one thing: his enemy's foolish heroics had made him order the other dwarfs to keep back while he dealt with the grey seer. No doubt Klarak wanted to save their lives from Thanquol's magic, trusting in his vest to do the same for him. Well, he would show the dwarf how little he knew about the power of the Horned Rat!

Swarming from every corner of the mine, summoned by the grey seer's irresistible magic, a living tide of vermin came screeching and skittering. Rats, rats by their hundreds, rats of every size and shape. Wary of having the frenzied animals repulsed by Klarak's resistance to magic, Thanquol ordered his minions away from the engineer. Instead he focused their crazed assault upon the wooden support beams.

Ordinarily, it would have taken a bunch of common rats hours to chew through the sturdy timbers. But these were common no longer. They were a living scourge enflamed by the malignance of Thanquol's will, goaded into a fit of crazed fury by his sorcery. Like the cannibal fish of forsaken Lustria, the vermin assaulted the beams, shredding them to splinters with their chisel-like fangs.

Klarak called out a warning to the other dwarfs, ordering them to leave. Thanquol gnashed his fangs. Fool-meat! Did he really think he could escape the magic the grey seer had unleashed?

The supports groaned, the earth above the shaft shifting as the weakened beams began to give way. Rats began dropping to the floor, their bodies smouldering from the frenzied magic blazing through them. Others rushed in to take the places of the fallen. Dirt and rubble began to rain from the ceiling.

Thanquol's chittering laughter raked across the ears of the fleeing dwarfs. They were brave enough against a bunch of frightened clanrats, but being buried alive by the fearsome sorcery of Grey Seer Thanquol was something else entirely! He watched the bearded wretches stumbling and scrambling down the tunnel, desperate to regain the gallery before the whole mine came crashing down about their ears.

Bullets continued to strike Boneripper. One crunched through the rat-ogre's ribcage to come sizzling past Thanquol's horn. He ducked, squinting from behind the brute's steel spine to gawp in amazement at the gold-bearded dwarf. With rocks and earth crashing down all around him, the madman was standing his ground and continuing to fire at the grey seer! The cold determination in Klarak's gold-flake eyes made Thanquol's glands spurt the musk of fear. The dwarf was insane! He'd be smashed to paste when the roof fell in! He should be running away, not standing there shooting at a lone skaven!

'Hurry-scurry!' Thanquol growled at Boneripper. Dropping to all fours, the grey seer scrambled down the tunnel, hoping to reach the closest bend before Klarak's deadly marksmanship could pick him off. A bullet crashed into the earth beside his right paw, splintering his staff. A second whizzed past his horn, causing the little bell to start jingling.

Crying out in horror, Thanquol threw himself flat. The next shot would smash through his skull, he was certain of it. The Horned Rat had forsaken him and now he would die an ignoble death because of some lunatic dwarf-thing!

The feared third shot never came. Instead, with a rumble and a crash, the roof of the mine collapsed. A cloud of dust and debris exploded down the tunnel, blinding Thanquol and filling his nose with dirt. When the grey seer was able to see again, the entire back of the tunnel was gone, buried under tons of rubble. He bruxed his fangs in triumph. Somewhere under all those rocks was the crazed dwarf-thing who had so stupidly persisted in trying to shoot him when he should have been running for his life. If only all dwarf-things would oblige Thanquol by dying so easily!

Brushing dust from his fur, Thanquol glared at the limping bulk of Boneripper. The lummox had barely escaped the collapse. Moreover it had been shot to pieces by Klarak's steam pistol. The grey seer snorted with contempt. So much for the genius of Clan Skryre engineering! He'd have expected their mechanical rat-ogre to be able to take at least a little abuse!

Swatting Boneripper for having the impudence to be damaged, Thanquol turned his thoughts to other matters. Taking stock of his situation, he vented a titter of anxiety. He was alone deep inside enemy territory with neither map nor guide to get him back to Bonestash. The only way out of the mines, so far as he could tell, was now choked by tons of rubble and hundreds of crushed dwarf-thing corpses.

It was a grim prospect. Not knowing how deep under the earth he was, Thanquol didn't even dare cast a spell to escape the situation. He might vanish through the aethyr only to reappear inside solid rock!

Suddenly, the grey seer turned his head. His nose twitched as he detected a faint scent. Scrambling towards it, he found that his senses were not mistaken. It was the scent of Grey Seer Skraekual. The filthy old rat was still somewhere in the mines, having high-tailed it the moment he betrayed Thanquol to the dwarfs.

Thanquol bared his fangs. Snarling an order to Boneripper, he began to lope down the tunnel, following Skraekual's scent. His situation might be miserable, but as every skaven knew, misery is more endurable when it has company.

Whatever hole Skraekual was hiding himself in, the traitor would soon have company.

Though he wouldn't have it long.

CHAPTER X

A BLACK CLOUD of dust spilled from the mouth of the mine shaft, sweeping across the dwarfs as they reached the safety of the gallery. Caked in dirt, coughing from the dust in their throats, the dwarfs were thankful to reach the solidly-built gallery alive. Many of them were miners themselves when not impressed to bear arms on behalf of the stronghold. There was no greater terror in the mind of a miner than the fear of being buried alive.

Unless it was the fear of being caught off their guard by their enemies and slaughtered without a fight. Such an end would shame them into the afterworld and condemn them to wander the halls of their ancestors as the lowest of servants without a place at the tables of their clans.

During their desperate race from the mine, the dwarfs half-expected a host of skaven to be waiting for them when they reached the gallery. Finding it deserted was a relief, but hardly an excuse to lessen their caution. Gruffly, Thane Erkii arranged a line of axemen to watch the mouths of the other mines.

'Take the wounded up to the Second Deep,' Thane Erkii ordered the warriors who had carried the injured out from the mine. He cast a grim look over the horrible injuries the dwarfs caught by the blast of warpfire had suffered. Plates of armour had melted into their flesh, burning clean through to the bone in some cases. If they'd been scalded by lava, Thane Erkii didn't think they could be any worse. 'Maybe the priestess of Valaya can help them,' he added in a doubtful voice. It was no slight against the ancestor gods, but he didn't see how anything could help a dwarf recover from such horrific wounds.

Thane Erkii turned around at the sound of rocks crashing into the gallery. For an instant, the frightening thought that the skaven magic had been so powerful as to undo the very walls of the gallery flashed through his mind. As Minemaster of Karak Angkul, such a shameful slight against the constructions under his care was doubly horrible. He would never be able to atone for such a humiliation.

His fear proved unfounded. The sound came from Horgar Horgarsson and the ranger Thorlek. The two dwarfs were attacking the mouth of the mine with frantic energy. Horgar's steel framework jetted great spurts of steam as the ex-hammerer ripped stones from the tunnel and hurled them aside as though they weighed nothing. Thorlek, unable to match the augmented strength of his friend, was doing his best by using the haft of his axe as a lever to roll stones from the rockpile. Azram Steelfoot, the old lorekeeper, was sitting on the ground drawing in the thick coat of dirt that now covered the floor. Lacking the strength of his companions, Azram was doing his part by trying to recall from memory the layout of the old workings and determine if there was some other way into the mine. There were tears in the lorekeeper's eye and a trickle of moisture seeped from beneath the edge of the lens-array he wore over his other eye.

Thane Erkii could sympathise with the sorrow of the three dwarfs. They had been part of Klarak Bronzehammer's Iron Throng, that select brotherhood of dwarfs who formed the eccentric engineer's closest aides and comrades. He knew they had travelled far with their master and shared many adventures with him. He could understand their despair at this moment, their unwillingness to accept that the brave hero had finally met his doom. It had been a valiant death, holding off the skaven wizard and buying the time the rest of them would need to escape the sorcerer's wicked magic.

Solemnly, Thane Erkii stepped towards the blocked tunnel. He laid a hand on Thorlek's shoulder, gently urging the ranger to give up his hopeless efforts. 'It's no good. He's in Gazul's keeping now.'

The ranger turned angrily on Thane Erkii, shoving aside his hand. 'I've seen Klarak pull himself out of worse scrapes than this,' Thorlek growled. 'Anybody who can trot through the lair of Malok in one piece isn't going to let some slimy ratkin finish him!'

Horgar ripped another rock from the pile, smashing it between his iron hands. 'We're not giving up on him,' the hammerer swore. 'He never gave up on any of us, no matter how bad things looked. We'll not give up on him now.'

Thane Erkii shook his head. 'It's hopeless,' he avowed. 'Grungni himself couldn't survive half the mountain coming down on his head!'

Horgar fixed the Minemaster with a menacing look. 'Leave us be,' he warned, tearing another stone from the rubble.

Suddenly, Thorlek leaped up, turning an excited face towards Horgar and Thane Erkii. 'I heard something moving!' he shouted.

'Stones settling,' Thane Erkii said.

'I know what stones sound like,' the ranger replied curtly. 'Ever know a stone to have rhythm as they settle?'

Thane Erkii was dubious, but he crouched down beside Thorlek and pressed his ear to the rubble. True to the ranger's claim, he could hear a regular tapping, strong and strident, emanating from behind the rubble. To his ears, the tapping seemed to be a sort of code, a signal used by miners to let any rescuers know they were still alive. Quickly the Minemaster rose to his feet, shouting for his warriors to help clear the blockage.

Working with a desperate haste, the dwarfs soon had a section of tunnel some twenty yards wide cleared. It was then that they hesitated. Something was stirring the rocks from the other side. The alarming thought belatedly came to them that whoever was moving about might not be Klarak but one of the skaven. The image of the skeletal rat-ogre suddenly bursting from the rubble gave even Horgar pause. They had all seen what the monstrous creature could do with its warpfire projector and none of them wanted to court such a fate.

The rocks jostled forwards with a crash, causing a cloud of dust to rise up, blinding the dwarfs. Thane Erkii called for his warriors to draw their axes and be ready. There had been times when skaven learned the miners' code and employed it to lure dwarfs into an ambush. The Minemaster wanted to take no chances.

When the dust cleared, however, Thane Erkii was

the first to lower his weapon. He sighed with relief as he saw Klarak Bronzehammer climbing out from the rubble. The gold-bearded engineer was bruised and bloodied by his ordeal, but at least he was alive. Images of King Logan's Book of Grudges gradually faded from the forefront of the Minemaster's thoughts.

Klarak's three aides rushed forwards, whooping with joy that their friend had escaped death in the cave-in.

'You have the luck of a drunken halfling!' Thorlek shouted, gripping the engineer's arm. Horgar went one better, embracing Klarak in a fierce hug and lifting him off his feet.

'That's a nice way to see if he's broken any bones,' Azram grumbled, adjusting the magnification of his lenses. The reprimand had its desired effect and both the ranger and hammerer released their battered victim.

Klarak patted his bloodied scalp, then smiled at the aged lorekeeper. 'Nothing broken, Azram, but I shouldn't like to go through that again.'

'You shouldn't have tried it in the first place!' Horgar swore. 'What was the idea of standing there taking pot-shots at a thaggoraki with the whole mine coming down about your ears?'

'What Horgar's trying to say is if there's anything stupid that needs doing, he's the dwarf for the job,' commented Thorlek.

Klarak shook his head. 'It was worth the risk,' he said, his tone grim. 'Grey Seer Thanquol poses too great a menace to Karak Angkul to be allowed to live. If it cost my life to bring him down, it would have been a fair trade.' The engineer clenched his fists, an angry light shining in his eyes. 'It didn't work though. Before the roof came down, I saw him scamper off deeper into the mine.'

'Then we've nothing to worry about,' Horgar said. 'The stupid ratkin has buried himself alive. A few days and the vermin will starve and save us the bother of smashing his skull in.'

'I wouldn't count on that,' Klarak cautioned. 'There's too much at risk to take any chances.' He thought about the warning from Altdorf and the horror that Grey Seer Thanquol would unleash unless he was stopped. Frowning, Klarak started to strip the scorched and tattered mail vest, dropping the blackened armour to the floor. 'This vest barely guarded me against Thanquol's magic,' he said.

'You'll have to have Kurgaz inscribe some tougher runes on the next one,' Azram suggested.

Klarak looked back at the blockage filling the tunnel. 'I don't think it would do any good. You weren't close enough to see how Thanquol powered that last spell of his. I saw him actually eat a piece of wyrdstone. He was fairly burning with energy, at any instant I expected him to burst into flames. The rats he summoned to gnaw through the beams did burn from the magic goading them to do Thanquol's bidding.' The engineer made a desultory wave of his hand. 'No,' he grumbled, 'I don't think I know enough to make a vest that could protect me from that kind of power. And I don't think any sorcerer capable of that kind of magic is going to let a few tons of rock keep him bottled up.'

'You sound almost like you're giving up,' Thorlek said, an incredulous note in his tone.

'Maybe it would be easier if I did,' Klarak told him. He gave his friend a grim smile. 'But when have you ever known me to do anything the easy way?'

* * *

GREY SEER SKRAEKUAL scurried through the old mine, the ratskin map clutched in his trembling paws, his whiskers maintaining contact with the earthen wall. His mind was a confusion of terrified instinct and avaricious ambition. A skaven needed the scent of his own kind in his nose in order to feel even slightly at ease. Alone, the ratman's natural fears rose to almost overwhelming levels. It was only by exertion of his hideous will that Skraekual was able to keep himself from fleeing in terror back to Bonestash.

He was playing for keeps now. Destroying that arrogant idiot Thanquol and the morons with him had been a step from which there was no going back. Skraekual had to succeed in the mission Seerlord Kritislik had entrusted to him. He would need the Seerlord's protection if either Clan Mors or Clan Skryre decided to take issue with the way he had handled his supposed superior. If the fools didn't manage to succeed in overcoming the dwarfs in their petty war, then Skraekual would make a convenient target upon which to fix the blame. For his part, it would be difficult to shift the responsibility back on the late and unlamented Grey Seer Thanquol.

Skraekual lashed his tail in anger as he thought about his scheming rival. The pompous maggot! He'd deserved to die! Thinking himself favoured by the Horned Rat! Acting as though he was the chosen child of the Horned One and lording it over anyone and everyone! Well, now Thanquol knew better. The Horned One did not favour fools!

How easily the dung-sniffer had been taken in by Skraekual's deceptions. It had been pup-play to make Thanquol think his rival was nothing but a burned-out, warp-witted addict. A few bottled scents applied at the right time, a few well-staged fits, and the idiot had been completely taken in. He would almost have liked to see Thanquol's face if the dullard knew Skraekual's nose hadn't rotted off from an excess of warp-weed. It had been bitten off by an over-enthusiastic breeder!

Chittering his amusement, the grey seer examined his map once more. It represented the labour of three months and a small fortune in warpstone incense to create that map, staring for days on end into his black mirror. But the mirror had shown him all. It had revealed to Skraekual the location of the old skaven warren of Festerhole, the first settlement to exist beneath Karak Angkul, predating Bonestash by nearly two thousand birth-cycles.

Disaster had come upon Festerhole when the mines of the dwarfs had broken into the skaven tunnels. The ratmen had fought tenaciously against the dwarfs, but at last they had been overwhelmed. The short-sighted dwarfs, however, hadn't moved to occupy the old warren. Instead they had collapsed every approach into the tunnels and entombed the last of the ratkin in their homes. Without the numbers to dig their way out again, the skaven had perished after a few weeks of infighting and cannibalism.

But Festerhole hadn't vanished completely. In the old records of the Order of Grey Seers, Skraekual had found reference to Festerhole's spiritual leader: Grey Seer Thratsnik. Thratsnik, it seemed, had departed Skavenblight with a potent talisman in his possession, a talisman of such power that Seerlord Kritislik was desperate to make sure it didn't fall into the wrong paws. He'd offered Skraekual wealth and position just to recover the thing and bring it back to him. It would be interesting to see if Seerlord Tisqueek could make an even better offer.

The Hand of Grey Lord Vecteek the Murderous, War-monger of Clan Rictus during the Black Death. It sent a thrill of fear down Skraekual's spine just to think of Vecteek's genocidal reign. Under his generalship the skaven had spilled out onto the surface and very nearly enslaved the wretched race of man-things. Only the betrayal of his subordinates had prevented him from achieving his ambitions and bringing about the Great Ascendancy foretold by the Horned Rat.

What a skilled grey seer could do with such an arte-fact! The mummified paw of one of skavendom's fiercest warlords! Surely Vecteek had been favoured by the Horned One, and by possessing even a bit of his remains, a grey seer would be able to augment his own connection to his god. What need for warpstone when the grey seer had such power at his fingertips!

Skraekual bruxed his fangs, imagining the might that would soon be his. Why should he kowtow to either Kritislik or Tisqueek? He could make himself Supreme Seerlord once he had the Hand of Vecteek!

Excitedly, the grey seer turned towards the wall of the mine. The dwarfs had been most thorough in disguis-ing this section of tunnel, but Skraekual's map showed him where the old skaven passageways had once been. He stared at the mass of rocks before him, visualising the long-lost warren behind the wall. He could see the trapped skaven dying in the darkness, beseeching Grey Seer Thratsnik for the intervention of the Horned One. If only Thratsnik had been more knowledgeable he might have saved them and himself with the relic he had stolen from Skavenblight. Now his stupidity had become Skraekual's gain.

Drawing a sliver of warpstone from his robe, Skraekual thrust the toxic rock between his fangs and ground it into powder. Swallowing the crushed warpstone, he felt the intoxicating rush of raw magic flooding through his veins. For an instant, he lost his focus, indulging in the maddening flow of aethyric energy. Then Skraekual remembered his purpose and asserted his will, quickly turning the rush of energy into fuel for a mighty spell.

Setting his paw against the rock face, Skraekual shaped the magical power filling his body into a tremendous spell. The entire tunnel began to shake as the rocks split before the grey seer's magic, vaporising beneath the black malignity of his will. Dust billowed out from the long-sealed passageway as the grey seer's spell ripped through the earth.

Soon he had an opening wide enough for twenty skaven, reaching as far back as that part of Festerhole the dwarfs had been unable to collapse. The air held a musty, dead quality that set Skraekual's fur on edge. With the warpstone energy still blazing through his body, he directed a second tremor deeper within the old warren, smashing apart another tunnel the dwarfs had demolished, one that would reconnect Festerhole to the Underway. After coming so far and risking so much, Skraekual wasn't about to be trapped in the tomblike maze of Festerhole and share the ignominious fate of Thratsnik.

Feeling a bit more confident with the back door opened, Skraekual scurried down the dusty tunnels of the warren. The gnawed bones of skaven littered the ground, evidence of the cannibalism that had consumed the settlement once the dwarfs had cut it off. Occasionally, the mummified husk of an intact body leered at him from the desolate passages, the sorry remains of the last ratmen to perish in the cataclysm.

Skraekual ignored the morbid husks, intent only

upon reaching his objective. Through his mirror, he had seen the burrow of Grey Seer Thratsnik and knew which way he must go to find the dead sorcerer's lair. He uttered a shrill squeak of triumph when he scuttled into the cave-like burrow. Most of Thratsnik's possessions had crumbled into dust, only a few stone cabinets cobbled together from old dwarf masonry and a handful of copper jars and trinkets remaining intact. However, behind a table crafted from the broken leg of a dwarf statue, Skraekual saw the shrivelled mummy of Thratsnik himself.

And resting before the dead grey seer, as full and fresh-looking as though it had been newly severed from its owner's arm, was a hairless skaven paw!

Skraekual rushed across the room. He hesitated before the table, freezing as he felt Thratsnik's dead eyes on him. He snickered nervously. The old fool had been dead for centuries. There was nothing he could do to cheat Skraekual of his victory now!

Making a quick grab at the table, half expecting the horned husk of Thratsnik to get up and try to stop him, Skraekual seized the severed hand. Springing away from the table, the grey seer made certain to keep his eyes on the old mummy while he inspected his prize.

The freshness of the paw was evidence that it had been endowed with potent enchantments, even the lowest skavenslave could have seen that. Sniffing the paw, Skraekual detected the odour of the warpstone which had been used to preserve the hand. It must have taken several pounds of the precious rock to so thoroughly saturate the paw. Further evidence that he now possessed a most potent artefact, a holy relic of the Horned One.

There was another smell too, one that was strangely

familiar to Skraekual's nose. Suddenly, the grey seer spun about. The scent he detected wasn't coming from the paw. It was coming from behind him.

Grey Seer Thanquol stood in the doorway of Thratsnik's lair, his fangs displayed in a threatening grin. Beside him stood the hulking figure of Boneripper.

'Burn-burn!' Thanquol growled, pointing a claw at Skraekual. 'Burn-burn with fire!'

'Wait-wait!' Skraekual shrieked. 'We can-will share-share!'

Thanquol motioned for Boneripper to stand down, then fixed Skraekual with an enraged stare, his foot tapping impatiently against the dusty floor of the burrow. Skraekual dipped his head in submission, making himself as unthreatening as possible. But there was a little grin tugging at the corners of his mouth.

'This is the Hand of Vecteek!' Skraekual announced, displaying the dismembered paw. He noted the way Thanquol's eyes boggled at the mention of the lost artefact. 'With this we can make-take what we want-like from Seer-fool Kritislik.'

Thanquol ran a claw through his whiskers, avarice creeping into his eyes. 'How can I trust you?' he hissed.

Skraekual seemed to sympathise with his rival's suspicions. Hurriedly, he tugged the dragon-head ring from his finger. 'A gesture-token of oath-bond,' Skraekual said, tossing the ring to Thanquol.

The motion surprised Thanquol, and awkwardly he bent about to catch the ring. It crumpled in his grasping fingers. A trick! Some cheap tin trinket! All this time it had been another of Skraekual's deceptions! From the start he'd never had Master Sleekit's ring!

'Die-burn, fool-meat!' Skraekual growled. A burst

of black energy leapt from the grey seer's paw, sizzling across the cave.

Thanquol squealed in horror, narrowly diving from the path of the deadly spell. Scrambling across the ground, putting Boneripper between himself and his enemy, he watched in horror as the wall behind him began to corrode, the rock turning to dripping mush beneath Skraekual's magic.

'Boneripper!' Thanquol shrieked. He pointed a claw at Skraekual. 'Kill-smash! Kill-smash!'

The rat-ogre vented warpsteam as its damaged mechanics ground into action. The huge monster charged straight towards Skraekual. The sorcerer's eyes glowed a brilliant green as the brute rushed him. At the last instant before Boneripper could reach him, he vanished in a puff of foul-smelling smoke. Unable to stop, the rat-ogre kept barrelling across the cave. It smashed headfirst into the stone table, collapsing it and hurling the mummy of Thratsnik from the seat it had occupied for centuries. A great cloud of warpsteam erupted from Boneripper and the brute collapsed amid the rubble.

Thanquol did not have long to take in the spectacle of his bodyguard's failure. A brutal impact against the back of his head sent him sprawling across the cave floor. Looking up, he saw Skraekual glaring down at him, his staff poised to smash the grey seer's head. Skraekual had used his magic to escape Boneripper's charge, but the vengeful sorcerer had not gone far.

The staff came smashing down, glancing off Thanquol's horn as the grey seer scrambled from its path. Skraekual bared his fangs in a vicious snarl. Extending the Hand of Vecteek, he sent a blast of pure aethyric force ploughing into his enemy. Thanquol was flung like a rag doll across the cave by the magical blow.

Skraekual tittered in amusement at his foe's helplessness and sent another blast of raw magic smashing into
him.

'Slow-slow,' Skraekual hissed. 'You are first-first victim
of Supreme Seerlord Skraekual and I want-will like-like
watch-smell you die-die!' In his bloodthirsty mania,
flecks of foam dripped from Skraekual's mouth and
madness burned in his eyes.

Thanquol took advantage of his rival's insane gloating to conjure his own spell. Lightning crackled about
the head of his staff, surging across the cave to strike
the other grey seer. Before the warp-lightning could
connect, however, Skraekual made a slashing gesture
with the Hand of Vecteek. As though it had been torn
to shreds by a thousand invisible fangs, the tatters of
Thanquol's spell were scattered across the burrow.

'Pain-suffer!' Skraekual snarled, gesturing once more
with the talisman. Thanquol attempted to fend off the
sorcerous attack with his own counterspell, but the
malignancy of Skraekual's magic was too powerful to
be resisted. All he could do was shriek in terror and
spurt the musk of fear as an invisible force closed about
him in a crushing embrace.

The crazed gleam shining in his eyes, Skraekual made
sweeping gestures with the Hand. At each gesture,
Thanquol was battered against the walls or dashed to
the floor. A long gash opened along his snout as his fur
was torn, a piece of his left horn went bouncing across
the floor as it broke against one of the stone shelves.

'Great-mighty Thanquol!' Skraekual screamed. 'Not-
not great-mighty now-now!' He raised the Hand,
the unseen power gripping Thanquol responding by
smashing him against the ceiling. Sparks flashed in
Thanquol's eyes as the wind was squeezed out of his

lungs. Coughing and spitting, he could only flail his legs in a feeble effort at escape.

Laughing, Skraekual made a dismissive wave of his paw. Instantly, Thanquol was flung to the floor with bone-jarring force. Before he could even think about trying to rise, a tremendous force crushed him flat again, feeling as though a giant had stepped on him. He squirmed in agony beneath the steadily mounting pressure, frantically trying to concentrate on a spell, any spell, that would keep him from being squished like an insect by Skraekual's magic.

The gloating Skraekual paced across the cave, chuckling evilly, his entire body twitching in a spasm of vermicidal glee. 'What-what does great-mighty Thanquol say-squeak now!'

Thanquol looked past his tormentor and a vicious grin spread across his face. 'Goodbye, Skraekual,' he snarled, provoking a confused look on Skraekual's face. 'Boneripper! Rip-tear-kill-crush!'

Skraekual had been so fixated on his torment of Thanquol that he hadn't noticed the skeletal rat-ogre stir from the rubble, or his own proximity to the hulking automaton. Before he could even turn around, Boneripper's immense hand closed about Skraekual's horned head. With one vicious tug, the rat-ogre pulled the grey seer's head from his shoulders.

The force pressing Thanquol against the floor instantly vanished. Painfully, he crept across the cave, kicking Skraekual's head. 'Traitor-meat!' he spat, giving it another kick. 'Scat-rat! Tick-popper! Warp-witted snake-suckler!' Thanquol cried out in pain as he cut one of his toes on Skraekual's horn. Glaring vindictively at the battered head, he focused his will and sent a blast of pure aethyric energy hammering down upon the object of his ire. Beneath the wave of raw magic, Skraekual's head burst into bloody splinters of fur and bone.

Panting from his fury and his exertions, Thanquol turned towards his enemy's body. Exhaustion was forgotten as he spotted the Hand of Vecteek still clutched in Skraekual's dead paws. Avarice again shone in Thanquol's eyes. Having been on the receiving end of the talisman's power, he was better able to appreciate its ability to augment the magic of its possessor.

With a trembling paw, Thanquol reached out to claim the Hand for his own. At the last instant, however, his natural caution reasserted itself. Skraekual had acted even more insane than usual at the end, a condition that Thanquol could only believe had been brought about by using the Hand. Granted, the fool had been nowhere near the sorcerer that Thanquol was, but still there might be some sort of curse on the thing. A skaven proverb maintained that he who sticks his neck out ends up in the larder.

Thanquol leaned back, staring suspiciously at the Hand. Again, greed and lust for power flared up in his black heart, driving back his instinctive fear. There was another skaven proverb that advised to take what you can when you can. It was sheer idiocy to leave anything so powerful just lying around. Besides, it would be safe enough to carry the Hand around. The danger would come from trying to use it. But a skaven of his stalwart resolve would hardly fall prey to that sort of temptation.

His paw trembling with an almost overwhelming mix of fear and greed, Thanquol seized the gruesome artefact.

Taking a sniff of warpstone-snuff to calm his nerves after his ordeal, Thanquol barked a sharp order at

Boneripper. With the traitor Skraekual dealt with and the Hand of Vecteek now in the possession of a loyal servant of the Lords of Decay, it was time to be quit of these gloomy old burrows. He was eager to be back in Bonestash. He could explain his associate's treason, make his apologies to Ikit Claw and Rikkit Snapfang and then be on his way back to Skavenblight. When he presented the Hand to Kritislik, the old villain would be forced to acknowledge the wisdom and cunning of his most faithful servant.

Creeping back down the passageway, Boneripper limping after him, Thanquol thought that it really was too bad Bokha had been killed. That idiot would have been just stupid and tractable enough to use the Hand on Thanquol's behalf, thereby solving the problem of any curse attached to it.

Still, Kritislik would reward him well. It wasn't every day an artefact like the Hand of Vecteek was returned to the Shattered Tower.

As Thanquol and Boneripper vanished around a bend in the tunnel, the dust kicked up by the fight in Thratsnik's lair slowly settled. Thrown from its ancient seat, the mummy of the old grey seer lay crumpled in one corner of the lair. Its robes had crumbled away, exposing its bony frame and the withered stump where one of its paws should have been.

There seemed an expression of vengeful amusement on the mummy's shrivelled face.

THE WAR-ROOM OF Karak Angkul was a frenzy of activity. King Logan and his generals were gathered about the massive granite table which dominated the centre of the room. Arrayed before their steely stares was a three-dimensional model of the dwarfhold and its labyrinth of tunnels, galleries and deeps. Scattered throughout the model were tiny iron statues of warriors, their chests each engraved with a different rune. The statues denoted the positions of the hold's warriors.

'If there is trouble, it will come from the Sixth Deep,' Thane Arngar, one of the king's generals, warned. He gestured with his hairy hand at a section of statues arranged in the twisting maze of mines beneath the Sixth Deep. 'We should concede the mines and concentrate our troops in the Sixth Deep.'

'Concede the mines!' roared the heavy-set Guildmaster Borgo Flintheart, head of the Miners' Guild. 'Leave the thieving thaggoraki down there with our gold? You must be bozdok!'

'The ratkin don't care about gold,' Thane Arngar told Borgo, 'and the mines are too numerous to mount a proper defence down there. No, the plan must be to concede the mines and lure the ratkin into the Sixth Deep where we can bring the full weight of our warriors against them.'

'We can move some of the reserves from the upper deeps as well,' opined another of the generals. 'There's no sense keeping them where they're not needed. The Overguard in the First Deep has to stay, of course, just in case the ratkin have stirred up some of the grobi tribes to cause us trouble.'

King Logan nodded as he considered the proposal. Weighing the benefits and dangers, he turned towards the one dwarf who had up until now been silent during the war council. 'What do you think, Klarak?' he asked. 'You've just come back from fighting these devils. Are they likely to strike out for the Sixth Deep if we pull out from the mines?'

Klarak Bronzehammer picked up one of the iron

statues standing in a section of the mine shafts. Grimly, he set the statue down. 'I would advise keeping the patrols in place and keeping the reserves where they are. It never pays to try to guess what ratkin will do. They are base, honourless creatures and their minds are as crooked as a goblin's heart. We have two choices. We can try to strike them first, which means taking the fight to their warrens. To do that, we'd have to take almost every able-bodied dwarf in the hold.'

'And the other option?'

'We try to eliminate their leader,' Klarak stated firmly. 'The ratkin are all cowards. They'll lose heart if we can kill their leader before the battle even begins.'

'That's why you want to keep the patrols down in the mines,' said Thane Arngar. 'You are hoping they can spot this Grey Seer Thanquol before he can slither back to his own kind.'

Klarak nodded. 'Eliminating Thanquol is vital if we are going to save Karak Angkul from destruction.'

Any further debate was interrupted by a disturbance at the door to the war-room. Two of King Logan's hammerers appeared, marching into the enormous hall with the practised precision of a steam hammer. Between them, they escorted a ragged, unkempt dwarf who wore only a set of ill-fitting breeches and the heavy blanket draped over his shoulders.

'Sire, this dwarf was discovered at the Great Gate petitioning for entrance,' one of the hammerers stated. 'He claims he has urgent information he must report to your highness.' The hammerer's face twisted into a crooked grin. 'He wants to warn us that the ratkin are going to attack Karak Angkul.'

The report brought a grim chuckle from some of the assembled dwarfs. Any warning about ratmen attacking the stronghold was very late in coming.

The bedraggled dwarf straightened his body when he noted the mockery in his escort's voice. Throwing off his blanket, he puffed out his scarred chest. 'I am Mordin Grimstone of Karak Izor,' he said. 'I was a prisoner of the skaven. For weeks I have been wandering the Ungdrin Ankor trying to make my way back to civilisation. While I was making my way here, I followed the ratkin warhost and overheard the plans of their leaders to attack Karak Angkul.'

'Did you get a good look at these leaders?' Klarak asked. It would go ill for the hold if Mordin had stumbled upon an entirely different army that was marching to join the one already threatening the hold.

'There were two who seemed in charge,' Mordin said. 'One was a horned ratkin they called Thanquol.' The escaped prisoner's voice dripped with venom as he named the monster he had sworn to destroy. 'The other was an iron-faced creature with a huge metal hand they called Ikit Claw.'

Klarak's face went pale when he heard the name of the second skaven leader. He turned towards King Logan.

'Sire, I am afraid I've been wrong,' the engineer said. 'If Ikit Claw is with our enemies then the peril is greater than I imagined.' Klarak cast his gold-flake eyes across the dwarf generals, fixing each of them with his steely stare.

'It is not just Karak Angkul which is now in danger,' he told them. 'But the whole of the Karak Ankor!'

CHAPTER XI

KLARAK BRONZEHAMMER LEANED against the table, his intense stare boring into the faces of the gathered generals and leaders of Karak Angkul. For once, even Guildmaster Thori kept silent, reading from the frightened pallor of Klarak's face that he was about to relate something of dire import. Even the engineer's worst detractors acknowledged that he was no coward.

'I first tangled with Ikit Claw when he raided Kraka Drak and tried to take many of the hold's engineers away as slaves,' Klarak began. 'Since then our paths have crossed several times. The last was in the dragon caves beneath Karak Azul. That time, he was trying to recreate an ancient ratkin weapon of vast destructive power, something he called the Doomsphere.'

'Typically grandiose ratkin name,' said Guildmaster Thori. 'Every piece of trash they knock together the vermin call the Big Sharp Stick of Exploding Death or the

Backscratcher of Infinite Destruction.'

'Except this time, the weapon could really do what the ratkin expected it to do,' Klarak said. 'I saw the thing with my own eyes, a great orb of steel the size of a steamship and packed with raw wyrdstone.'

The description brought a few gasps from Runelord Morag and the other runesmiths. More than any of the other dwarfs present, they understood the connection between warpstone and dark magic. They had some inkling of the destructive potential for a device such as the one Klarak described.

'What did the ratkin expect to use this weapon for?' King Logan asked, fearing he already knew the answer.

'Destroy every dwarfhold in the Worlds Edge,' Klarak told him. 'Ikit Claw constructed his wyrdstone bomb over the fault running beneath Karak Azul. If he'd been able to unleash the power of his weapon, he could have precipitated an earthquake the likes of which no dwarf has seen since the Time of Woes.'

Cries of alarm spread through the war-room, the magnitude of what Klarak described shaking many of the assembled dwarfs to the very core.

'How did you stop him?' asked Thane Erkii.

Klarak's expression became even more dour, a haunted quality entering his eyes. 'I'm not sure that I did,' he confessed. 'Myself and my companions fought our way through Ikit's minions, slaying scores of the ratkin. The Claw saw us coming and in his craven wickedness, he activated the Doomsphere moments before we could reach it. The huge machine shuddered into hideous life, the stink of skaven engines venting from its exhausts in a caustic cloud of green gas. If not for the protective gear I'd ordered my companions to bring along, all of us would have met our ancestors in that moment. I saw ratkin without protection doubled-over beside the weapon, coughing out pieces of their own lungs as the gas scorched their innards.

'A rearguard of ratkin continued to protect the Doomsphere, each wearing a heavy respirator. While my comrades fought these vermin, I charged through their ranks and assaulted the hell-machine itself. Employing a steam hammer, I tried to smash my way through the steel shell to get at whatever mechanisms were inside.

'I had only just begun my assault before I found myself attacked by Ikit Claw himself. The ratkin had strengthened his frail body with an exoskeleton of iron powered by infernal skaven sorceries. His left arm had been fitted with an enormous metal claw within which had been built one of the ratkin's diabolic fire-throwers.'

The engineer closed his eyes and sighed deeply. 'I managed to elude the ratkin's fire, but the iron frame he wore protected him from my pistol. The filthy beast then tried to crush me with his magic, but the ancestor badges I wore guarded me against his spells. I was able to close upon the monster, bringing him low with blows from my hammer until his metal claw was an unrecognisable mass of scrap. Before I could finish him, however, the Doomsphere began to shriek and shiver. One of the steel plates from the machine's roof was ripped free, flung across the cavern as though shot from a cannon. A searing blast of greenish light burst from the resulting tear in the Doomsphere's skin, scorching the roof of the cavern and raining rocks down upon those below.

'Ikit Claw broke away from me, but the ratkin had lost the appetite for battle. He turned his gaze to the hole in the top of his machine, and in his eyes was an expression of such wrath as I've never seen. I moved to close upon the ratkin once more, but even as I did, a panel in the side of the Doomsphere was blown loose, a stream of burning light erupting from the rent and blocking my path to the warlock.

'By this time, the entire cavern was coming apart. Rocks fell like rain from the savaged roof and the vibrations of the Doomsphere were making the ground quiver and quake. The ratkin were fleeing in their multitudes, slinking back into the dark, trying to escape the disintegrating machine. More steel plates burst as the power within the sphere continued to mount. As an engineer, it was obvious to me that the machine was going to self-destruct, that no power could restrain its raging energies now.

'I quickly gathered my companions and together we fled from the cavern. My last look back found Ikit Claw still struggling at the controls of his Doomsphere, trying to induce it to power-down. A few minutes later, and I was bowled over by the shock wave of a tremendous explosion. The cavern, and everything within it, was buried by tons of rock.'

'But it appears that Ikit Claw escaped the destruction of his machine,' King Logan observed.

'That is what concerns me,' Klarak said. 'From Mordin's description, there can be no doubt he saw Ikit Claw.'

'You think this creature would be crazed enough to repeat such a fiendish experiment?' Guildmaster Thori asked.

'For what the records tell us,' Lorekeeper Azram answered, 'we know that the ratkin are given to obsessions. Once it has entered their mind to do a thing, they will try to do it, regardless of their own losses or the obstacles in their way.'

Klarak paced along the table, staring at the three-dimensional map. 'More to the point, we can't afford to assume Ikit Claw doesn't intend to construct another Doomsphere. The situation of Karak Angkul is much like that of Karak Azul. The same underground fault links us. Detonating his weapon here might serve the same purpose as detonating it beneath Karak Azul.'

'You can't be sure of that,' Guildmaster Thori said. 'There is no basis upon which to base your theory.' The old dwarf snorted with disapproval. 'But I've grown used to your unproven theories.'

King Logan ran his hand along the length of his beard, thinking hard about what Klarak had said. The dwarfs were always a cautious people, but they also weren't prone to abandoning themselves to imaginary terrors. 'How can we know if this ratkin warlock is up to something?'

'You might look for anything unusual,' Klarak said. 'Anything that is abnormal. Something that doesn't fit the model of ratkin raids.'

'You mean like the mines?' Thane Erkii asked. All eyes turned to the Minemaster, fixing the undivided attention of the war council upon him. The thane shifted uncomfortably in his seat, unaccustomed to having the king and his advisors hanging on his every word.

'The last two patrols in the mines have reported some strange things,' Thane Erkii explained. 'They've found some of the support beams missing.'

'Ratkin are always vandalising our diggings,' observed Guildmaster Borgo.

Thane Erkii shook his head. 'Not in this fashion. The beams were removed, but the ratkin had built new supports to replace them and prevent the tunnel from

collapsing. Naturally, their crude constructions were
spotted right-off but…'

'Where did this happen?' Klarak demanded, an
urgency in his voice.

Thane Erkii thought for a moment, then drew the
connection Klarak feared. 'All the beams they stole were
the ones from your workshop. The ones you sent…'

'Have your dwarfs remove every beam that is still
down there before the ratkin can steal them!' Klarak
ordered, forgetting his place in the magnitude of the
fear growing inside him. He shot an apologetic look
at King Logan. The king waved aside his remorse and
repeated the engineer's orders to Thane Erkii.

'Why the need for haste?' wondered Guildmaster
Thori.

'Because I was right to doubt my sabotage was enough
to destroy the Doomsphere,' Klarak told him. 'It was a
design flaw that caused the machine to destroy itself.
The steel plating wasn't tough enough to contain the
energies of the Doomsphere as it started to power-up.'

Klarak slammed his fist against the table, knocking
over some of the iron statues. 'That is why Ikit Claw has
come here! He means to make another Doomsphere
and this time he intends to use a tougher metal to contain it.

'He's come here for my barazhunk!'

THE TUNNELS OF Bonestash were in turmoil. The air
reeked of blood and musk, but beneath these there
was the tang of warpstone, a scent that had not been
quite so prominent the last time Thanquol had passed
through the warren. Ratmen scurried about in confused packs, squeaking their agitation at anyone and
anything that came too close to them. Clan Skryre

skirmishers, heavy warplock pistols gripped in their paws, kept vigil at the mouth of every tunnel. Skaven bodies were scattered through the rat-runs, some of them scorched by what had obviously been an application of warp-lightning, others lying with their skulls shattered by warpstone bullets.

It gave Thanquol pause to return to such confusion. Unrest meant uncertainty, and that was the last thing any skaven wanted to walk into. Briefly he thought about simply turning around and making his way back to Skavenblight without putting in an appearance at Bonestash. He lashed his tail in annoyance at the idea of retreating before he found out what was going on. Besides, he now had the Hand of Vecteek. With that artefact in his possession, he was more than a match for anything Ikit Claw or Rikkit Snapfang could throw at him.

He patted the breast of his robe, ensuring that the artefact was still where he'd hidden it. Yes, it was still there, clammy and cold. Thanquol tugged at his whiskers. Did he dare use its power? He was still mindful of the maniacal madness that had settled upon Skraekual. If there was some curse on the relic, he certainly didn't want to risk bringing it down upon himself. Then again, he didn't have to actually use the Hand to browbeat the other skaven. He could merely threaten to use it to get them in line.

Pleased with this train of thought, Thanquol strode boldly through the tunnels, shoving aside those ratmen too slow to get out of his way. Boneripper dutifully followed in Thanquol's wake, the rat-ogre's damaged mechanics venting steam at every step. Squeals of protest and pain wailed as the steam scalded some of the closely-packed ratmen. Boneripper's gait displayed an almost tipsy quality as its rattled cognisance struggled to regain its centre of balance. The brute's battle with Skraekual had left its marks.

Two Clan Skryre skirmishers stepped out into the mouth of the tunnel, moving to block the passage. Thanquol simply glared at the two skaven until they bobbed their heads in a suitably subservient manner.

'Where is the Claw?' Thanquol demanded, baring his fangs in a threatening display.

'Chief Warlock Ikit Claw makes big-big squeak-speak with Clan Mors,' one of the skirmishers answered.

Given the state of things, it made sense that Ikit Claw would be trying to coordinate with Rikkit Snapfang to restore order in Bonestash. Thanquol wondered what had caused the breakdown. Likely some sort of dwarf attack, one that threatened the warren itself. Again, the impulse to flee coursed through his mind. Fighting a bunch of dwarfs was something he wasn't eager to do, at least not without some substantial gain waiting for him at the end of the battle.

Still, it might be worth it to see the exact lay of the land first. Thanquol wouldn't want to scurry back to Skavenblight and then find out the skaven of Bonestash had managed to pull out some zero-hour victory.

Following the directions given to him by the skirmishers, Thanquol headed for the central storage burrow. It was an odd sort of place for the leaders of Bonestash to be holding a meeting, though Thanquol imagined it must be among the most secure caves in the entire warren. As he proceeded through the cramped tunnels, he began to notice an increase in the Clan Skryre guard posts. Armoured stormvermin were now in evidence too, racing through the tunnels in vicious packs, brutalising just about every skaven they came across.

Behind each gang of stormvermin, Thanquol saw mobs of shackled slaves, each slave laden down with a variety of foodstuffs and other supplies.

While he watched, a pack of brown-furred clanrats set upon the stormvermin, trying to get past them to the slaves and the supplies they carried. Two of the armoured ratmen were dragged down before the rest of them could fend off their attackers. Snarling and displaying their fangs, the defeated clanrats withdrew, but from their attitude, Thanquol felt they wouldn't go far before making another attempt to steal the supplies.

Disorder was quickly consuming the warren, upsetting the strict social hierarchy. The downtrodden masses were forgetting their obligations to their superiors. Worse, they were forgetting their fear of their superiors.

At least the vermin hadn't forgotten their fear of the Horned Rat. Thanquol went unmolested as he prowled the tunnels, rampaging clanrats and escaped skaven-slaves taking one sniff of the grey seer's scent and then quickly scrambling out of his way. Those who dared to stare at him for too long, Thanquol clubbed down with the head of his staff. If he once showed any sign of timidity, he knew the rioters would fall upon him like starving wolf-rats.

Deeper into the warren now, Thanquol could see how far the unrest had gone. He saw a pack of skaven-slaves, chains still looped about their necks, munching on a clutch of squealing grey meat while behind them a gang of clanrats were trying to herd brood-mothers away from their birthing nests. The immense, almost brainless female skaven would waddle out a few steps, then swing about and try to retreat back to the familiar smells of their nests. More than a few of the rustlers had been crushed beneath the flabby paws of the breeders, their comrades callously indifferent to the fate of the stricken thieves.

A group of piebald ratmen came scampering down the tunnel, their backs bent almost horizontal by the heavy sacks of mushrooms they carried. These were hotly pursued by a squealing mob demanding a share in the loot.

Another pack of brown-furred skaven emerged from one of the side-passages. These bore an array of weapons and wore bits of bloodied armour. At their head marched a skinny white-faced ratman who carried a long spear, the head of a black-furred stormvermin spitted upon its tip like some gruesome standard.

Thanquol skirted well clear of the marching brown-furs and their snarling leader. He ducked down a side-tunnel, then frowned as he discovered it was choked with shivering ratmen, scrawny little wretches too timid to take part in the general looting. Angrily, the grey seer ordered Boneripper forwards. The hulking rat-ogre seized two of the cowering skaven in its bony claws, crushing them in its steely grip.

Thanquol bared his fangs at the rest of the cringing ratmen. 'Out-out!' he growled. The skaven didn't need to be told twice, rushing past Thanquol and Boneripper in a terrified river of fur and musk. Pushing his way through the fleeing verminkin, the grey seer stalked down the tunnel. There was a scent of warpstone in the air. If Rikkit Snapfang was anywhere, the warlord would be with his warpstone, protecting it from the rampaging rat-packs that would steal it.

The scent led Thanquol into the vast cavern that had served Bonestash as a central supply cache. There were gangs of stormvermin posted everywhere, their halberds and swords at the ready, their armour stained with black skaven blood. Mobs of slaves, under the stern supervision of warriors, continued to emerge from the cavern with bundles of food. The sound of hammers, the smell of hot metal, the shriek of drills against stone, all of these drifted out to welcome the grey seer as he forced his way past the sentinels and into the cavern.

What he saw froze Thanquol in his tracks. The vast cavern was being emptied of its stores by a veritable army of slaves. While they hurried to clear the area, a second horde of slaves was bringing in a wild assortment of machinery the function of which he couldn't even begin to guess. Wooden scaffolds and gantries were being erected all about the cavern. Teams with warp-powered drills were gouging great pits in the floor while other skaven hurried about transforming the holes into crude forges and smelters.

At the very centre of the activity, Thanquol saw an immense ovoid machine, a great sphere of exposed gears and levers. At the heart of the machine was some sort of furnace from which billowed a quantity of green smoke. The grey seer felt his heart flutter in shock as he saw a pair of ratmen in strange metal coveralls shovelling warpstone into the furnace. He couldn't know how long they'd been feeding the machine, but just from a moment's observation, he saw them cast a small fortune into the flames.

The sight was such a wasteful outrage that Thanquol roared at the vandals, demanding them to stop. He lifted his staff, fully prepared to visit the wrath of the Horned One upon these heretic maggots.

'Grey Seer Thanquol,' the steel scratch of Ikit Claw's voice rose from across the cavern, arresting the sorcerer's spell. Thanquol shifted his gaze to find the Chief Warlock watching him. The Claw was situated beside one

of the forges. Thanquol was surprised to find the two
warlock-engineers who had deserted his patrol standing to either side of the Claw. On the ground between
them rested one of the strange metal beams Thanquol
had seen in the dwarf mines.

'Have you considered what would happen if you sent
a bolt of warp-lightning into such a large quantity of
warpstone?' Ikit Claw demanded. The Chief Warlock
made a sidewise motion with his metal claw, the scythe-
like digits snapping together with a grinding click.

Slowly, Thanquol lowered his staff. Truthfully, he
wasn't sure what would happen if a stray spark of warp-
lightning were to strike the cart of warpstone Ikit's
minions were feeding into the furnace. He also wasn't
willing to gamble that the Claw was bluffing when he
claimed that he did know.

'They-they   destroy-ruin   warpstone!'   Thanquol
shrieked, pointing angrily at the furnace-tenders.

Ikit Claw stepped away from the forge. His head
bobbed in a gloating manner. 'Yes-yes,' he hissed. 'The
essence of the warpstone feeds my machine. To create,
one must-must destroy! To destroy, one must-must create!' The warlock-engineer waved his monstrous claw
towards the smoking, shuddering machine. 'This will-
will be great-best invention!' he explained, his metal hiss
becoming slurred and debased in his excitement. 'Make-
force all skaven bow-grovel! Destroy-kill all-all enemies!'

Thanquol bruxed his fangs. There was the fanatical
gleam in Ikit's eyes that reminded him uncomfortably
of the plague monks of Clan Pestilens. The grey seer
patted the breast of his robe, reassured by the dead
touch of Vecteek's hand. For all of the Claw's postur-
ing, the tinker-rat's invention was just a toy beside the
power Thanquol had at his fingertips.

'Mad-crazy!' squealed Rikkit Snapfang. The warlord of Bonestash came scurrying to Thanquol's side, leaving the tangle of clawleaders supervising the removal of the warren's supplies. 'The Claw is mad-crazy!' he repeated. 'Speak-squeak that all must be moved! Speak-squeak that breeder-nest not big enough!'

In an instant, Thanquol saw why the warren had been thrown into such chaos. The removal of the food stores hadn't been an organised affair, but rather one hastily imposed upon Rikkit by the Clan Skryre skaven. Without proper preparation and warning, the inhabitants of the warren had been thrown into a panic, believing as Thanquol had that the dwarfs were on their way. They saw the removal of the supplies as a sign that their leaders were abandoning the warren – and them along with it! No wonder the ratmen were rioting, trying to take for themselves whatever they could lay their paws on.

Thanquol's lip curled in contempt for Clan Skryre's foolishness. Their tunnel vision had provoked disorder in the warren at a time when they would need every available skaven to fight the dwarfs! It was like being handed a gift from the Horned Rat himself! He could head back for Skavenblight and lay all of the blame on Ikit Claw, but now he could do so and know he would be backed by Clan Mors when he made his allegations!

'Great-mighty Grey Seer,' Rikkit was saying, exposing his throat in a gesture of submission to Thanquol's authority. 'Make-stop the Claw. Tell-say the Horned One will-will smite-smash him if he won't stop-stop.'

'Don't presume what the Horned One will do,' Thanquol upbraided Rikkit for his blasphemous presumption. The grey seer's eyes narrowed. He was planning on leaving Bonestash anyway, but now that Rikkit had begged for his help, he had to make a token gesture of publicly disapproving of Ikit Claw's antics. He'd spew out a bit of mumbo jumbo about the Horned Rat and curses and such, then scurry off in a huff. He chuckled, patting the morbid artefact once more. When he returned to Skavenblight, he'd force Seerlord Kritislik to elevate him to the rank of seerlord, maybe even replace Tisqueek. From there he'd be only one convenient accident from becoming the Supreme Seerlord and occupying Kritislik's seat on the Council of Thirteen.

Ikit Claw was still prancing about his invention, squeaking and babbling about it like a man-thing with a new pup. It was a revolting display, but at the same time made Thanquol uneasy. He dug out his snuff-box and took a little pinch to fortify himself against the coming unpleasantness.

'Mad-meat!' Thanquol snarled at the Chief Warlock. 'You've wrecked–'

Ikit Claw spun about, baring his fangs in a feral snarl. 'Mad? Mad? You squeak-say I am mad-mad?' The warlock-engineer chittered, his laughter sounding like a knife being sharpened. 'Yes-yes! Only mad-mad would make-bring the Doomsphere!'

Thanquol stood still, as rigid as a statue. Had the Chief Warlock really just said he was making another Doomsphere? The first had been built ages past by the sorcerer-engineers of Clan Skryre to crack open the roots of the mountains and annihilate the kingdoms of the dwarfs in one fell swoop. It hadn't worked out quite the way they had planned. While the dwarf kingdoms had suffered immense destruction, the rampant energies unleashed by the Doomsphere had rebounded against the skaven. Skavenblight had been cast into ruins, the plain around it flooded by the sea to become the Blighted Marshes. In the wake of this destruction, the despots who had ruled skavendom up until that point had been overthrown and replaced by the Grey Lords, predecessors of the current Lords of Decay.

The Doomsphere! Here was a weapon that could, as Ikit Claw claimed, exterminate the enemies of the Under-Empire and bring the bickering clans to their knees! From fear of the Doomsphere, all skavendom could be united, forced to set aside their petty intrigues and work towards the fulfilment of the Great Ascendancy! They would answer to one voice! One will! One vision! No longer would there be a Council of Thirteen, no Lords of Decay! The skaven would answer to the Horned Emperor!

The magnitude of the glorious vision sent an icy thrill of fear coursing through Thanquol's mind. Reason struggled against the enormity of such ambition, pleading with him that such thoughts were but the delusions conjured up by a bad batch of warp-snuff.

The grey seer grimaced. He did not need warp-snuff to tell him his destiny! His glory was foreordained by the Horned One! The very fact that he was here, present to witness the construction of Ikit Claw's weapon, and that he did so armed with the tools to seize control of it – these were incontrovertible signs of the Horned Rat's favour!

Yes! All skavendom would grovel before Thanquol the First! No, Thanquol the Only, for there would be no other Horned Emperor! By magic or through the arcane technology of Clan Skryre, Thanquol would ensure the Under-Empire would never be deprived of his selfless leadership. He'd use the Doomsphere and blast skavendom to smithereens first!

The grey seer stroked his whiskers and chuckled to himself. It didn't even matter if Ikit Claw's contraption worked or not. Simply the threat that it would work would be enough to bring the Council to its knees. The Hand of Vecteek! Bah! A worthless bit of carrion beside the awesome power the Claw now offered him!

'Feared Thanquol, you must stop-stop this insanity!' Rikkit Snapfang pleaded.

Thanquol glanced aside at the desperate warlord. 'Shut up,' he ordered before scurrying across the cavern to confer with the most noble and brilliant visionary Ikit Claw.

'You think-want make-make new-better Doom-sphere?' Thanquol asked, unable to keep a trickle of drool from dripping off his fangs.

Ikit Claw's eyes narrowed behind his metal mask. He scratched at his white fur with his good hand. 'This time-time all be good-perfect!' he hissed. 'No-none mistake-trouble!' The Chief Warlock reached down, lifting the stolen beam from the ground with his steel claw, holding it as effortlessly as an old mouse bone. 'Last experiment-test, housing-skin was weak-bad. Now use-take new-better dwarf-metal!'

That was the reason Ikit Claw had come to Bone-stash! One of the mercenaries Clan Mors had hired before must have been a spy for the Chief Warlock. The spy had discovered the dwarf-metal and reported it to his master. The Claw must have had most of his Doom-sphere already constructed, waiting only for a housing strong enough to restrain its immense energies until they were needed. That was what the Claw's minions had been dragging through the Underway – the par-tially assembled apparatus of his weapon!

'Thanquol stop-stop him!' Rikkit protested. 'He will ruin-wreck Bonestash!'

The grey seer swatted the grovelling warlord with his

staff. There were far bigger things to consider now than one idiot and his three-flea warren. Conquest of the Under-Empire, for a start. The complete genocide of the dwarf race for another.

Thanquol looked around the cavern, nodding in approval at the frantic pace of work. However, they could certainly do better with more labourers. 'Good-smart plan-plot,' the grey seer said, his words clipped and excited. With an effort he forced a bit of dignified reserve into his voice. He didn't want to seem too eager to exploit Ikit Claw's invention. He would need to adopt the poise of a wise old grey seer who saw an opportunity to better skavendom through the Claw's genius. That way the Claw wouldn't see it coming when fate caught up with him and left Thanquol with a free paw to claim the Doomsphere as his own.

'We need more workers,' Thanquol said. He pressed his claw against his breast, making a half-bow towards the metal-faced warlock-engineer. 'I shall go out into the tunnels and bring order among the Horned One's misguided children. I will make them see-scent that the Horned One expects them all to devote themselves to this grand endeavour. They will know that they can aspire to no greater thing than to help Mighty Ikit Claw the Great in his noble work.'

The grey seer bared his fangs in a vicious snarl. 'And any of the flea-bitten scratch-sniffers that don't listen to me will have their bones blasted into ash and fed to the whelps!'

CHAPTER XII

THANQUOL'S EYES GLEAMED as he stared out across the vast horde of skaven who had been assembled in the tunnels of Bonestash. Here was mustered the might of the warren, thousands of clanrats and skavenslaves, hundreds of armoured stormvermin. He could smell the odour of refined warpstone rising from the skirmishers of Clan Skryre. Warplock jezzails, Poison Wind globadiers, ratling guns and warpfire throwers. The malignant power of skavendom was spread before him, anxiously awaiting his every command.

He found the spectacle invigorating, even if it was but a taste of the authority he would soon possess. Once Ikit Claw completed his devilish machine, Thanquol would be able to bring all the Under-Empire to its knees. He wondered if it would be possible to employ the Doomsphere in a limited capacity. He'd use it to smash a few warrens for a start. Destroy the holdings of a few

lesser clans, perhaps even annihilate the city of one of
the greater clans, just to show that he made no distinc-
tion. Then he'd turn the Doomsphere loose against the
dwarfs. He'd break their miserable little kingdom like a
rotten tooth, bury the whole lot of the fur-faced scum
in their own halls. That would be a fair recompense for
all the trouble that ginger-furred maniac and his man-
pet had caused him. Never again would anyone have
the temerity to trifle with Thanquol the Tyrannical!

The grey seer sneezed, shaking his head as a stray
bit of warpsnuff was dislodged. He had to keep a clear
head now. It was important to ensure his wits were
sharp when the inevitable time came to separate Ikit
Claw from his new toy. And the Chief Warlock's head
from his shoulders.

The time of the Claw's usefulness would soon be
over. This raid would bring the warlock-engineer everything he needed to complete the Doomsphere. That
would be the moment when he would be at his most
vulnerable. While Ikit was gloating over his invention,
Thanquol would strike. Afterwards, he would say a
dwarf assassin had caught the Chief Warlock unawares.
He would be able to find plenty of witnesses to back
him up, especially once he controlled the Doomsphere.

Thanquol bruxed his fangs. He was being foolish.
Once he had the Doomsphere, he'd never need to
worry about what another skaven thought ever again.
He'd tell the vermin what to think! He'd tell them what
to say! The entire Under-Empire would be his plaything
to gnaw and abuse as he wished!

Wiping the drool from his mouth, Thanquol turned
and stared down at Fangleader Frothrend. Normally,
the black-furred stormvermin would have towered
over the grey seer, but out of deference to Thanquol's

dominance, he'd kept his posture appropriately hunched and submissive. Since the cowardly desertion of Warlord Rikkit Snapfang, Frothrend had become de facto leader of Bonestash. Or, at least as much of a leader as Ikit Claw's demands for labour and resources allowed. Frothrend probably had expected more power when he'd linked his ambition to that of Clan Skryre. His defection placed him in a bad spot if things didn't work out. Clan Mors would learn of his betrayal and seek retribution, sooner than later if Rikkit had scurried off to tattle, as Thanquol was fairly certain the craven flea had.

In the short term, however, it meant Frothrend was as loyal and dependable as any skaven could be. His only hope of escaping the wrath of Clan Mors was for Clan Skryre to protect him. Unless, of course, he fell under the protection of an even mightier skaven than Ikit Claw. Frothrend had a wonderfully over-developed sense of religious fervour. It stemmed from an incident when he'd been shot by a dwarf jezzail. The bullet had barely singed the fur on his breast, something Frothrend had taken as nothing less than the Horned Rat reaching up from the depths of the earth to protect him. Thanquol found the story puerile, as though the divinity had nothing better to do than bother about the pelt of some inconsequential fangleader. Still, it made Frothrend especially tractable where the grey seer was concerned.

'Are all my warriors here-here?' Thanquol asked.

'Yes-yes, Blessed Gnawer of Heaven,' Frothrend said. 'All-many skaven ready-wait for wisdom of Wise-holy Thanquol.'

The grey seer smoothed down his whiskers. Frothrend had a tongue for flattery that might yet serve him well.

It was pleasant to have underlings who were so vocal in their appreciation of their master's genius.

'Strong-smart Thanquol, greatest of grey seers,' crowed Twitchtail Burnpaw, his simpering voice rasping from behind the steel mask of his helmet, his beady little eyes gleaming from the shadows of his goggles. The warlock-engineer had been specifically appointed to obey Thanquol and execute the grey seer's orders without question. A situation which made his loyalty all the more suspect in Thanquol's eyes. Twitchtail had been one of Kaskitt's pack before Ikit Claw took over the expedition. There was probably little the weasel wouldn't do to get into the good graces of his new overlord. Thanquol would have to keep an eye on him, or at least have Boneripper ready to accidentally step on him.

'Most murderous one!' Twitchtail continued, deciding he needed to add more grovelling to his efforts to ingratiate himself. 'Clan Skryre stand-wait for your blessing-command. All dwarf-things burn-die for glory of the Horned One!' Twitchtail bobbed his head in enthusiasm as he spoke. Noting the surly look on Thanquol's face, he hastily added, 'and for the glory of most-dread Thanquol!'

Yes, Thanquol thought to himself, he'd have to arrange something nasty for Twitchtail before things went much farther. Any warlock-engineer who started to show a religious streak and expected a grey seer to take it at face value was simply too stupid to be allowed to breed.

Waving aside all thoughts of Twitchtail and any secret plans for treachery the Claw had given him, Thanquol stepped out from the little circle of chieftains and warlock-engineers to address the teeming masses of skaven soldiers packed in the tunnels. The ratmen were wonderfully simple, with a pup-like, unquestioning faith in the Horned Rat and his prophets. They were so utterly unlike the cynical, scheming skaven who ruled them. The faith of the ratmen in their god was the one joy in their miserable lives, the knowledge that one day they would scamper among the Horned Rat's burrows and feast from the cornucopia which he would provide them. Never again would they know hunger or fear once they became one with their god.

It was pathetic superstition, but one the grey seers encouraged. There were times – such as now – when such beliefs could be manipulated. The Horned One would understand. He liked nothing better than watching the feebleminded being exploited by those with craftier minds.

The ringing of a bell brought the squeaking horde of ratmen to silence. Thanquol shook his head, trying to clear the clamour from his ears. He glared balefully at Nikkrit Twistear, the brown-furred clanrat who had been chosen to bear the grey seer's standard. Affixed to the iron pole was a cage crafted from dwarf bones, a large bronze bell suspended inside. Nikkrit happily swung the standard from side to side, causing the clapper to bang against the insides of the bell. Thanquol couldn't decide if it was religious zeal or a simpleton's fascination with a new sound that made the clanrat attack his new duties with such over-exuberance, but he was certain he'd wring the scum's neck if he kept ringing the bell.

Delivering a savage thrust of his staff against Nikkrit's foot ended the problem. In the soothing silence that followed the clatter of the bell, Thanquol bestowed his pious wisdom upon the warriors who would follow his lead and precede him into battle against the hated dwarf-things.

'My bold-strong litter-kin!' Thanquol shouted, using a small measure of his magic to project his voice deep into the tunnels. 'Shame-disgrace has been the ruin-wreck of Bonestash! Too long have traitor-meat led the warriors of your warren astray! They have allowed the dwarf-things to oppress you and keep you from the great halls and tunnels that have been promise-gifted you by the Great Horned One! No more! Rikkit Snapfang is gone-fled and now the blessing of the Horned One is allowed to preen you once again. Coward-traitors are no more and once again the strong-strength of Clan Mors shall bring terror-fear to the dwarf-meat!'

Thanquol leaned on his staff, enjoying the rapt attention of his audience. He savoured the moment, rolling it over on his tongue like a choice bit of spiced toad-flesh. 'My bold-strong litter-kin! Thank-praise that you have been chosen to redeem the glory-might of Bonestash! We have borne-suffered much-much, but all is past-gone! Now there are no more traitor-meat among us! Now we march-fight against dwarf-meat! With the blessing of the Horned One, we shall overcome! We shall be victorious! Long-long have I wanted to tell the Horned One that Karak Angkul belongs to him. Now I squeak-say to the Horned One that my litter-kin have made it so!'

A roar of squeaking applause echoed through the tunnels, the chittering cacophony of an excited horde. Thanquol bruxed his fangs, pleased at this reception to his words. Ikit Claw might know a thing or two about slapping a few bits of metal together and calling it a weapon, but he knew nothing about how to stir the hearts of his fellow skaven and mould them into a living tide of destruction.

'My bold-strong litter-kin! The hard-long battle will be difficult. Many-many will sacrifice for the glory of the Horned One! Never will their scent be forgotten! Though the dwarf-things use fire and lightning, though they cut you down in your hundreds with steel and iron, you will-will overcome! Those who die-fall will be martyrs to skavendom! They will…'

Thanquol glanced aside in irritation as Twitchtail started tugging at his sleeve. The grey seer glared at him, ripping his robe from the warlock's hand.

'Maybe tell-say there's food up there,' Twitchtail suggested.

Thanquol scowled at the impertinent flunky. How dare the maggot suggest a grey seer needed prompting! He knew exactly what the warriors of Bonestash needed to hear! If Twitchtail thought he was going to sabotage Thanquol's speech…

Sniffing at the air, Thanquol detected the sour musk of fear. Straining his ears, he could hear the pad of feet retreating down the tunnels.

'Dwarf-things have much-much flesh-food!' Thanquol exclaimed. 'Much-much corn and grain and goats and ponies and chickens and crickets and octopuses and…' The grey seer put a bit more magic into his voice, letting it carry even further through the tunnels as his ears told him more skaven were starting to desert his command. 'All gift-gift from the Horned One! All for my litter-kin when they slay-kill coward-sick dwarf-things!' Thanquol's mind raced, picking about for a lie that would keep any more of the skaven from slinking away into the darkness. 'Clan Skryre make-make dwarf-water bad. Poison-sick all dwarf-things!'

Twitchtail grabbed at Thanquol's paw as he spoke. The grey seer could hear some excited squeaks again and there seemed to be a more positive smell now. He glanced at the warlock-engineer.

'We didn't...' Twitchtail started to whisper.

'Finish that sentence and you'll have the nasty pleasure of seeing what your intestines look like wrapped around your neck,' Thanquol threatened in a low hiss, the sound almost blasting Twitchtail off his feet. Thanquol rolled his eyes, having forgotten the magic magnifying the power of his voice.

Fortunately, it seemed none of the other ratmen understood the importance of his last words. Their attention was fixated upon the promise of food and loot and enemies already half dead from poisoned water.

Lifting his voice again, Thanquol made a hasty conclusion to his speech. 'Squeak-swear to the Horned Rat to be faith-loyal to Grey Seer Thanquol! Rise! Rise from tunnels and kill-slay! Kill-slay all dwarf-meat! Kill-kill! Kill-kill!'

Thanquol dissipated the spell he had conjured, revelling in the fury he had whipped up among the credulous idiots of Clan Mors. They were frothing at the mouth, goaded into a bloodthirsty frenzy by their priest-prophet. With such a horde, Thanquol would sweep aside the puny dwarf defenders, even if they hadn't really been poisoned.

It would just cost a few hundred extra skaven to get rid of them, but that was a sacrifice Thanquol was prepared to make. So long as he secured the dwarf-metal Ikit Claw needed to finish the Doomsphere, then there wasn't a skaven in Bonestash Thanquol wouldn't send into the enemy axes.

* * *

THE DWARFS WERE waiting when the skaven emerged from their tunnels to assault the Sixth Deep. On the way up from the bowels of the earth, the ratmen had encountered several of the unmanned sentry guns. Dozens of slaves had been lost before Twitchtail's engineers and skirmishers could blast the dwarfish contraptions apart with their own arcane weaponry. After his own encounter with a sentry gun, Thanquol was perfectly willing to let the warlock-engineers take all the risks. At this stage in the campaign, it would be disastrous for the army to be denied his leadership because of some reckless display of battlefield valour. Besides, he needed to husband his magic powers for the inevitable confrontation with Ikit Claw.

Entering into the Sixth Deep, however, the skaven found their progress blocked by more than a few automated guns. An entire dwarf army was waiting for them, rank upon rank of armoured warriors with broad shields and shiny axes. There were war engines too, a number of cannon and crude fire-throwers and ranks of dwarfish jezzails. A roaring mob of half-naked dwarfs with red fur and swirling tattoos caused Thanquol to spurt the musk of fear, his nose straining to detect the hated scent of the one-eyed madman who had dogged his track ever since Nuln.

It was with some relief that Thanquol failed to detect the scent of his hated foe among the trollslayers, but even so he found his gaze constantly wandering back to them, watching to make sure none of the crazed dwarfs had a human tagging along with him. He muttered a quiet prayer to the Horned One and reached beneath his robe to caress the Hand of Vecteek. The artefact made him feel a little safer.

A moment later, Thanquol's assurance faltered. He

caught the smell of magic rising from the dwarfs. Under his gaze, he saw the dwarfs lift a large altar up onto their shoulders. A grizzled old dwarf wearing scaly armour stood upon the altar, clutching an ornate hammer in his hands. An anvil rested before him on the altar, exuding an aura of malignance that made the grey seer cringe. Seldom had he ever seen such a dwarf, one who possessed an affinity with the world of sorcery. He gnashed his fangs at the thought that this was one of the high priests of the despicable bone-cult of the dwarf-things, the insane coven that made the dwarf-things lock their dead inside tombs to rot instead of employing their meat towards more practical uses.

A growl rattled through Thanquol's teeth. His nose twitched again. Treachery! He could scent it! An entire dwarf army waiting for him here, and one of their exceedingly rare bone-mages with them! It could only mean they had been warned, told of his impending advance! That back-stabbing rat Ikit Claw had never intended to share the Doomsphere with anyone! He'd betrayed Thanquol and his entire expedition to the dwarfs!

The dwarf throng bellowed a fierce war-cry, the sound rumbling through the great hall like thunder. 'Dwarfs got axes', or some such nonsense, but it sounded imposing enough to dampen some of the fighting spirit of Thanquol's horde. The grey seer glared at his minions.

'Fight-kill!' he snarled, trying to work them back into a frenzy. The unexpected sight of hundreds of dwarf warriors waiting for them had slowed the initial charge up into the Sixth Deep. The dwarf war-cry threatened to turn it into a rout. The crack-boom of a dwarf marksman's musket and the sudden gory death of a slave pawleader was the spark that almost sent the whole horde scurrying back into the mines.

'Fight-kill!' Thanquol screeched. Selecting a nearby ratman, he drew a portion of the Horned Rat's malignance into his body, unleashing the magic in a burst of destruction. His victim shrieked in agony, collapsing in a shrivelled husk, black smoke rising from the twitching carcass. 'I'll flay the fur from all coward-flesh!' the grey seer promised.

The threat had its desired effect. The skaven horde surged forwards, the scrawny slaves pushed across the great hall by the better fed and better armed clanrats behind them. Fangleader Frothrend and his brawny stormvermin began to march after the clanrats, but a sharp snarl from Thanquol brought him up sharp.

'Wait-see,' Thanquol hissed. 'Dwarf-things might have trick-trap. Let fool-meat spring it.' The grey seer glanced over at Twitchtail and the small teams of Clan Skryre skirmishers with him. 'Go help brave-strong war-pack,' he ordered the warlock-engineer.

Twitchtail blinked at him in shock and confusion. 'But you said…'

Fangs gleaming in a threatening smile, Thanquol pointed his claw at Twitchtail's nose. 'Are you coward-flesh?' the grey seer asked.

Twitchtail didn't need to be asked again. Turning about, he snapped orders to the other Clan Skryre ratmen, sending them scampering after the packs of clanrats. A lingering glance at Thanquol, a dejected look towards the tunnel leading back to the mines, and Twitchtail made a half-hearted effort to catch up to his skirmishers.

From the dwarf lines, the thunder of guns sounded. The dwarf marksmen with their ridiculously oversized jezzails sent a withering shower of bullets smacking into the front ranks of the skaven horde. The stink of gunpowder was quickly overwhelmed by the stench of fear-musk. Dead and wounded skavenslaves crumpled under the fusillade, their black blood staining the granite floor. Forced forwards by the crush of bodies behind them, the surviving slaves trampled their dead and dying kin.

Now the great hall shook with the bellow of dwarf cannons. The gunners loaded their artillery with chainshot, small iron cannonballs linked by lengths of stout chain. The result was a whirling scythe of death and destruction, cutting down dozens more of the weakened skavenslaves. The shrieks and squeaks of the scrawny ratmen rose to a sickening wail, some of them flinging themselves back upon the swords of the clanrats in their terror. Mercilessly, the clanrats cut down the unfortunate skaven, knowing that if the slaves fled they would lose the living shield which protected them.

Another volley from the dwarf jezzails and then the skaven mob was beset by the ferocity of their enemy's most hideous weapon. Situated at the centre of the dwarf line, an immense war engine had been biding its time, waiting for the ratkin to come in range. As the chittering horde continued to advance, the dwarf engineers sprang into action, hastily working the massive pump fitted to the rear of the barrel-shaped chassis of the weapon. From its dragon-shaped mouth, a sheet of dripping fire shot out across the onrushing skaven. Skavenslaves burst into flame as the liquid fire washed over them, transformed into living torches that squealed and howled in terrified agony.

This last attack did not go unanswered. Thanquol watched as Twitchtail popped open the mask of his helmet and stuffed something that looked suspiciously like warpstone into his mouth. An instant later, the warlock-engineer pointed his claw at the dwarf flame cannon. From his fingertips, a flickering stream of energy sizzled through the cavern. Several skaven were between Twitchtail and his target, each of them becoming a smouldering heap of fur and rags as the warp-lightning passed through them.

Whatever effect passing through a half-dozen skaven had, there was still enough potency in Twitchtail's spell to fulfil its purpose. The violent energies crackled about the dwarf weapon and its crew. The heavy armour of the dwarfs betrayed them, the metal acting as a conductor for the murderous magic. They fell to the ground, charred bones rolling free from their smoking armour.

The cannon itself blew apart, its volatile fuel ignited by Twitchtail's magic. Shards of bronze and iron, splinters of oak and wutroth were sent slicing through the massed troops of both sides. The thick armour of the dwarf warriors protected them from most of the shrapnel, but they were momentarily stunned by the blast.

The skaven fared more poorly, a score of slaves and clanrats injured in the explosion. The worst of the wounded were trampled underfoot by the chittering mass of ratmen following behind. The scent of dwarf blood in their noses, the skaven had found their courage and were now eager to rend and slay.

With a howl, the trollslayers obliged them. Scorning armour in their effort to court a glorious death, the slayers had suffered worse from the explosion than their fellows. Not one of them was unmarked by the shrapnel, but such was their ferocious determination that they paid their wounds little heed.

The ferocity of the skaven collided with the berserk

fury of the slayers. Steel axes hacked through verminous bodies while rusty swords and sharp fangs ripped at dwarfish flesh. The slayers cut down their foes, dropping them by fives and tens for each of their own that was brought low. The floor of the great hall became strewn with the carnage, the floor turning black from skaven blood.

EVEN THE MOST optimistic ratman could see numbers alone would not prevail against the crazed slayers. One dwarf, stabbed through the gut by a spear, a crooked sword thrust through his collar bone, continued to fight on, a maniacal laugh shuddering from his blood-flecked lips. Another, his hand pinching tight a throat torn by skaven fangs, had strength enough to batter his enemies with the haft of his axe. Dying, the slayers refused to quit the fray while a single spark of life still pulsed in their veins.

Thanquol was far from the most optimistic ratman. As he saw the slayers hacking their way through his troops, he imagined the crazed dwarfs routing his entire army. Such had happened before. Carefully he sniffed the air, trying again to detect the hateful scent of the one-eyed lunatic from Nuln.

Prudence was called for, and before things took a turn for the worse. Already the other dwarfs were rushing into the fight to support their beleaguered maniacs. Once a dwarf shield wall was supporting the slayers, they would be almost impossible to bring down. At least not without some help from the Horned Rat.

And maybe a sliver of warpstone for good measure.

Fangs crunched against the tiny shard of green stone, grinding it into dust. Thanquol swallowed the fiery residue, drawing its power into his veins. The grey seer's eyes burned with eldritch energies, his staff crackling with sorcerous power. He felt the intoxicating rush of magic flooding his mind.

What did he need to fear the dwarfs for? He was Thanquol the Magnificent, Great Pestilence of the Overworld! With a snap of his claws he could bring the whole dwarfhold crashing down, smash to bits every last one of the fur-faced vermin! He would sink the entire mountain into the steaming pit of Karak Angkul!

Thanquol forced himself to calm down. Degrees, he reminded himself, everything must be done by degrees. Caution was as important as power. A safe pelt was more important than a dead enemy.

Grinding his teeth against the power-crazed impulses still trying to tempt him, the grey seer forced his mind into focus. He could see the dwarf battle line, now hope-lessly mixed with that of his own troops. Twitchtail's skirmishers were starting to fire into the melee, lobbing globes of poison gas and discharging warpfire throwers into the swirling confusion of dwarfs and skaven, heed-less of which side was slaughtered by their weapons. It was the sort of ruthlessness that never failed to take the enemy by surprise and several dwarfs had already been felled by the ploy.

Thanquol intended to do better. Focusing the power burning through his body, the grey seer slapped his paws against the floor. He pictured the position of the slayers, evoking the might of the Horned Rat to burn them where they stood.

The great hall shook, trembling to its very founda-tions as Thanquol's magic coursed through its stones. A great conflagration erupted from beneath the battle line, a massive fire that immolated dwarf and skaven alike in a holocaust of annihilation. The sorcerous blaze expanded, consuming troops from both sides, throwing the dwarfs into confusion and spurring the skaven into retreat.

Angrily, Thanquol broke the spell, allowing the flame to dissipate. Where his spell had burned the granite had turned black, peppered with scores of charred corpses. He chittered with amusement as he heard the dwarf leaders trying to restore order to their panicked warriors. Then the grey seer's eyes narrowed with fury as he saw the horde of ratmen scampering towards his own position.

'Ring-ding the holy bell!' Thanquol snarled at Nikkrit, finding his standard bearer gripped by the same awed fascination as Frothrend's imbecile stormvermin. 'Rally-stop my army!' He added a few choice threats and was pleased when the discordant clatter of the bell began to sound. Spinning about, he snapped more orders at Frothrend. 'Form-make line-wall! No skaven leave-flee!'

Twitchtail and his skirmishers came scurrying ahead of the mob of clanrats, moving with surprising speed for all the bulk of their weaponry. The warlock-engineer uttered an angry snarl when he saw the line of stormvermin blocking his way.

'Move-move!' Twitchtail howled. 'Hurry-scurry before dwarf-things come!'

Frothrend cast an imploring gaze at Thanquol. The fangleader wasn't happy about the number of guns and bombs the skirmishers were carrying. Thanquol considered letting the more dangerous Clan Skryre ratmen past. Then he noticed the fresh loyalty-scars branded into Twitchtail's fur. As one of Kaskitt's former retinue, it was natural that Twitchtail had been compelled to receive Ikit Claw's brand. What Thanquol found less natural was that every Clan Skryre ratman clamouring to escape back into the mines also bore new brands.

They had all been Kaskitt's followers! That scheming offal Ikit Claw had tricked Thanquol! The maggot had never intended Thanquol to secure the dwarf-metal for him, he was using the grey seer as a distraction to keep the dwarfs' attention!

Thanquol lashed his tail, his blood boiling. He was getting very tired of being used as a decoy by every scheming crook-back he came across!

'Back-back!' Thanquol snarled. He would show the Claw! He'd break through the dwarfs, find the metal and then force the Chief Warlock to come begging…

'Fool-meat!' Twitchtail spat. At a gesture from the warlock-engineer, one of the skirmishers aimed his jezzail at the grey seer.

Reflexively, Thanquol ducked, clapping his paws across his face and shouting at his bodyguard. 'Boneripper! Burn-kill!'

The order brought caustic laughter from Twitchtail and the skirmishers. They knew the mechanical rat-ogre wasn't able to hurt any skaven from Clan Skryre. Their laughter vanished in squeaks of terror as Boneripper limped forwards and sent a gout of warpflame sizzling through the jezzail, turning him into a burning heap in the wink of an eye.

Thanquol grinned at the unexpected turn his thoughtless panic had taken. Gloatingly, he glared at the crestfallen Twitchtail. 'Get-take tinker-rats back to fight-fray!' he ordered. 'Make-take all clanrats too!' he added, seeing the mass of panicked warriors surging towards them.

Twitchtail glanced at the swarm of routed skaven and began to shiver. 'They won't stop-stop!' he said. The image of being trampled did wonders for the warlock-engineer's imagination. Shrieking orders to his own ratmen, Twitchtail set his two ratling guns into position and opened fire on the fleeing clanrats. The revolving guns churned out a fusillade that tore through the rat-kin, butchering them by the bushel.

Faced with a fresh source of gruesome death, the routed skaven turned about, flying back towards the dwarf lines straight into the ranks of their vengeful pursuers. Trapped between their cruel masters and their remorseless foes, the skaven became frenzied kill-ers, fighting with the viciousness of cornered rats. The abrupt shift from vanquished enemy to amok fighter caught the dwarfs unprepared. Without the time to form into a shield wall, several of the bearded warriors were dragged down and torn to ribbons by verminous claws and fangs.

'Keep them there,' Thanquol warned Twitchtail. A blast of lightning suddenly arced out from the dwarf lines, smashing into the warlock-engineer and hurl-ing him across the great hall. Thanquol cringed as he heard Twitchtail's bones snap when his body smashed against the far wall. The tang of magic was in the air and belatedly the grey seer recalled the bone-mage he had spotted among the dwarfs at the onset of the battle.

Well, the fool had chosen the wrong enemy to strike down with his craven attack! Now Thanquol would obliterate the dwarf before he even had time to know what was happening. The grey seer climbed onto Bone-ripper's leg, peering above the swirling combat to sight the altar and the old dwarf with the hammer. While he watched, the dwarf brought the rune-hammer crashing down on the anvil, sending little bolts of lightning flar-ing across the great hall.

A horrible purpose motivated the lightning, and each spark swept towards one another as it escaped the anvil, becoming a single lance of magic. Thanquol slipped around behind Boneripper as he saw the lightning speed in his direction. The bolt electrocuted one of Frothrend's warriors, melting the stormvermin's feet to the floor.

'Kill-slay dwarf-mage!' Thanquol howled at the late Twitchtail's comrades. They didn't seem too happy about the idea, but came around when Boneripper's warpfire projector took aim at them. Thanquol chortled as a barrage of fire, gas and warpstone bullets sailed into the melee. He was less pleased when he saw the chaotic barrage kill more skaven than dwarfs. He was still less amused when another bolt of lightning came sparking out from the anvil to shock a stormvermin uncomfortably near where he was standing.

It was all Ikit Claw's doing! That flea-spleen traitor-meat had planned this! He thought he would use the dwarfs to eliminate the one skaven cunning enough to save the Under-Empire from his megalomaniacal plan to threaten it with his hellish weapon! Well, now the claw would be on the other paw! Thanquol didn't want his Doomsphere now. He could reap just as much benefit by bringing evidence of the Claw's treachery back to Skavenblight. The Lords of Decay would hail him as the saviour of skavendom and the mightiest grey seer since Gnawdoom!

'Frothrend,' Thanquol snarled. 'I must report-tell this setback to Ikit Claw. I put-make you warlord in my absence. Kill-slay all dwarf-meat!'

The fangleader didn't seem too happy about his promotion, but knew better than to argue with Thanquol. Bowing his head in submission, Frothrend started snapping orders to his minions.

The grey seer didn't stick around long enough to listen in on Frothrend's plans. He had more important things to worry about, such as what Ikit Claw was up to and what sort of evidence he would need to steal to expose his sordid little scheme before the whole Council. Taking a firm grip on his staff, he ordered Boneripper to lead the way back into the mines.

Nikkrit watched the grey seer scurry into the darkness, then took one glance back at the battlefield. Still ringing his bell, the standard bearer scampered off in pursuit of his departed master.

CHAPTER XIII

THE SMELTHALL OF Karak Angkul was nestled at the core of the stronghold, its immensity stretching through the stronghold's Third and Fourth Deeps. Immense columns of stone, their surfaces plated in bronze, reared up from the granite floor to support the ceiling two hundred feet above. The floor, pock-marked by slag pits and cisterns, was covered in mosaics of red stone, depicting the life of the ancestor god Smednir the Shaper of Ore, showing him teaching the ancient dwarfs how to smelt iron and copper. Giant blast furnaces fed by enormous sets of bellows were arranged along the walls of the smelthall, each furnace connected by a clockwork conveying belt to the ore-heaps situated throughout the chamber. Towards the middle of the smelthall were the refining furnaces, monstrous coke-fed ovens in which ground ore would be further purified. A massive slaghearth stretched along one

corner, a low stone table upon which waste slag would
be re-smelted, a bed of charcoal blazing beneath it.
Reducing furnaces and orehearths were lined across
another wall, situated close to where the sand moulds
of the metal-casters would shape the molten lead or
silver into ingots.

Throughout the smelthall, clockwork conveying belts
of leather and tin deposited ore onto the oreheaps or
carried coke to the furnaces. Hooks and chains fitted
to mechanised pulleys swung from iron gantries and
stone causeways far overhead, creating weird draperies
of steel and bronze. Giant copper pipes brought water
down to the kilns while a fast-flowing culvert snaked
its way across the floor to remove waste. The shudder
of great steam-driven fans formed a perpetual susurrus
as the atmosphere within the smelthall was rotated and
fresh air was sucked down from the surface by fluted
vents.

Within the smelthall, the heat was tremendous, each
furnace and kiln burning with the fires of industry.
The quartz glowstones hanging from the pillars were
hardly a match for the hellish red light belching from
the chimneys of the furnaces and the mouths of the
ovens. Strange shadows flickered throughout the hall
as dwarfs from a dozen clans worked the raw ore of the
mines and recovered the precious metals locked within
the stone.

Around one of the small forges arrayed throughout
the smelthall, Klarak Bronzehammer and his assistants
worked feverishly to rework the beams of barazhunk
that had been recovered from the mines. The pounding
hammers of the dwarfs rang out as each of the beams
was slowly reshaped into a thin sheet of metal.

Only Kurgaz Brightfinger, the runesmith, did not

partake in the frenzied labour. His face pale, sweat beading upon his brow, the dwarf had his own task to perform. Seated on the floor, he employed a long rune-etched burin of gromril to engrave the still hot plates of barazhunk. Kurgaz worked in silence, his face drawn and pale, his breath barely stirring his body as he focused on his work. Fixated upon the rune he had studied in Runelord Morag's chambers, Kurgaz had no attention to spare for anything else. Time and again he attempted to recreate the magical symbol, time and again he failed, each time feeling a little more of his vitality drain away. It was no small thing to fail in the crafting of a Master Rune. Even to make the attempt was normally a matter of weeks of the most careful preparation. Kurgaz had been given only a few hours. Only the knowledge that Klarak desperately needed the rune-magic kept him at his work. With true dwarfish stubbornness, the only way he would accept defeat was when he collapsed from sheer exhaustion.

Klarak sympathised with his friend. He knew how great was the effort he was demanding of Kurgaz. When he'd originally set the runesmith to learning that particular Master Rune, he'd thought he'd have more time before ever needing it. Now, however, the presence of Ikit Claw and the threat of the Doomsphere was too great to brook any delay. It might mean the salvation of the entire Worlds Edge Mountains.

'You shouldn't push him like that,' Kimril observed, a touch of disapproval in the physician's voice. 'The strain on him is too great to maintain. Something must give way.'

Klarak nodded. 'I know,' he said, 'but Kurgaz is the only chance. None of the other runesmiths would dare even try and Runelord Morag would insist on a

month of rituals and preparation before going ahead.
By then it would be too late. I wanted this magic for my
own inventions. Now I need it for Ikit Claw's fiendish
machine.'

'How can you be so certain the ratkin will come?'
Azram objected as he brought his hammer cracking
down against the heated surface of the barazhunk
beam stretched across his anvil. 'If the beast is as smart
as he seems, now that he's stolen some barazhunk, he
could study it and make his own.'

'You forget skaven nature,' Klarak said. 'They are all
thaggoraki, thieves who will never make something for
themselves if they can steal it from someone else. The
Claw will come for the rest of the barazhunk. It's our
job to be ready for him when he does.'

Klarak shifted his gaze to study the complicated instrument set close by his anvil. It was a curious arrangement
of tubes and rods, a variant upon the water clocks still
employed by the most tradition-minded dwarfs. This
clepsydra, however, was not designed to measure time.
Klarak had made several changes to its workings, the
most important of which were the copper stakes which
bolted the machine to the floor. Sunk to a depth of several feet, the stakes acted as divining rods, feeling the
vibrations in the earth below. The glass tubes would act
as a gauge for these vibrations, giving a visual impression of their magnitude and intensity.

A gang of dwarfs marched from one of the other furnaces, depositing a load of barazhunk sheets upon the
growing stack at one side of the refining furnace. They
saluted Klarak as they passed. The engineer had warned
the workers of the dangers he expected, insisting that
only volunteers remain behind to help reshape the
alloy. Not a single one of the metalworkers had been

lacking the courage to stay and help. It had taken King Logan and a formal edict to thin their ranks, leaving only a solid core behind. The metalworkers were willing to act as bait, but King Logan wasn't quite so eager to risk the industry of his stronghold just to spring a trap.

Klarak reflected upon the danger of his plan. If anything went wrong, the consequences could be dire. The smelthall had been chosen only after careful deliberation; the size and scope of its furnaces and the heavy smell of their smoke was an important aspect of Klarak's plan. The skaven were ruled by their noses, scent was their key sense, far more vital to them than either sight or sound. Deprived of that sense, the ratkin would be disorientated. Hopefully they'd be confused enough to miss the trap until it was too late.

There was a contingency, however – if Kurgaz could just manage to inscribe the Master Rune upon one of the barazhunk plates. In that event, should the skaven make off with their prize, there would still be a chance to stop them.

'Looks like we have word at last,' Thorlek observed, turning away from his anvil to watch as a wiry dwarf in the livery of a royal messenger came rushing across the smelthall. The runner dashed straight towards Klarak, bowing his head when he came to a halt.

'I bear tidings from His Highness King Logan Longblade, Sovereign of Karak Angkul and all its domains,' the messenger announced.

'Less of the jewellery-talk and more information,' growled Horgar, more interested in hearing the tidings the messenger bore rather than who'd sent them.

The messenger flushed, but kept facing Klarak. 'The ratkin have broken into the Sixth Deep,' he reported.

'Klarak told you they'd be hitting the Sixth Deep again when the sentry guns in the mines started to fail,' Thorlek said. Though it was true that the destruction of the sentry guns had given enough warning for the dwarf army to assemble in the threatened section of the Sixth Deep, it annoyed the ranger to maintain the fallacy that the guns themselves had malfunctioned. There was only so much patronising of Guildmaster Thori's pride he was willing to suffer.

'The ratkin host is being led by one of their horned sorcerers,' the messenger continued.

Klarak's expression became grim. The horned ratman was likely Grey Seer Thanquol, a creature he had been warned posed a tremendous threat to Karak Angkul. Against this menace, he had to balance the danger of Ikit Claw and the Doomsphere. There was no question which evil was the greater. Even if Karak Angkul was lost, Ikit Claw had to be stopped.

'Can Thane Arngar stop them?' the engineer asked.

The messenger nodded. 'The king has sent reinforcements to bolster Thane Arngar's command. Runelord Morag is with them and has stated he will make every effort to destroy this creature called Thanquol.'

'Then may the ancestors smile on their battle and may their axes strike true,' Klarak said, but not without a note of uncertainty in his voice. Had he been wrong? Was Thanquol truly the greater menace? If Ikit Claw didn't make an attempt to steal the rest of his baraz-hunk, then what foolishness would it be to stay here while the real battle was being fought hundreds of feet below?

'King Logan requests the use of any troops you can spare,' the messenger said. 'He fears this is but the opening skirmish in a concentrated attack to seize the Sixth Deep.'

An ugly feeling began to grow in Klarak's gut. 'Or it could be a diversion,' he said, convinced of his theory as he made it. 'Tell His Highness that I am sorry, but I still need every warrior.'

The messenger made a deep bow, then hastened to bear Klarak's answer to King Logan.

'Don't think the king is going to like you telling him no,' Kimril observed.

'Aye,' agreed Horgar. 'Maybe we should be down there in the Sixth Deep smashing skaven skulls!'

A sharp bellow rose from the nearest of the slag pits. The top of the pit was abruptly thrown back, revealing itself to be nothing but a piece of canvas with lumps of charred ore glued to it. In the now exposed hole, five armoured dwarfs now stood revealed. A sixth dwarf scrambled up the ladder leading down into the pit. Unlike his companions, he wore no armour, only a pair of leather breeks and iron-shod boots. Swirling tattoos stained his naked torso, forming complex patterns within which was depicted the Rune of Grimnir. The dwarf's beard had been stained a bright orange, the same colour as the long crest into which his hair had been shaved.

There was fury on Mordin Grimstone's face as he stalked towards Klarak Bronzehammer. 'The Sixth Deep!' the slayer roared. 'That vermin Thanquol is attacking the Sixth Deep!'

Horgar shifted about, moving to place himself between Mordin and his master. Sternly, Klarak waved his bodyguard aside. The engineer stared into Mordin's hostile gaze. The dwarf had taken the slayer oath almost the moment he'd left the war council, vowing to destroy Grey Seer Thanquol and atone for his brother's death. To the bitter Mordin, nothing else would wash away the disgrace which held him in its grip.

'You insisted on joining us,' Klarak told the enraged slayer.

Mordin's expression became livid, his hand closing about one of the hand axes tucked beneath his belt. 'I came because you told me the greatest danger would be found here! Only it isn't! Thanquol is down there and I'm up here!' The slayer ripped the axe from his belt and threw his arm back as though to deliver a blow with the keen-edged blade.

Klarak didn't move, just continued to gaze into the slayer's eyes. 'The danger is the greatest here,' he said. 'In that, I told you no lie. What the ratkin want is here and they will come for it.' The engineer shifted his gaze, watching the clepsydra.

'I don't care about the ratkin!' Mordin swore. 'I only care about avenging my brother!'

Returning his gaze to Mordin, Klarak's face became bitter. 'Then you are the most wretched zaki who ever took up the slayer oath,' he swore, the fury of his voice taking his assistants by surprise and shocking even Mordin. 'If the ratkin succeed here, then the entire Karak Ankor may be threatened! Every dwarf, woman and child in the Worlds Edge Mountains! But all Mordin Grimstone can think about is his own shame! Where is the sense of duty that led you to Karak Angkul to warn us of the skaven threat? Where is the dwarf who understood that loyalty to his people comes before loyalty to his pride?'

Slowly, the fire ebbed in Mordin's eyes. Gradually, the slayer lowered his axe.

'Do not fear,' Klarak said, his tone becoming sympathetic. 'You may yet get your chance. The ratkin do not fight honourably. Just because they have sent some of their horde into the Sixth Deep doesn't mean that's where they intend to make the real fight.'

'A diversion?' Mordin grumbled, suspicion in his eyes.

'I'm certain of it,' Klarak replied. He pointed to the clepsydra. The water in the tubes was visibly agitated now, indicating powerful and persistent vibrations in the ground below.

A vicious grin spread across Mordin's face. The dwarf ripped a hair from his crest and split it across the edge of his axe.

'Best get back to your place,' Klarak advised. 'Even the ratkin know enough to be suspicious if they see a slayer working over an anvil.'

Mordin nodded. 'All right,' he said, 'but remember: Thanquol is mine!' The slayer turned on his heel and quickly sprinted back to the slag-pit, hooking the edge of the canvas with his axe as he jumped down into the hole. A moment later, the camouflage was tugged back into place.

'Valaya!' exclaimed Kimril. 'I thought he was going to split your skull! You must be as crazy as he is to talk to a slayer like that!'

'I just encouraged him to keep things in perspective,' Klarak said, shrugging off the concern of his friends. 'Whatever oaths he has made, Mordin Grimstone is still a dwarf. Just because he's shaved his head doesn't mean he's forgotten his duty.'

'Still, to take such a chance...'

'Enough,' Klarak decided, waving his hand. 'We have more important things to worry about.' He watched as the violence being exhibited by the clepsydra continued to increase.

'Any moment now we'll be receiving guests,' the engineer warned. 'Let's make sure we're ready for them.'

* * *

STONE SHRIEKED AS parts of the smelthall's floor began to melt. Wisps of foul-smelling smoke rose from the melting stones and an unholy green glow began to shine through the fractured granite. The dwarfs at the furnaces drew back in alarm, shifting a little closer to where each had secreted his own weapon.

'Steady!' Klarak bellowed, his voice carrying above the sound of crumbling stone. The engineer gave only passing notice to the glowing craters forming in the floor, his eyes locked on the still violently quivering clepsydra. 'Hold your places!'

From one of the glowing craters, a pair of chittering skaven emerged, the foremost holding a weird pronged instrument not unlike an oversized tuning fork bolted to the end of a long spear. Between the prongs of the fork, a fist-sized chunk of glowing black rock had been fitted, dark energies sizzling about its carved surface. Heavy hoses of ratgut and leather ran from the oversized spear, connecting it to the massive generator lashed to the back of the second ratman. Both skaven snickered with amusement as they saw the stunned dwarfs.

From the pit the warp-grinder had gouged from the floor, a rabble of verminous creatures sprang, loathsome skavenslaves, their skinny bodies covered in scars and sores, crude spears and rusty knives clenched in their paws. They sprang into the smelthall with an eagerness born of terror. Before the last of them had cleared the hole, there came a groaning rumble and the pit collapsed in upon itself. The skaven did not twitch as the squeals of their trapped kin rose from the rubble. Instead they flung themselves towards the nearest dwarfs, a slavering pack of fangs and claws.

Other warp-grinders cut their way into the smelthall, disgorging scores of emaciated skavenslaves into the chamber. The dwarfs at the furnaces dived for their weapons, drawing a wild array of axes and hammers. The sight of weapons made the slaves hesitate, forcing the warp-grinders to goad them onwards with snarled threats.

'Steady!' Klarak called out once more, still watching the clepsydra. Now the water was sloshing about so violently that it had almost been whipped into foam. There was no need to explain his call for patience, however. Every dwarf in the smelthall could feel the quiver in the earth, not unlike the tremor of an earthquake.

The dwarfs at the furnaces were now beset by the slavering skavenslaves. While the ratmen engaged the metalworkers, dying upon their vengeful hammers, the warp-grinders circled around the melee, seeking to assault their enemies from the rear.

'Cowardly cheese-thieves!' Thorlek snarled. The ranger drew one of the steam pistols Klarak had armed him with. The engineer set a restraining hand on his friend.

'We can't interfere,' he said, the words bitter as wormwood in his mouth. 'We can't do anything that will make the ratkin suspect a trap. They mustn't warn their master.'

One of the warp-grinders successfully completed its circuit of the melee. The strange machine whirred into life, a nimbus of green light gathering about the stone fitted between the forks. As the energy gathered, it was drawn out by the forks, crackling and sparking in a blaze of electricity. Chittering with sadistic amusement, the warp-grinder's wielder thrust it towards the back of a dwarf. The victim cried out, his scream wailing through the smelthall. He crumpled to the floor, a ragged hole melted through his torso.

'Klarak!' shouted Horgar. 'We have to stop them!'

The engineer shook his head. 'We'll get our chance,' he said, pointing to a pack of slaves charging towards their own position. 'But until their chief arrives, no shooting. We don't want them scurrying away and warning the rest.'

The injunction was hardly popular among Klarak's bold-hearted comrades, but each of them understood the necessity of his warning. Firming their holds upon their weapons, the dwarfs made ready to meet the enemy.

'Keep them off Kurgaz,' Klarak said, gesturing with his thumb at the runesmith. Unlike the rest of them, Kurgaz had made no move to arm himself. Instead, he was still set upon his task of engraving.

'No thaggoraki is getting past me,' Thorlek swore.

'Bad as you smell, they'll probably take you for one of their own,' Horgar laughed.

Thorlek might have replied to the insult, but at that moment he was too busy separating a ratman from his head. Other slaves flung themselves at the rest of the dwarfs. Horgar smashed one down with his hammer, cracking its skull in a dozen places, then broke the spine of a second in his metal hand. Azram slashed the legs out from under another ratman, breaking its neck with a kick of his boot when the maimed skaven tried to bite him. Kimril took his walking stick, breaking it open to reveal a slender gromril blade. Plying the stick like a Cathayan spear-fighter, he dropped three more of the scrabbling ratmen.

Klarak Bronzehammer didn't wait for the skaven to come to him. Vaulting over his anvil, he pounced upon the oncoming pack like an enraged lion. His strong fists smashed out, cracking snouts and breaking ribs. The engineer's objective wasn't to kill the ratmen, but simply to debilitate them as quickly as possible. He rushed past his crippled enemies, intent upon the warp-grinder crew beyond them. Already the warp-grinder was trying to circle the combatants, to come upon the rear of the fray.

The crew saw Klarak as the engineer broke the leg of the last slave standing between himself and the warp-grinder. Frantically, the ratmen activated their weapon, setting energy crackling from the stone and dancing about the prongs of the fork.

Before they could fire, Klarak threw himself into a long dive, his momentum carrying him past the two skaven. He turned his dive into a roll, tumbling past the warp-grinder. As he came back to his feet, the dwarf sprinted back towards his comrades.

Laughing wickedly, the ratman operating the warp-grinder raised his weapon, prepared to unleash the corrosive energy against his fleeing enemy. A squeal of terror from the skaven behind him, the one lumbered down by the heavy generator, brought the other ratman up short. Turning his head, he saw arcs of green lightning crackling about his comrade's body and the ratman frantically trying to adjust the dials on the sides of the generator. A torn hose flopped obscenely from the side of the generator. The operator stared stupidly at his now inert warp-grinder, then squeaked in horror as he understood what had happened. In diving past the warp-grinder, Klarak had ripped the hose conducting energy into the weapon. With nowhere to go, all the energy was building up inside the generator!

The warp-grinder operator turned to flee almost the same instant the damaged generator decided to explode.

* * *

THE DESTRUCTION OF the warp-grinder sent the last surviving slaves attacking Klarak's comrades scurrying away in retreat. The ratmen stumbled and slid as the floor continued to quake. Suddenly, a green glow began to rise from the ground a few hundred yards away. The dwarfs watched with a feeling of dread as the stone started to melt, creating a pit easily ten times as vast as the holes carved out by the warp-grinders.

Across the smelthall, the embattled metalworkers suddenly found themselves alone. With their master coming, the skaven withdrew, forming into a tight knot of squeaking flesh that eagerly cheered the underlord whose brand they bore.

The shriek of dying stone shuddered the walls of the smelthall, setting chains swaying and gantries rocking. A great stream of foul smoke billowed upwards as a giant metal snout erupted from the floor. Shaped like some immense gemstone, the metal snout crackled with the same green energy as the much smaller warp-grinders. To the destructive energies had been added a cruel mechanical augmentation. Rings of metal teeth circled the snout, rotating in opposing directions at an almost blinding speed. A pair of mammoth-sized ratmen pushed the immense drill upwards, its wheels clattering on the jagged lip of the hole. The rat-ogres had suffered horribly under the ghastly influence of arcane science: each of them had had their arms replaced with metal hooks that had been bolted into the back of the drill and crude engines had been inserted into their bellies, glowing with the eerie green resonance of warpstone. Rusty smokestacks were stapled to their backs, belching the fumes from their mechanical stomachs. A ghastly ratman wearing an insect-like mask sat on a little chair between the rat-ogres, throwing levers and turning wheels as he directed the drill onwards.

Behind the drill, a swarm of ratmen came scrambling into the smelthall. These weren't naked slaves but armed clanrats, each skaven bearing a notched sword or spiked mace in his paw. Upon their shields, the symbol of Clan Skryre shone and the fur of each ratman bore the brand of Ikit Claw. Small packs of strangely garbed ratmen scurried after the clanrats, wearing heavy coats of ratgut and leather, their faces enclosed within strange bug-like masks, their paws hugging big ratskin bags to their chests.

Bringing up the rear of the invasion were still more weirdly equipped skaven, some of them bearing oversized multi-barrelled guns while others lugged bulky contrivances that looked like the nozzles of pressure hoses. Still others of the weapon specialists were carting huge brass tubes upon their backs and wearing the insect-like face-masks. As the specialists fanned out, moving to support the onrushing clanrats, a small cadre of robed ratmen appeared, their bodies draped with belts and wires, their backs fitted with metal harnesses from which mechanical dendrites arched menacingly over their shoulders.

It was among the warlock-engineers that Klarak saw the foe he had been hoping to see. Ikit Claw had changed his armour since their last encounter, replacing and upgrading the iron frame which supported his withered body. The Chief Warlock had refined the monstrous claw that enclosed his shrivelled left arm, had made further cog-driven enhancements to his ruined body, but for all of his changes, Klarak recognised his foe. There was no mistaking the aura of ruthless evil the ratman exuded, no forgetting the insane ambition which shone in his eyes.

Ikit Claw recognised his enemy as well, locking eyes with Klarak across the immense sprawl of the hall. Hatred burned in the skaven's gaze, his scarred lips peeling back to expose his fangs. Uttering a sharp snarl, the Chief Warlock gestured with the halberd he carried. In response, the skaven troops gave voice to a savage cry. The next moment, the entire horde was swarming over the smelthall, converging upon the few clutches of defenders still standing.

Klarak grinned back at Ikit Claw. Reaching to his belt, the engineer drew a fat-mouthed pistol. He saw the Chief Warlock instinctively flinch as the dwarf's weapon came free of its holster. A coward like all of his breed, Klarak thought, though he doubted any bullet could pierce the iron skin the ratman had forged for himself. It didn't matter, the shot within his dragon-belcher wasn't for the Claw.

'Now!' Klarak roared, holding his pistol high and squeezing the trigger. A flare of fire exploded from the weapon, streaking high into the vastness of the smelt-hall before bursting in a violent flare of brilliant light. The most craven of the ratkin shrieked in fear at the sudden illumination. A moment later they had something to really fear.

From hiding places on the catwalks and gangways, scores of dwarfs appeared. Each of the hidden warriors bore a heavy crossbow or long-barrelled handgun. Mixed among them were fat-bellied engineers carrying heavy satchels filled with iron-skinned bombs. Guild-master Thori had not approved of Klarak's trap, but his disagreement had been overruled by King Logan, forcing the Engineers' Guild to cooperate with their rebellious colleague. Whatever their feelings, however, the engineers would play their part in the coming battle.

Throughout the smelthall, the tops of the camouflaged slag pits were thrown back and dozens of armoured dwarf warriors burst onto the scene. The onrushing skaven recoiled as they saw the grim-faced dwarfs suddenly appear, their superstitious minds finding the manifestation as inexplicable as the conjuration of a sorcerer. The snarling clanrats faltered, no longer quite so eager to come to grips with their enemies. Happy to ply their swords in a massacre, they were less thrilled about engaging in a real fight.

First blood was still struck by the skaven. Snapping orders to the ratmen closest to him, Ikit Claw knew the only way to stir the quailing courage of his troops was to get the smell of blood in the air. Fiercely, the Chief Warlock raised his halberd overhead, pointing it at the armed dwarfs above. Energy crackled about the blade of the ratman's weapon, soaking up the light all around it. A bolt of dark lightning shot from the blade, hitting the iron walkway above.

Storm Daemon, the Chief Warlock had named his weapon, endowing it with a hideous magic and then augmenting its destructive powers with a warp generator fitted just below the blade. The black lightning exploded across the iron gantry, crackling through the bodies of the dwarf crossbowmen positioned there, the metal acting as a conductor for the malignant sorcery. The stricken dwarfs didn't have time to scream, only to twitch and writhe under Storm Daemon's assault. After an agonising moment, the scorched bodies came hurtling downwards, their corrupted flesh splashing across the smelthall as they struck the granite floor.

Vengeful dwarfs unleashed a volley from their crossbows and thunderer handguns. Bolts crunched down into the skulls of ratmen, bullets from the thunderers ripped through skaven bodies. Engineers lit their bombs, dropping the explosives down into the massed ratkin. With the precision of their craft, the engineers fitted short fuses to the bombs, causing them to detonate above the heads of their enemies and send a withering burst of shrapnel slashing into the verminous bodies.

Ikit Claw's shrieked commands echoed above the turmoil. Mobs of sword-armed clanrats converged upon the metalworkers and the dwarf warriors from the slag pits. Teams of jezzails turned their guns upon the catwalks, sniping at the dwarfs shooting down at them. Warpfire throwers played their ghastly flames across the lowest of the catwalks, incinerating every dwarf within reach of their fire.

It was the ghastly ratmen with the hollow brass tubes lashed to their backs who took the most murderous toll on the dwarf marksmen. There was a reason the specialists were garbed in the same protective gear as the bomb-tossing globadiers, for it was the same toxic Poison Wind which they employed. Loading the brass tubes with the deadly glass spheres, the mortar teams lobbed certain death over the battlefield. The Poison Wind globes shattered against stone causeways, unleashing clouds of toxic gas that slowly drifted downwards. Even when the mortars missed their original targets, the gas would often settle upon dwarfs on a lower walkway, striking them down without warning.

The skaven had walked into the dwarfs' trap. The question now was whether they would stay trapped.

KLARAK AND HIS comrades drew their steam pistols. Ahead of them, a horde of snarling ratmen came charging towards their position, hate and bloodlust blazing in their eyes. Five dwarfs against dozens of ravenous clanrat warriors, odds that would test the valour of any human knight. Yet the defenders unflinchingly faced the onrushing tide.

At Klarak's signal, the dwarfs unleashed a volley from their steam pistols. The repeating weapons sent a fusillade of lead punching into the rodents, spilling their mangled bodies to the floor. Taking more careful aim, Klarak targeted the masked skaven lurking about the fringes of the ratpack. With eerie precision, the engineer sent a round smashing into the heavy satchel of gas bombs one of the globadiers was carrying.

Instantly, the globadier vanished in a cloud of green gas that billowed outwards to claim the nearest ratmen. But Klarak did not wait to see the results of his shot. Without hesitating, he spun around, clipping a second globadier, one that had been braced to hurl a gas bomb at the engineer. The second globadier flopped to the ground, shrieking as the gas bomb he had been holding shattered against the granite floor. The corrosive Poison Wind spread like a low-hanging mist, searing the legs of the clanrats. Some of the skaven unwisely stopped to discover the source of their hurt, dropping as the toxic fumes burned their way into their bloodstream. Others shrieked and leaped, scrambling over dying comrades in their frantic efforts to get clear of the gas.

A lone dwarf charged into the panicked skaven, his axes cleaving limbs and smashing ribs at every turn. Bitter laughter bellowed as Mordin Grimstone slaughtered his foes, cutting them down without mercy. The slayer's body dripped with the black gore of skaven blood and viscera, his axes slick with the slime of his enemies. Ten, fifteen, twenty of the ratkin fell before his crazed onslaught, but it was not enough to slake his lust for vengeance, to drown the guilt that twisted his heart.

'He'll be killed,' grumbled Thorlek. The ranger holstered his pistol, intending to join the berserk slayer in his crazed charge, but Horgar's steely grip stopped him.

'Even for you, that's stupid,' the hammerer scolded. 'Mordin's looking for a glorious death. He doesn't need any company.'

Thorlek twisted free, scowling at his friend. 'He might not need it, but he'll have it!' the ranger vowed. 'No dwarf, even a slayer, should have his bones gnawed by the ratkin!'

Horgar shook his head, but he holstered his own pistol and unfastened the massive hammer tethered to his steam-powered harness. He glanced aside at Klarak. 'How about it?' he asked.

'We stay our ground as long as we can,' Klarak answered. He let his exhausted steam pistol drop to the floor and drew a fresh weapon from his belt. He was looking past the reeling clanrats, watching as a fresh horde of skaven emerged from Ikit's tunnel. These were no fighters, but instead were a rabble of naked skavenslaves. Overseers with barbed whips lashed the wretches mercilessly, driving them towards the furnaces where some of the barazhunk beams were still waiting to be reshaped. Several of the slaves fell as crossbows and thunderers picked them off, a dozen of them were caught in the blast from an engineer's bomb. The overseers, however, did not relent in their brutality, forcing the slaves across the smelthall to seize the precious metal.

Klarak felt his stomach churn. Most of the barazhunk was piled nearby. As long as they could stop the skaven from capturing those supplies, he didn't think Ikit Claw would have enough to complete his hellish invention.

The problem was, it didn't look like there were enough dwarfs to keep the Chief Warlock from escaping their trap.

'Kurgaz,' Klarak called out.

The runesmith didn't look up, his eyes still focused on the sheet before him, his burin still trying to engrave the complex Master Rune into the metal. Klarak watched his friend labouring, concentrating with the grim determination of a true dawi, ignoring even the clamour of battle raging all around him. Time was growing short if the engineer was going to manage his contingency plan. If Kurgaz could just get the Master Rune enscribed in time, then Ikit Claw's victory would become the ratkin's defeat!

'We'll buy you more time, old friend,' Klarak swore. Turning around, he repeated his order to the other dwarfs. Whatever happened, they had to make sure Kurgaz was undisturbed.

'It doesn't look like the ratkin agree,' Azram remarked. The routed clanrats Mordin had been pursuing were being swept aside, bowled over by a pack of brawny vermin, their bodies protected by thick armour plates. Even under the layers of paint and filth staining it, the lorekeeper could tell the skaven had scavenged the armour from dead dwarfs. What was less obvious was the purpose of the curious pistons and cogwheels fitted to the suits of armour.

Klarak gave the armoured skaven only a brief glance, staring past them at the grisly figure of Ikit Claw. 'No, it doesn't,' he said. His hand played across the dials of his chain vest, adjusting the settings of its mechanisms, trying to judge the intensity of Storm Daemon's deadly magic. After the near failure of his other vest, Klarak had a better idea of what the device could withstand.

Mordin's war-cry rang out. The slayer had also sighted the gruesome warlock-engineer. Carving his way through the fleeing clanrats, the lone dwarf rushed to confront Ikit Claw.

The armoured skaven interposed themselves between Mordin and their master, acting with an eerie, machine-like precision. The slayer's axe bit through the leg of one of his attackers while he lopped the paw from another. Neither of the ratmen gave so much as a squeal of protest. What spurted from their wounds was too thick for even skaven blood and possessed a weird glow to it. Mordin stared in disbelief as his crippled foes swarmed over him, beating him down with armoured fists.

'Zombies,' Kimril cursed, not without a shudder. For the ancestor-worshipping dwarfs there was no greater abomination than the restless dead.

'Automatons,' Klarak corrected him. 'Ratkin who have had their blood replaced with chemicals and their souls replaced with steel.' The engineer sighted along the barrel of the long pistol he'd drawn. It was a bulky weapon, not unlike a pared-down thunderer. He sighted along the barrel, then quickly sent a shot slamming into the head of one of Mordin's attackers. The explosive shot detonated as soon as it struck the ratkin, popping its head and sending a spray of chemicals and gears spattering across its comrades.

Ikit Claw snarled at his guards, cursing their uselessness. The Chief Warlock glared at Klarak, recognising the gold-bearded dwarf as the enemy who had foiled him in his previous attempt to build a Doomsphere. This time, his enemy would not stand in his way!

Gripping Storm Daemon in both hands, Ikit Claw activated the weapon's warp generator, throwing it into full power. Crackling energies formed about the black blade, a nimbus of dark power expanding from the tip of the halberd.

'Scatter!' Klarak ordered his assistants. 'Get behind cover!' The engineer did not take his own device, instead coldly sighting down the barrel of his pistol. While he stood in the open, there was every reason to expect the Claw to ignore his friends. There was a chance his vest would be able to save him from the crazed warlock's magic. Just as there was a chance that one of his explosive bullets might be powerful enough to penetrate the monster's iron frame.

Muttering a quiet prayer to his ancestors, Klarak squeezed the trigger, the pistol belching fire as the volatile bullet was sent speeding on its way. In the same instant, Ikit Claw unleashed the ferocity of Storm Daemon upon the dwarf.

Klarak shrieked in pain as black lightning crackled across his body. He could feel his teeth being pulled from his mouth, his hair being ripped from his scalp. The pistol fell from his hand, the reinforced steel glowing red hot as it struck the floor. The engineer's clothing caught fire, his skin blistered, his beard began to shrivel. Sparks flared through his vision as the pain impossibly intensified.

Abruptly, the black lightning dissipated. Klarak Bronzehammer crashed to the floor, smoke rising from his battered body.

CHAPTER XIV

HORGAR HORGARSSON ROSE from behind the cover of an anvil, berating himself for listening to Klarak instead of watching what the engineer was doing. It wasn't the first time his master had sent his assistants scrambling for shelter while he lingered behind to face danger alone. Perhaps Thorlek was right, maybe his injuries had made him thick-witted.

The hammerer glared across the smelthall. Klarak's last shot had struck Ikit Claw. Thick black smoke rose from the warlock's body, but the monster's iron frame looked to be intact and whatever hurt the skaven had suffered, he wasn't too injured to snap orders at his minions. The weird metal-limbed ratmen in the scavenged dwarf armour began to advance, their heavy steps clanking against the granite floor. Spurts of green gas erupted from engines lashed across their backs. It was with a feeling of horror that Horgar realised the vermin were wearing crude parodies of the steam-powered harness he himself wore.

Cursing the ratkin and their fiendish talent for copying the inventions of others, Horgar turned his concern towards Klarak. The engineer's body was still smoking from Ikit Claw's sorcery. For a terrible moment, he thought his master was dead, but then the engineer's body shuddered in a cough.

'Kimril! Thorlek! Help me!' Horgar called out. The ranger and physician scrambled out from behind their own shelters, hurrying to the side of their prone chief. Azram followed behind them, loading a fresh tube of pressurised steam into his pistol.

'Get him moving,' the lorekeeper warned, aiming his weapon at the oncoming skaven. The shots smashed into their armoured bodies, but the stolen dwarf mail was too tough to be pierced at such distance.

'He's alive,' Kimril said, making the quickest of examinations. Truthfully, he counted it a miracle that Klarak hadn't been killed, even if the engineer was disorientated. 'We have to get him to cover.'

Thorlek cast about him for any spot of refuge. All around the smelthall, bullets from jezzails and thunderers were pinging from the walls, debris from bombs pelted the furnaces. What they needed was a way to get below the ricochets and shrapnel. The ranger smiled as an idea came to him. He reached down, gripping Klarak's arm. 'Let's get him to the slag pit,' he said, nodding his beard at the hole where Mordin had been hiding. Kimril didn't argue, wrapping his arm about the engineer's waist. The two dwarfs and their burden quickly scrambled for the shelter of the hole.

Horgar and Azram hung back to cover the retreating dwarfs. The pack of mechanical skaven were nearly upon them now. Horgar snarled at the oncoming rat-kin. Crouching down, wrapping his reinforced arms about the anvil beside him, the hammerer strained to lift it from the ground. Grunting with effort, he raised it over his head.

'This is for Klarak!' Horgar shouted, hurling the massive anvil full into the face of his foes. Augmented by skaven cog-wheels and warp generators, the armoured skaven were still crushed beneath the heavy missile. The anvil smashed through them with the violence of an avalanche, snapping limbs and crumpling armour, crushing gears and bursting organs. The anvil rolled through the massed skaven, felling six of them before it came to a rest.

Unfortunately for the dwarfs, that left far too many still closing upon them. Horgar glanced at Azram. 'You'd better get to cover too,' he said as he recovered his warhammer from the ground.

The old lorekeeper grinned at Horgar. 'Let a little beardling like yourself have all the fun?' he scoffed, drawing the sword from his belt.

Horgar gave Azram a look of concern, but knew better than to try and force his friend to retreat. There was no time in any event. The first of the ratmen were already upon them. Horgar's warhammer came smashing down into the snarling face of an armoured ratman, smashing its skull like a melon.

'First to ten buys the beer,' Horgar shouted, swinging his hammer around to collapse the ribcage of another ratkin.

'As long as we don't count the ones you got with the anvil,' Azram said, thrusting his blade into the belly of a skaven trying to exploit Horgar's flank. 'Just like the Last Stand of Karak Varn!' the scholar exclaimed as he stabbed his wounded foe a second time.

Horgar brought his hammer swinging around, caving the side of the skaven's head, finishing it off. 'You should know,' he said. 'You're old enough to have been there.'

Suddenly, a sheet of green fire washed over the battlers. The mechanised skaven twisted as the flames scorched their fur and melted their armour. Azram gave voice to a single shriek as his face dripped into his beard.

Beset on all sides by his foes, Horgar was spared the lorekeeper's fate, the skaven blocking most of the warpfire. Still, enough of the virulent flame reached him to corrode the engine of his harness. The hammerer's steam-powered limbs locked up, freezing into place as the motivating power jetted from the ruptured tanks. Unbalanced by the sudden stop, Horgar crashed to the floor.

The dwarf struggled to turn his head. He clenched his teeth as he saw his attacker striding through the destruction. Wisps of smoke rose from the nozzle set into the metal talon of Ikit Claw. The ratman's evil eyes glared down at the stricken Horgar. Burnt lips peeled back to expose a mouthful of fangs in a sadistic grin. Pointing his metal claw at the defenceless hammerer, Ikit Claw reached with his other hand to pull back the warpfire projector's activation lever. Horgar closed his eyes, deciding he didn't want to see the skaven gloating over him as the Claw melted the flesh from his bones.

Horgar heard the whoosh of the warpfire projector, could smell the corrupt stink of its flames, yet strangely, there was no pain. Daring to open his eyes, he stared in amazement to find Kurgaz standing over him. The runesmith held a heavy gromril mattock in his hands, a single rune blazing upon its surface, looking as though it were burning from within. The green flames of warp-fire broke around the runesmith like waves breaking against a boulder.

Kurgaz looked down at the crippled hammerer. 'Tell. Klarak. It. Is. Done,' the runesmith said. Then, calling upon the names of Grungni and Valaya, Grimnir and Thungni, the dwarf charged Ikit Claw.

The runehammer Kurgaz held burst into flames as he approached the skaven warlock, tongues of yellow fire crackling about the enchanted weapon. The runes inscribed upon the hammer not only guarded against fire, but could unleash the same force against a foe.

Ikit Claw snarled at the lone dwarf, calling for his minions to stop the runesmith. The Chief Warlock's shrieks became even more frantic when he discovered there were none close enough to stop Kurgaz. The only ratmen who might have helped him had been burned down by the Claw's own weaponry.

Furiously, Ikit Claw stabbed at Kurgaz with Storm Daemon, the enchanted halberd scraping across the runesmith's gromril breastplate. The dwarf brought the haft of his hammer swinging around, the granite ancestor badge chained to its butt cracking against the warp generator fixed just beneath Storm Daemon's black blade.

Protective runes carved upon the ancestor badge met the raw malignance of Ikit Claw's weapon, the deathly power trapped inside the generator. The confusion of energies sent a shudder sweeping through both combatants, passing through their bodies in a spasm of shaking limbs and shivering bones.

The warp generator crackled as its power was vented in a great spray of corrosive steam. Hastily, Ikit Claw flung the damaged Storm Daemon from him before its unleashed power could turn against him. Snarling, the Chief Warlock drew his warplock pistol and turned to exact revenge upon his foe.

Kurgaz's runehammer crashed against the warlock's iron-bound body. The skaven squealed in pain, staring in disbelief as the hammer's magic pierced his iron frame. Slivers of torn metal stabbed into the furry body underneath, the fires of the hammer shrivelled the ratman's flesh.

Howling in panic, the rage of a cornered rat filling him with an amok courage, Ikit Claw flung himself upon the dwarf, moving with almost blinding speed. The warplock pistol's muzzle belched smoke and flame as it was pressed close against Kurgaz's belly. The warpstone bullet ripped through the runesmith, burning its way through armour and flesh, erupting from the dwarf's back in a spray of blood.

The dwarf's runehammer came smashing down one last time, Kurgaz's face filled with the fierce determination to take down his killer before passing into the halls of his ancestors. If he could end the villainous career of Ikit Claw, then Karak Angkul would be saved. It was the sort of heroic offering that would earn him a place near the table of Grungni and Valaya and the other ancestor gods.

Before the burning runehammer could strike, Kurgaz's hand was caught in a steely grip. The huge metal hand of Ikit Claw held the dwarf's weapon at bay. The ratman's beady eyes glared at the runesmith from beneath the head of the frozen hammer.

'Die-die, fool-flesh!' the skaven snapped. As he spoke, Ikit Claw snapped the scythe-like fingers of his metal hand. Kurgaz screamed as the bladed fingers sliced through his own hand, leaving only a spurting stump behind. The runehammer smashed to the floor, its fires fading the moment it came to rest.

The runesmith clutched his maimed arm against his chest, his other hand fumbling at his waist, trying to staunch the blood spilling from his belly. There was nothing Kurgaz could do when the triumphant Ikit Claw reached out with his metal hand and closed the bladed fingers about the dwarf's head.

Ikit Claw licked the mix of blood, bone and brains from his hand as he limped away from the headless Kurgaz. Angrily he shrieked for his underlings. A mass of skavenslaves and warlock-engineers came scurrying at his call, doing their best to dodge the fire raining down upon their heads from the walkways above.

'Fetch-bring all dwarf-metal,' Ikit Claw snarled, gesturing imperiously at the furnace where Klarak and his aides had been working. The skaven stared back at their master, greedy lights gleaming in their eyes as they considered his injuries. Baring his fangs, the Chief Warlock pointed at one of his minions. A stream of caustic words slipped off the Claw's tongue as he evoked one of the many hexes he'd learned in his travels.

The victim squealed in agony as magical energies exploded inside his chest, causing his heart to burst. The skaven around him took note of their comrade's destruction with whines of contrition and simpering assurances of loyalty. Suddenly, Ikit Claw's injuries didn't look so inviting.

The Chief Warlock pointed at the furnace. This time his minions were falling over one another in their eagerness to carry out his command. Ikit Claw watched them scamper off, catching hold of one of the warlock-engineers as he passed. 'Get-bring Storm Daemon,' he ordered, flicking his tail towards the damaged weapon.

His henchrat took one look at the corrosive steam venting from the ruptured warp generator and spurted the musk of fear.

'Mercy-pity, Mad-genius! Scrap-master, Junk-lord! Most Calamitous of Scavengers! Abominable Bringer of Abominations!'

Ikit Claw kicked his fawning minion away. 'Fetch Storm Daemon,' he hissed through clenched fangs. 'Or I'll kill you and get-find someone else to do it.'

The Chief Warlock's threat sent the other warlock-engineer scurrying away to recover the damaged weapon. Ikit Claw turned away, limping back towards the digging machine. It was time they were quit of this dwarf-thing smell-hall.

The infiltration hadn't worked quite as successfully as he had planned. The attack should have come as a complete surprise to the dwarf-things. Instead, his troops had suffered losses far in excess of what Ikit Claw had expected.

Still, they were small sacrifices. Once the Doomsphere was complete, Ikit Claw wouldn't need armies any more. Once the Doomsphere was complete, he would control a power far more destructive than all the armies in the entire world.

And with the captured dwarf-metal, the Doomsphere would be complete!

AWARENESS RETURNED TO Klarak Bronzehammer, breaking through the fog of confusion that befuddled his mind. One moment, the dwarf inventor rested helplessly at the bottom of the slag pit, his concerned friends watching over him. The next moment, there was clarity in the gold-flake eyes. Klarak surged to his feet, his expression grim. Shaking off Thorlek's restraining grip, the engineer scrambled for the ladder. Kimril cried after him, vainly trying to stop Klarak's desperate momentum.

Ikit Claw would escape the trap. This terror twisted through Klarak's guts like a knife. The engineer had gambled much on stopping the skaven here, before the beast could complete his hideous invention. For the Claw to escape now, the consequences would be apocalyptic. The name of Klarak Bronzehammer would be recorded among the most villainous oathbreakers – if anyone was left to write of his failure!

The engineer leaped up from the slag pit. He stared out across the devastated smelthall. Dead dwarfs and dead skaven littered the ground, great craters pockmarked the floor where bombs had shattered the stone. Strips of gantry and walkway drooped down from the heights, scorched by skaven warpfire or corroded by the awful touch of Poison Wind. Klarak felt his heart go cold as he saw the mutilated body of an old longbeard dangling from the wreckage.

The old dwarf's sacrifice would not be for nothing. Klarak clenched his fist and vowed that the skaven would pay for every drop of dwarf blood they had spilt this day. His eyes grew hard as he noticed a large group of the ratmen retreating back into one of their holes. Snatching a war-axe from the dead fingers of a metalworker, Klarak dashed across the ravaged smelthall.

Bullets continued to rain down from the ceiling as the remaining thunderers tried to thin out the ranks of the fleeing ratmen. Several teams of skaven jezzails lingered behind to return their fire, cowering in the shelter of big oak shields when the dwarfs tried to shoot back. Klarak ran straight into one of the jezzails. His axe licked out, opening the throat of the rodent sharpshooter, his fist smashed the muzzle of the ratkin shieldbearer.

Klarak didn't linger over his victims, but was off again, rushing towards the retreating ratmen. He could see now that many of them bore plates of barazhunk with them as they vanished down into the tunnel. The engineer roared, bellowing a war-cry that shuddered through the smelthall. As he roared, he waved his arms towards the retreating skaven.

Warpstone bullets whizzed past Klarak's ears, smashed into the columns and pillars he darted behind as he crossed the hall. The jezzails, noting the death of their comrade, hearing the crazed screech of the lone dwarf madman, trained their guns on Klarak. Futilely they tried to bring down their nimble target.

Given a respite from the punishing fire of the jezzails, the dwarf marksmen above the smelthall were free to loose a salvo into their foes. Noting the figure of Klarak as he dashed through the havoc, waving his arms, the thunderers chose their mark. The fusillade poured down, not into the scattered jezzails, but full into the mob of fleeing ratkin.

Yelps and squeals rose from the savaged throng as the thunderers spat stone bullets into their close-packed ranks. Furry bodies thrashed on the floor, black blood pouring from their wounds. The stink of raw fear spurted from the ratkin. Many cast aside their burdens, clawing and snapping at one another as they tried to force their way through the pack and into the safety of the hole.

The despair of the embattled skaven made itself known to those who had gone before, the ratmen who had already fled into the tunnel. From the depths, a loud rumbling made itself felt, shaking the entire smelt-hall. Klarak was knocked from his feet as the tremor rattled the ground. Skaven screams filled the air as a thick cloud of dust rose from the yawning mouth of the hole.

With callous treachery, to prevent pursuit the ratmen had collapsed their tunnel right on top of their own fleeing comrades!

Klarak regained his feet, watching as the few surviving skaven began to pull themselves out from among the dust and debris. Bullets and bolts rained down upon the wretches, picking them off with bitter vindictiveness. The ratkin who had escaped being buried alive had only traded one kind of death for another.

The engineer turned away, pacing back towards the furnace where he and his comrades had made their stand. He could see Thorlek and Kimril labouring to pull Horgar Horgarsson upright, the hammerer's steam-harness making the task difficult for even two dwarfs to manage. Klarak shook his head sadly. If either Azram or Kurgaz had been able, they would be helping tend Horgar. The fact that he didn't see them sent a knife of bitter sadness cutting through his heart.

The skaven had been thorough in their attack, better armed and prepared than Klarak had anticipated. He'd underestimated Ikit Claw, a failing that had cost many dwarfs their lives.

Klarak paused, noticing a movement among the heaped bodies of the dead ratkin. Tightening his hold upon his axe, the dwarf stormed vengefully towards the ratkin. These were the hideously augmented war-rats who had served Ikit Claw as bodyguards. It would be in keeping with the Claw's evil genius that these creatures should have greater vitality than their verminous kin. A flash of guilt gnawed at Klarak as he considered that the skaven might have been inspired by Horgar's steam-harness when he decided to create his loathsome shock troops.

Seizing the topmost of the bodies, Klarak rolled the heavy bulk away, noting as he did the horrible injuries the skaven had suffered, the way its flesh and even its armour had been burned and melted. Caught by the warpfire of its master's hand. Klarak clenched his teeth at this vivid display of skaven cowardice and treachery.

Rolling away another of the armoured skaven, Klarak jumped back as a third body started to move. Bracing himself to attack the maimed ratman, the engineer sighed with relief as the body sagged against its comrades. A thick dwarf voice snarled curses from beneath the heavy corpse.

'I'll kill you again, you yellow-backed flea nest! By Grimnir, get your carcass off me!'

Klarak set aside his axe, helping the trapped dwarf extricate himself from the pile of corpses. Mordin Grimstone's body was coated in blood, both his own and the black filth of his enemies. Ugly patches of burnt flesh peppered his skin where melting blobs of skaven fat had dripped down through the heaped dead. A livid gash marked his brow where a ratman's sword had glanced across the slayer's shaven head. One of the dwarf's shoulders had the claws of a dismembered skaven hand embedded in it.

But the most disturbing aspect of Mordin's countenance were his eyes. Pools of fire, blazing with murderous ferocity, they glared across the smelthall, darting from shadow to shadow looking for foes to slay. Except for the few jezzail teams and abandoned slaves, the enemy was gone. Mordin clearly felt that the few dregs being picked off by the marksmen on the walkways weren't worth his time. He fixed his fiery gaze on Klarak.

'Where's that metal-masked scavenger?' the slayer growled. He stooped and ripped one of his axes from the belly of a dead ratman. 'There's a blade here eager to taste his blood!'

'Gone,' Klarak frowned. 'Fled back into his hole.'

Mordin sneered, spitting a blob of bloody phlegm onto the floor. 'Some trap,' the slayer scoffed. A wracking cough gripped him, causing more blood to drip into his beard.

'Come along,' Klarak said. 'Kimril will tend your wounds.' Mordin pulled away at Klarak's touch. 'This is no way for a slayer to die,' the engineer told him. 'What of your vow to kill Thanquol?'

The slayer's face flushed crimson. 'What of your promise that the cur would be here?' Mordin growled. 'You are right when you say it is wrong for a slayer to die because of a lie.'

Klarak's face darkened. 'There is more at stake here than your revenge,' he reminded Mordin.

'Tell that to Kurgaz,' the slayer snarled, waving his axe ahead of him.

Klarak followed the direction of Mordin's gesture. A great sorrow settled about him as he saw the rune-smith's armoured body lying stretched out in a pool of its own blood, only a torn stump of neck where his friend's head should be. He had asked so much of Kurgaz, depended so much upon the runesmith's wisdom and magic. In the end, he had demanded too much and it had cost his friend his life.

'I saw him die,' Mordin said. 'Peeping through the pile of corpses, I watched him battle the ratkin with the metal claw. A fine fighter, his runehammer burning like the sun. Such an end! Such a death!' The slayer ran his hand through the filth caking his beard. 'If he'd only

managed to kill the villain, he'd be able to hold his
head high when he steps into Gazul's vaults.'

Klarak turned away from the vision of his friend's
corpse. 'Now we both have someone to avenge,' he told
Mordin as he helped support the slayer. 'And by Morgrim's Hammer, Ikit Claw will pay for the evil of this
day!'

'Thinking of shaving your head?' Mordin laughed,
then fell silent as a blood-flecked cough wracked his
torn body.

Klarak didn't answer the slayer. His eyes were cold,
his thoughts dark. He had risked much to trap his
enemy. The responsibility was his, and even the Slayer
Oath would not efface his guilt.

KING LOGAN LONGBLADE surveyed the carnage of the
smelthall, his eyes heavy with emotion. A hundred
and twelve dwarfs were dead, a score and more were
maimed or wounded. The smelthall had suffered
structural damages that would place it out of com-
mission for weeks, perhaps even months. It would
be years before the furnaces were again operating at
full capacity. The clans of the metalsmiths would seek
compensation for their dead, reparations for their lost
custom. The shadow of this black day would linger
over the stronghold for generations.

'This is what comes from flouting tradition.' Guildmaster Thori's voice echoed the troubled thoughts
boiling inside the king's brain. 'I warned against allowing Klarak to proceed with his reckless plan.'

'Enough,' King Logan told the engineer. 'I will not
have my decisions questioned by hindsight. Whatever
the consequences.' He turned away from the view of
the dwarfish dead, their bodies draped in the mantle of

their clans, a wizened priest of Gazul folding the hands of each corpse about a gilded ancestor stone – an offering for the dour Lord of the Underearth. The craftsmen of Karak Angkul would be busy carving new mournstones to replace the ones given to the dead this day.

The king's mind turned back to the battle in the lower deeps, the fierce struggle against the massed skaven horde. At the time, he had thought Klarak was wrong, that the real ratkin attack was in the deeps. Right up until the moment when a messenger brought him word that the smelthall was under assault, he had felt confident that Klarak's grim predictions weren't real. The ratkin had been assaulting Karak Angkul for generations and each time the vermin had been driven back. As his army smashed the skaven down in the Sixth Deep, he had allowed himself to believe this time would be no different.

Now, the king had to concede it was different. The attack in the Sixth Deep had been a deception, just as Klarak had warned. But if the king had underestimated the foe, so too had the hero of Karak Angkul. Disaster seemed too light a word for the carnage that had raged in the smelthall.

King Logan circled the heap of skaven dead. Already five cartloads of the vermin had been loaded up and removed to be burned outside the stronghold, yet still the ratkin dead numbered in the hundreds. It was always the same. The dwarfs could slaughter their foes by the bushel and hardly make a dent in their numbers, yet each of their own dead was a wound from which the stronghold would be slow to recover.

Ahead of him, King Logan could see Thane Erkii and a throng of miners digging away at a rubble-choked hole in the floor. An enormous grinding machine, steam venting from its pipes, chewed into the blockage, sending a spray of dirt and rock shooting behind it. The machine was another of Klarak Bronzehammer's inventions, one that the engineer had offered to the Miners' Guild over the protests of the Engineers' Guild who maintained that the machine needed a few more decades of tests before it was deemed stable enough for development.

Guildmaster Thori cursed into his beard when he saw the forbidden machine in operation. 'By Morgrim! The reckless debaz goes too far!' He pointed a jewelled spanner at the mechanised drill, gesturing angrily at the machine. 'That contraption isn't authorised! It isn't safe!'

A lone dwarf turned away from the dig at the sound of Thori's voice. There was a menacing intensity in Klarak's eyes as he approached the Guildmaster. 'My rockchewer is the fastest way to excavate the ratkin tunnel,' he told the older dwarf. 'Authorised by the Guild or not. Unless maybe you think it would be safer to leave Ikit Claw down there undisturbed.'

Thori's face pulled back into a scowl of disapproval. 'You'll be expelled from the Guild,' he warned, tapping Klarak's chest with the end of his spanner. 'Cogged and tossed out on your ear! If you would have followed accepted traditions, obeyed the proprieties of invention, none of this would have happened!' Thori waved his arms wide, indicating the damage the smelthall had suffered. 'The ratkin came because of your new metal!'

'Give thanks to Grungni that he did,' Klarak said. 'Because that has given us our only chance to stop him.'

'Stop him?' Thori gasped. 'Look around you! The thaggoraki has come and gone, and taken your barazhunk with him!' The Guildmaster's eyes hardened into chips of ice. 'Tell me, without your metal, could this ratkin have any hope of completing his machine? No! It would have blown up in his face and saved us the problem of digging him out!'

Klarak shook his head. 'Ikit Claw would have found a way to make his own,' he insisted. 'He would have slunk off to some hole far away and finished his Doom-sphere where we would never find it.' He shook his fist at the hole the miners were excavating. 'At least now we have a chance of following him and stopping him.'

'Stopping him from building a weapon with your new alloy,' Thori reminded, spite rolling off his tongue.

'Enough,' King Logan ordered. 'There is blame to spare. I still think Klarak had the right of it in trying to entice the ratkin out and trap him here.' A hard edge crept into the king's voice. 'But the trap failed. That responsibility can be placed on no one's head except that of the dwarf who made the plan. Klarak Bronze-hammer, I am compelled to record grudge against you for the death of my subjects and the defilement of my smelthall.' The king stared into Klarak's gold eyes. 'Recompense for this grudge is set as five hundred rat-tails and the head of Ikit Claw.'

Klarak bowed his head as he heard his king pronounce judgement upon him. 'I accept this burden as just and fair,' he said. 'Let my spirit never walk the Halls of the Ancestors if I fail to balance the debt I owe to Karak Angkul and King Logan Longblade.'

Guildmaster Thori smiled to see the bold Klarak humbled. 'Now you must drag that unproved contraption away from the dig,' he ordered.

Klarak fixed the older engineer with a withering stare. 'Guilt and responsibility don't change reality,' he said. 'The rockchewer is still the fastest way to follow Ikit

Claw. As you've pointed out, he has my metal now, so we need to catch him before he can finish his machine.'

'Maybe you won't have to.' The interrupting words came from Horgar. The hammerer's gait was unsteady as he came marching towards them, his head wrapped in bandages, his steam-harness shuddering at every step. He bowed respectfully to King Logan, cast a hostile glance at Guildmaster Thori, then faced Klarak.

'You should be letting Kimril and the healers tend your wounds,' Klarak admonished his bodyguard.

Horgar's face spread in a lopsided grin. 'Since when have I ever done the sensible thing?' he asked. 'Besides, most of my problems are with this steam-harness you made me, not my battered bones.' The hammerer's face grew serious. 'Kurgaz spoke to me before he died. He wanted me to tell you that he finished what you wanted him to do.'

Horgar's words had the effect of lightning on the engineer. From morbid melancholy, Klarak became energised with determination. Hastily, he drew a set of goggles from his belt, the lenses possessed of a curious purple hue. Staring through the goggles, Klarak hastened to the small pile of recovered barazhunk, examining each piece in rapid succession. The other dwarfs watched him in confusion, wondering if the loss of his friends had addled the adventurer's wits.

Klarak turned away from his labours, shouting hasty words to Thane Erkii and his miners. 'Be careful to recover each piece of barazhunk,' he told them. 'Set each aside for me to inspect.' The engineer turned back to his confused sovereign.

'When I was first warned about Grey Seer Thanquol,' Klarak told King Logan, 'I conceived a plan to guard my inventions from the skaven.' King Logan nodded, aware of this part of the story. It had been his assistance that had given Kurgaz access to the secret lore of the runemasters. 'At the time, I believed the danger lay with the theft of my inventions. Kurgaz agreed to help me by learning one of the Master Runes and using its magic to prevent my devices from falling into the wrong hands.

'When Mordin brought us word that Ikit Claw was involved, and when Thane Erkii reported the theft of barazhunk from the mines, I saw a different way to employ the knowledge Kurgaz had gained.' Klarak paused, holding up the burin the runesmith had used. 'This burin was treated with a chemical that leaves a residue behind. Each plate Kurgaz tried to inscribe will have a trace of the chemical upon it.' He tapped the goggles. 'With these, I can tell which plates have been treated and which have not.'

'More foolishness,' Thori scoffed. 'What does it matter if the ratkin have taken inscribed metal or plain metal?'

Klarak favoured the Guildmaster with a grim smile. 'Because if Ikit Claw uses the plate Kurgaz inscribed the Master Rune on, then the skaven will do our work for us.'

King Logan sighed, glancing back at the rows of dwarf dead. 'We can't trust that he will.'

'No,' Klarak agreed. 'That's why it's doubly important we excavate the tunnel. We have to find Ikit Claw's lair and make sure he's used the inscribed plate. We have to follow his trail back to the Doomsphere and see that it is destroyed.'

'Hurry-scurry, fool-flesh!' Ikit Claw glared at the horde of skavenslaves and clanrats rushing through the tunnels. He had lost a lot of the dwarf-metal when the tunnel into the smelthall collapsed. The thought

that he'd sacrificed too much of the metal was one
that vexed the warlock-engineer and he was impatient
to have this particular fear dispelled. Once back in his
workshop, he'd be able to make certain exactly how
much of the stuff he'd acquired.

The skaven poured into the now quiet tunnels of
Bonestash. Between his attack on the smelthall and
the diversion attack on the Sixth Deep, the warren had
been almost completely depopulated. Except for the
most vital sections of the warren, not a ratman had
been left behind. Troops of stormvermin had ensured
a complete muster of the settlement's strength. The ratmen of Clan Mors weren't particularly bright, but Ikit
Claw had to admit their efficiency was useful. It had
been almost a pity to send them out to be slaughtered.
But a device like the Doomsphere wasn't built without
a few sacrifices.

The Chief Warlock rubbed his hands together in
greedy anticipation. Once the Doomsphere was completed, he would be reckoned the most brilliant mind
in all skavendom. Even Warplord Morskittar would
acknowledge the genius of his chief acolyte. A weapon
the likes of which no skaven had dared contemplate in
thousands of generations! Soon it would be his! The
Doomsphere of Ikit Claw!

Allowing he'd managed to steal enough of the dwarf
metal. Ikit bruxed his fangs in annoyance at that
thought. It might take him years to fabricate any of the
stuff on his own and the stupid dwarf-things would be
on their guard to keep him from stealing any more. The
stone-witted scum had nearly foiled his plans already,
coming alarmingly close to snuffing out the Under-
Empire's greatest mind. Gingerly he probed the rent in
his iron frame with his paw, wincing as he felt blood

spurt over his fingers. The wound would need see-ing to, but he wasn't so sure he could trust any of his apprentices. The short-sighted maggots had been get-ting uppity since his injury. One of them even had the audacity to suggest if there wasn't enough dwarf-metal that he should downsize the Doomsphere! If not for his injuries, he would have had the rat roasted alive for such insolence!

But it would be enough! It had to be! Destiny would not cheat the mighty Ikit Claw!

Ahead, the sprawl of the old storage cavern opened before Ikit Claw's triumphant horde. The Chief War-lock pushed his way to the forefront, eager to behold his magnificent weapon. Once he saw its unfinished beauty, he knew he could confidently say that he had enough dwarf-metal to complete it.

Ikit Claw's eyes lingered on the Doomsphere for only a moment, then his gaze was drawn downwards. Like every member of his entourage, he found himself staring at the horned figure standing upon the Doom-sphere's platform.

Grey Seer Thanquol glared down at him, the priest's tail lashing back and forth. What was the prayer-gnawing parasite doing here! The idiot should be lying somewhere in the dwarfhold with an axe in his chest or a bullet in his brain! Part of being a decoy meant getting killed by the thing you were supposed to be decoying!

A bell clanged, its discordant notes ringing out across the workshop. Thanquol cast a smug look at the scrawny clanrat bellringer perched beside him, then turned his snarling face back towards Ikit Claw.

'Off-flee!' the Chief Warlock growled. 'Away-away! Get away from my Doomsphere!'

An evil light shone in Thanquol's eyes. 'My Doom-sphere,' the horned ratman hissed.

Ikit Claw's lips pulled back in a feral snarl. 'Kill-kill!' he shouted, pointing with his metal claw at the grey seer.

A pack of warriors drew swords and rushed towards the platform. Skaven of Clan Skryre, they chittered with amusement when they saw Boneripper's skeletal bulk lurch into their path. They knew the measures the warlock-engineers had taken to ensure their creation didn't turn against them.

'Boneripper!' Thanquol's voice snapped like a whip. 'Burn-kill!'

The clanrats weren't laughing when a gout of warpfire erupted from the rat-ogre's third arm. Five of the rat-men were immolated instantly. Six others raced about the cavern, their burning fur making them into living torches. A squeal of horror rose from the rest of Ikit Claw's minions. Somehow Thanquol had disabled his bodyguard's safety valve.

Ikit Claw didn't care. Rat-ogre or no, he wasn't about to hand over his invention to some corrupt sorcerer-priest! Angrily, he ripped Storm Daemon from the warlock-engineer carrying it. The broken warp generator had stopped venting corrosive gas, making the halberd reasonably safe to handle. The weapon wouldn't be able to shoot lightning at his enemies, but that didn't bother Ikit. He would prefer chopping Thanquol's treacherous head from his scrawny neck.

Thanquol took a step back when he saw Ikit Claw advance from the horde of Clan Skryre skaven. There was a note of fear in the grey seer's eyes, a momentary softening of his posture. Then the horned ratman reached beneath the folds of his robe, drawing forth a severed skaven paw. Ikit Claw stared in alarm at the gruesome talisman, his sorcerously attuned eyes able to see the magical energies swirling about the desiccated paw.

'Behold!' Thanquol crowed. 'The Hand of Vecteek!'

To every other skaven in the cavern, the name meant nothing. But to Ikit Claw, it spelled doom. He was familiar with the legacy of the artefact, the paw of Clan Rictus's feared war-chief. In the possession of a murder-minded traitor like Thanquol, such a potent talisman could unleash untold havoc and destruction. Thanquol had demonstrated a callous disregard for his fellow skaven and wouldn't care how many died in any duel between himself and the Chief Warlock. For the good of his minions, Ikit Claw couldn't afford to provoke the weasel-spleened traitor.

'Wise-mighty Thanquol,' Ikit Claw said, lowering Storm Daemon. 'Happy-glad am I that you escaped the dwarf-things. I had worry-fear something happened to you.'

Thanquol grinned down at the suddenly unctuous warlock. 'Save your worry-fear for yourself,' he advised. The grey seer turned his head, raising his snout as he smelled the dwarf-metal Ikit's slaves carried. He licked his fangs.

'You were going to finish your weapon,' Thanquol said. He grimaced as his standard bearer punctuated the statement with an especially frenzied burst of bell ringing. Grinding his fangs together, the grey seer continued. 'It is my wish-order that you will finish it. If it works, the Horned One tells me that I may spare your lives.'

Thanquol brandished the Hand of Vecteek so all of the skaven could see it. Even those who didn't know what it was understood the menace it posed after seeing the way Thanquol had threatened their own terrifying master with it.

'Work fast! Work hard! Work accurately!' Thanquol cried. 'If anything goes wrong with my Doomsphere, I'll flay the fur from your skins!'

CHAPTER XV

THE WARLOCK-ENGINEER's pathetic mewing was silenced when Boneripper crushed the craven little weasel's skull. Thanquol wasn't certain the wretch had really been up to anything, but it was prudent not to take any chances. Besides, the only one of the parasites he needed to keep around was Ikit Claw himself. The rest of the Clan Skryre tinker-rats were a liability. The Claw might forget his place if he started believing he had strength in numbers on his side. Thinking it over, Thanquol was of the opinion he should probably exact a few more object lessons to put his new minions in a more pious and obedient frame of mind.

The grey seer leaned back in the throne he'd ordered brought down from Rikkit Snapfang's abandoned lair. It was a remarkably comfortable seat, crafted from dwarf bones and upholstered in only the softest whelp fur. A pair of exceedingly energetic skavenslaves were crouched at the foot of the throne trimming Thanquol's claws while another rubbed a sweet-smelling liniment into the grey seer's scaly tail. Standing beside the throne, Nikkrit rang the holy bell, sending the dolorous voice of the Horned One racing through the cavern. Knowledge that their god was watching them would help spur Thanquol's henchlings to better effort.

Thanquol's eyes gleamed evilly in the green light cast by warp lanterns. The Doomsphere was quickly taking shape. Already the exposed mechanisms and supports were covered by plates of tough dwarf-metal. Teams of workers were crawling all over the shell, ensuring that each plate was firmly in place with no gaps or weaknesses. Other teams of workers inspected the inspectors, ensuring there were no mistakes or sabotage. Third and fourth teams continued the routine of inspection. For all his submission to Thanquol, Ikit Claw was proving a most methodical and zealous overseer.

It made Thanquol nervous to watch the fearsome Chief Warlock accepting his new role as lackey and servant with such graciousness. The Claw was up to something, Thanquol was certain of it. He felt a great temptation to err on the side of caution and blast the warlock with a bolt of magic every time his back was turned – or better yet, have Boneripper do the job while Thanquol watched from a safe distance.

Only Ikit's repeated claims that he was the only one that could complete the Doomsphere kept Thanquol from acting upon his murderous impulses. If there was only one thing the Chief Warlock said that the grey seer believed completely, it was that the Claw hadn't trusted the secret of his superweapon to anyone else. It was easy to believe because in the same position, Thanquol would certainly have done the same. The secret of such a weapon was too important to trust to any minion.

And that was why Ikit Claw would have to die once the Doomsphere was complete. Thanquol couldn't take the chance that the Chief Warlock might betray him and make a second Doomsphere. That would upset all of the grey seer's plans. The threat of one Doomsphere would make him the unquestioned tyrant of all skavendom, but if someone else had an identical weapon it would confuse the issue. The teeming hordes of the Under-Empire wouldn't know which way to present their throats. Worse, the threat of the Doomsphere would be diminished if Thanquol's enemies had their own weapon which they could threaten to detonate if he used his. Mutually assured destruction would dull the menace of the Doomsphere, rendering it impotent and almost inconsequential.

No! Thanquol would not be denied! He would be the unquestioned ruler of skavendom, the Horned Emperor, Scourge of Skavenblight, Lord of the Ratkin, Master of the Underearth! He was the beloved of the Horned Rat, most favoured and powerful of the rat-god's servants. It was the will of the Horned One that he should be present to seize the product of Ikit Claw's heretical genius. It was the Horned One's decree that the power of the Doomsphere should be entrusted into the claws of the one ratman who would use it for the betterment of the Under-Empire. It took a skaven of Thanquol's humble and unassuming nature to be trusted with a weapon like the Doomsphere.

Stroking his whiskers, Thanquol watched the treacherous Ikit Claw snapping orders to the scurrying warlock-engineers and skavenslaves. Only a raticidal lunatic would dare try to recreate a weapon that had nearly obliterated Skavenblight. The Claw was a danger to all skaven everywhere! It was the duty of any right-minded ratman to exterminate the threat he posed! As soon as the Doomsphere was finished, Thanquol would have the Chief Warlock killed. It was his civic responsibility as a servant of the Lords of Decay to get rid of this threat to their power.

Thanquol bruxed his fangs as he contemplated the manner in which he would be welcomed back to Skavenblight. He would be the hero who had saved skavendom from the machinations of a mad scientist! The Council of Thirteen would be falling over themselves in their efforts to reward him. And if they didn't, Thanquol would still have the threat of the Doomsphere to get them in line. They would proclaim him Horned Emperor of All Skavendom! He would sit upon the thirteenth throne, symbolically kept vacant for the Horned Rat himself. Well, such superstition would have no place under Thanquol's reign. What better way to show that he was superior to the Lords of Decay than by claiming the throne they dared not touch? He would be venerated as the living manifestation of the Horned Rat, adored and feared throughout the world!

Thanquol sneezed as a little fleck of warp-snuff caught in his nose dislodged itself. He really was sorry he'd been manipulated into killing Lynsh Blacktail by the pirate's mutinous crew. He'd really like to know where the yellow-spined buccaneer had come upon such a fine grade of snuff.

'Most Abhorrent One,' the wheezing voice of a warlock-engineer interrupted Thanquol's ruminations. The grey seer looked up, glaring at the snivelling tinker-rat. He glanced over at Boneripper, motioning for the rat-ogre to squash this annoyance. Then he reflected that he should probably hear what the weasel had to say first. Squishing might prove too kindly a death if the vexing little flea had something particularly repellent to tell him.

'Squeak-speak,' Thanquol hissed, putting an impatient and threatening gleam of teeth behind his words.

The tinker-rat scratched at some of the wires bolted into his scalp, then cast a nervous look over his shoulder at the Doomsphere and particularly at the spot where Ikit Claw was acting as supervisor. 'Great and Horrible Thanquol, Wondrous Smiter of the Impious, Most Dread Bane of...'

Thanquol kicked his foot out, his newly cleansed claws scratching across the warlock's snout. 'Before I lose my patience,' he snarled.

'Great Thanquol,' the warlock-engineer said, dropping his voice to a barely audible squeak. 'I have watched the work. The Doomsphere is finished. Ikit Claw is trying to trick you by insisting it isn't ready.'

Thanquol's eyes narrowed. He should have expected such a ploy. Ikit Claw was no fool, for all of his heretical ideas about science. He knew that as soon as the Doomsphere was finished, Thanquol would have no reason to keep him alive. The treacherous rat was playing for time, waiting for the opportunity to hatch some plot against his beneficent master. Well, Thanquol wasn't about to give the maggot the chance!

Snapping his claws, Thanquol dismissed his attendants. A wave of his paw had Boneripper smashing its foot down upon the warlock-engineer's neck. Thanquol had no sentiment for spies and traitors, especially when they turned on their own masters, most certainly when they could be of no further use. The squashed tinker-rat died without uttering a shriek, so sudden was his demise.

One traitor down, one to go. Thanquol reached into his robe, bringing forth the Hand of Vecteek. He was still loath to use the hideous artefact, but Ikit Claw wouldn't know that. While the stupid warlock was worrying about the Hand, he'd never see Boneripper until the rat-ogre sent a blast of warpfire scorching through his scabby hide.

The clatter of his standard followed Thanquol as he crossed the cavern to where the Doomsphere was being constructed. Had been constructed, the grey seer corrected himself. His informant had said the weapon was finished.

The sound of Nikkrit's bell caught Ikit Claw's attention. The metal-faced warlock turned, staring down at Thanquol as the grey seer approached.

The grey seer cast a look of fury upon the bell-ringer, a look that promised nasty things for Nikkrit in the not-too-distant future. So wrapped up in his own thoughts of power, Thanquol hadn't bothered to consider that the clatter of his standard would betray his approach. The grey seer returned his attention to the Claw. Thanquol felt a flush of annoyance as he noted the Claw's position high above him on the wooden platform. It wasn't proper for an underling to stand higher than his master. If for no other reason, that impudence marked Ikit as worthy of death.

'Stay your paw, Thanquol,' Ikit Claw called out, mockery in his voice. He gestured with his metal claw, sweeping it across the shell of the Doomsphere. 'It would be unwise to kill me before the weapon is finished.'

'The weapon is finished,' Thanquol growled. 'And so are you!' He raised the Hand of Vecteek, pointing its dead claws at the warlock. From the corner of his eye,

Thanquol could see Boneripper circling to one side. Just a few more steps and the rat-ogre would be in position to burn the Claw to a crisp.

Ignorant of his peril, Ikit Claw continued to mock Thanquol. 'Finished? Who says it is finished?' The warlock tapped the metal shell with his claw. 'The outside is complete, but the weapon is not operational. It needs power.'

Thanquol lashed his tail in annoyance. He didn't like the turn this conversation had taken. 'You take-make fuel!' he accused. 'Crush-grind much-much warpstone!'

Ikit Claw's eyes were cold as he glowered down at the grey seer. 'But it wasn't enough,' he said. 'The Doomsphere won't work without more warpstone.'

Panic started to seep into Thanquol's belly. It wasn't possible, the Claw was just lying again, playing for time! Unless… maybe the informant had been trying to betray Thanquol as well as Ikit Claw! Maybe the villain had been a secret spy for the Council of Thirteen! The idea of it! A spy from the Council trying to trick a loyal servant of the Council!

'I wouldn't kill me, Thanquol,' the Claw was saying. 'Don't think you can make the Doomsphere work without me. If it has too little warpstone, the machinery will be ruined. Too much…' The Chief Warlock flexed the metal blades of his claw open, evoking the image of a mighty explosion. 'Only I know the correct measure. Without me, you have nothing.'

Thanquol ground his fangs. There was too much assurance in Ikit Claw's posture for it to all be a bluff. The scheming tinker-rat had tricked him! Now there wasn't a chance for him to simply execute the rat!

Thanquol groaned in horror as he saw Boneripper lurch into position. The rat-ogre levelled its warpfire projector straight at Ikit Claw. Before the grey seer could howl a countermand, the automaton sent a sheet of searing green flame shooting across the platform. Skavenslaves and warlock-engineers hurtled from the walkways, their bodies transformed into blazing torches. For a moment, Ikit Claw vanished behind a curtain of fire.

Cursing the Horned Rat, Thanquol leapt towards the inferno. This close to achieving his wildest dreams of power and domination, he wasn't about to be cheated! Not because some brainless rat-ogre had taken it into its mind to attack his valuable ally just when their plans were coming to fruition! He ignored the flames that licked about him as he scrambled onto the platform. Somewhere amid the inferno, his great friend and loyal comrade Ikit Claw was in peril!

'Ikit Claw!' the grey seer cried out. 'Don't die-die! My magic heal-fix all burn-hurt!' After all, Ikit Claw had survived a worse fire in his own laboratory, surely he'd be able to escape a stupid accident like this! Thanquol glanced down as his paws broke through the charred husk of a skavenslave, the body crumbling into ash beneath his toes. 'Ikit Claw!' he cried out, panic hammering at his heart. 'Good-good friend! Don't die-die!' What was the use, the grey seer thought, of being Chief Warlock of Clan Skryre if you let yourself get killed by some brainless rat-ogre!

A shape stepped out from the smoke, its metal mask and iron frame glowing red from the heat of the warpfire. It seemed to Thanquol that even more of Ikit Claw's white fur was burned away than he remembered, but at least the Chief Warlock looked mostly intact. Clearly the warlock's magic had been great enough to preserve him from Boneripper's idiotic attack.

'Ikit Claw!' Thanquol squealed in relief. 'Are you hurt?'

There was an ugly look in Ikit Claw's eyes. 'Not-not as bad-hurt as you will be!' the warlock snarled. Ikit pounced towards Thanquol, his huge metal claw raking against the Doomsphere's shell as he tried to disembowel the grey seer.

Squeaking in terror, Thanquol leapt back. His jump carried him too far, bringing him past the edge of the platform. The grey seer's arms waved frantically as he fell to the floor of the cavern some dozen feet below. Crashing on his backside, he yelped in pain as something in his tail broke. He didn't have long to consider his injury, however. Ikit Claw loomed above him, a warplock pistol in his hand. Savagely, the Chief Warlock squeezed the trigger.

Thanquol blinked in disbelief as Ikit Claw's pistol exploded in his hand, misfiring in the most dramatic fashion. That would teach the faithless flea the folly of pointing his heathen weapons at a priest of the Horned Rat! Before the grey seer could crow about his escape, he was scrambling across the cavern floor, fleeing as Ikit Claw discharged the warpfire projector built into the palm of his metal hand. The green flames pursued Thanquol as he scrambled for cover.

'Peace-friend! Thanquol cried out. It occurred to him that while he needed Ikit Claw, the Claw didn't need him. That gave the Chief Warlock the edge. Glancing about the cavern, Thanquol also came to the ugly realisation that almost all of the watching skaven were cheering his adversary. The only ones who didn't seem to share that sentiment were Boneripper and Nikkrit, the latter still ringing his bell as though it were the most important job in the Under-Empire. Thanquol was beginning to think his standard-bearer wasn't quite right in the head.

Upon the platform, Ikit Claw snarled orders at the other skaven. From dozens of hidden caches, a veritable arsenal of pistols, jezzails and even stranger weapons emerged. One of the warlock-engineers scurried towards the Doomsphere, the menacing Storm Daemon clutched in his paws. Chittering with malicious mirth, Ikit Claw snatched the magic blade from his underling. A gang of ratmen were already crawling over Boneripper, pulling the rat-ogre to the ground. Without receiving orders from its master, the machine didn't even move to defend itself.

'Now, Thanquol-meat die-burn!' Ikit Claw screeched, raising Storm Daemon overhead. A bolt of crackling black energy erupted from the halberd, the new warp generator fastened to the weapon shuddering as it fed power into the blade. Thanquol spurted the musk of fear as the malignant energy scorched a hole through the pile of scrap he was sheltering behind.

'Hand of Vecteek!' Thanquol shouted, waving the artefact through the air, trying to remind Ikit Claw of the power he still possessed.

Ikit Claw laughed again. The Chief Warlock slapped his metal hand against the shell of the Doomsphere. 'Kill me and you lose the Doomsphere!'

Thanquol rolled his eyes. The damn litter-runt! By the Horned One, he'd suffer for this! After the Doomsphere was finished, of course. The grey seer wracked his brain for some way to extricate himself from the situation without hurting Ikit Claw. Almost choking on the words, he called out, 'I let-allow you to share the Doomsphere.'

His answer was a fusillade that blasted the scrap

pile and sent shards of metal flying about the cavern. Thanquol was forced to hug the ground, cringing as warpstone bullets whistled over his head and Poison Wind globes shattered against the wall behind him.

Clenching his eyes closed, Thanquol prayed to the Horned Rat. Surely his god could see the trouble he was in. These deluded, misbegotten heretic tinker-rats were standing in the way of progress, obstructing the natural order of dominance that had maintained the Under-Empire for thousands of years. They were trying to upset the careful structure of leadership the Horned Rat himself had established at the Great Summoning. If they weren't stopped, the cruel warlocks of Clan Skryre would seize control of the Under-Empire for themselves and initiate an unprecedented age of despotism and wickedness! Thanquol was the only chance there was to stop Ikit Claw's monstrous machine from being put to such a villainous purpose! Surely the wise and beneficent Horned One could see that!

Squeaks of fright suddenly sounded through the cavern. Thanquol opened his eyes. For a moment he expected to see a legion of the Horned Rat's daemons come to rescue him from the treachery of Clan Skryre. He was a bit dismayed to see the source of the disturbance was just a pack of grubby skaven, leftovers from Bonestash's resident population. His ears pricked up when he caught the nature of their whines.

Dwarfs! There were dwarfs in the tunnels! Somehow the fur-faced rabble had tracked Ikit Claw down, using a great boring machine to chew their way into the skaven warren. Thanquol chittered happily to himself. All he had to do now was sit back and let his enemies annihilate each other!

* * *

THE DWARFS RUSHED through the dirty, ramshackle tunnels, their fierce war-cries echoing through the warren. Despite the ferocity of their cries and the gleaming axes in their hands, the warriors made no effort to attack the verminous creatures that came scurrying out from every dark passageway and black cave. The orders they had been given had been blunt in their directness. They were after big prey and the quickest way to find that prey was to follow the stragglers.

Any dwarf with experience fighting the ratkin knew of their natural cowardice. Confronted by a foe, the skaven would flee unless they far outnumbered their enemy. And where would they run? To someplace where they felt they would be safe. Such as the lair of the despotic monsters who ruled over them.

Klarak Bronzehammer was thankful the warriors were so disciplined. The skaven nest was a confusing labyrinth of boltholes and ratruns, dark and narrow, a place where an army might lose itself for weeks. There was no rhyme or reason behind the layout of the warren, new tunnels and chambers appearing wherever space allowed. Klarak suspected the ratkin themselves didn't know the layout of their home, using scent rather than memory to guide them through the confusion. One thing a dwarf lacked was the keenness of a skaven's nose, but by flushing the ratmen out from their holes and following them, they could still exploit the olfactory advantage of their enemy.

Four hundred dwarfs marched with Klarak, as many warriors and miners as Karak Angkul could muster without sacrificing the guards watching the surface gates or those still hunting skaven in the lower deeps. Among the company were King Logan and his hammerers as well as Runelord Morag, a company of longbeards carrying the hold's Anvil of Doom through the skaven tunnels. It was a testament to just how seriously Klarak's warnings about Ikit Claw and his weapon had been taken. The Anvil was one of the dwarfhold's most prized relics. To risk its loss in the murk and slime of a skaven burrow was not the sort of chance any dwarf would take lightly.

'They're all scurrying in the same direction,' Horgar Horgarsson observed. He had stubbornly refused to be left behind in the smelthall, insisting that he was fine after Klarak made a few spot repairs to his steam-harness. By long experience, Klarak knew it was useless to argue with his friend.

'So now you're the tracker?' scoffed Thorlek, the ranger's furs oddly bulky. The oddity was caused by the wire vest Klarak had compelled his surviving aides to wear. The deaths of Kurgaz and Azram had struck the inventor especially hard. He wanted to take no chances of losing any more of his Iron Throng.

'Never mind following them,' snarled Mordin Grimstone. Like Horgar, the slayer had flatly refused to be left behind. Unlike Horgar, however, there was no question about the gravity of Mordin's wounds. Kimril's hasty surgery might have stopped most of the bleeding, but the slayer's body still looked like a piece of chewed meat. 'When do we start killing them?' Mordin fingered his axe, a murderous gleam in his eyes.

'A bit more patience,' Klarak cautioned. 'The ratkin lead us to their leaders.' The engineer felt a twinge of dread as he spoke. The warning from Altdorf rose clear in his mind. Morag and the others who had fought in the Sixth Deep were certain they had seen a horned priest among the skaven. They were equally certain the creature had escaped. That meant Thanquol was alive and likely still helping Ikit Claw with his hellish weapon.

It was not too late. Klarak could still turn back, leave the destruction of Ikit Claw and the Doomsphere to King Logan. The engineer sighed. Even with the warning, he couldn't turn back. Ikit Claw had to be stopped and his presence in the battle could mean the difference between victory and disaster. If Thanquol was there, then Klarak had to take his chances.

Sometimes, even prophecies went wrong.

Klarak had to be there, had to make certain that, one way or another, the Doomsphere was destroyed. If the dwarfs had to, they would demolish the infernal machine themselves.

The increased sound of skaven squeals and squeaks was the first warning the dwarfs had that they were near their goal. The cramped tunnel gradually opened outwards, linking to a network of broader tunnels. Klarak drew his steam pistol, warning those with him to likewise get their weapons ready. The fight the dwarfs had been spoiling for was almost upon them.

'You should keep back,' Horgar advised as they watched the last pack of skaven scuttle down the tunnel and around the corner all the noise was coming from. 'There could be almost anything in there.'

Klarak patted his bodyguard's shoulder. 'If anyone has to be up front, it's me,' he said. He produced the special goggles, slipping them down over his head, leaving them on his forehead so they could be dropped over his eyes when needed. 'I have to see if the ratkin have used the treated plates. I have to know that the Master Rune has been fitted to the Doomsphere.'

'One of us can do that just as easily,' objected Thorlek.

The gold-bearded engineer shook his head. 'My plan,

my neck,' he said. 'Just keep the ratkin off me long enough to make sure.' He cocked his head to one side, listening as the squeaks of the skaven suddenly took on an angry tone. Some leader, probably Ikit Claw, was trying to whip the frightened mob into some sort of defence. If the dwarfs were going to strike, the best time was before the ratmen got themselves organised.

'Bring the thunderers to the fore,' Klarak advised Thane Erkii. The Minemaster nodded his head, conveying the order down the line. Klarak waited only long enough for the dwarf gunners to push their way through the press of warriors. They presented a grim, menacing appearance, their armour sooty and bloodstained from the fighting in the smelthall. They had lost kith and comrades in the battle, losses they were eager to avenge on the ratkin. It was only right that first blood should be theirs.

Klarak Bronzehammer led the way, flanked by Horgar and Mordin. Running after the last of the fleeing ratmen, the dwarfs soon found themselves at the entrance to a vast cavern. From floor to ceiling, the chamber was littered with a riotous confusion of ratwalks and platforms. Skaven were scattered throughout the elevated tiers, a motley arrangement of sinister weapons clutched in their hairy paws. The armed ratmen glared down at the invaders, their eyes gleaming with a volatile mixture of hate and fear.

Klarak gave the skaven only the briefest notice, his eyes drawn to the sinister round bulk which dominated the centre of the cavern, surrounded by wooden platforms, teams of skaven still crawling over its superstructure. The engineer felt a chill run down his spine as he gazed upon the hideous weapon. Ikit Claw had made some improvements on his previous Doomsphere. This one was easily twice the size of the last, nearly as large as a steamship, and the smell of warpstone rising from it was enough to make Klarak gag. He didn't want to think about the kind of destruction such a weapon could unleash.

Thunderers dashed into the cavern, coming up short as they stared in fascinated horror at the sinister machine. The skaven squeaked anxiously as they saw the massed ranks of gunmen spilling into their lair. For a moment, both sides stood frozen, gripped by shock and indecision. Silence spread across the cavern.

Into that silence, came a scratchy voice. 'Dwarf-things! Drop-leave weapons! Surrender-submit! Fight and all dwarf-meat will die-die!'

GREY SEER THANQUOL rose from behind the pile of scrap he had taken shelter behind. The onset of the dwarfs had turned the attentions of Ikit Claw's murderous crew to more important matters. Thanquol saw an opportunity to escape, to slink away while the ratmen turned their guns on the dwarfs. It was a very tempting idea, but one that made the grey seer's mouth taste sour. This close to achieving his wildest dreams, to attaining the destiny which was his birthright as the favoured prophet-sorcerer of the Horned One – no, he would not slink off like a wounded wolf-rat! The Doomsphere was his! All he had to do was impress that fact upon the heretic vermin trying to kill him!

Thanquol saw the confusion and fear in the postures of the skaven as they hastily climbed into the ratwalks and prepared themselves for the attack. Ikit Claw had some talent for knocking together contraptions of steel and bronze, but the Chief Warlock was a poor leader. He could threaten and bully his subordinates, but he couldn't instil anything like courage and valour, he couldn't fire the ferocity of his underlings by invoking the holy words of the Horned Rat.

Thanquol could and he would. He would snatch leadership of these maggots away from Ikit Claw, he would fire their craven souls with the fury of the Horned One and drive them to victory over the dwarfs. They would praise him as their saviour, as their guardian and protector. Then, a twitch of a whisker, and they would turn against Ikit Claw. Under torture, the Claw would reveal everything he knew about the Doomsphere down to how many bolts it took to hold the thing together. Thanquol would enjoy teasing his secrets from the Claw's torn flesh.

First, however, there was the annoying matter of the dwarfs to consider. Thanquol felt a flash of fear as he saw the gold-bearded dwarf from the mines leading the invaders. That insufferable animal had survived some of the worst magic the grey seer could conjure, and Thanquol wasn't terribly happy to see the dwarf still possessed the horrible pistol that had riddled Boneripper with holes. His quick glance showed him the dwarf's weaknesses as well as his strengths. There was an unmistakable expression of terror in the invader's eyes as he stared at the Doomsphere. Thanquol could use that terror. He bruxed his fangs as an idea came to him.

Stepping out from his cover, Thanquol called out to the dwarf-things in their harsh, cumbersome language. The grey seer felt his fur crawl as the eyes of the dwarfs turned on him. He appreciated just how exposed he was, but it was a necessary risk if he was going to impress the treacherous Clan Skryre skaven. They had to know he was a brave and imposing war-leader, unafraid of the things that sent yellow fear slithering down their spines.

Thanquol's heart pounded against his ribs as the eyes of Klarak Bronzehammer fell upon him. The grey seer cast a covetous gaze at a stack of timbers close by. They would make a convenient shelter. A sidewise glance at the Doomsphere made him dismiss the thought. The dwarf was more afraid than he was. That made him the stronger.

'Surrender-submit!' Thanquol hissed. 'Or I start-begin Doomsphere! Destroy-kill all dwarf-burrow!' The grey seer gestured imperiously towards the weapon. It looked complete. There was no way the dwarfs could know it wasn't. He could see from the way the colour drained out of Klarak's face that the dwarf understood the havoc the machine was capable of.

A scuffle broke out among the dwarfs. A shaven-headed maniac tried to charge Thanquol. The grey seer spurted the musk of fear when he saw the ginger-furred dwarf and the hate gleaming in his eyes. Thanquol quickly jerked his gaze across the rest of the throng, looking to see if the slayer had a human pet tagging along with him.

The threat was quickly subdued, a big dwarf with a curious metal framework supporting his body grappling the slayer in a fierce bearhug. Thanquol chittered maliciously to see the frustrated fury on the slayer's face. After the dwarfs laid down their weapons, that fanatic would be the first one to die. Thanquol might even do the job himself, if it looked reasonably safe.

'Drop-leave weapons!' Thanquol cried out, pointing impatiently at the ground.

Klarak glared back at the grey seer. 'No,' the dwarf spat.

Thanquol lashed his tail angrily. Why was it that dwarfs were never as stupid as they looked? He pointed his staff at the Doomsphere, reminding Klarak of its menace. 'Start-start Doomsphere! Kill-kill all dwarf-meat!' he threatened.

The engineer shook his head. 'No,' he repeated. His gold-flake eyes became as cold as the black aethyr itself. Thanquol instinctively cringed under the gaze. 'I have been warned that you are my doom. But perhaps, I am yours.' Klarak raised his steam pistol.

Fixated upon the menace of the dwarfs, Thanquol did not hear the shot until the bullet went zipping through his robes. The grey seer leaped into the air, landing on all fours, shivering in terror. A sharp squeak of agony sounded from nearby, punctuated by the discordant clatter of a bell striking the ground. Thanquol swung his head around to see Nikkrit topple to the floor, a bloody hole gaping in his chest. The grey seer fumbled at his robes, noting with horror the blackened burn marks where the bullet had passed, missing him by the width of a whisker.

Thanquol's would-be killer snarled, hurling the spent warplock pistol at the grey seer's head. Ikit Claw's eyes gleamed with outraged fury. Twice frustrated in his efforts to kill the grey seer, the warlock gnashed his fangs and spun around to retrieve Storm Daemon from where it leaned against the side of the Doomsphere.

IKIT CLAW'S SHOT threw the cavern into pandemonium. The tense standoff was shattered in a deafening din of gunfire and the hideous whoosh of warpflame. Skaven shrieked as dwarf bullets smashed into their bodies, pitching them headlong to the cavern floor. Dwarfs screamed as their armour was gouged by warpstone missiles, the poisonous stones searing through their bodies. A swath of the entrance became an inferno of green fire as a ratkin warpfire projector doused it in flame.

Where lesser foes would have broken, the dwarfs remained steadfast. The thunderers returned the erratic fire of the skaven skirmishers while squads of axe-bearing warriors rushed into the cavern, climbing into the ratwalks and taking the fight to their cringing foes.

Klarak watched Thanquol scramble across the floor, seeking shelter behind a pile of timber. The engineer started after the fleeing grey seer, then stopped himself. His own peril wasn't important. The greater threat to the whole of the dwarf kingdom had to be confronted first. He lowered the goggles over his eyes, smiling coldly as he saw the engravings shining out from the Barrazhunk plates that formed the Doomsphere's shell. Most of the engravings had been scratched out, obliterated by Kurgaz's burin when he failed to complete them. One plate, however, had not been defaced. Standing out bold and bright, it bore the Master Rune.

Activity at the base of the Doomsphere drew the engineer's attention. Klarak felt his heart go cold with hate as he saw Ikit Claw throw away his pistol and reach for the black length of Storm Daemon. Here was the killer of Kurgaz and Azram and so many other dwarfs. Here was the monster who had built this hellish machine, the fiend who would destroy the mountains themselves in his obscene lust for power.

Klarak aimed his pistol at the Chief Warlock. Destroying the Doomsphere was only a half measure. While Ikit Claw lived, there was a chance the monster could build another.

* * *

THANQUOL SCRAMBLED BEHIND the pile of timbers, clapping his paws against his horns as bullets whistled around him. He wasn't certain if the shooters were dwarfs or ratmen, but at the moment he didn't much care. Things had spiralled out of control, beyond his ability to recover. It was all that traitorous weasel Ikit Claw's fault! There was a time for disputing leadership positions, but to do so in the face of the enemy! Any decent skaven would set aside such petty squabbles and form a common front against their foes! What Ikit Claw had done was tantamount to treason against the whole of skavendom!

A thrill of satisfaction swept through the grey seer's body as he heard the distinct discharge of Klarak's steam pistol and saw Ikit Claw struck by the dwarf's marksmanship. The Chief Warlock's iron frame deflected most of the bullets, but a few struck spots not protected by his magic armour. The Claw wilted to the floor of the platform, blood gushing from wounds in his legs and shoulder. Only his grip on his halberd kept him from collapsing completely.

Good! Let the faithless maggot die! The dwarf-things were welcome to him. Thanquol might even help them if they looked unable to finish the job!

The grey seer's nose twitched as a horrible realisation came upon him. Finish the job! Ikit Claw still had to finish the Doomsphere! It was worthless without him! Fishing a tiny piece of warpstone from his robe, Thanquol frantically ground the pebble into dust between his fangs, drawing its energies into his body.

Hastily, the grey seer formed the energy into a spell, evoking a sorcerous shield to stand between the brave Ikit Claw and his murderous persecutors. A shimmering haze of yellow fog formed in front of the wounded warlock. The hail of bullets coming from Klarak's pistol struck the fog but went no farther, stuck like flies in amber.

Thanquol grinned at the success of his spell. Ikit Claw would be grateful for his rescue and his gratitude would place him even more firmly under the grey seer's control. Now he'd freely offer up the secrets of the Doomsphere and then...

A fierce dwarf war-cry brought Thanquol whipping around. Ikit Claw, Klarak Bronzehammer, the Doomsphere, all of these were forgotten as a crazed, half-naked dwarf came screaming across the cavern. The dwarf's eyes blazed with maniacal fury. Thanquol was surprised to note that the creature had a familiar smell about it. Again, he glanced nervously for any sign of a human tagalong.

'Thanquol!' the slayer howled, brandishing the axes filling each of his powerful hands. 'I am Mordin Grimstone! You killed my brother! For that, you die!'

CHAPTER XVI

THANQUOL FELT RAW fear squirming through his innards as the crazed dwarf dived at him. Mordin brought both of his axes slashing down, their sharp edges shining in the green warp-light. In a panic, the grey seer threw all of his magical energies into erecting another shell of aethyric force to repulse his attacker. The yellow haze leapt into existence between himself and the slayer. Mordin struck the barrier as though it were a solid wall, rebounding from it and crashing to the floor.

Any hope that the dwarf maniac had broken his own neck vanished a few moments later when Mordin lurched back onto his feet. The dwarf's face was a mask of blood, his nose squashed into an unrecognisable mush, but the slayer's eyes continued to burn with the raw fury of unbridled hate. He crashed his axes together and rushed towards Thanquol, slashing his blades against the magic barrier, as though he might cut his way through the grey seer's sorcery.

Such unreasoning insanity made Thanquol's glands clench. What had he done to warrant such obsessed hate? Killed the dwarf-thing's litter-kin? Surely the deranged beast had plenty of others! Why did he have to get so emotional about it?

Thanquol realised with horror that the slayer was doing the impossible. He was making progress. Step by step his axes were cutting through the barrier. For the first time, Thanquol noticed the faint smell of magic about the axes, his eyes spotting the runes gleaming in the axe blades. Cursing all dwarfs and their sneaky magic, the grey seer summoned his fading energies for another spell. He'd have to be a good deal more proactive about destroying his would-be killer.

A crackling stream of green lightning erupted from the head of Thanquol's staff, snapping around the slayer's body. Mordin howled in agony, electricity dancing across his axes and blazing about his teeth. Smoke rose from the dwarf's beard and headcrest, blood boiled about his open wounds. The grey seer chittered with amusement as his enemy crumpled to the ground. So would fall all who opposed the might of Grey Seer Thanquol and the Horned Rat!

Chittering laughter died in a squeal of fright. The dwarf raised his head, his hateful eyes glaring at Thanquol. Painfully, Mordin gained his feet, spitting a blob of blood onto the floor. 'You killed my brother,' he growled. 'Now you die.'

With a lunge, the slayer hurled himself towards Thanquol. Desperately, the grey seer raised his staff, pouring his fading magical energies into strengthening its wooden substance, rendering it tougher than steel. In his panic, Thanquol dissolved the sorcerous shell protecting Ikit Claw, channelling the reclaimed energies into his own defence. The Chief Warlock would have to fend for himself now, Thanquol had more pressing concerns to worry about.

Mordin's axes rebounded from the strengthened staff, sending the dwarf stumbling backwards. Thanquol swung the heavy metal head of his staff at the slayer, the sharp edge slashing across the dwarf's breast. Satisfied that he'd gained at least a few seconds, the grey seer scrambled onto the pile of timbers, trying to reach one of the overhanging ratwalks. Behind him, he heard the slayer's angry voice. The timber pile shuddered as Mordin used his axes to hack away at Thanquol's refuge.

The grey seer made a frantic leap for the lowest of the ratwalks, his flailing claws missing the edge of the platform by inches. Squeaking in fright, he crashed to the floor, his staff knocked from his hand, the breath crushed from his lungs. Thanquol rolled onto his back, his terrified gaze turning back towards the timber pile. Mordin stood there, crashing his axes together, vengeance burning in his eyes. Uttering a savage war-cry, the slayer leapt down upon his foe.

A frightened squeal rose from the grey seer as he rolled away, scurrying across the floor on all fours. Mordin's axes gouged the earth as he landed. The slayer roared with frustration when he found there wasn't a furry body beneath his blades. Ripping the axes free, he rounded on the cringing Thanquol.

'Run, vermin! You won't escape death, and you won't escape me!'

Thanquol fingered another shard of warpstone. So soon after drawing upon the aethyric energies trapped inside it, he wasn't anxious to take the risk of taking any more. The image of his body disintegrating into a puddle of twitching flesh wasn't a pleasant one. Then again, the image of being hacked to ribbons by a crazed dwarf-thing wasn't appealing either.

'Boneripper!' Thanquol cried out in desperation. 'Save-guard your master-lord!'

Mordin's axes came slashing down, one of them ripping the sleeve from Thanquol's robe, another glancing off the side of his horn. The embattled grey seer kicked out with his legs, his claws slashing across Mordin's belly. The dwarf grunted in pain, but the feeble attack wasn't enough to stop his relentless assault.

The immense shape that loomed up behind him, however, was. Boneripper's skeletal claws closed about the dwarf's body before he knew the rat-ogre was there. Mordin cried out in rage as the mechanical monster lifted him from the ground. His axes chopped at the brute's arms, chipping the bone and denting the steel. Boneripper gave no notice of the dwarf's frenzied attack, oblivious to the hurt being inflicted upon it.

'Grimnir!' the slayer shrieked, hurling one of his axes full into the face of his attacker. The gromril blade bit deep into Boneripper's fleshless skull, catching fast in its mechanical brain. For an instant, the rat-ogre shuddered, its body freezing. Thanquol cursed the stupid contraption, allowing itself to be destroyed before it had disposed of his enemy. Mordin laughed, a cruel sound filled with murderous mirth, and turned his remaining axe against the rat-ogre's claws. One of the bony digits went spinning away, followed soon after by a second. In a matter of moments, the slayer would free himself.

Then Boneripper suddenly lurched back into motion, its mechanisms recovering from the trauma of Mordin's axe. Savagely, the rat-ogre lifted its victim into the air and began to twist the dwarf's body. Blood cascaded down the monster's claws as it wrenched the slayer apart.

KLARAK BRONZEHAMMER RACED towards the Doomsphere, determined that this time Ikit Claw would not escape. The bullets from his steam pistol clattered against the warlock's armour, but a few shots managed to strike the gaps in his defences. Unfortunately, the Claw had more than his insidious technologies to protect him. Before Klarak could finish him off, a magic barrier sprang up between the engineer and his enemy, trapping the bullets that would have ended the monster's evil.

Klarak tossed the spent steam pistol aside, unslinging the steam hammer lashed across his back. Around him, the battle raged. Dwarf warriors fought the teeming hordes of ratmen across the cavern, up in the rickety ratwalks and platforms, wherever their verminous foes could be found. The skaven took a deadly toll on their attackers, warpstone bullets burning through even the heaviest armour, Poison Wind smothering the fiercest of fighters. Entire ratwalks came crashing to the floor, torn from their moorings by the weight of those fighting upon them or else burned loose by the green hell-flame of the warpfire projectors.

The battle hung in the balance. The dwarfs were limited by how many of their number could charge through the cavern entrance at one time and many of their best troops were still confined to the tunnels outside. Entering the cavern, the invaders presented opportune targets for the jezzails clustered about the highest tiers of platforms. The marksmanship of the skaven was slovenly, but in the press of armoured bodies at the entrance, even the worst shot couldn't fail to inflict harm.

If the dwarfs were to be certain of victory, then they needed to shatter the cornered courage of the ratkin. The best way to do that was to remove their leader. It was doubly important now that Klarak eliminate Ikit Claw quickly.

The engineer rushed across the cavern, his steam hammer lashing out and crushing the skull of a black-furred ratman who lunged at him from a pile of scrap. A second skaven, a glowing sword clutched in its paws, made a dive for Klarak's back. Before he could sink his blade home, the ratman found himself smashed down by the hammer of Horgar Horgarsson.

'You don't make it easy on your bodyguard,' Horgar grumbled, shaking the crushed ratman from the head of his hammer.

'Nothing worth fighting for is easy,' Klarak replied. He pointed at the Doomsphere. 'I'm going after Ikit. Keep the rest of the ratkin off me.'

Horgar nodded, his steam-powered armour venting vapour as he charged ahead of his friend. A tangle of ratmen leapt out of hiding to assault the dwarf and keep him from reaching their master. Horgar laughed as he drove his hammer into the bestial mob, breaking limbs and crushing skulls at every turn. Several skaven held back, trying to train the lethal length of a warpfire projector on the hammerer, heedless of their own comrades who would be caught in the blast.

Before they could unleash the fury of their weapon, a concentrated barrage of bullets smashed into the ratmen's ranks. Thorlek snarled as he unloaded his steam pistol into the cringing monsters, crying out jubilantly as one of his shots punctured the fuel canister for the projector and engulfed the slinking killers in a spray of burning liquid.

Klarak exploited the violence to run past the rat-men defending the Doomsphere. Throwing himself up the ramshackle ladder, the adventurer brought his steam hammer cracking into the chest of a last skaven who scurried out from hiding. Then he turned his eyes towards his real enemy.

Ikit Claw glared at Klarak from behind his metal mask. The Chief Warlock leaned heavily upon Storm Daemon, using the deadly weapon as a crutch to support his weakened body. Black blood coated the rat-man's tattered robes and stained the plates of his iron frame.

'Bronzehammer,' Ikit Claw hissed. 'You try to stop me, but you cannot stop-kill progress!' The skaven tapped his metal claw against the Doomsphere's shell.

'This madness ends now,' Klarak growled back. He rushed the injured skaven, but his charge turned into a wild sprawl when his foe suddenly sprang to one side.

The steel rasp of Ikit's laughter stung Klarak's ears. 'Fool-meat! The only thing ends here is your life!' The warlock lunged at Klarak, slashing the dwarf's vest with his steel claws. The adventurer kicked out with his boot, smashing the side of the skaven's sensitive snout.

Ikit Claw limped back, leaning against Storm Daemon. The warlock had feigned weakness to make his foe overconfident, but he was still in no condition for a protracted fight. Snarling in rage, he pointed his metal claw at Klarak, the blades opening outwards and exposing the nozzle of the warpfire projector built into the palm.

Klarak rolled away, throwing himself over the side of the platform an instant before the Claw's fire came for him. His fingers closed about the edge of the scaffold-

ing, holding him just beneath the lip of the platform.
He waited until the sound of Ikit's weapon faded, then,
with a display of strength incredible even for a dwarf,
he pulled himself back onto the charred platform.
Before Ikit could unleash a second gout of warpfire,
Klarak flung a small, egg-shaped grenade at the ratman.
It exploded against the metal claw, coating the weapon
in white powder.

The Claw's nose twitched and a snarl of unbridled
rage screamed through his clenched fangs. He recognised the scent of Klarak's smother-dust and knew what
would happen if he tried to send another burst of warpfire after his enemy. The skaven lashed his tail in fury,
his eyes blazing with a mad light.

'Fool-meat! Now all-all dwarf-thing die!' Ikit Claw
sprang away as Klarak dived for him. The warlock
turned, slashing the blades of his claw at the engineer's
head. Klarak ducked beneath the murderous sweep
of his enemy's talons, wincing as he heard the sharp
blades grind against the shell of the Doomsphere.

Klarak tackled the crazed warlock, locking his arms
about the ratman's waist and spilling him to the floor
of the platform. The talons of Ikit's feet raked against
the dwarf's legs, scratching uselessly against the engineer's armour.

'All-all dwarf-thing die!' Ikit Claw raged. The warlock
brought his head smacking full into Klarak's face, the
metal helmet cracking into the dwarf's skull with the
force of a hammer. Klarak reeled back in pain, loos-
ening his grip enough for his foe to squirm out from
beneath him.

Ikit Claw stumbled away, lurching towards a panel of
levers and gears projecting from the side of the Doomsphere. 'Now all-all dwarf-thing die!' he squealed

triumphantly. Scratchy laughter shook the ratman as he saw Klarak stagger to his feet. 'Too late, Bronzehammer! Your dwarf-metal was all I needed!

'My Doomsphere is fully operational!'

THANQUOL CHORTLED WITH glee as Boneripper twisted Mordin in half. The deranged slayer deserved such a fate, obsessing over something as trivial as the demise of a litter-mate. No skaven would have ever been so petty in his hatred.

The immediate threat of the slayer removed, Thanquol turned his attention back to Ikit Claw. If the idiot had gotten himself killed in the last few minutes, the grey seer hoped the Horned One had an especially nasty hell arranged for Ikit's soul! Cheating Thanquol of his rightful destiny, what greater depths of treachery could a skaven sink to?

Thanquol breathed a little easier when he saw Ikit Claw standing beside the Doomsphere, the gold-bearded dwarf bleeding and helpless at his feet. There was still some life in the dwarf, which meant Thanquol still had a chance to strike down the fool and put himself into the Claw's good graces. Then it would just be a small matter of assassinating the warlock once the Doomsphere was complete.

Summoning up a small measure of power, just enough to send a flicker of warp-lightning searing through Klarak's heart, Thanquol hesitated when he heard Ikit's steel voice. The grey seer's fangs snapped together in a snarl when he heard the warlock boast that the Doomsphere was operational.

The scheming flea had been lying to him all along! The weapon was already complete! There was no reason now to suffer the warlock-engineer's insufferable heresy and treason! Hissing malignantly, Thanquol pointed his staff at Ikit Claw.

Before the grey seer could unleash his magic against the traitorous rat, he heard the Claw speak again. Something about killing all of the dwarfs. Thanquol's empty glands clenched as the warlock's true intentions struck his brain.

The mad, psychopathic maniac was going to activate the Doomsphere! In all of his plans for the weapon, Thanquol had never intended to actually use it! He'd smash the very empire he wanted to conquer!

Surely Ikit Claw wasn't crazed enough to think he could activate the Doomsphere and not wreak untold destruction upon skavendom! The answer came to Thanquol in a burst of fear. The Claw was crazy, obsessed with his science and his technology. He didn't care what happened to the Under-Empire, so long as he could boast about unleashing the most destructive force ever known to ratkin! The Claw would ruin all of skavendom just so he could measure the power of his bomb!

Thanquol sent the bolt of warp-lightning sizzling across the cavern. The malignant magic crackled over Klarak's prone body, streaking straight towards Ikit Claw. The warlock's body was engulfed in the discharge, snakes of electricity writhing about him. But the fury of Thanquol's spell was quickly spent, draining away into the warp generator fitted to Storm Daemon's blade. An unharmed Ikit Claw turned, fangs bared beneath his metal mask. His beady eyes fixed hatefully on his horned attacker.

'Die-die, fool-meat!' Ikit snapped, his metal claw closing about one of the levers and thrusting it upwards. The metal-faced warlock chittered maniacally as the

immense Doomsphere shuddered into life, warp-steam
venting from its sides, electricity crackling about its
shell. Still laughing, Ikit Claw pressed his paw against
his belt. The next instant, the warlock vanished in a
cloud of purple smoke.

Squeals of horror shuddered through the cavern as
the embattled skaven became aware of their master's
treachery. Better than anyone, they knew the awful
potential of the Doomsphere. Sheer terror sent them
scurrying down from the ratwalks, fleeing across the
cavern straight into the waiting axes and hammers of
the dwarfs.

Thanquol glanced at the entranceway, not terribly
keen to share the fate of all the skaven being so dra-
matically cut down by the dwarfs. There was always the
possibility of using his magic to escape. He fingered a
piece of warpstone, knowing that if he could control its
energies he'd be able to skitterleap through the void.
The only problem was doing so would possibly result
in his reappearing inside a solid wall. That sounded
about as messy as anything the Doomsphere would do
to him.

The Doomsphere! There was still a chance! If he
could just shut the thing down, he'd overcome Ikit's
treachery and possess the most powerful weapon in
skavendom! Thanquol nervously took a pinch of warp-
snuff to quell the terror coursing through his veins. The
difference between a leader and a slave was making sure
greed was never stifled by fear.

Scurrying across the cavern, Thanquol rushed to
stop the Doomsphere. He leapt onto the bucking work
platform, the energies of the machine causing the scaf-
folding to roll and shiver like an angry sea. As he tried
to gain his footing, he saw Klarak dive down from the

platform. The dwarf was wearing strange goggles over his eyes and kept glancing back at the Doomsphere's shell. Thanquol contemplated sending a blast of magic burning through the dwarf's back, but quickly suppressed the murderous urge. First he had to stop the Doomsphere, then he could worry about the dwarf-things.

Horns blasted throughout the cavern, the deep brazen notes of dwarf trumpets. They were withdrawing from the chamber, fleeing back into the tunnels. Thanquol could hear Klarak's voice raised in warning, urging his comrades to run, as though the fools could escape the destructive might of the Doomsphere by running! Thanquol was almost tempted to let the bomb detonate just to show the dwarfs what fools they were.

The grey seer clapped his paws to his horns. That was the warp-snuff talking!

Frantically, Thanquol raced to the control box. He stared stupidly at the bizarre array of buttons, levers and gears, trying to maintain his footing as the Doomsphere bucked and shuddered around him. The violent vibrations emanating from the machine were causing the walls to shudder, knocking great chunks of rock from the roof and collapsing the confusion of ratwalks and platforms. Thanquol's glands clenched as the whole cavern groaned. He risked a look over his shoulder, watching as the last of the dwarfs hurried back into the tunnels. He'd have never believed the creatures could move so fast.

Fear pounding in his chest, Thanquol cursed the confusion of controls and turned his thought to some other way of disabling the amok Doomsphere. He'd never made it a point to study the workings of Clan Skryre's obscene technology. The only proper magic for skaven to study was that which had been taught to them by the Horned Rat. Yet he remembered snatches of conversation he'd had with Heskit One Eye before the Battle of Nuln. He recalled something about the warlock-engineers using different coloured wires in their machines and how any of their devices could be shut down by pulling out the red wires.

The Doomsphere's vibrations sent a hill-sized chunk of rock smashing down, gouging a deep pit in the cavern floor. Warp-steam exploded from the machine's vents, corroding the walls. Fingers of lightning whipped about the platform, nearly scorching Thanquol's tail.

The grey seer needed no further prompting. Grinding his fangs together, he lunged at the control box, slipping his claws beneath the brass covering and ripping it free. The red wire! All he had to do was rip out the red wire!

Thanquol cursed the name of Ikit Claw and the perfidy of the Horned One! All the wires were black! That deranged maniac had ensured his machine couldn't be stopped by using only one colour wire!

The lightning storm emanating from the quaking Doomsphere increased in its fury, throwing Thanquol from the platform. He was hurled across the quivering ground, ratwalks and boulders crashing down all around him. The grey seer popped the sliver of warpstone into his mouth, grinding it beneath his fangs. He felt the intoxicating rush of aethyric power surge through his body. Then his eyes were drawn upwards.

A boulder the size of a village came crashing down from the ceiling, dropping straight towards the grey seer.

* * *

AT THE CENTRE of the cavern, the immense Doomsphere continued its crazed revolutions. Warp-steam erupted from its broken casing, scorching the walls and chewing apart ceiling and floor. Skaven shrieked as boulders continued to rain down, but the rocks falling towards the whirling mechanisms of the Doomsphere shattered as they came into contact with the murderous cloud of steam.

The plates upon the Doomsphere began to buckle, sucked into the churning maw of its vengeful heart. Even the wondrous alloy which was the pinnacle of dwarf metallurgy could not resist the pull of the weapon's churning belly. Gradually they were torn loose from their fastenings, dragged into the boiling maw of the void-engine.

As the plate marked with the Rune of Power was torn free, the entire machine crumpled, folding in upon itself. A final terrific scream rose from the warp-furnace as the Doomsphere completed its self-annihilation in one last bellow of violence.

THE SKAVEN WARREN shook as a tremendous explosion rumbled through its tunnels. The dwarfs covered themselves with their shields, blocking the shower of rocks and earth that rained down upon them. As the tremors grew, so did the anxiety of the dwarfs. In their own deeps, with good dwarf construction over their heads, they wouldn't have been so scared, but none of them trusted the ramshackle skaven tunnels to withstand such violence.

Thane Erkii and his miners sprang into action, hurriedly fixing braces to the shoddy skaven construction, trying to bolster the strength of the trembling walls. Familiar with the hazards of skaven warrens, the expedition had descended into the depths fully prepared to dig their own shafts to reach their quarry as the cowardly ratmen were prone to collapse their own tunnels. Now that foresight served the dwarfs well.

As the shudders gradually passed and the cramped tunnels began to settle, King Logan and Runelord Morag picked their way through the press of dirt-covered dwarf warriors. The two lords had been too far back in the tunnels to take part in the fighting, but they were eager to get an account from those who had.

'Engineer Klarak,' King Logan addressed the adventurer when he reached the mouth of the tunnel. Klarak bowed respectfully to his sovereign. 'This expedition has been a success? You have settled the grudge laid down against you?'

Klarak shook his head. 'I fear not,' he confessed. 'The Doomsphere is destroyed, but Ikit Claw used his filthy magic to escape.'

Runelord Morag nodded as he heard the engineer's account. 'This was why you requested that Runesmith Kurgaz be allowed to study the Master Rune of Unmaking?'

'No,' Klarak told the white-bearded dwarf. 'Originally I planned to use the Master Rune to protect my own inventions. To keep them from falling into the hands of our enemies.'

'The magic of the Master Rune would do that,' Morag conceded. 'It was created to guard the most potent of runeweapons and to destroy them if any hand but that of a dwarf sought to use them.' The Runelord's expression became bitter. 'I do not believe that allowing such a potent rune to be used upon an abominable construction of the ratkin is either proper or respectful.'

Klarak shook his head. 'Such was not my intention. When I was warned about Thanquol, I felt the need to guard my inventions. That was my only purpose in asking Kurgaz to learn the Master Rune. When I learned that Ikit Claw was also threatening Karak Angkul, I knew there was another way the Master Rune could be used to safeguard the Karak Ankor.'

'You let the skaven finish their machine knowing the Master Rune would cause it to destroy itself the moment it was activated?' Thorlek was astonished by the subtlety of his master's plan.

'First we had to be sure they used the plate with the rune upon it,' Klarak said, tapping the goggles resting across his forehead. 'Once I was certain of that, I knew the skaven were finished.'

'But you said Ikit Claw escaped,' King Logan observed. 'Can you be certain he won't just make another one?'

'He will never be able to build another on such a scale without my barazhunk,' Klarak said. 'And I will never forge the alloy again. Every trace of it will be taken to the smelthall and melted down. The danger it now poses to our people is greater than any benefit it can provide.'

There was a sad tone of resignation in Klarak's voice as he spoke, acknowledging the terrible danger his alloy had brought upon his people. It was ever the way with the dwarfs. Every step forwards only seemed to bring them that much closer to their own doom.

Klarak's eyes grew cold as he thought about doom. Ikit Claw was gone, but there was still the threat of Thanquol hovering over Karak Angkul. If one skaven sorcerer had used magic to escape the Doomsphere's destruction, it was possible the other had done the same. The only way to make certain was to go back into the cavern and dig out Thanquol's corpse.

'We'll have to collect every scrap of barazhunk from the cave,' Horgar said. 'Might take weeks to dig it all out.'

'The Master Rune will have taken care of it,' Runelord Morag said. 'Its power will have reduced the entire machine to dust.'

'There is something just as vital for us to find,' Klarak said, his voice like an icy wind. 'When I ran from the cavern, Thanquol was trying to shut down the Doom-sphere.'

'Clearly he didn't,' Horgar said. 'And if he stayed around any longer than you did, then the whole cavern must have come crashing down about his ears.' The hammerer made a graphic illustration by smashing a rock between his steam-powered gauntlets.

'We can't leave it to chance,' Klarak said. 'We have to dig through the rubble and find his body.'

'And if we don't?' asked King Logan, disliking the worried look in Klarak's eyes.

'Then I'm afraid Karak Angkul is still in danger,' the engineer told him. 'We've saved the rest of the Karak Ankor from the skaven, but our own homes are still threatened.'

THANQUOL HUGGED HIS arms against his sides, the chill of the void clinging to him like a cloak of frost. His empty glands kept clenching, trying to spurt the musk of fear, his mind racing with the raw terror of his passage through the aethyr. Every time he invoked his magic to sunder the veil between worlds he was certain he'd never emerge safely. The void was populated by numberless legions of damned spirits and ravenous daemons, each of them eager to ravage a mortal intruder.

Never again! He'd never put himself at such risk again! Next time he would find some clean way out of his troubles, plan an escape route that wouldn't end with him in the belly of a daemon!

He hoped that Ikit Claw hadn't been as fortunate. If the warlock's spell had employed the same principles as Thanquol's, then it might not be too much to hope that the traitor had paid for his crimes. Torn asunder by daemons, his spirit doomed to wander the void until it was finally devoured by some nightmarish phantom.

The braggart weasel! Boasting about his vaunted science! Claiming his Doomsphere could reshape the world, place the skaven who possessed it at the very pinnacle of power! The useless contraption! What was the use of having a superweapon if the first time you tried to use it the thing blew up in your face?

There would be a reckoning. Thanquol would lay this sordid scheme out before the Council. Clan Skryre would suffer for what they had done, threatening to upset the whole hierarchy of the Under-Empire!

Thanquol forced himself to calm down long enough to take stock of his surroundings. His spell had sent him into the Underway, but his nose told him he was no great distance from the refuse piles outside Bonestash's tunnels. He'd been forced to leave Boneripper behind when making his escape, but that was inconsequential. His faith in Clan Skryre technology had been shaken of late.

Still, his journey to Bonestash wasn't a complete loss. The two-scented traitor Skraekual was dead. The Hand of Vecteek was recovered. Thanquol still wasn't sure about the artefact. The more he thought about it, the more wrong the thing felt. He'd certainly need to find a pliable dupe to harness its powers for him.

Thanquol's head jerked around as a curious scent struck his nose. Sniffing at the dank air of the old dwarf road, the grey seer was impressed by a heavy, musky smell. Skaven of Clan Mors, there was no mistaking their scent. Most likely refugees from Bonestash returning to see what was left of their homes.

Thanquol straightened his posture, preening himself so that he would look his most intimidating. He wasn't eager to make the long journey back to Skavenblight alone. A bit of brow-beating, some threats of divine retribution from the Horned Rat, and he'd have this pack of wretches eating out of his paw. They'd follow him straight back to the Shattered Tower if he told them to, though Thanquol's recent experiences made him consider he'd only need to take them as far as the slave market.

The grey seer's whiskers twitched with uncertainty as the smell continued to grow stronger. There were certainly a lot of refugees. His ears could pick up the squeaks and snarls of a large number of skaven, the tromp of many marching feet, the rattle of armour and weapons.

Into the dim light of the Underway, a vast army of ratmen marched into view. Thanquol could see from their banners and the designs on their shields that they belonged to Clan Mors. Belatedly, he remembered Rikkit Snapfang's desertion. His worries that the warlord was going to tattle to his superiors had been well founded.

The army came to a halt when the pickets caught Thanquol's scent. Their leader pushed his way through the pack. Thanquol found himself staring at Rikkit Snapfang. The warlord stared back. It was all he could do, his eyes frozen in an expression of terror, his severed head spitted on a spike. Other decapitated heads grinned from the trophy rack lashed to the crimson armour of the army's leader. Thanquol bruxed his fangs nervously as the dark-furred warlord glowered at him.

The grey seer knew this warlord, the most fearsome of Warlord Gnawdwell's henchrats. Within the Under-Empire, the name of Queek Headtaker was infamous. Tales were told about the warlord's fits of violence and crazed bloodlust that would have a hardened Eshin assassin spraying the musk of fear.

'Traitor-meat,' Queek snarled, pointing the spiked maul in his hand at Thanquol. The ranks of red-armoured stormvermin behind the warlord growled menacingly.

'No! No!' Thanquol whined. 'Loyal-true! Servant of the Council! Prophet of the Horned One!'

Queek's eyes lost none of their malignance. 'Rikkit-meat says you betray Bonestash to Clan Skryre.' The warlord cocked his head, pushing one of his ears against Rikkit's cold lips. 'Yes-yes, he say-squeak you betray Clan Mors!'

Thanquol grimaced at this display of Queek's madness. He turned a hopeful look at the skaven warriors, but if any of them thought their leader was deranged, none of them were about to do anything about it. There was an empty spike on Queek's trophy rack.

'No! No!' Thanquol grovelled. 'Ikit Claw is my enemy too. He try to trick-lie, but I find out what he was up to.'

The warlord waved his paw and a dozen black-furred stormvermin closed upon Thanquol. The grey seer's mind raced, trying to recall everything he'd ever heard about the Headtaker.

'I can take-lead you to Karak Angkul,' Thanquol squealed. 'Most of the dwarf-things are down in

Bonestash. Their own burrows are unprotected.'
Thanquol was gambling on the pathological hatred
Queek was said to hold for all dwarf-things.

The gamble paid off. Queek raised his maul, motioning for his stormvermin to stay back. 'If this is a trick,
you die,' he snarled.

'No! No! No trick!'

Queek grinned, lips pulling away from his fangs.
'Good. Kill the traitor-meat, then we march on the
dwarf-things.'

Thanquol scurried between the advancing stormvermin. 'Wait-listen!' he cried. 'I have mighty sorcery!
This is the Hand of Vecteek!' Thanquol brandished the
artefact, hoping Queek would be intimidated by it the
way Ikit Claw had. Unfortunately, it seemed the warlord had never heard of it. The stormvermin rushed
at Thanquol, stabbing at him with their swords and
halberds. The grey seer was forced to duck and dodge
between their blades, desperately seeking any way past
the closing ring of steel. His magic spent escaping the
Doomsphere, he knew that only his cunning would
save him now.

'I can help you!' Thanquol shouted. 'I can help kill-
slay dwarf-things! I can call upon the Horned One to
kill-slay all-all dwarf-things!'

Queek uttered a savage cry. At the sound, the stormvermin fell back. The warlord approached Thanquol,
his fierce eyes glaring at the horned priest. 'Kill-slay all
dwarf-things?' he growled.

'Yes! Yes!' Thanquol exclaimed. He held the severed
paw of Vecteek up so that Queek could see it. 'I can
use this to call up great-mighty magic! Spells powerful
enough to kill-slay all dwarf-things!'

There was a fanatical gleam in Queek's eyes. The

warlord tilted his head, pressing his ear first to Rikkit's lips, then to the toothless skull of an orc. Thanquol shuddered as he heard Queek whispering to his trophies, conferring with them, seeking their council.

'Good-good,' the warlord decided. 'Thanquol will help kill-slay dwarf-things.' Queek pressed the spiked end of his maul against the grey seer's snout. 'Make good magic, Thanquol. If you don't...' Queek twisted the maul around, pointing to the empty spot on his trophy rack.

Thanquol swallowed the lump in his throat. All things considered, he would rather be dealing with his good friend Ikit Claw again.

CHAPTER XVII

'MORDIN GRIMSTONE HAS found his doom,' Thorlek said, a tremor in his voice. A path had been cleared through the worst of the rubble by Thane Erkii's miners. Klarak and his aides had followed close behind, inspecting each of the crushed, mangled skaven carcasses, desperately hoping to find the horned carcass of Grey Seer Thanquol amongst the dead. It was ugly, nasty work, the sort to test even a dwarf's resolve. Yet even the dwarfs could not repress a shudder when a pile of rocks collapsed under the miners' picks and exposed the fearsome sight of the slayer's death.

By some fluke of chance, none of the crashing boulders and falling platforms had disturbed the frozen tableau. The skeletal bulk of Boneripper stood erect amid the destruction, its bony claws closed about the mutilated wreckage of the slayer's body. Mordin's face was contorted in an expression of agony, his lip bitten through by his own clenched teeth.

The dwarfs reached for their weapons, waiting for the grotesque rat-ogre to turn upon them, but the skeleton remained stolid as a statue. Cautiously, Klarak approached the immobile monster. Muttering complaints about the engineer's boldness, Horgar lumbered after his master.

'Looks like Mordin killed it before it killed him,' the hammerer said, pointing at the axe buried in Boneripper's skull.

Klarak turned away from his inspection of the grotesque beast. 'It wasn't alive to begin with,' he said. 'It's another of the ratkin's infernal machines.' He shrugged his shoulders. 'As you say, it seems Mordin was able to destroy it, even if he was too late to save himself.'

'Mordin Grimstone has found his doom,' Thorlek repeated.

'Yes,' agreed Klarak. 'But unless we find Thanquol's body, we cannot be sure he's had his revenge.'

Thorlek and some of the miners attacked Boneripper's bony claws, cutting away at the bladed fingers until they were able to free the twisted corpse of Mordin Grimstone. Reverently, they laid the slayer's body upon their cloaks. He would be borne with honour back into the halls of Karak Angkul, from there to be sent on to Karak Kadrin and interred in the Shrine of Grimnir with other fallen slayers.

Klarak and the rest of the throng redoubled their search. True to Runelord Morag's words, there was no trace of the Doomsphere, not even a twisted beam or a crumpled plate, only a great heap of rust-coloured dust. A few plates of Barazhunk, excess that Ikit Claw had not used to create the shell of his machine, were uncovered. Of Grey Seer Thanquol, however, there was no trace.

'He might be under one of the big rocks,' Horgar suggested.

Klarak shook his head. 'No, the vermin has escaped.' As he spoke, the adventurer's voice became heavy and there was sombreness about his eyes. 'The menace to Karak Angkul remains.'

A dwarf runebearer, his body damp with sweat, came rushing into the cavern, glancing about the rubble with frantic eagerness. When he spotted Klarak, he dashed across the cave with an unseemly haste.

'Klarak Bronzehammer,' the runner gasped when he stood before the engineer. 'I have been dispatched from the Sixth Deep to bear ill tidings from King Logan.'

The engineer felt his blood go cold at the runebearer's words. King Logan, along with many of the dwarf warriors, had started a thorough search of the ratkin tunnels, scouring them for any lurking skaven, hunting through them for any caches of stolen gold or weapons looted from the fallen warriors of Karak Angkul. Only a matter of the greatest import could distract the king from the sombre duty of reclaiming the honour of the dead.

'By the king's decree, I repeat my message,' the runebearer continued. 'A vast horde of skaven have risen up from the depths. They have swarmed past our defences in the lower deeps and now run amok through the Sixth Deep. If we would not lose the entire hold, the army must return at once.'

'Hashut's Bald Beard!' Horgar cursed, spitting the name of the profane Dark Father. 'The filthy ratkin are above us! Between us and our homes!' Similar oaths of alarm and outrage echoed through the cavern as word spread among the miners.

'King Logan has ordered all dwarfs to make speed through the tunnels,' the runebearer reported. 'He does not hold out hope that the army can return in time to save the hold, but at least it will be there to avenge those killed by the ratkin.' There was an unmistakable tone of accusation in the messenger's voice as he finished. Klarak wondered if that was also something the king had told him to convey.

'The king is right,' Klarak said. 'We will never reach the hold in time if we use the tunnels.' The engineer's words brought roars of fury from the miners. He held up his hand, motioning for silence. 'I said, if we use the tunnels. But there is another way. We can dig our own.'

'Guildmaster Thori is right,' Thane Erkii snarled. 'You are mad! Even with your steam drill, we'd never move enough rock to get back into the upper deeps ahead of the skaven! We were lucky the tunnel from the smelt-hall waited until we were out from under it before it collapsed!'

'And we'll need still more luck if we are to save Karak Angkul.' Klarak turned and faced the runebearer. 'Tell King Logan that I know a way we can reach the upper deeps ahead of the ratkin. Tell him we will use the skaven's own digging machine to burn our way through the mountain.'

The runebearer looked unconvinced, but bowed his head and hurried away to take Klarak's message back to the king. Klarak shifted his attention back to the sullen miners surrounding him. 'We'll have to fetch the skaven drill from the cave where they abandoned it.'

'Klarak, it took two of their rat-ogres to push that thing,' Thorlek objected.

'I know,' the engineer said. 'It'll mean a fair bit of exercise for all of us, but that machine is the only chance we have to cut past the skaven and get ahead of them.'

'And what about Thanquol?' Horgar asked, dropping the boulder he had been moving.

Again, a grim cast crept into Klarak's eyes. 'Unless I am much mistaken,' he said, 'I think we will find him leading the ratkin against our homes.'

THE SMELL OF blood in the air made Thanquol's mouth water. Fresh blood! Dwarf blood! The grey seer's stomach growled as his mind formed the image of dwarf-steaks garnished with mushrooms and sautéed in skalm, perhaps with just a hint of squeezed bat thrown in for added flavour. He'd wash the meal down with a strong warp-wine, preferably of at least ten-generation vintage. The best warp-wines were those that made the drinker eager to devour the warp-worm hiding at the bottom of the bottle. The really good ones were so old that the warp-worms could fight back.

Shrill screams disturbed Thanquol's culinary daydream. Angrily, he turned his eyes on a mob of crimson-armoured stormvermin. The ratmen were dragging a fat old dwarf breeder from between a pair of monstrously oversized beer kegs. There was a little mewing thing clutched in her arms. The grey seer snarled an oath at the stormvermin, demanding they lower their swords.

The fangleader bared his teeth, not the slightest trace of deference in his posture. 'Warlord say-tell all-all dwarf-thing die-die!' the black-furred ratkin snapped. In the next moment, the blades of the stormvermin came chopping down into the dwarf breeder and her whelp.

Thanquol bruxed his fangs, his eyes narrowing with hate. Queek was a lunatic and so were all of his warriors! Since reaching the dwarfhold, the vermin had gone completely amok, rushing about in a frenzy of bloodlust! What happened to traditional skaven values! What became of simple practicality! He'd led them into the dwarfhold for a regime of pillage and plunder, not to watch a pack of crazed beasts butcher and burn everything they came across!

Sadly, the grey seer stared down at the butchered mess at the base of the kegs. Dwarf pups were worth their weight in warpstone, deemed an exquisite delicacy back in Skavenblight. Dwarf breeders weren't easy to come by either, and notoriously difficult to keep. But Thanquol had never turned his genius to the problem of mating dwarf-things in captivity. Certainly with an intellect such as his own devoted to the problem, he'd find a solution in short order. Indeed, if the dwarf-things produced only a few litters a year, he'd have enough dwarf pups to corner the market. He'd become the wealthiest meat-grower in Skavenblight!

More screams banished Thanquol's ambitions. He glared at another gang of stormvermin rushing down the hall in pursuit of a long-haired dwarf breeder. Of course, there'd be small chance of becoming a prosperous dwarf-herder if Queek's idiots kept killing everything!

Once again, Thanquol gnashed his fangs and lashed his tail. Had a skaven ever been given such an amazing opportunity? An entire dwarfhold ripe for the taking! And Queek's maniacs were just throwing it all away!

When Thanquol led the army up through the old mines and the tunnels of the lower deeps, following the route of his previous expedition into Karak Angkul, the skaven had encountered only the most marginal of resistance. Dwarf pickets scattered throughout the mines, sentinels who were supposed to bear word of any attack back to the upper levels of the hold. The watchers had been spread too thin, however, never arrayed in the numbers necessary to delay Queek's horde long enough to allow any messenger to be dispatched to carry the warning. The dwarf wasn't born who could outrun a skaven, and the spectacle of watching a pack of enraged ratmen drag down a fleeing messenger had been one of the great amusements on the march up from the mines.

A larger force of dwarfs had been waiting in the Sixth Deep, gathered in the very hall where Thanquol had led the diversionary force while Ikit Claw ransacked the smelthall. Well-armed, stubbornly disciplined, the dwarfs could have caused Queek's horde serious trouble had any warning reached them. As it was, they were poorly organised and caught unprepared. Thunderers were cut down while they loaded shot into their guns, cannoneers were hacked to ribbons as they struggled to shift their weapons and train them upon the skaven. Such a massacre should have been enough to quench any ratman's thirst for battle, hundreds of dwarfs chopped to pieces at the cost of only a hundred or so skaven.

Not the Headtaker though! Oh no, not the crazed Queek! Such was his hate of the dwarfs that he shunned the traditional place of leadership far behind the troops and away from the hazards of the fighting. No! Queek was right there at the front, slashing dwarf throats with his sword, crushing dwarf skulls with his maul, the gruesome weapon he called Dwarf Gouger. Axes flashed before the warlord's eyes, hammers cracked against his crimson armour, and all the time Queek was laughing his murderous hate at his foes.

Thanquol didn't mind Queek trying to get himself

killed. In fact, it was something the grey seer thought should be encouraged. What he didn't like was the warlord's paranoid insistence that Thanquol stay close beside him. He'd been forced to expend what little magic he felt strong enough to muster turning aside bolts and bullets or blasting the face of the most persistent of his attackers.

They'd broken the dwarfs at last, running down dozens as they tried to withdraw from the Sixth Deep and flee into the upper hold. A hundred or so of the dwarfs had managed to escape, spreading the alarm through their halls. But the call to action came too late to save the Fifth Deep and the skaven had caught entire clans of the face-furs as they tried to evacuate their homes.

Thanquol grimaced as he glanced about the shambles of the brewhall in which he found himself. Dwarf beer sprayed from ruptured casks, wutroth furnishings had been piled and burned, bronze tankards lay smashed, sacks of barley and hops lay slashed and befouled. The grey seer couldn't keep a quiver from his lips as he considered the value of everything the war-rats were destroying.

'Stop-stop!' Thanquol growled, shaking his staff at a stormvermin who was trying his best to wreck a heavy bronze mallet by smashing it against the rock walls of the brewhall.

The grey seer got no further in his threatening. A steely grip closed about the back of his neck, lifting him onto the balls of his feet. The rancid scent of Queek Headtaker and the decaying reek of his trophies filled Thanquol's nose.

'Break-smash all dwarf-things,' the warlord snarled, flecks of blood dripping from his whiskers. 'Make all dwarf-meat long-suffer!'

Thanquol noted with some alarm that Queek, at least, had not been looting the dwarfhold. A collection of disembodied dwarf heads circled his waist, tied by their beards to his belt. The freshest of them continued to drip blood onto the warlord's legs. Arguing with somebody who took the time to hack off heads while letting perfectly good loot be destroyed would require a good deal of cunning.

Fortunately, for all his psychotic rage and hate, Queek was still a skaven, and no skaven liked to pass up weakened prey.

'Tremendous War-bringer, Overmaster of Sword and Maul, Gnasher of Fangs and Cutter of Throats,' Thanquol whined in his most fawning and ingratiating voice. 'I only mean-want to remind that there are more-many dwarf-things above. It would be wrong-wrong if they escaped.'

Queek released Thanquol, dumping the grey seer onto the sodden floor. 'Coward-scum!' he raged at the vandals. 'Gather all warriors! We march on dwarf-things! Hurry-scurry!'

Cursing under his breath, Thanquol wrung out his robes, wincing at the pungent smell of dwarf beer. He spun about as an uneasy feeling gripped him. He wasn't reassured to find Queek staring at him with a dangerous gleam in his eyes.

'Thanquol has mighty magic,' the warlord hissed, his fingers tapping the handle of Dwarf Gouger. 'Where is great-strong magic of Thanquol-meat?'

Hastily, Thanquol drew the Hand of Vecteek from his robe. 'I still have-carry the Hand!' he insisted, feeling a flicker of fear writhe through his glands when Queek's attitude remained unmoved. 'I can call-summon great-strong magic! The Horned One watches over me and helps me!'

Queek bared his fangs. 'Pray-hope hard-much, Thanquol,' he warned. 'I want better magic when we kill-slay dwarf-things.'

Thanquol stiffened his spine. 'You threaten a prophet of the Horned Rat?' he growled.

'I give-gift Horned One many dwarf heads,' Queek snarled. 'He won't miss one grey seer.'

Thanquol bent down, paws kneading his suddenly aching back. 'Great-strong magic,' he said in a meek voice. 'Yes-yes, I will cast-call many-many spells. Kill-slay many-many dwarf-things.'

Queek continued to glare at the grey seer. His ears twitched and he cocked his head to one side as the clatter of armoured bodies rushing through the corridors of the Fifth Deep echoed through the dwarfhold. The marauding skaven were returning from their rampage, hastening to the summons of their ferocious master.

'Stay close-near,' Queek told Thanquol. 'Stay where I can keep an eye on you.'

The warlord turned about, presenting his back to Thanquol. It didn't take a genius to know what Queek expected of him. Bobbing his head in a series of contrite bows, the grey seer hastened from the brewhall, leading the way as Queek marched out to take command of his army.

'THE FIFTH DEEP is lost and I don't know if we can hold the Fourth.' Thane Arngar ran his hand through his beard, trying to brush away the clotted blood that stained it. A gash in his cheek continued to bleed from beneath its bandage. The general's voice was heavy with shame. He had been entrusted with defending the Sixth Deep by King Logan. Now he'd lost not only the Sixth but the Fifth Deep as well. Looking out over the small throng mustered in the Fourth Deep, he wasn't terribly optimistic about their chances to keep even this level from the ratkin.

'You are not to blame,' Guildmaster Thori consoled the general. 'Klarak Bronzehammer talked King Logan into taking the bulk of our warriors down into the ratkin tunnels when their place was up here, protecting the hold. The responsibility for all that has happened is his, not yours.'

Thane Arngar shook his head. 'Blame won't help us hold the Fourth Deep,' he grumbled. The general looked out across the rag-tag throng assembling in the Fourth Deep's central hall. Masons, architects, stone-cutters, sculptors, rune-scribes, every available dwarf who could swing a hammer or wield an axe had been impressed into Arngar's force. Many of the dwarfs he looked upon were mere beardlings with barely an inch of hair on their chins. Others looked old enough to be living ancestors. None of them were professional warriors. The only experienced fighters he had were those of the Fourth Deep Guard and the survivors from the army the skaven had overwhelmed down in the Sixth Deep.

'We could withdraw to the Third Deep,' Thori proposed. 'The powder rooms of the Engineers' Guild are situated on the Fourth Deep. We could detonate the powder stores and collapse the entire level, bring it crashing down on the heads of the ratkin.'

Arngar's face went pale. 'We... we would destroy half of Karak Angkul by doing that! The work of our ancestors, the halls of our forefathers lost forever!' The general shook his head. 'No, I can't do that! Better to let the ratkin take the deeps than destroy them! What has been taken can always be reclaimed!'

'Very well,' Thori said. 'Then we should fall back to the Ruby Gate. That is the most defensible position in the Fourth Deep. It will allow us to protect the ramp up to the Third Deep and also keep the king's vault from the ratkin.'

Arngar removed his helmet, scratching at his scalp. A file of immense stone statues lined the central hall, each the representation of one of the dwarfs' ancestor gods. As he looked up at them, the general could feel their cold eyes staring down at him, weighing his every action. What he did today, the decisions he made, would be with him always, following him into the halls of his ancestors. He was determined they would do him credit, not shame.

'We can't fall back to the Ruby Gate until the rest of the Fourth Deep has been evacuated,' Arngar decided. The image of the dwarfs they had been forced to abandon in the Fifth Deep was one that plagued the general. He wouldn't have it compounded by the lives of those who dwelt in the Fourth Deep.

'We can't delay!' Thori protested. 'It is only by the grace of Valaya that we've been given this much time! If the ratkin weren't busy plundering the Fifth Deep, they would already be at our throats!'

'Position your gun crews over there,' Arngar told the engineer, unmoved by his objections. 'That will give them a clean line of fire when the ratkin come up from the Fifth Deep.'

Guildmaster Thori bowed his head, favouring Thane Arngar with a look that said 'I hope you know what you're doing'. The engineer hurried to relay the general's orders to the small number of cannoneers who had joined the motley throng. Arngar watched as the crews began to push their cannons into position. Again, the general felt a tremor of doubt. He'd had six cannons to defend the Sixth Deep. Now he had only half that number and a single organ gun brought down from the proving halls on the Second Deep. He could only hope the skaven wouldn't be expecting a fight and that the mere presence of a defence would send them packing. He certainly didn't have enough to stop them if they pressed the attack.

Arngar turned his head, watching as a pair of women herded a dozen children past his line of defence. The general smiled bitterly. Whatever happened, he would hold this hall. The ratkin wouldn't drive him off this time. He bellowed to his aide, a grizzled longbeard named Norgrin. 'Fetch down the oathstone of the Arnrim Clan.' He saw the flash of surprise in the longbeard's eyes. To fight beside an oathstone was no small thing for a dwarf lord. It would mean no retreat, however the battle turned. Even if it meant certain death, no dwarf would dishonour himself by abandoning his clan's oathstone.

'Here I make my stand,' Arngar said, his voice raised so it might carry to his troops. 'Let the ratkin come, if they dare. They shall be broken upon our shields and die beneath the eyes of our gods.'

THE ROAR OF cannon thundered through the massive corridor. The stink of gunpowder and black skaven blood spilled across the ramp. Mangled bodies were flung through the air, cartwheeling over the heads of the close-packed skaven as they surged up from the depths of Karak Angkul. Fangleaders snapped reprimands as their troops squealed in panic, some of them using the flat of their swords to keep their warriors in line, others not bothering with the flat and using the edge to lop off the ears of the nearest malcontents.

'Perhaps we should be in the second wave?' Thanquol squeaked, knowing as he did so that his words were falling on deaf ears. Queek's eyes were ablaze with the sort of red madness Thanquol had thought only the eyes of an orc could ever possess.

Before them, at the head of the ramp, a cluster of dwarf cannon pointed down into the Fifth Deep. As soon as the skaven had reached the halfway mark, a concentrated volley from the cannons had smashed into them, cutting through their massed ranks like a cleaver through rotting man-flesh. Now, a file of dwarf jezzails marched out from behind the cannons while the crews reloaded their weapons.

Thanquol felt hideously exposed as the dwarfs began firing into the swarming skaven. But he'd feel even worse if one of the bullets zinging past his horns found its mark. The yelps of the skaven around him as the bullets found other victims didn't help the grey seer's valour. Ducking and bobbing, weaving between the armoured stormvermin, Thanquol tried to gradually let himself sink into the onrushing mob. As long as he could keep a few bodies between himself and the dwarfs, his own prognosis for survival would be markedly enhanced.

Queek, damn his mangy hide, seemed oblivious to all danger. The warlord was lost to his crazed bloodlust now. He didn't even flinch when a dwarf bullet shattered one of the skulls on his trophy rack. The warlord reared up, smashing his sword and maul together, roaring like some escapee from Clan Moulder's Hell Pit.

Then the dwarf cannons spoke once more, bellowing like giants as they spat death down the rampway. Thanquol shrieked as a cannonball went careening through the ratmen on his left, passing so close that his side was splashed with skaven blood. Squeals of terror rose from the rear ranks of the horde as mangled bodies were hurled into their midst. Again, Thanquol cursed the foolishness of Queek. A leader's place was in the rear, where he could quell such panic as soon as it started.

And, of course, avoid getting too close to whatever caused such panic to begin with.

The dwarfs clearly expected the skaven attack to falter in the wake of a point-blank discharge of their cannons. They had not reckoned with the frenzied hate of Warlord Queek Headtaker. The maddened skaven warlord leapt through the cloud of smoke billowing from the mouths of the cannons. Perched atop the bore of one cannon, he brought his sword slashing down, tearing the arm from a gunner. Dwarf Gouger crashed into the face of a second foe, splashing blood and brains across the neighbouring cannon.

Queek howled his challenge, pouncing upon the dwarf warriors who came charging forwards to protect the embattled cannons. Again and again the warlord's weapons struck, bringing death with every blow. Dwarf Gouger tore through even the thickest gromril plate as though it were cheesecloth, smashing the leathery bodies inside.

One doughty longbeard, more determined than the rest, pressed his attack even after a blow from Dwarf Gouger broke his arm. The dwarf's blade raked across Queek's armour, the crimson coating fracturing in a spray of metallic splinters. The longbeard screamed as the splinters dug into his flesh, sizzling as they came into contact with his skin, their warpstone content eating away at the dwarf's body like the most vitriolic acid.

Now other skaven surged forwards, goaded on by their master's example. It wasn't loyalty or courage that made them hasten to Queek's side, but rather the fear that their warlord would win his way clear and come looking for any ratman who had been too timid to press the fight.

The cannons were finished now, their crews scattered or slain. The thunderers retreated through the ranks of their own warriors, trying to form a fire line from which they could cover the eventual retreat of their comrades.

Thanquol pressed himself against one of the walls, watching as Queek's warriors tore into the reeling dwarfs. There was little question that the skaven would overwhelm their foes now, but the dwarfs would take a lot of killing and a lot of ratmen would go down with them. Thanquol did not intend to be one of them.

Satisfied that Queek Headtaker would have his paws full killing dwarfs for a while, Thanquol began to sidle back down the ramp. He'd had more than his fill of Clan Mors and its maniacal leadership. It was time for all prudent grey seers to cut their losses and scurry back to Skavenblight. Besides, he still had the Hand of Vecteek. That would be enough to set him up good with Seerlord Kritislik. Or Seerlord Tisqueek, if it looked like Kritislik's rival might prove a more generous patron.

A quivering sensation against his spine sent Thanquol springing away from the wall. The grey seer drew back, his staff held defensively across his chest, his beady eyes glaring at the wall. There was nothing there. Irritated at his unreasonable fright, Thanquol stepped back to the wall, placing his hand against the stone. He immediately pulled his paw back. There was a noticeable tremor running through the wall. His mind pored over the possibilities of earthquake and sabotage. Perhaps that traitorous rat Ikit Claw was back and trying to get his revenge by collapsing the ramp and sealing Thanquol up with Queek's lunatics!

Thanquol cast a worried look back at Queek and the raging battle with the dwarfs. It still looked like a bad idea to get involved in that scrap, even if he just lingered at the edges of the fighting. He cast his gaze back at the wall. It was noticeably shaking now, little trickles of dirt running down from between the blocks. There might still be time to race back down into the lower deeps and beat a hasty retreat.

Then again, Thanquol thought as the violence acting against the wall increased, there might not be time to get clear before the whole thing came crashing down. He'd already had a near escape from that sort of thing. He wasn't about to repeat the experience.

A stone block suddenly broke loose, smashing into the floor of the ramp and rolling down into the darkness of the Fifth Deep. Another soon followed, and then still another. Thanquol straightened himself, smoothing back his whiskers.

Why should he be afraid? Ikit Claw was the one who should be afraid! Unlike that dullard Queek, the Claw knew all about the Hand of Vecteek and what it could do. And this time the maggot didn't have a malfunctioning Doomsphere to try and bluff his way past Thanquol's wrath!

Oh yes, Thanquol thought as the reek of warpstone began to billow out from the expanding hole in the wall, there would be a reckoning when the Chief Warlock showed his ugly face! If the Claw didn't grovel just right, Thanquol would snuff out his worthless life like a mouse in a troll-trap!

'So-so,' Thanquol snarled as he saw the grinding

drillhead tear through the rock. 'You come back to beg the Great Thanquol to forgive-forget your...'

Thanquol shook his head, his nose twitching as an impossible smell struck his senses. He blinked, trying to make sense of the scent. Surely there weren't dwarfs hiding in the walls of their own stronghold?

The drill crashed to the floor of the ramp, slowly sliding down towards the Fifth Deep. After it came a grimy, dirt-covered dwarf. Despite the dirt, however, Thanquol couldn't fail to notice the pitiless hate shining in the creature's gold-flake eyes.

Klarak Bronzehammer drew the steam pistol from his belt, unleashing a barrage of bullets at the grey seer. Only Thanquol's twitchy reflexes preserved him from the fusillade, the skaven sorcerer flinging himself to the floor the very moment the dwarf fired at him. Scurrying across the ground on all fours, squeaking in terror, he watched in mounting horror as more dwarfs emerged from the hole in the wall.

The army he had thought safely lost in the maze of Bonestash was back!

BEFORE KLARAK COULD reload his weapon and fire again, Thanquol picked himself up and raced for the safety offered by Queek's massed warriors. Pushing and shoving, biting and clawing, he forced his way through the horde. The more of them he put between himself and the revenge-crazed dwarfs, the better. Especially that gold-furred maniac! That one seemed unnaturally obsessed with killing the grey seer. Thanquol was beginning to think the creature had been set on his tail by some jealous rival. Or perhaps a scheming superior. Or maybe even some uppity underling.

Thanquol's passage through the teeming stormvermin

and clanrats became a maddened dash when the sounds of battle began to sound from the area of the ramp. Klarak and his warriors were attacking the rear of Queek's force, trying to cut their way through the press of bodies in their vindictive persecution of the grey seer. His one hope was that Queek's mob had managed to hack their way through the rest of the dwarfs blocking the way into the Fourth Deep. Once clear of the dwarfs, Thanquol would have an entire level of their stronghold to hide himself in.

Abruptly, Thanquol found himself free from the press of bodies. His paws almost slipped out from under him as he discovered a pool of dwarf blood underfoot. Glancing around, he saw a mass of butchered dwarfs and skaven. Some distance away, a small, ragged group of dwarfs was trying to form a shield wall. Thanquol could see them rallying around some elaborately armoured dwarf standing on a ridiculous-looking block of stone. It seemed the dwarfs had lost their taste for battle.

Or maybe they were just trying to keep the skaven from escaping now that their full army was coming out of the wall. It was an unpleasant thought, but one that Thanquol was forced to consider as he looked at the grimly defiant faces of the dwarf-things.

'Fight-die, coward-meat!' Queek cursed the distant dwarfs, hurling the severed head of his last victim at the withdrawing enemy. Something, perhaps a cry, perhaps the smell of death, made the warlord suddenly turn. His eyes went wide when he saw the throng of dwarfs rushing from the wall and attacking the rear of his horde. His nose twitched, singling out the scent of the ratman who had told him the dwarf army was gone.

Queek pounced upon Thanquol, smashing the grey

seer to the floor. 'Traitor-meat! Snivel-scat!' the warlord raged, fury in his eyes, froth falling from his fangs.

Thanquol scrambled out from under the warlord just as Queek's sword came flashing down. 'No-no!' the grey seer whined. 'Not my fault! Dwarf-trick! Sneaky dwarf-things!'

Queek's fangs glistened as he brought Dwarf Gouger smashing down, missing Thanquol by the breadth of a whisker. The grey seer cringed away, his head darting from one side to the other. Either end of the hall was blocked by a wall of angry dwarfs. If he stayed where he was, the deranged Queek would either gut him like a mouse or smash his skull like an egg.

There was only one thing left. The Hand of Vecteek! He had to use its power. If he could impress Queek, if he could drive away the dwarfs, then he might still snatch victory from the paws of disaster.

'Wait-listen!' Thanquol pleaded. 'Hand of Vecteek! I can-can make mighty spell! Kill-kill all dwarf-things!'

The words had lost their ability to impress Queek. The warlord's sword flashed so close to Thanquol's neck that he felt his fur bristle. Thanquol needed to cast a spell and cast it quick. He needed to evoke such an impressive feat of sorcery that even the crazed Queek wouldn't dare lift a claw against him.

More than that, he needed an ally who would stand by him against Queek should the warlord refuse to see reason. Thanquol grinned as he considered the perfect solution. Vecteek. In life, he'd been Supreme Warmonger of Clan Rictus, chief rival of Clan Mors. Vecteek would have no love for Queek and his ilk.

The Horned Rat sometimes rewarded his most powerful servants. When a mighty skaven died, his spirit was reborn as one of the Horned One's sacred harbingers, one of the dread Vermin Lords. A skaven of such might and power as Vecteek, whose very paw had become a profane relic, was certain to be numbered among the Horned One's daemons.

Ordinarily, Thanquol would be loath to call upon a Vermin Lord. It was a humbling experience to be in the presence of such a divine manifestation. Cowards might even describe the experience as terrifying.

The proper procedure to summon a Vermin Lord from the Horned Rat's domain was through a lengthy ritual involving complex sacrifices and elaborate ceremonies. Thanquol didn't have the time for all that. What he did have was a part of Vecteek's mortal remains. There was no surer way to summon a daemon than possessing a part of it.

Thanquol gnashed a sliver of refined warpstone between his fangs and drew the dark energies of the aethyr into his mind. He muttered an appeal to the Horned One that he might lend his divine assistance in the grey seer's endeavour to summon one of his Harbingers of Doom.

Queek backed away as Thanquol's entire body began to glow with unholy energies. Bullets from a few dwarf marksmen glanced away from the coruscating shell of energy that rippled about the sorcerer. A dull, keening moan began to whistle through the hall, the shriek of an invisible veil being torn asunder.

Thanquol focused his entire mind upon the relic he held in his paws. The slightest stray thought, the merest hint of doubt, and the spell would be broken; the energies would snap back and sear his body to a cinder. Only by using the Hand of Vecteek as a focus was Thanquol able to keep his concentration. He merged his own power with that vested in the artefact.

In his mind, Thanquol could see the wall between the mortal and immortal worlds crumble, fracturing as surely as the wall the dwarfs had broken through. He could smell the electric tang of the void, hear the shrieks of the damned, the hungry howls of hunting daemons. Swiftly, he blotted out the impressions, fixing his mind solely upon the powers of the Hand.

'Vecteek,' Thanquol snarled. 'Mighty Vermin Lord. Prince of Ruin and Desolation. Heed the summons of Grey Seer Thanquol. Harken to the Voice of the Horned One's Prophet.'

An icy chill swept through the hall as the void poured through the rent in the veil. Thanquol felt fear hammer at his heart, a terror greater than anything he had ever known.

'Vecteek!' he cried. 'I, Thanquol, servant of the Horned Rat, demand you to pass through this tunnel between worlds! Obey!'

Now Thanquol could see something, a black essence, pouring through the torn veil. His glands clenched, the musk of fear dripping from his fur. There was a stench in his nose, a foul mixture of blood and steel, the smell of a dozen wars smashed together into a single reek. The sound of laughter rolled through his mind – deep and booming and utterly malignant.

Vecteek couldn't come, a voice like fire blazed through the grey seer's brain. *So I came instead.*

Images swirled through Thanquol's mind. He could see the old grey seer sealed away inside Festerhole by the dwarfs. He could see the bitter old priest slowly starving away in his lair, his every thought turned against the Under-Empire which had forgotten and abandoned him. He could see the villain setting the Hand of Vecteek upon the table before him. He watched in disbelief as the long-dead sorcerer sank his fangs into the mummified artefact. In a few moments, the Hand was no more, consumed utterly by the starving grey seer.

The entire hall shook, trembling as though a titan lumbered across its floor. Embattled skaven and dwarfs broke away from their foes to stare in bewilderment at the shuddering walls, the quivering ceiling. An intense dread passed through them, drawing colour from faces, scent from glands. Swords faltered, axes lowered as a nameless terror swept through the hall.

In Thanquol's mind, other images presented themselves. He could see Grey Seer Thratsnik, his body ablaze with magical energies from his consumption of Vecteek's paw, leaning across the table once more. The grey seer laid his hand upon the table. Gradually, the power burning through him began to seep down his arm, gathering in his outstretched hand. Thratsnik raised his knife…

Now the thunder of footsteps sounded through the hall, the tromp of monstrous feet. Eyes lifted as an immense shadow began to form, wisps of smoke billowing from nothingness to slowly coalesce into something with shape and substance.

'Is… is that-that Mighty Lord Vecteek?' Queek stammered, even his hate of the dwarfs forgotten as worms of terror raced down his spine and through his glands.

Thanquol barely heard the question. In his mind's eye, he was watching Thratsnik put the final touch to the trap he had left behind, the snare for any who would seek to recover the Hand of Vecteek. The grey seer's own dismembered paw lay before him on the table, saturated with magical energy. It might still serve as a potent talisman for anyone with the knowledge to tap into its energies. But Thratsnik had planned his revenge too well for that. He set his knife against the severed hand. Across the palm, so faintly that it might be overlooked, he made a mark, scratched a symbol which no sorcerer could gaze upon without a feeling of terror.

'Squeak-say!' Queek shrieked. 'Is that Lord Vecteek?'

Thanquol slowly raised his head, staring up at the gathering shadow. The smell of blood and havoc was even more pronounced now, threatening to choke the breath from his lungs.

You have called and I have answered. You sought the Harbinger of Doom. I am he, little sorcerer. I am your Doom.

I am Skarbrand.

I am your death.

CHAPTER XVIII

THANQUOL'S BODY QUIVERED as though gripped by a seizure, pain shot through his bowels as his empty glands continued trying to spray the musk of fear. With an effort of supreme will, he forced his eyes away from the shadowy manifestation spilling out through the door his magic had opened. He felt something wet dripping down his claws. The Hand of Thratsnik was dissolving, turning into runny streamers of blood, losing all shape as it oozed to the floor. Only the symbol cut into the palm remained intact, mockingly defying the dissolution of its surroundings.

Disgusted, Thanquol threw the cursed artefact away. It landed on the floor, palm upwards, the Skull Rune glowing balefully from its setting of corroded flesh.

The Skull Rune! Emblem of the Blood God of Chaos, Khorne, Lord of War and Slaughter! Well had the vengeful Thratsnik set his trap! The wrathful Khorne was a god of warriors and murderers, the patron of sword and claw. For all sorcerers, all who would ply the craft of spell and hex, the Skull Lord was their bane. Khorne had nothing but loathing and scorn for magicians and wizards – only an insane fool would use magic to draw the Blood God's attention.

Thanquol wasn't particularly happy to think of himself as an insane fool. Yet as he watched the Hand of Thratsnik dissolve into a puddle of crimson muck, he understood how completely he had been taken in. By his own actions he'd opened the gateway into the Blood God's realm and drawn the attention of one of his great daemons.

Given enough time, Thanquol was certain he would figure out exactly how everything was Skraekual's fault, but just now, he had more pressing concerns. For instance, there was the nasty matter of a giant shadow that was becoming less shadowy with each passing breath. He could see shoulders now, and great black wings. Horns and claws, and terrible pounding hooves.

'Did… did… you-you call-summon… that?' Queek's voice was as soft and mewing as that of a whelp torn from a breeder's teat. The warlord's eyes were immense pools of terror as he cringed beside Thanquol.

You have called, and I have come.

The voice of Skarbrand thundered through Thanquol's mind. Raw terror pulsed through his body. He glanced at Queek, then back at the horrifying manifestation. There was really only one thing to do.

'Keep it busy while I get help!' Thanquol snarled at Queek, shoving the warlord towards the manifestation. The grey seer didn't even wait to hear Queek's angry snarls, but spun about on his heel and scurried across the hall. Darting and weaving between awestruck dwarfs and shivering skaven, he drove straight towards the inner gate, certain he could find some small opening to squirm through. He'd feel a lot better putting a big thick dwarf wall between himself and Skarbrand.

A coward dies a thousand deaths. All of them slow and very painful.

Thanquol clapped his paws against his ears, trying to block out the daemon's growl. Maybe he'd keep going once he was through the gate. If one wall between himself and the daemon was good, then two would be better. Actually, it might be nice to have seven or eight. In fact, Thanquol was feeling a decidedly un-skavenlike desire to be out in the open sky and well away from tunnels and dwarfhalls.

Run, fleshling! You cannot hide!

Thanquol cried out in horror as he caught sight of the Ruby Gate. The way was shut! The treacherous, cowardly dwarfs had closed the gate already!

Some of the dwarfs around him began to stir from their horrified stupor. An axe flashed past Thanquol's ear, a hammer smashed against the floor beside his foot. The grey seer's staff smacked out, cracking into the hairy face of a dwarf guard, splitting his lip and breaking his teeth.

The insufferable idiots! Death itself was marching through their burrows and the moron dwarfs had the gall to bother about a lone, defenceless little skaven! If Thanquol escaped from this indignity, he'd come back with an entire army and put every one of these bearded fools to the sword!

Thanquol ducked and dodged, scurrying on all fours between the legs of his attackers. The very numbers of the dwarfs around him played against the efforts of his enemies to catch him. They couldn't swing a hammer without the risk of hitting a comrade. It was a moral failing with the dwarf-things that they were too timid to pursue an enemy if it meant hurting one of their own.

For his part, Thanquol missed no opportunity to lash out at his confused foes. He smashed toes and bit fingers, used his tail to trip legs and his staff to bludgeon anything else that had the misfortune to come within reach. His scurrying progress through the dwarf throng was easily tracked by the trail of cursing, hopping warriors he left behind.

A voice suddenly roared out across the hall, sounding out above the frightened squeaks of the skaven and the angry snarls of the dwarfs. 'The grey ratkin is the focus!' the voice was shouting and Thanquol recognised the voice of his gold-bearded tormentor. 'Kill him before the daemon takes form! Kill Thanquol!'

Hearing his own name spoken by a lowly dwarf-thing caused Thanquol to freeze. He spun about, glaring across the hall, fixing his malignant gaze on the gold-bearded dwarf. How had that creature learned his name? It was a question that vexed the grey seer, a question that made his mind turn to thoughts of betrayal and corruption. No crude dwarf-thing was smart enough to bedevil him the way this gold-fur had!

Eyes narrowed with hate, Thanquol looked for Queek, his suspicions turning instantly to the only rat-man present crazy enough to betray him. He bared his fangs as he saw the warlord and his bodyguard cutting a path through the dwarfs, retreating back to the ramp and the darkness of the lower deeps. It was too late for Thanquol to share the warlord's escape route. There was the small matter of a gigantic daemon standing between himself and the ramp leading back into the lower deeps.

Conspiracy! Thanquol writhed out from beneath the clutching fingers of a dwarf warrior and slashed his claws across the nose of a second dwarf who was trying to catch the ratman's legs. The grey seer kicked and squirmed out from the press of his foes.

Treachery! Queek had launched this attack solely to destroy the mighty Grey Seer Thanquol! The scheming maggot had forced this chaos upon him, forced him to draw upon the malignant power of Thratsnik's cursed relic! Now the cowardly Headtaker was fleeing, running off into the darkness, abandoning Thanquol to face the dwarfs and the daemon alone.

The daemon. Thanquol could feel Skarbrand's malignance growing, swelling, expanding. He could smell the stench of the bloodthirster's wrath, hear the fires of its hate. The grey seer felt very small beside that infinite wellspring of atrocity and carnage. His heart banged against his ribs, threatening to burst from sheer terror. The pain of his clenching glands made him want to scream.

But he would not scream. Not now. Not when the daemon was so near. Not when Skarbrand was so close and so hungry.

Thanquol dodged the butt of a dwarf's gun as the thunderer tried to club him down. The grey seer's staff smashed up between his attacker's legs, doubling the wretch over in pain. Without hesitation, he sprang over the body of his stunned opponent, scurrying from the flailing hammers and axes of his enemies.

No longer did the dwarfs hesitate, but targeted the ratmen with enraged abandon. Warriors cried out in agony as the blades of their comrades missed Thanquol and gouged their flesh. A crazed light burning in their eyes, the stricken dwarfs fell upon their former friends, tearing at them with clawed hands, cutting at them with knives and hatchets, gnashing their teeth as they snapped at the throats of their kinsmen.

Thanquol scrambled away from the fratricidal fray. Even wracked by the black hunger, he had never seen skaven overcome by such bloodthirsty madness. The dwarfs attacked one another with the mindless ferocity of a cornered wolf-rat. The grey seer watched as one old longbeard continued to strangle the life from his younger enemy despite the axe stroke that had disembowelled him. A leather-cloaked engineer drove a heavy mattock into whatever came near him, uncaring of the red ruin dripping from his gouged eyes.

The grey seer could feel the same madness trying to snake its way into his own mind, trying to seduce him into berserk self-destruction. He drew upon every scrap of his occult knowledge to drive back the tempting cries of the daemon, clinging to the tatters of his sanity as Chaos tried to consume him.

Thanquol scrambled past a knot of fighting dwarfs, retreating into the shelter between a statue's immense legs. The dark shadow beneath the dwarf ancestor god seemed to welcome him, enveloping him in the protective embrace of darkness. The grey seer rested his paws against the cold stone ankle, sucking breath back into his panting lungs. If he could just concentrate, just recover his strength…

As the grey seer began to think about the escape spell he would use to elude the daemon, his body was wracked by a searing pain. He cowered against the foot of the statue, blood oozing from his nose. He forced himself to keep his eyes focused upon the floor, resisting the almost overwhelming urge to gaze up at the manifesting daemon.

No, you shall not escape me so easily. You will burn, mage-rat, and then you will scream. And scream. And scream.

Thanquol's will faltered. Slowly, he lifted his horned head, gazing up towards the roof of the dwarfhold. Staring into the face of Skarbrand.

KLARAK BRONZEHAMMER WATCHED in mounting horror as the daemon conjured by Thanquol's sorcery seeped through the rupture between worlds. The entity's evil swiftly flooded the hall, flowing like a river of malignance into every heart and mind subjected to its presence. A scum of hoarfrost gathered upon the ceiling, streams of blood bubbled from bare stone walls. The light of torch and lantern flickered, smothered by the clammy clutch of Chaos. Upon the floor, dead bodies twitched, spilled blood began to boil. Steam rose from bloodied blades. Snakes of red lightning sizzled through the air.

At the core of the manifestation was the shadow. Great and terrible, growing with each heartbeat, becoming more solid, cladding itself in a shape of terror. Klarak had seen such things before, in the infernal workshops of the daemonsmiths, but even the horrors of the dawi-zharr paled before the wickedness of the horror now spilling into Karak Angkul.

This was the danger Klarak had been warned of, the unspeakable destruction Grey Seer Thanquol represented. They had stopped Ikit Claw's Doomsphere and saved the greater Karak Ankor from destruction, but now an even more terrible doom stretched forth its claws to visit ruin upon Karak Angkul. The daemon's taint would spare nothing. Not a man, woman or child would escape its wrath, the very foundations of the dwarfhold would be tortured and corrupted by its malignance.

There was only one chance. Klarak was no wizard, no scholar of the occult, but he knew daemons required sustenance to materialise. For the daemon to manifest, it needed a focus, an anchor to bind it to reality and keep it from slipping back into the void. If that focus could be broken before the entity's evil could fully gather itself the dwarfhold might yet be saved.

With an effort, Klarak pulled his gaze away from the forming daemon, staring out across the ranks of awestruck dwarfs and terrified skaven. Desperately he searched for the individual whose destruction would send the monster back. The engineer bit back a cry of triumph as he saw Thanquol trying to slip away between the stunned dwarfs. 'The grey ratkin is the focus! Kill him before the daemon takes form! Kill Thanquol!'

Klarak just had time to see his words galvanise some of the dwarfs into action before a wave of almost palpable malevolence smashed down upon him. He could feel the daemon's rage slam into him, crushing him to his knees. The feral howl of a bloodcrazed beast snarled through the corridors of his soul. His body heaved with revulsion. When he looked back at the shadow, a pair of immense eyes glared down at him, blazing like volcanic fires in the gathering blackness.

Concentrated into the daemon's eyes was a quality of violence and havoc that made Klarak's flesh crawl. He could see the fountainhead of all atrocity, the nucleus of all carnage, the cornerstone of all brutality smouldering behind the daemon's gaze. The lust of blood and destruction began to grow inside him, feeding from his every memory. He saw the goblins who had tortured and murdered his mother. He was there as his father was smashed beneath the claws of a troll. He experienced the lynching of his grandfather by human bandits as though wearing the skin of his long-dead ancestor. Each memory cried out to him with a voice of wrath, urging him to vengeance, demanding blood and slaughter as the price to wash away their pain.

The dwarf threw back his head, screaming in anguish. In that howl of agony, Klarak embraced his pain. The daemon did not need the subtlety of lies to fan the embers of rage in the engineer's soul. How easy it would be to listen to its seductive voice, to cast aside reason and to wallow in the mindless joy of wrath! Pain would be forgotten when the world was painted red with the blood of the damned! Cast aside suffering and abandon himself to battle unending!

No! It took all of Klarak's willpower to manage that single word, that single spark of defiance. He was a dwarf! A dwarf was nothing without his past, without his traditions and his ancestors, without the glories and the sorrows of his race! The very pain which the daemon had evoked to seduce him, to drag his mind down into a wallow of violence and massacre, now became the dwarf's strength. What his kin had endured, what his race had endured, these became like a sword in Klarak's fist, driving back the daemon's call to carnage.

Blood streamed from Klarak's eyes as he fought free of the daemon's influence. All about him, he could see other dwarfs shaking their heads, wiping gore from their faces. There was a haunted expression in their eyes, but they had managed to cling to their sanity. By drawing the focus of the daemon's ire, Klarak had preserved his companions from the worst of the entity's malevolence.

Skarbrand Rage Feaster, Bloodthirster of Khorne. In that brief moment when the daemon's gaze had pierced his soul, Klarak discovered its name and its purpose. Karak

Angkul would drown in blood. Every living thing within its walls would be butchered, an offering for Bloody Khorne upon his throne of skulls. And if the offering was great enough, if the slaughter pleased Skarbrand's god, then the entire hold would be consumed, ripped from the face of the earth and dragged into the Blood God's realm of rampage and barbarity.

'What... is...' Horgar's voice trembled as he tried to speak.

'Death for Karak Angkul unless we can send it back,' Klarak told him. He raised his voice so that the other dwarfs could hear him. 'We have to kill Thanquol before the daemon can manifest itself fully.'

The dwarfs nodded grimly, moving to engage the skaven once more. A large body of the ratmen were pushing their way back to the lower deeps. Klarak could see the trophy rack of the hated Queek Headtaker rising above the mass of armoured skaven. The Headtaker had many a grudge recorded against him. It would mean glory and honour to any dwarf who could bring about the ratman's destruction.

'Stop!' The command rang out above the cries of skaven and the crash of blades. Runelord Morag stood at the mouth of the tunnel, his hammer raised above his head. The venerable dwarf seemed bathed in a soft blue radiance and there was a feeling of unquestionable authority in his voice. 'Let the vermin pass! Do not touch them!'

Reluctantly, the dwarfs started to pull back. The skaven, however, took their retreat as weakness. Instinctively they lunged after the warriors, cutting several down with their rusty halberds. Roaring with indignation, the dwarfs surged back, their axes felling many of the ratkin.

'Let them pass!' Morag shouted once more. This time, Klarak could see the reason behind the Runelord's order. Every drop of blood that was shed, be it from dwarf or ratkin, bubbled and steamed as it struck the floor, vanishing in a crimson mist. Dread gripped Klarak as he turned his eyes to the bloodthirster's black shadow. There was no mistaking it, the daemon's shape was more distinct now and becoming even more so with each wisp of red vapour rushing into it.

'The daemon draws strength from death!' Klarak cried out. 'Let the skaven run! It's the daemon we must stop!'

The threat posed by ignoring Klarak's words was not lost on the dwarfs. Sheltering behind their shields, they withdrew for the second time, leaving a path open for Queek and his bodyguards. The dwarfs cursed the skaven warlord as he scurried off into the darkness with his retinue. Many vengeful oaths were sworn before the last of the stormvermin scurried away. It was a hard thing for any dwarf to suffer such an infamous enemy to escape justice.

If Thanquol had been among Queek's retinue, the dwarfs could have risked engaging them in battle, but to do so when every drop of blood fed the daemon was suicide.

Klarak turned away from the retreating skaven, drawn by the clamour of battle. All across the hall, Thane Arngar's defenders were locked in battle once more with the skaven Queek had left behind. There were still hundreds of the dark-furred vermin scattered about the hall, trapped between the two dwarf throngs. Klarak cried out to his kinsfolk, urging them to disengage, hoping against hope that the cowardice of the ratmen would lead them to quit the battlefield.

A new horror gripped Klarak when he saw that his

words went unheeded. Studying the battle more closely, he could see that it was not a simple matter of ratkin versus dwarf, but a confused melee that pit ratkin against ratkin and dwarf against dwarf. The fighters slashed away, uncaring of who they came against, cutting down their own as happily as they did their enemies. The engineer remembered the horrible madness that had done its utmost to overwhelm him. Nearer to the daemon, those he now watched had been unable to resist the bloodthirster's call to battle. Only a small cluster of dwarfs gathered about Thane Arngar and his oathstone appeared to still be in possession of their faculties. They did their utmost to fend off their crazed attackers without harming them, a restraint that went unreciprocated.

Red fog rose from the battle, streaking above the heads of the dead and dying, rushing across the hall to lend their substance to the malignancy taking shape. From shadow, the daemon became a thing of solidity, a goliath monstrosity of tattered pinions and leathery flesh. Massive thews rippled beneath the daemon's scarred skin, strings of gore swayed from the tips of its black horns. Plates of brass were bolted to the daemon's crimson skin, each segment of armour scored with the Skull Rune of Skarbrand's fearsome lord and master. In each of its mighty claws, the bloodthirster bore an immense axe of dark, lustreless metal that seemed to writhe and howl beneath its gripping talons, eager to taste mortal blood upon their sharp blades.

Skarbrand's hound-like face split in a baleful grin, its eyes blazing with unbridled savagery. The bloodthirster's cloven hoof smashed against the floor, cracking the flagstones and causing the very mountain to shiver. The daemon's laughter thundered through the dwarfhold, blood trickling from the ears of all who heard it.

The daemon exulted in the stench of blood and terror that its laughter provoked. Lustily, the bloodthirster swept its axes down across the crazed ranks of the little creatures that fed him with their maddened fury. Scores of skaven, dozens of dwarfs were massacred in the blink of an eye, Skarbrand's axes tearing them asunder. The daemon blades wailed in ecstasy as the blood of their victims was absorbed into their metal skins.

Klarak could watch no more. 'It has to be stopped,' he snarled, feeling again the murderous fingers of the daemon probing his mind. Glutting itself upon its bloody harvest, Skarbrand would soon grow powerful enough to sustain itself without the focus of Thanquol's life-force. If that happened, the daemon would only fade back into the world of phantoms when it ran out of victims to slaughter.

'By Grungni, it will be stopped,' Runelord Morag vowed. Moving with surprising speed for a dwarf of his age, he hurried back to the mouth of the tunnel where King Logan and his hammerers were bringing forth the stronghold's Anvil of Doom. The Runelord scrambled onto the litter, taking his place behind the ancient relic. Hurriedly, he brought his magic hammer smashing down onto the black surface of the anvil. Blue sparks of lightning erupted from the pounding hammer, crackling across the hall to strike the rampaging daemon.

'Khazuk! Khazuk! Khazuk!' Morag roared, foam flecking his beard as he uttered the famed dwarfish war-cry. The shout was taken up by the warriors around him. Sternly, the armoured dwarfs formed ranks before the Runelord, King Logan taking his place among the vanguard. The daemon might bring destruction to their homes, but it would not do so without knowing it had been in a fight.

As the magic lightning sizzled against its crimson flesh, Skarbrand turned about. The bloodthirster's face spread in a gruesome snarl. Rearing to its full height, spreading its torn wings, the daemon bellowed its challenge to the dwarfs. Clashing its wailing axes together, Skarbrand stormed across the hall, heedless of the crazed warriors it trampled beneath its hooves.

Gunfire cracked from the muzzles of a hundred thunderers, the barrage smashing into the charging daemon's body. The daemon roared onwards, unfazed by the bullets that tore at its flesh. A sheet of lightning danced from Morag's hammer, scorching the bloodthirster's face. Skarbrand's nostrils flared as it snorted in amusement. It enjoyed destruction so much more when its prey tried to fight back.

Seeing the uselessness of their bullets, the thunderers clubbed their guns and rushed at the daemon, determined to drive the beast back by simple force of arms. Many of the warriors broke ranks, charging forwards alongside their comrades. This day they might walk the halls of their ancestors, but they would not do so knowing they had spent their final moments as cowards.

Klarak rushed alongside King Logan's bodyguard. If he would die, then it would be alongside his sovereign. Thorlek and Horgar accompanied their master, relishing the chance to fight beside him in one last battle.

Lightning from the Anvil of Doom crackled overhead as Morag continued to draw upon the relic's magic. The bolts seared the daemon's hide, leaving behind ugly dripping scars. But instead of weakening, the bloodthirster seemed to draw strength from its injuries, savouring the smell of even its own foul blood.

A small mob of crazed skaven lingered between the dwarfs and the daemon. The charging warriors smashed

into the amok ratmen, cutting them down before the
creatures could turn away from their fratricidal mania.
Verminous spines shattered beneath the blows of hammers, rodent limbs were hewn beneath the biting steel
of axes. One ratman, more crazed then the rest, lunged
at Klarak, ending its existence when Horgar's steam-
powered hand squeezed its head into pulp.

As the dwarfs broke through the ranks of the skaven,
they hesitated. Skarbrand glowered down at them, the
daemon's eyes like glowing pits of blood. Nothing
now stood between the dwarfs and their ghastly foe.
Nothing save the grisly carpet of butchered bodies the
bloodthirster trampled beneath its hooves.

The hound-like muzzle parted in a bark of murderous laughter. Then the daemon's snarling axes came
hurtling downwards.

Before the daemon's hellish weapons could reap their
harvest of blood, Klarak sprang forwards. The engineer
reached to his belt, hurling a small egg-like oval straight
into Skarbrand's bestial visage. The grenade exploded
as it smacked against the daemon's forehead, a bright
flare of fire erupting across the bloodthirster's face. The
daemon staggered back, its axes dangling limply from
their chains as it pawed at its burning face.

Klarak knew the grenade had done little damage to
the bloodthirster, causing it more surprise than injury.
Yet as the beast drew away, its gargantuan body suddenly contorted in agony. Skarbrand's fanged mouth
fell open in a howl, the chemical fire flickering across
its snout forgotten as it reeled about with pain. A great
swathe of the daemon's back was torn and bloodied,
burned black by some incredible force.

Klarak ignored the daemon's wails of rage, his keen
eyes seeking out whatever had done such damage to the

seemingly invulnerable beast. He considered the way
Skarbrand had recoiled from his bomb, the direction in
which the daemon had retreated and the location of its
grisly wound. The engineer's gaze rose, staring in wonder at the stone face of one of the statues which flanked
the hall. The dour countenance of Valaya stared back at
him, the goddess's granite eyes frozen in an expression
of defiant watchfulness.

From the face of the statue, Klarak turned his attention to the mighty axe clutched in Valaya's outstretched
hand: a masterful representation of Kradskonti, the
famed Peacebringer. The engineer could see Skarbrand's
boiling ichor dripping from the statue's weapon.

The dwarf's mind raced, stunned by the implica-
tion of what he saw. Immune to mortal weapons and
unfazed by Morag's magic, the daemon had proven
itself vulnerable to this stone figure, this effigy of the
dwarfish goddess of protection and healing. Klarak did
not question the source of this power, whether it lay in
some enchantment cut into the stone by the statue's
sculptor or whether the power might be a manifestation of Valaya's divine strength. It was enough that the
statue held the power to hurt the daemon.

'Thorlek! Horgar!' the engineer called out. He did
not wait to see if his friends had heard him, instead
rushing across the hall, hurdling the dead and dying.
The engineer's eyes kept drifting back to Valaya's statue,
studying the angle of her outstretched arm and the distance between her axe and the enraged Skarbrand.

A crazed dwarf lurched into Klarak's path, the heavy
iron length of a cannon worm gripped in his bloodied
hands. The gunner thrust the corkscrew-shaped head
of the worm at Klarak, trying to impale him upon its
barbed tip. The engineer twisted aside, driving his fist

into his attacker's throat. The gunner staggered back, gasping for breath, the worm falling from his hands.

Before Klarak could fully disable his foe, a filthy weight pounced upon him from behind. The sharp nails of a ratman's claws tore at his neck while chiselled fangs worried at his ear. A second skaven, fully as mad as the first, rushed at Klarak from the side, slashing at him with a notched sword.

The sword-rat's blow never landed. An axe whistled through the air, slamming into the beast's back and sending its broken body rolling across the floor. The skaven on Klarak's back squealed in agony as powerful hands ripped it from the dwarf's body and smashed its face into the unyielding stone floor.

'Daemons aren't foe enough for you?' Horgar asked as he finished crushing the life from Klarak's skaven attacker.

'Watch out!' cried Thorlek, pointing to the crazed dwarf gunner. His throwing axe gone, the ranger could only watch as the berserk gunner charged his friends.

Klarak met the gunner's attack, driving his fist into the other dwarf's face. The gunner crumpled, his jaw broken by the powerful blow. Even so, he struggled to rise until Klarak brought both hands smashing down into the gunner's skull. The gunner slumped to the floor as consciousness fled his body.

'If this madness does not pass, it would be more merciful to kill him,' Klarak said, turning the gunner over and examining his body. 'Please to the gods that I do not have the blood of my kinfolk upon my hands.'

The engineer stared intently at the belt circling the gunner's waist. It was the leather workbelt of a cannoneer. Quickly, Klarak's hands searched the belt, an idea forming in his mind. He cursed when he did not find what he was looking for. Sometime before attacking Klarak, the gunner had battled other foes. One of them had slashed the belt, spilling its contents somewhere on the battlefield.

'Klarak,' Thorlek said, his voice low with dread. 'The daemon is moving again.' The ranger gestured across the hall with his thumb. Skarbrand had recovered from its injuries and was once more moving against King Logan and his warriors. The bloodthirster's twin axes licked out, butchering brave dwarf soldiers with every sweep of the daemonic blades.

'Search the battlefield,' Klarak ordered, glancing frantically at the dead bodies strewn all about them. 'Find another cannoneer!' Even as he gave the order, his eyes were drawn to the little circle of dwarfs surrounding Thane Arngar and his oathstone. The engineer's gaze hardened when he saw Guildmaster Thori among Arngar's dwarfs. Standing beside Thori was a black-bearded dwarf in the soot-stained clothes of a gunner, the broad workbelt of a cannoneer straddling his waist.

Klarak raced across the battlefield, dodging the small knots of crazed dwarfs and skaven still prowling among the carnage. Again, his eyes kept straying back to the statue of Valaya and the axe she held. He judged the distance between statue and daemon, the murderous progress Skarbrand was making through the ranks of King Logan's warriors. With every sweep of its axe, the daemon took another thunderous step away from the statue and the one thing that might end its monstrous rampage.

The adventurer redoubled his efforts. He could hear Thorlek and Horgar behind him, savagely beating back any of the berserkers who took an interest in their master. Klarak could give only scant notice to their efforts, his mind focused upon reaching Thane Arngar's hold-outs and the cannoneer.

Klarak fought his way through the small cluster of maddened dwarfs and skaven which yet surrounded the oathstone. The warriors within the circle nearly brought him down with their axes until they heard the engineer cry out, until they saw the intense, yet wholly sane, expression in his eyes.

'Bronzehammer!' Thane Arngar exclaimed, shocked by the engineer's sudden and dramatic appearance beside the oathstone. 'You bring news from the king?' the general asked, trying to fathom what could have sent the adventurer rushing across a hall filled with dae-mons and madmen.

'I am on my own mission,' Klarak said, turning from the perplexed general and dashing to an equally con-fused Guildmaster Thori.

Mistaking the engineer's intensity and excitement as a threat, Guildmaster Thori drew away at Klarak's approach, his hands clenched about the haft of a warhammer. 'Don't even think about touching me!' Thori threatened.

Klarak gave the Guildmaster a withering look. 'I'm not thinking about you at all,' he growled. He turned his back to the indignant Thori and set upon the gun-ner beside him. Quickly, Klarak ripped the workbelt from the dwarf's waist, his fingers deftly probing its many pockets and pouches for what he needed.

'This is all your fault!' Thori raged as Klarak spun around, eyes locked on the distant figures of Skarbrand and Valaya's statue. 'If not for your recklessness, the ratkin would never have besieged our halls with such viciousness!' The Guildmaster shook his fist in rage as Klarak sprinted back towards the battlefield. 'You are expelled from the Engineers' Guild!' Thori bellowed. 'You are finished! Through!'

Klarak ignored Thori's threats. He did not have the time to worry about such trifles, not when the very existence of Karak Angkul depended upon him. As he again charged through the ring of deranged attackers laying siege to Thane Arngar, the engineer's face broke into a grim smile. Fighting their way through the crazed dwarfs and amok skaven, Horgar and Thorlek shouted a hurried greeting to their master.

'Stay with Thane Arngar,' Klarak told them.

'Our place is at your side,' Horgar objected.

'Not this time,' Klarak said.

Thorlek eyed his friend with suspicion. 'You've some idea to destroy the daemon?'

There was no point in lying to them. Both of them knew him too well for that. 'Yes, I have a plan,' Klarak said. 'And it needs only one dwarf to do it. If this doesn't work, the daemon is sure to take its revenge.' He raised his hand, silencing any other protests. Staring at Horgar, Klarak made a request of his bodyguard. 'I'll need your hammer, old friend.'

Horgar looked sadly at the steam hammer, a weapon that had become as close to him as his own skin. Yet he did not hesitate to hand it over to the engineer. 'Need the weapon but not the hand that holds it,' he grumbled.

Klarak looped the heavy weapon's strap over his shoulder and gripped the former hammerer's arm. 'Not today,' he said.

Horgar and Thorlek watched as their master rushed away, sprinting across the gory battlefield.

'Why do I feel like we're not going to see him again?' the hammerer said.

'For once,' Thorlek replied, 'I think you're right.'

* * *

KLARAK CHARGED ACROSS the hall, his heart pounding in his chest. His eyes kept roving between the daemon and the statue, his mind calculating distances and velocities. There was yet a slight window of opportunity, a small chance to put his plan into action. He clenched his teeth against the pained screams of those being butchered by the bloodthirster, tried not to hear the daemon's murderous bellows. If this didn't work, then nothing would. The taint of Skarbrand would mark Karak Angkul forever.

The dwarf raced to the feet of Valaya. Without hesitation, without thinking too much upon the imposing height of the statue above him, Klarak reached to his belt and withdrew a set of spiked crampons. Hurriedly, he tied the spikes to his boots, then produced a similar set of climbing claws which he slipped over his hands. Drawing a deep breath, Klarak started to mount the leg of Valaya's statue.

As he started to climb, Klarak did not notice the grey shape huddled behind the statue's ankle or the spiteful eyes that glared at him as he made his ascent. The dwarf's thoughts were focused upon the task at hand, upon the terrible act of desecration and destruction which had become the only hope of stopping Skarbrand's rampage.

Higher and higher the engineer climbed, his eyes constantly drifting back to the daemon and the mutilated corpses strewn about its feet. The sight urged Klarak to greater effort, forcing him to exact still more speed from his fading strength. Every breath, every heartbeat brought death to another dwarf.

When he finally reached Valaya's outstretched arm, Klarak could only sag wearily against the stone sleeve. It was the sound of Skarbrand's roars that urged him

to the final effort. Gazing across the hall, he could see
the daemon pressing onwards. Another few steps and
it would be beyond reach. If he were to act, it must be
now or never.

Hurrying across the uneven surface of Valaya's arm,
Klarak drew a spike from his belt. The engineer studied
the statue's arm with a practiced eye, judging where he
must make his mark if he would bring destruction to
the daemon. For an instant, his mind rebelled against
the unforgivable vandalism he was contemplating. But
the image of crazed dwarf-wives strangling their own
children, of daemons and skaven running rampant
through Karak Angkul's desolate halls, fought against
his moral objections.

Setting the spike against the statue's elbow, Klarak
brought Horgar's steam hammer smashing down. The
stone beneath the spike cracked, a small fissure opening beneath the fang-like length of steel. Klarak cast
aside his tools, reaching now for the small packet he
had taken from the cannoneer. It was a little square
of leather, a length of fuse projecting from one side, a
lumpy mass locked between the packet's folds.

The thing was a blasting charge, a more specialised
and powerful sort than those employed by miners.
Dwarf gun crews carried such charges in order to spoil
their weapons in the event of defeat and prevent their
cannons from falling into enemy hands. Judging the
distance between Valaya's axe and Skarbrand, Klarak
cut away most of the fuse, then savagely tamped the
blasting charge into the crack he had made.

With a last prayer to the ancestors for their forgive-
ness and understanding, Klarak lit the fuse and dived
for what shelter Valaya's shoulder might offer him.

A roar more violent and thunderous than that of

the daemon boomed through the hall as the charge ignited. Chips of granite smashed against wall and ceiling, a cloud of debris pattered to the floor. All eyes turned to the source of the explosion and even Skarbrand's blood-crazed awareness was distracted. The daemon turned, its glowing eyes glaring at the goddess, its nostrils flaring with challenge.

Then the statue's arm came apart. The explosion had done its work. The forearm snapped clean from Valaya's elbow, hurtling downwards, tons of stone rocketing towards the floor hundreds of feet below. Standing in the path of the falling arm stood the brutish figure of Skarbrand. The daemon howled wrathfully as the massive stone axe chopped down, sinking between its curled horns and cleaving its bestial skull in half.

To the dwarfs, it seemed almost as though Valaya herself had struck down the bloodthirster. The carved representation of the Peacebringer cut down the exultant daemon, spilling its steaming ichor in a cataract of boiling blood. The glow in Skarbrand's eyes died, the malignant power of its spirit faded. Torches flickered back into life, frost faded from the roof and walls. Before the stunned eyes of the dwarfs, the daemon's body began to wither, to sink into a quickly spreading pool of gore. The daemon's disintegrating body twisted and writhed, the axe of Valaya slowly sinking with its victim to the floor far below.

Cries of 'Valaya!' and 'Peacebringer!' echoed through the hall as the surviving dwarfs began to recognise their deliverance. Soon another name rang through the hall as sharp-eyed dwarfs spotted a lone figure standing upon the statue's shoulder.

'Bronzehammer!' the dwarfs roared, extolling the hero who had brought destruction to the daemon.

Klarak stood upon the statue's shattered arm and accepted the adulation of his kin. For the moment, he was their champion, their saviour. It was a moment he knew he would savour all his life.

GREY SEER THANQUOL cringed behind the dwarf goddess's foot, his mind shivering with the anguished scream of Skarbrand. The daemon was far from happy about its fate, about being banished back to the void before it had glutted itself upon mortal blood. Yet even in its rage, the bloodthirster spared a thought for the skaven sorcerer who had summoned it.

When you call for me again, I shall be waiting.

The daemon's words were far from comforting to Thanquol. Indeed, he found the prospect of crossing paths with Skarbrand again more terrifying than meeting up with Deathmaster Snikch in a dark alley. Somehow, he didn't think the bloodthirster's words were just an empty threat.

Bitterness grew in Thanquol's throat as the cheers of the dwarfs rang through the hall. He glared balefully from the shadows, wishing the daemon had finished its work before being banished. The filthy fur-faced dwarf-things! They had conspired with his enemies, allowed themselves to be used by Ikit Claw and Queek Headtaker in a craven plot to discredit and destroy the mightiest mind in all skavendom!

Well, their nefarious scheme had failed! Thanquol lived! He had survived the worst his enemies had thrown at him! Bravely defying even the daemonic malevolence of Skarbrand!

As Thanquol heard the name of Klarak Bronzehammer being shouted, he crept out from behind the statue's foot. So, the gold-bearded dwarf had survived and now his people cheered him as a hero. The credulous fools thought the dwarf had somehow vanquished the daemon! He could readily imagine how Klarak would exploit such fame!

The grey seer reached into the pocket of his robe, withdrawing a sliver of warpstone. He hadn't dared draw upon such power with Skarbrand's voice thundering through his head, but now he felt it was safe enough to partake of the stone's energies. A quick spell, and he'd be beyond the reach of the murderous dwarfs and their treacherous intrigues.

Thanquol's fangs ground the sliver into dust, the burning energies of the warpstone rushing through his body. His mind blazed with power, his eyes glowed with a green light. He felt his entire being saturated with the limitless power of the aethyr.

Yes, he could use his magic to escape. But first he would teach the dwarf-things a lesson. He would remind them of the heavy cost for daring to trifle with Thanquol!

Emboldened by the warpstone, Thanquol scurried out into the open. He tilted his horned head upwards, glaring at Klarak standing upon the statue's broken arm. He felt a thrill of excitement as the dwarf spotted him. There was no mistaking the fear in the creature's eyes.

'Die-burn, dwarf-thing!' Thanquol shrieked. Raising his staff, he sent a bolt of green lightning searing into the dwarf's body. Klarak's vest crackled as it struggled to dissipate the malignant energies, but it could do nothing to prevent his body from being thrown back by the impact. Klarak cried out as he lost his footing and hurtled to the floor far below.

Stunned silence held the Fourth Deep as the dwarfs

watched their hero fall, as they saw his body smash upon the flagstones.

Thanquol chittered in triumph, hopping up and down in glee as he saw his enemy's body crash to the floor. So perish all who defy Thanquol!

A bullet whistled past the grey seer's ear, snapping him from his revelry. Another shattered against the foot of the statue, and a third tore splinters from the side of his staff. Thanquol spun about, his eyes going wide as he saw a vengeful throng of dwarfs charging towards him.

Of course, it would be a small thing for a sorcerer of his stature and power to annihilate the scruffy villains, but Thanquol was too humble to abandon himself to such gratuitous abuses of his magic. It was better to retire and leave the dwarfs to contemplate the lesson he had taught them.

Another bullet smacked into the foot of the statue. Frantically, the grey seer focused his mind on the spell that would part the veil between worlds. If he happened to find Skarbrand waiting for him, he hoped the daemon would be grateful that Thanquol had slain the gold-furred dwarf.

Only foul-smelling smoke met the dwarfs when they reached the feet of Valaya.

EPILOGUE

SILENCE REIGNED IN the Fourth Deep as the surviving dwarfs gathered their dead. The assault by Queek Headtaker had wrought havoc among Thane Arngar's defenders, but even these losses paled beside the daemon's toll. Hundreds of dwarfs had been struck down by the bloodthirster's axes. Even the slightest wound defied the efforts of Karak Angkul's physicians and chirurgeons to heal, the injuries refusing to be staunched. Blood drained from the stricken dwarfs until their flesh was white and their breath faded into a ragged gasp. The priestesses of Valaya recited the litanies of mercy over each dying warrior, beseeching the goddess to ease their passing. The sombre priests of Gazul burned sacred incense in the hope that the Lord of the Underearth would guard the spirits of the dead and protect them on their journey to the Halls of the Ancestors.

Trains of wagons drawn by stout mine ponies carted the skaven dead away. There seemed to be thousands of the butchered ratmen, many of them killed by the claws of their own kind when the madness of Skarbrand conquered their feral minds. The skaven dead would be burned outside the walls of Karak Angkul, where the stench of their foulness would be borne away by the wind and their ashes washed away by the rain.

Across the hall, the saddest casualties of all sat huddled in blankets, their eyes gazing emptily at the walls, their ears deaf to the soothing voices of the priestesses. These were the survivors of Thane Arngar's army, those who had not been protected from Skarbrand's influence by the magic of the oathstone. Though the daemon's madness had passed, it had left deep scars within the mind of each dwarf. With care and compassion, it was hoped the warriors might recover, but such hopes were tempered by the grim reality etched into the haunted face of each victim. The horrors that had raged through their minds would never heal. However many years the gods saw fit to give them, they would remain mad idiots.

King Logan watched his subjects labour to remove the broken arm of Valaya. Though the arm of the goddess had smote the daemon and brought about its destruction, Runelord Morag had urged the massive debris be removed from the hold and cast into a deep chasm. The stone axe had touched the vileness of Skarbrand, there was no telling how much of the daemon's essence had seeped into it through that contact. He recalled the saga of Uzki Ranulfsson, the famed daemonslayer whose axe became a cursed thing eager to taste the blood of friend as well as foe. Uzki's fame crumbled into infamy and he was remembered in the Book of Grudges as Uzki Kinslayer.

King Logan's thoughts turned to another dwarf whose fame would leave debts in the Book of Grudges. He glanced away from the broken arm and stared at the bier where the battered body of Klarak Bronzehammer reposed. Even in death, there was a powerful dignity about the adventurer. Each dwarf bowed his head as he passed the bier, leaving a gold coin at Klarak's feet as a token of their gratitude for his sacrifice.

There was no question that Klarak had saved Karak Angkul. His plan had destroyed Ikit Claw's machine. His boldness and bravery had vanquished Thanquol's daemon. Yet King Logan could not still the doubt that nagged at his heart. The words of Guildmaster Thori and Runelord Morag stoked the embers of conflict in his mind. True, Klarak had saved the stronghold and perhaps all of the Karak Ankor, but had he not been the one to place it in jeopardy? Thori had always cautioned against Klarak's impetuous flouting of tradition, his reckless innovation and invention.

King Logan had always believed Klarak's position that great good could come from casting aside the cumbersome restrictions of tradition. Now, he was not so sure. Klarak himself had said Ikit Claw was drawn to Karak Angkul only to steal the alloy he'd created, that without the alloy the skaven Doomsphere would be impossible to complete. Klarak had saved Karak Angkul, but perhaps without the engineer's recklessness, the hold would never have been threatened to begin with.

It was a grim thought, but one which the king could not cast aside. He watched Horgar Horgarsson and Thorlek and Kimril, the only survivors of Klarak's Iron Throng, standing in mournful silence about their dead master. Horgar and Thorlek had acquitted themselves well in the battles against Skarbrand and the skaven. Kimril had served with equal honour tending the many injured in the battle in the smelthall. King Logan felt the weight of the decision he would need to make. It left a bad taste in his mouth, but the duties of kingship were not always pleasant.

Klarak would be buried with the honour of a fallen hero. The dwarfs of Karak Angkul would demand nothing less. But then the engineer's name would be stricken from every record. His inventions would be confiscated and handed over to the Engineers' Guild for proper testing and evaluation. His workshop would be dismantled and its apparatus locked away.

Only in one place would the name of Klarak Bronze-hammer linger. It would be found in the Book of Grudges, charged with the misfortunes which had nearly destroyed Karak Angkul. The debt against him would not be cancelled until the heads of Queek and Ikit Claw were set before the Silver Throne and until the horned pelt of Grey Seer Thanquol was pinned to the Ruby Gate.

As he made the decision, King Logan knew how Klarak's surviving friends would react. Their master had no clan to redeem the grudge laid out against him, so they would take up that task as their own. They would not rest until the spirit of Klarak Bronzehammer could enter the Halls of the Ancestors with honour.

King Logan shook his head as he observed the three dwarfs standing over Klarak's bier. Perhaps his decision was not such an imposition. After the cowardly way Thanquol had struck down their master, revenge against the grey seer was written upon the face of each of them.

Whatever hole Thanquol had crawled into, King

Logan was certain the friends of Klarak Bronzehammer
would find him.

THE STINK OF death was all around Grey Seer Thanquol
as he picked his way through the deserted tunnels
of Bonestash. Any skaven left alive by the vengeful
rampage of the dwarfs were long gone, fleeing into
the Underway to seek refuge at some other outpost
of the ratkin. There was no sign of the dwarfs either;
they'd withdrawn all of their warriors to reinforce the
defenders of the Fourth Deep. The only sign of life in
the entire network of tunnels and burrows were the
slinking rats nibbling at the dead skaven scattered
throughout the warren.

Thanquol gave the noxious vermin a sharp kick when
one of them tried to gnaw on his toes. Spitefully, he
expended some of the magic still flowing through his
veins. With a squeak of surprise and pain, the inquisitive rat exploded in a burst of fire and smoke.

Immediately, the grey seer regretted his action, a
headache pounding against the inside of his skull. After
taxing his sorcerous powers to skitterleap far from the
halls of the dwarf-things, Thanquol knew better than
to place any strain upon his magic. He blamed the irra-
tional hate and viciousness of the dwarfs for setting
his nerves on edge. It was their maniacal vindictiveness that had caused him to abuse his powers, casting
such powerful spells without the proper preparations
and ceremonies. It was a testament to his mastery of
the arcane arts that even under such distressing circum-
stances he'd been able to successfully evoke the aethyr
and bend it to his will. A lesser skaven would have tel-
eported himself smack into the centre of a stone wall.
But where such a feckless wretch would have perished,

Thanquol had succeeded, rematerialising in the dank passages of Bonestash.

In case the Horned Rat had played some small part in his escape, Thanquol made the sign of the Horned One with his claws and mumbled a prayer of gratitude. Just to be on the safe side, he struck down a creeping rat with the edge of his staff, offering its blood to the Blood God. After all, there was just a chance Skarbrand's essence was lingering close and there was no sense antagonising the daemon needlessly.

His prayers made, the grey seer began scurrying down the cramped tunnel. It would be a long journey back to Skavenblight and a far from pleasant one. He had no slaves to carry provisions for him, no guards to protect him from goblins and spiders and the multitudinous other terrors of the underworld. Worse still, he didn't even have enough warp-tokens to buy what he needed. Indeed, considering the warpstone shards he'd used to fuel his spells, he was more destitute now than he had been when he left Skavenblight!

Thanquol gnashed his fangs at the thought. Angrily he pointed his finger at a black-furred rat picking the eye from the skull of a stormvermin. The rat burst apart in a flash of green light. The grey seer groaned as he felt his headache worsen.

They were all to blame, those scheming cowards who had thought to exploit the renown of skavendom's greatest hero! Kritislik and Ikit Claw, Queek and thrice-damned Skraekual, Snikch and that decapitated maggot Rikkit…

Thanquol's thoughts broke off in mid-curse. Rikkit Snapfang! Of course! That greedy little weasel would never have come back to Bonestash without good reason. He must have had an excellent one to take his problems to Queek Headtaker and risk getting his head lopped off. Even more if he was going to try and play Queek's army against the weird science of Ikit Claw. Granted, even with the unpredictability of Clan Skryre's corrupt inventions, Rikkit knew he would be facing the awesome sorcery of Thanquol upon his return. It would take a lot to make a ratman take such a risk.

The answer was clear and bright in Thanquol's mind. Rikkit had left a stash of wealth behind when he fled. A cache of warpstone big enough to put some steel into the coward's spine! The same treasure that had lured Kaskitt Steelgrin into making the journey from Skaven-blight!

Thanquol hesitated, staring down the tunnel which would lead him back to the Underway and a dangerous, ignominious return to the Under-Empire. He glanced back over his shoulder at the corpse-strewn warren of Bonestash. If he was Rikkit Snapfang, where would he hide his treasure? Of course, it was a difficult thing for a skaven of Thanquol's brilliance to try and imitate the intellect of a half-wit mouse-chewer like Rikkit...

Uttering a bark of excitement, Thanquol turned and dashed off through the winding corridors of the warren. If he was a spineless rat like Rikkit, he would have taken his treasure with him when he fled! The moment Ikit Claw had started taking over, he would have gathered his warpstone and headed for Skaven-blight. Since Rikkit had tried to get Queek to come and reclaim the warren, obviously the warlord had been unable to recover his treasure. And that meant he'd hidden it in a place constantly under Ikit Claw's observation, a place that afforded him no chance to steal in and get his loot.

There was only one such place! The great storage

cavern where Ikit had assembled his woefully defective Doomsphere!

Thanquol raced through the narrow corridors, leaping over dead skaven and darting around fallen boulders. It took him a moment to recognise the smell of the cavern over the lingering smells of dwarf-scent and the ill vapours of the Doomsphere's dissolution. Yet, after a bit of scrutiny and some guesswork, he reached the half-collapsed chamber. He ground his fangs together as he looked over the destruction. The dwarfs had put the cavern into some semblance of order, rolling aside many of the rocks in their morbid mania to take away their own dead.

Thanquol glanced fearfully at a particular boulder. No mistaking that one, it had come very near to smashing him. The grey seer lashed his tail in annoyance, angry at the twinge of fear he felt. Well, the damnable thing wouldn't hurt him now! He'd use it as a marker to maintain his bearings while he searched the cave.

Scurrying across the cavern, Thanquol didn't quite reach the boulder before his eyes caught a gleam of metal off to his right. Instinctively, he sprang back, raising his staff to beat in the brains of whatever scavenger was lurking down here.

Bitterly, the grey seer lowered his staff. What he'd seen was simply the steel armature of his late bodyguard. The rat-ogre stood frozen in place, its paws broken, its bones chipped, its mechanics dripping oil and fluids. Clan Skryre's vaunted science! Bah! This shoddy contraption hadn't even the sense to lay down when it died, or the decency to have some meat on its bones to feed its hungry master!

Imperiously, Thanquol strode towards the unmoving rat-ogre. It was annoying to him that the brute should be standing there like it was. He didn't like having the gruesome thing looking down at him with its empty eyes. A good kick would solve the problem, and there might even be a few bits of warpstone left in its fuel tanks.

As soon as he came within five steps of the rat-ogre, the brute shuddered into life. Boneripper's crouched body straightened itself and green lights blazed from the sockets of its skull. A hiss of warpsteam erupted from the rat-ogre's damaged engine.

Thanquol scrambled for cover, diving behind his boulder. The frightened grey seer peered out from behind his refuge, staring wide-eyed at Boneripper. The huge beast stood where it was, its shoulders shuddering as the vibrations of its mechanics pulsed through its bones.

What was the monster waiting for? Why didn't it attack?

Slowly it dawned on Thanquol what Boneripper was waiting for. Lashing his tail in anger, the grey seer stood up and brushed the dirt from his robes. Stalking towards the rat-ogre, he swatted its fleshless snout with his staff.

'Bone-brained tick-popper!' Thanquol snarled at Boneripper, striking it again. In mute silence, the rat-ogre bore its master's abuse, waiting patiently for the grey seer to give it orders.

Panting, his anger spent, Thanquol leaned against his staff and glared up at the skull-faced rat-ogre. 'Bone-ripper! Find-search warpstone!' he commanded.

Obediently, Boneripper began shifting the rubble, searching for the treasure its master coveted. Thanquol watched his bodyguard toil away, uncaring for the toll its exertions were taking upon its already damaged mechanics. Either the brute would find Rikkit's treasure or it would break down.

The grey seer accepted both possibilities. If Boneripper did break down, he would at least be able to recover the warpstone from its fuel tanks.

ABOUT THE AUTHOR

C. L. Werner was a diseased servant of the
Horned Rat long before his first story in
Inferno! magazine. His Black Library credits
include the Chaos Wastes books *Palace of
the Plague Lord* and *Blood for the Blood God*,
Mathias Thulmann: Witch Hunter, *Runefang*
and the *Brunner the Bounty Hunter* trilogy.
Currently living in the American south-west,
he continues to write stories of mayhem and
madness set in the Warhammer World.

Visit the author's website at
www.vermintime.com

Also by C. L. Werner
THE RED DUKE

Paperback ISBN: 978-1-84970-073-3 Digital ISBN: 978-1-85787-258-6

After a thousand years, the monstrous Red Duke rises from his grave and brings death to the lands he once ruled. As the Knights of Bretonnia muster to defeat the vampiric fiend, battlelines are drawn for an epic conflict between the dead and the living.

An extract from The Red Duke
by C.L. Werner

THE VAMPIRE NOTED the knight's approach, tearing his
mouth from the wound on Jacquetta's neck. The creature hissed wrathfully at the man, his face shriveled
and pale where it was not smeared with the witch's
blood. Angrily, he threw the dying witch aside, flinging
her across the altar with such force that her spine broke
upon impact with the stone obstruction.

Jehan received a good look at his foe for the first
time. The vampire's body was withered, but from its
desiccated husk there was fastened the armour of a
Bretonnian lord, armour stained as red as the blood
smearing the creature's fangs. A thick-bladed sword
hung from a chain about the vampire's waist, the
golden pommel cast in the semblance of a grinning
skull.

In a blur of steel, the vampire drew his blade, springing
towards the knight with bestial fury. Contemptuously,

he swatted aside Jehan's guard, crumpling the edge of the man's blade with the superhuman power of his blow. Jehan reeled, staggered by the violence and suddenness of the attack. The monster allowed him no quarter. The serrated blade he held licked out, smashing through the knight's arm, slashing the chainmail as though it were cheesecloth. Blood bubbled up from the mangled flesh beneath the armour.

Snarling, howling like a beast of the wilds, the Red Duke fell upon the wounded Jehan. The powerful warrior was crushed by the vampire's clutch, held as helpless as the witch had been while undead fangs tore at his mangled arm. Struggling, kicking, screaming for help, the knight could do nothing as the vampire engorged himself upon the man's lifeblood.

It was a drained, lifeless husk the Red Duke let fall to the ground minutes later. He wiped the back of his hand across his mouth, licking the blood from his fingers, savouring the intoxicating tang of fear trapped within the sanguine liquid. After so many centuries, there was nothing like the taste.

He would never suffer such privation again, the vampire promised himself. He would gorge himself, fatten himself, stuff himself until the hunger was sated, until he was acquitted of the long centuries of starvation and torment.

The Red Duke bared his fangs in a ravenous snarl. There was more blood nearby, he could smell it coursing through terrified hearts, thundering through shivering veins.

All of it would be his, a feast of blood to drown the years of deprivation and agony. Not a man, not a woman, not a child would leave the graveyard. Peasant or noble, they were people no longer, but cattle to be tracked down and slaughtered. Fodder for their dread liege, the Red Duke, rightful master of Aquitaine.

EARL GAUBERT HAD fled along with the rest, dragging Aldric with him. The nobleman's heart pounded with terror as he blundered through the maze-like darkness, uncaring of direction so long as his steps took him away from the monument and the monster his madness had set free.

Yes, the earl admitted, it was his fault, the responsibility was his alone. In his insane lust for revenge he had allowed himself to treat with the forces of darkness and the unholy powers had betrayed him. Instead of evoking the Red Duke's spirit, instead of stealing from that spectre its skill with the blade, Jacquetta and Renar had resurrected the vampire himself in all his terrible glory. Earl Gaubert felt his skin crawl as he remembered the sight of the undead gorging himself upon Jacquetta's blood, of the vampire tossing about one of his bravest and boldest knights as though he were a child.

'My lord, we must hurry,' Aldric advised him when the crippled nobleman's endurance faltered and he leaned upon the cold back of a headstone. There was fear upon the knight's face, only his sense of duty and obligation kept him by the old man's side.

Screams rippled through the night, obscene cries of agony that pierced the very stars with their horror. The vampire was hunting the members of Jacquetta's cult, stalking them among the tombs, battening upon their diseased blood.

Earl Gaubert crumpled beside the headstone, the strength deserting his legs. He covered his face with his hand, tears falling from his eyes. What had he done?

What kind of monster had he set loose? The enormity of his shame turned his stomach and he retched into the weeds.

'My lord,' Aldric grabbed his master's shoulder and shook the sick nobleman. 'That thing is still out there, killing everyone it can find! We have to get out of here before it finds us!'

The earl turned bitter eyes on his vassal. 'I deserve to die,' he said. 'For hate's sake, I sent my sons to their deaths. For hate's sake I spat upon my oaths to the Lady and the blessings of the grail. I have committed an unforgivable sin. Without the promise of my protection, the witch and the necromancer would never have dared such an outrage. I am the guilty one. I am ready to pay for my crime.' Earl Gaubert smiled weakly at the knight. 'You have been loyal to the last, Sir Aldric. Run now, escape while you can. Consider your oaths fulfilled and leave an old man to meet the doom he has brought upon himself.'

Aldric shook his head. 'It would be the craven act of a knave to abandon my lord.' The knight helped Earl Gaubert back to his feet. 'We will return to the chateau and muster your knights. Even the Red Duke does not have the power to stand alone against the might of your soldiers.'

His knight's words of martial pride stirred some hope in Earl Gaubert's heart. There was still a chance to undo the evil he had unleashed. They could return with a company of cavalry and scour the graveyard until they brought the vampire to ground. They would destroy the monster and hide the shame Earl Gaubert had brought upon the name d'Elbiq.

A sudden chill gripped the nobleman. He watched as the weeds around the headstone began to wilt.

Turning his head, he gasped as he saw a grisly shape standing atop one of the tombs. It was just a dark silhouette, a shadow framed by the sickly light of Morrslieb, but Earl Gaubert could feel the creature's malignant gaze fixed upon him.

'Behind me, my lord!' Aldric shouted, pushing his master around the back of the headstone. The knight brandished his sword, shaking it at the watching shadow. 'Hold your ground, fiend! Sup upon the peasants, but think not to touch my master or I shall send your rotting carcass back to its grave!'

No sound came from the menacing shadow, the creature seeming content to crouch and watch the two Bretonnian nobles. Then with the speed and abruptness of a lightning bolt, the vampire leapt upon his prey, lunging at Aldric with the ferocity of a pouncing lion. The knight's sword was knocked from his grasp as the vampire's shrivelled body smashed into him, the force of the undead monster's impact bearing him to the ground.

The Red Duke's claws gripped either side of Aldric's head. With a single twisting motion, the vampire broke the man's neck. A hiss of satisfaction slithered through the Red Duke's fangs as he rose from the twitching corpse and fixed his fiery gaze upon the cowering figure of Earl Gaubert.

Frantically, the earl tried to draw his sword, in his terror he forgot the infirmity of his crippled arm and tried to grip his weapon as he had before his fateful duel with Count Ergon du Maisne. The palsied fingers refused to close around the sword, the trembling arm refused to draw the blade from its scabbard.

In two steps, the Red Duke reached the pathetic cripple. A sweep of his hand ripped the sword from

Earl Gaubert's feeble clutch. The nobleman screamed, stumbling across the graves, trying to keep a line of headstones between himself and the vampire.

Before he had gone twenty feet, the earl collapsed, grabbing at his chest, trying to ease the burning pain that pounded through his body. An old, sickly man, he was not equal to the ordeal he had been put through. Now the earl's terrorized flesh failed him, his weak heart sending waves of pain and weakness through his body.

The Red Duke stared down at the panting, wretched figure of Earl Gaubert. There was no pity in the vampire's eyes, only the merciless hunger of the damned.